# VESSELS

By

# John Bowen

Story contributions from
Iain Grant

# Copyright John Bowen, 2021

Text and pictures copyright © 2021 John Bowen

**All Rights Reserved**

This book is a work of fiction. References to real people, events, establishments, organisations, or locations are intended only to provide a sense of authenticity, and are used factitiously. All other characters, incidents and dialogue are drawn from the author's imagination and are not to be construed as real.

For
Vera and Ken.

# Chapter One

*The banks of Sognefjord, Norway.*

*The house stands in the belly of a valley on the banks of a fjord.*

*Inside the dwelling, a man named Torsten, tall, strong and hard as a knot, hair red as freshly spilt blood, stares out through a large window. From his vantage point, the water cutting through the valley appears sheer as glass, a mirror, offering a perfect reflection of what lies above: the stars and the moon, the unfathomable reaches of the cosmos, a realm in which time is measured on a different scale from that imposed upon the creatures who inhabit the small blue rock beneath. Those who gaze up count their existence in years, the other in aeons.*

*Torsten's allotment lies somewhere in between.*

*The window pane is thick, a mix of laminated glass and polycarbonate which renders it impressively resilient; bulletproof, even. The walls surrounding it are similarly stout. The house is a fortress, not because Torsten is an especially fearful soul, but because he is a cautious one. He is guardian to something wonderous and powerful, and has been so for a very, very long time.*

*He is unaware that outside the house, a group of men is closing in.*

*The party have hiked from over four miles away. Each man is clothed in matt black combat gear, a mixture of ultra-high-molecular-weight plates and a super-lightweight Kevlar derivative. Between them, they carry enough firepower to take down a small army.*

*Or one very formidable adversary.*

*They mean to kill Torsten and take what he has.*

*The security system designed to alert Torsten to trespassers has failed to detect their approach. It has been hacked and disabled — not a simple task. The system is highly sophisticated, but like all technology, vulnerable to an attacker with the right tools and expertise, with access to better technology and more skilled minds than those who conceived and designed it.*

*The assault squad scurry like beetles to the outer walls, converging around the architectural weak point they have chosen as the ideal spot to breach. The house has been the subject of intense study, sonic resonance imaging harvested by drones under the cover of darkness. One of the men primes the explosives and rejoins his squad a judicious distance away.*

*The squad's commander, a large man, a head or more taller, and wider than any of his men, counts down from three. They hear him over the coms, and are ready when he activates the detonator upon uttering 'one'. Like a sorcerer's incantation, the word conjures an explosion.*

*The blast echoes through the valley, a throaty, reverberating bark of thunder. It also rips a hole clear through the half-metre-thick reinforced wall. Torsten, who stands a short distance away, is hit by the force and the resulting debris and hurled clear across the room into the far wall. Disoriented, ears ringing, he staggers to his feet, and through a tick-tock, syrupy slow-motion surge of adrenaline sees figures stepping out of the smoke and over the rubble.*

*One spots him and raises an automatic rifle. Torsten rolls out of the way as bullets smash into the wall inches from his head. He keeps moving, knowing what they have come for, determined to reach it first. A few strides are enough to offer a brief audit of his injuries, among which he counts broken ribs, a broken wrist, and innumerable lacerations...*

*He makes for the spiral staircase but does not take the winding steps down. Instead, he vaults over the rail. With his right hand injured he is forced to execute the vault hurriedly and with his left. In a few minutes, two, three at most, Odin's blood would mend his shattered bones, knit the ruptured tendons, tissue and cartilage, but he doesn't have minutes. The resulting manoeuvre is not graceful. He drops and hits the floor below hard and clumsily. He rights himself and sprints for the door to the basement, barging through and taking the steps four at a time.*

*He can hear the intruders on his heels and exits the lower basement door with gunfire in his wake.*

*He barrels onward, through subterranean rooms burrowed into the hillside. Set deepest is the vault. Boots and bullets are close behind him. One discharge finds him and rips through his thigh. He stumbles but keeps moving. Another burst of gunfire finds its mark and tears greedy chunks from his shoulder and arm. These wounds too will heal, if he can just reach the sanctuary of the vault. Odin's blood would make him whole, and what lies inside would even the odds.*

*He would give these men a taste of what they came to steal.*

*At last, he arrives at the vault door and slams his palm to the reader, rousing its machinery from slumber. Gears deep in the wall rumble and roll, and the large steel door retracts.*

*Torsten dives through the opening and strikes the inner lock as bullets split the air, hammering the vault's interior wall and smashing into the thick steel door as it halts and then reverses to roll back into place. He breathes a sigh as the door thumps closed and the din outside falls to a muted rattle for a few seconds, and then ceases.*

*Once again, time is his ally, for a spell at least.*

*The vault is a cube filled with paintings, sculptures, rare books, ancient coins. A monitor is fixed to the wall in one upper corner, showing a constant live feed of the area outside the vault.*

*More than a dozen figures in black combat gear are assembled there. Heavily armed, they stand poised, weapons trained on the vault door. The figure centremost, a tall, heavily built man, gestures and turns his head. His mouth moves, something is said, but the vault's feed lacks audio and its door is too thick for any of his words to penetrate.*

*They are at a stalemate.*

*Torsten sits for a spell, his back against the cool steel door.*

*In theory, he could remain in the vault indefinity. It would not be pleasant, extremely tedious, but possible. If the vault were truly impenetrable, he could sit until these men, and their offspring, and their offspring's offspring withered into old men. He doubts any vault is truly impenetrable, and these men would seek to prise him from his shell, employing whatever brute force or ingenuity was necessary. That they have got this far indicates they almost certainly have the means.*

*Torsten has no intention of awaiting such an eventuality. He will not cower until they come for him.*

*He climbs to his feet, walks to the statue at the centre of the room, the itch of his healing wounds erasing the pain of his injuries with every step. He shakes out his right hand, the bones once again whole.*

*The intruder's bullets have blown chunks from the five-hundred-year-old marble figure, a crime in itself. He pushes the base and the statue slides back, exposing a recessed handle in the floor.*

*He grasps it and executes a sequence of left and right turns. There is a pneumatic hiss and a steel pillar rises from the ground.*

*Inside the pillar is a cavity, in which rests an impossible treasure.*

*Mjolnir belongs to another world. If one believes the legends, it was forged in Svartalfheim, the realm of the dark elves. In its sleeping form its skin is impossibly smooth, slightly asymmetrical, shaped almost like a vase, with an opening on one side of its flared base. The portion of the exposed base bears indentations that seem to invite one who gazes upon it to feed his hand through the barrel and lie an open palm within. The collection of razor-sharp blades nestled inside the barrel above render such a course of action less inviting.*

*Mjolnir is undoubtedly made of metal, but what manner of metal is less clear. It resembles no material Torsten has seen throughout his long existence, whether forged by smith or by science. Likewise, the finely etched markings that skin the treasure's curves, converging into rich pockets of detail, are unique.*

*These men on the far side of a thick wall of steel are not the first to have learnt of Mjolnir's existence and grown to covet it. Over the centuries, others had, too, and been foolish enough to come for it, bearing arms, thirsty for power and glory. Their axes, swords, bows and arrows, did not bring them success. Few who set out to take it survived to tell the tale. The contingent outside the vault is more formidably armed, but that will not deter Torsten from seeking to deliver them the same fate.*

*What those long dead raiders had not known, what perhaps is not known by these latest intruders, too, is that the treasure they seek is more than a source of immortality. What lies before Torsten is Mjolnir at rest.*

*He moves to wake it.*

*A warrior, Torsten is the last of a people who cut through seas in longboats, doing what they became infamous for, taking what they wanted by force, from farms, from villages, from monasteries. One day his clan had returned home with a treasure of inestimable value, imbued with a magic which made them gods among men. At first, the treasure had concealed its true identity, but the clan had eventually teased it out: and come to believe they possessed Mjolnir itself.*

*Blessed with its gift, the clan had prospered and endured, until Arne's madness had infected not just his own mind, but spread among others, divided them, set brother against brother. The split was bloody and sustained, time and violence whittling their numbers until eventually only Arne and Torsten remained.*

*And then Torsten alone.*

*In the ages since, he has kept Mjolnir safe, and will continue to do so until his dying breath.*

*Torsten drives his hand into the treasure's throat. The foremost blades taste his blood, find it familiar and retract. His open hand falls within the indentations ready to receive it. With his other hand, he traces a pattern upon Mjolnir's skin. The treasure immediately responds and melts to shift into a new shape. It takes the form of a bracer around his forearm, a skin-tight fit, enclosing elbow to wrist.*

*He glances up at the monitor. His foes are still in place. They believe they have him cornered, are waiting to see what he will do.*

*He strikes the lever to open the vault door, and falls back against the wall. Gunfire erupts as the door retracts, deafening, filling the basement, as bullets pour into the vault, shredding and destroying centuries of art. Torsten waits until the gap in the half-metre thick door is wide enough, and plunges low and fast into the basement. As he does so he traces another gesture across the intricate markings on the bracer. They cause Mjolnir to shift again. The bracer extends to enclose his knuckles, forming a flared ridge that stands proud.*

*The rage he has held in check thus far finds itself untethered, permitted free rein.*

*A bullet slams into Mjolnir and ricochets off, leaves not a mark. He reaches the first of the soldiers and kicks him clean off his feet into one of his companions standing behind him, then whirls to smash Mjolnir into the chest of a third.*

*This blow is significantly more potent. When Mjolnir connects, the soldier is not only launched off his feet but swatted clear across the room. The force delivered is closer to being struck by a speeding truck than by a fist. The soldier's short journey ends with the basement's concrete wall, which he meets with bone-shattering force, and slides to the ground.*

*For an instant the group seem frozen, struggling to process what they have just witnessed.*

*Torsten capitalises on their inaction and moves further into their midst.*

*The basement imposes close quarters upon all, but whereas they cannot fire indiscriminately for fear of injuring or killing their own, he is not similarly confined. So long as he can claim the centre-ground, he holds this advantage. He is faster than they anticipate, too; he seizes the barrel of an automatic rifle, wrenches it from its owner, and swings it like a club, taking another of their number down. A particularly enthusiastic foe leaps on his back and tries to jam a pistol to his throat. Torsten grabs the fool's arm, hurling him over his shoulder while his cohorts jostle to find space to draw a clean aim on him.*

*He tugs the reins of his berserker rage, assesses the odds.*

*Perhaps a dozen opponents remain, but they are backing away now, warier of what they have unleashed. He pivots, moves upon the nearest of them, the slowest to respond. He ducks under the man's rifle muzzle and the burst of fire it releases to deliver an uppercut with Mjolnir, which sends the man crashing into the ceiling and swiftly back down, in no shape to get up. The rest of the squad continue to spread out, acknowledging and seeking to correct their error.*

*One of them finds the opportunity to deliver a sustained burst of fire; Torsten feels leaden teeth rip into his shoulder, causing his left arm to explode with pain and fall numb. Mjolnir, on his right, will have to earn it time to heal. He grits his teeth and keeps moving.*

*He advances on a soldier to his left, swinging to land a blow as another burst of fire from his right bites into his leg and forces him onto one knee. He raises Mjolnir to deflect a burst of fire to his left.*

*The group closes back in, training their weapons down on him, sure of their line of fire.*

*He is pummelled, and loses the feeling in his legs.*

*Bullets pour into him as he falls to his face. His body becomes a canvas of screaming red agony. There is no relent in their assault. He is meat, just meat, now, and yet he knows Odin's blood will be striving to stitch the meat back together.*

*It takes him a moment to notice when the firing finally ceases. His grip on consciousness is spare.*

*A boot kicks under his chest, lifts and rolls him onto his back.*

*Torsten stares up into the dispassionate face of its owner, one of the soldiers. The man is tall, heavily built, and wielding a heavy blade. His boot comes back down, pinning Torsten's bicep. What meagre strength Torsten can still rally, he marshals to his right hand, his grip on Mjolnir.*

*If they wish to take it, they will have to prise it from his cold dead fing—*

*The soldier swings, and the blade parts Torsten's arm above the elbow. The man reaches down to collect his prize, shaking Torsten's severed hand and forearm free. He seems surprised when Mjolnir melts in his hand, shifting from a weapon of war into a state of rest, a strange vase-like object.*

*Then he raises the blade again, this time above Torsten's head.*

*And Torsten knows his long life is at an end.*

*There are injuries even Odin's blood cannot reverse.*

# Chapter Two

*The University of Arizona. Tucson, Arizona, The United States.*

Mervin advanced his presentation to the next slide. The projected PowerPoint image showed a large Norse copper alloy pendant, dated to around 700 AD. Intricately worked into the pendant's face was a strange but distinctive vase-like object, with what appeared to be an opening at its base.

Mervin gave the room a few moments to digest the image before advancing to the next. This picture showed an ancient Greek patera dish with handles, dated to around 340 BCE. The dish depicted an armoured figure; holding aloft an object which shared the same features as the one on the pendant.

He progressed to the next photo, of an object sculpted from pitted marble, believed to be from the reign of the Roman emperor Augustus, dated from between 27 BCE to AD 14. The item bore a striking similarity to the previous two.

Mervin progressed to the next image, which showed a portion of a Mayan jade plaque; dated to around 500 BCE. One side was damaged, forever lost, but the surviving detail on the remaining portion was stunning. It featured a seated figure, clearly exalted, flanked by kneeling subordinates. The figure had one arm extended, palm facing up. Sitting atop his open palm was the now-familiar object.

Mervin's next slide showed all four of the previous images side by side. The art styles, arising from cultures worlds apart both geographically and temporally, were, of course, starkly different, but if a viewer allowed his mind to take the fundamental details and proportions of the central object into account...

This object, and the theories that attempted to explain what it was, what it might represent, and the resulting ramifications, had been the subject of Professor Mervin Pickering's studies and research for the last eight years. He faced the lecture theatre, crammed with anthropology students and other interested attendees, hoping, as he increasingly did in recent years, that young minds were naturally more fertile, open minds.

It was somewhat ironic his lectures were so well attended these days. His audiences had grown steadily, and inversely to his standing among his peers. A few years ago, when he still commanded the respect of his fellow academics, this same auditorium would have been scarcely a quarter full.

He turned his face to the image. "Four depictions of an object, continents and centuries apart," he said, his voice dominating the room. He had always been a good speaker, he thought, aware that an effective lecture was always part theatre. "Each connected to cultures whose myths speak of a race who walked the earth in advance of, or alongside, man. This race goes by many names: giants, the fallen, the Nephilim...

"Many scoff at the possibility this race was real, and yet it is not so incredible." Mervin turned back to face his audience, "The overwhelming bulk of our own genealogy is shared by a plethora of species, hominids whose DNA is separated from ours by the barest fractions of a percentage. We are just one surviving branch of a common ancestor, and the progression is not clearly delineated. Homo neanderthalensis and Homo sapiens shared the earth for over a hundred thousand years.

"Civilisations rise and fall, and are viewed by later civilisations through what survived, a picture that is open to interpretation, incomplete, founded on fragments. To dismiss the possibility of a race that predates our own, or which existed contemporaneously until its extinction, is to recklessly calcify our understanding of the history of life on this planet, and possibly our own earliest history too.

"Consider this." Mervin deployed a well-judged pregnant pause, "Man, Homo sapiens, has existed in his current form for more than *two hundred thousand years*, and yet his grasp of recorded history reaches back a meagre five thousand.

"Numerous cataclysms predate this picture. If Man has enjoyed all the evolutionary benefits of his present composition for over two hundred thousand years, why is it that only in the last five thousand we find evidence of civilisations?

"What prevented it earlier? Why, given he was possessed of the same biology, the same hands, the same fiercely inventive brain for the preceding ninety-five thousand years, did he fail to organise beyond simple tribes? Consider this also: the relative infancy of our current civilisations in this context, and how rapid their journey to their present technological peaks.

"The microcomputer is scarcely half a century old, and yet its impact has transformed our world. The same can be said for other technology we accept as commonplace, which are far more recent: sophisticated machine learning AI, cloud computing, genetic engineering, electric vehicles… Edifices we view as iconic, from Buckingham Palace to the

Empire State Building, are scant centuries old. Hundreds of years, in a story spanning tens of thousands. And how long would these edifices survive without constant maintenance? Left alone, how long would it take the elements and nature to tear them down? Certainly, a far shorter period than they have existed. What would survive of them after five thousand, ten thousand, one hundred thousand years or more?

"What would a sufficiently intelligent race who may come later, perhaps to rise from the ashes of our own, make of the fragments they found? Stripped of our history, our culture, our tools and technology, would they struggle to credit we had reached the same heights they have, or even higher?

"Would these beings, perhaps a new branch on the hominids' evolutionary path, be ready to accept a superior race might once have inhabited their world? Or would their ego become an obstacle? Is ours? We like to think of those who came before us as more primitive, but this may not be the case.

"Our picture of the past must not be myopic or cast beyond alteration. We have to allow for our view of it to be incomplete, to allow space for discovery and change…"

—

The lecture had been well-received, at least Mervin thought so. Once he had been more confident to judge. Those who had listened were easier to categorise, history students and professionals. Now it was a more eclectic mix.

He had always attempted to make his presentations entertaining, but these days he was oftentimes left with the uneasy feeling he had become an entertainer first and an educator second. Upon emerging from the auditorium, his path was barred by a group of young men waiting for him, students, he guessed, who had attended the lecture. They looked friendly and excited.

"Professor Pickering?" The youth at the head of the group was grinning at him. "We're big fans of your work. We hoped we might get a picture with you?"

Mervin felt awkward. In the past, attendees of his talks had not been in the habit of requesting snapshots, or worse 'selfies', with him, but to refuse seemed rude.

"Of course." He nodded.

The youths briskly coalesced around him, save for a tall pimply one who backed up to take the picture. From his new position a few metres away, the youth directed the assembled to 'squeeze in' to fit everyone in shot. Mervin, who was at the centre, found himself surrounded. When the youth urged everyone to crunch up further still, Mervin found himself trapped in something of an undignified scrum and regretting his decision not to have found an excuse to get away.

"Ready?" asked the youth, beaming.

There was something about the quality of the grin, a darkly mischievous bent, which gave Mervin the distinct impression he was missing something. It was then he caught a glint of light from the corner of his eye. Too late, he noticed the youths had all slipped something shiny onto their heads. Several snaps had already been taken before he identified the offending headgear. The young men were all sporting tinfoil hats, spun into a peak at the top to form a sort of silly aerial. Before he was able to protest, the scrum was already disbanding.

The youths dispersed, laughing. One clapped him on the shoulder and thanked him before scuttling off. The group was out of sight before his anger was even given the chance to properly ferment. He was left standing alone, knowing it was too late to go after them, and that even it if hadn't been, there was nothing to gain from causing a scene.

He stormed towards the exit. His car awaited. He wanted nothing more than to be inside it and driving away.

How dare they?

Was this truly what he was now, a joke? Once he had been a respected expert in his field, his work as an archaeologist and historian published in prestigious journals and magazines. Then, he had unwittingly committed a professional crime and strayed too far from his tribe, diverging too far from their established scripture of historical consensus.

When the paper he had submitted had been rejected in peer review, he had been genuinely shocked then slighted, and then annoyed. Indignant, he had approached several publishers to get his work seen. He felt the material, which had taken a great deal of time, passion and research, was progressive, daring and important work.

One publisher, of a more mainstream bent, had been remarkably receptive. They had paired him with an editor, an energetic, if pushy, fellow, who seemed determined to focus on the more speculative areas of his research.

Truth be told, Mervin had felt a little bullied by the chap, but he was unfamiliar with the cut and thrust of the commercial publishing world, and the project had been set on such a tight deadline there simply hadn't been time to argue every point. The editor had massaged the book's content to court the broadest audience possible. *'Mervin. People should learn this stuff! Their interest will force your stuffy colleagues to reassess it!'*

Whatever Mervin's misgivings, the editor's approach had undoubtedly proven successful, and 'THOSE WHO CAME BEFORE' quickly escaped the bounds of the academic literature niche Mervin had envisioned for it. True, the cover, which Mervin had not seen until the presses were virtually rolling, was something which would not have looked out of place on a science fiction novel, …and the accompanying blurb and marketing were perhaps a little too strident in presenting his sober speculation and fragmentary evidence as cast-iron proof of an ancient civilisation lost to history. But his work was being seen, and by a lot of people.

The publisher was even able to secure appearances on some radio and television shows. It was during these interviews he got his first real taste of how far he had veered from his familiar, comfortable world of academia.

He discovered himself lumped in with the nutty fringe, treated as a pseudo-scientist, among the conspiracy theorists and wackos. It was rudely apparent in the questions put to him, the levity with which his ideas were treated, and it rankled. His research *was* sound, and his theories, approached from the correct perspective, couched with the appropriate amount of caution, were more than reasonable. Somehow, though, the more dignified and sober he remained in these interviews, the more the hosts liked it, and the more blatantly patronising their questions became.

Worse still were the interviews his publisher had arranged with less mainstream outlets, internet live streams and podcasts. In these, he was commonly faced with hosts who believed things, or pretended to believe things for the sake of sating their gullible audiences, which he viewed as utter nonsense.

Mervin did not believe the moon landing was faked, that aliens built the pyramids, or shadowy lizard men secretly orchestrated the earth's affairs.

The book's promotion campaign had spanned just two months, eight weeks which left Mervin exhausted and mortified. His reputation, if not in tatters, was significantly frayed and soiled.

He remained, however, a scientist. Evidence was evidence.

Troy had long been viewed as a myth until excavations in northwest Turkey located its ruins. Now historians overwhelmingly accepted the existence of the bronze age city. Mervin assured himself that if only he remained steadfast, and resolutely continued to soberly argue his case, the growing weight of evidence would ultimately vindicate him. It would see him not only brought back into the fold, but recognised as a visionary who had played a key role in expanding mankind's understanding of its greater history.

This was what he told himself, forced himself to believe. The alternative was too agonising to contemplate.

Face burning, embarrassed and furious in equal measure, he finally extricated himself from the building, whereupon he made a beeline for the car park. His hired sedan lay within sight across the lot. Before he could reach the sanctuary of the vehicle, however, a man in a smart suit hurried over and intercepted him.

"Professor Pickering, may I perhaps have a moment or two of your time?"

Mervin didn't break stride, "Very sorry. Afraid I can't stop."

The man kept pace with him, "Please, Professor?"

Mervin stole a glance at the man, looked him up and down. His suit was expensive, and the request seemed genuine, but then so had the youths'. The truth was that at the present moment, Mervin just longed to be somewhere, anywhere, else.

"I'm sorry I really don't—"

"I represent Benedict Fine. Of Fine Technologies? Mr Fine is eager to discuss your work with you, with a view to funding your future research."

Mervin hadn't meant to stop. His legs seemed to make the decision for him.

"Look, if this is some sort of practical joke, I can assure you—"

"It's no joke, Professor. Mr Fine takes your work very seriously."

"I'm really not—"

"Perhaps if you spoke to Mr Fine yourself?" The man took out his phone. "Please?"

A moment later its screen was in Mervin's face, displaying a live video stream. The face of the smiling billionaire on the other side would have been instantly recognisable across the globe.

"Professor Pickering."

"Erm, Mr Fine, hello. I—"

"Please, call me Ben. Could we perhaps have a chat?"

Mervin could hardly say no. Benedict Fine was a powerful man, and not just because he was one of the wealthiest individuals on the planet. Fine Technology's revolutionary and patented battery innovations had earned the company a presence in virtually every tech industry one could mention.

Fine Automotive had set about eating the old giants of the car industry for breakfast. Its proprietary battery technology had made combustion engine vehicles look expensive, limited, and antiquated almost overnight. The firm had then rapidly expanded its horizons, taking a huge bite from the markets of tech giants like Google, Apple and Microsoft.

Benedict Fine himself had a reputation for being somewhat eccentric, but he was also respected and admired. If he was to take Mervin's work seriously... It was as good as instant credibility.

"Erm, yes. Of course, I'd be delighted to make myself available to—"

"Wonderful, wonderful. My chef is preparing cuttlefish paella for lunch. Do you like paella?"

There was a pause, during which Mervin worked out that by 'have a chat', Fine hadn't meant 'my people will talk to your people and we'll arrange a meeting'. The meeting was now.

Fine must have seen Mervin catch up, and smiled. "I'm currently at home. Scarcely an hour from where you are."

Mervin nodded. Fine said "Wonderful", and the call ended.

The suit pointed to Mervin's case. "If you have all your things, we have a car and a chopper waiting."

# Chapter Three

*Brooklyn, New York City, The United States.*

Reluctantly, Gabe abandoned the hunt.

He was forced to accept the store didn't have what he was looking for. Granted, he had only popped into the bodega on the off-chance, aware that among its near ceiling-high aisles of goods, density matched only by variety, rare treats from his homeland might occasionally be found.

On this occasion, however, the McVitie's chocolate digestives he had been hoping to find were nowhere to be seen. Holly had more than once pointed out that he could just order this stuff online, but really, where was the fun in that? He liked discovering them in the wild, like some rarefied, exotic delicacy, and after years spent living away from Britain, the last twelve months here in New York, that was precisely what they had become.

If something was going to be dunked in his tea this evening, it would have to be a biscuit of domestic origin. He settled upon a pack of Oreos and left the bowels of the store to pay for them at the checkout in the front kiosk.

As he strolled down the aisle and neared it, he found the clerk beside the till staring out, strangely. The kid, who couldn't have been older than twenty, seemed rooted to the spot. Gabe's first thought was that, despite his youth, he was having a stroke. Then his eyes flitted to the aisle and settled on Gabe, and gave him a small, tight warning shake of his head.

At which point things quickly went south.

A figure stepped into view at the end of the aisle, a man, wearing a grubby knee-length coat over an equally distressed looking hoody. A shaky hand poked out from the coat's filthy right sleeve, holding a pistol. Gabe read a dangerous cocktail of mean, twitchy and high-strung.

Part way through a stick-up job, it was obvious the man had not missed the clerk's attempted warning and consequently learned the store was not as deserted as he had believed. When he spotted Gabe along the aisle, he started jabbing the pistol towards him and screamed, "You! Get here, down on the floor there. NOW!"

Gabe lifted his hands, as was customary in such a situation, and dutifully appeared to comply, his feet moving slowly, his mind doing its best to think fast.

The clerk spotting his approach, the inelegant warning, the gunman noticing and turning to scream instructions – all this had taken maybe four or five seconds. A brief time in some circumstances, but plenty enough time for a fan to start whirring and the brown stuff to begin its journey towards the blades in a situation like this.

What had served it up this time was the clerk's next move.

While the gunman was preoccupied screaming at Gabe, the youth had carpe'd the diem and bent to reach under the counter. When the stick-up guy glanced back to the kiosk, he caught the clerk partway through pulling out a pistol of his own.

He got as far as bellowing, "You! Empty that fucking register n—" when he noticed, and immediately swung his pistol back towards the clerk.

Gabe was a couple of strides away.

He rushed the guy.

Two gunshots sounded in quick succession.

The clerk got his shot off first, but, terrified and panicked, it was a clumsy effort. Even before his finger squeezed the trigger Gabe saw the shot was destined to miss its mark by a mile. While the gunman appeared similarly flustered and erratic, his arm was at least out straight and pointing in the right direction as he squeezed his pistol's trigger.

Gabe crashed into him, connecting maybe a fraction of a second before the shot fired. Gabe and the stick-up guy crashed to the floor, whereupon Gabe introduced the man's nose and teeth to his right fist, numerous times in quick succession.

Then the weapon between them discharged two more shots.

Gabe felt both of them tear into him. One in the gut, one in the chest. The shock hit him like a lead shovel, and created room for the stick-up guy to wriggle free. He kicked Gabe backwards, and he collided with a snack display stand, utterly demolishing it.

Slumped back on a bed of crunchy foil bags, a dislocated part of Gabe's mind took note of the logo. Lay's potato chips. In a more serene moment, he might have found the discipline to admonish himself; *crisps*, not potato chips... This was the peril of being away from the British Isles for a few years, and it was a slippery slope. If he didn't watch himself, he'd soon be calling bums fannies, or tramps, bums... Or, worse yet, trousers, pants.

The initial shock of being shot was receding; pain rushed in to fill the vacuum.

His gut and chest were home to two big pockets of roaring fire.

Propped awkwardly against a bed of crushed snacks and the broken display rack, he surveyed the damage, the holes in his shirt where the bullets had punched through quickly lost as the surrounding fabric soaked with blood.

The stick-up guy scrambled to his feet, eyes wide as hubcaps. They darted from Gabe to the counter, behind which the youth had taken refuge. He jabbed the gun towards it and started yammering. His Adam's apple was bobbing nervously like a piston.

"Fuck, fuck, fuck fuuuuuck... You better throw that fucking strap over here, kid, before—" here, he faltered, "Just throw it over and empty that register or so help me I'll fucking blow a couple of holes in you too! You better fucking believe it!"

It was the babble of a man caught way out of his depth. A stick-up robbery was one thing, homicide was another.

Down amid the snack-strewn remains of the display, Gabe's stomach cramped, but those two pockets of fire were beginning to cool.

The clerk tossed his weapon as directed. A 9mm Smith and Wesson sailed over the counter to land on the shop's floor.

The stick-up guy yelled, "Get up, where I can see you!"

The clerk appeared, rising slowly, arms aloft.

The stick-up guy shouted, "Money! NOW!"

The kid nodded, popped the till, and began pulling notes out and stuffing them into a grocery bag. The amount didn't look like it was worth the trouble caused.

Gabe was trying to weigh up how much longer he needed, against how long he had.

Each extra second spent playing possum would see him in better shape and more agile. On the other hand, once the guy who had already put two holes in him was close to having his money, what he would decide to do next was anyone's guess. Patently unstable, and in over his head, he might conclude that leaving witnesses was a bad idea.

The clerk handed over the bag of cash.

Gabe was far from match fit, but whatever shape he was in, it would have to be good enough.

He plucked a can of greens from the bottom of a nearby shelf and let out a pained groan to attract the robber's attention. He pitched the can as the man turned, putting, to use an American phrase, some English on it. It was intended to serve more as a distraction than a weapon, so it was a satisfying bonus to see it strike bullseye and ricochet off the bridge of the gunman's nose.

Gabe propelled himself forward and swept the man's feet from under him. The stick-up guy flipped almost comically over, hit the ground hard a short distance away, his head bouncing off the linoleum. His gun hand settled close enough for Gabe to bring his heel down on it, mashing the man's fingers between the floor and the pistol's grip. His fingers sprang open. Gabe kicked the weapon away. It went skidding beneath one of the bodega's tall stacks of shelving.

When it was retrieved, hopefully the prints would help ensure its owner wouldn't be getting up to any other mischief for a while. The stick-up guy attempted to get up, but Gabe's second heel strike, this time coming down hard on his solar plexus, cut short the attempt.

While the guy was busy gulping for breath, Gabe climbed painfully to his feet. He pulled the cuff of his shirt over his hand and picked up the clerk's Smith and Wesson 9mm. Handed it back to him, grip first, over the counter.

"If he moves tell him to stay put, and if he keeps moving shoot."

The youth nodded.

"Got any large zip ties?"

The clerk's eyes never left the gasping stick-up guy, "Aisle three."

Gabe fetched them, returned, and bound the robber's hands and feet. As he got up the kid pulled out his phone.

"Police?" the youth asked.

Gabe looked down at himself and shook his head. His shirt was soaked with blood from the chest down, and his jeans were badly blood-stained, too. Beneath the shirt he could still feel the itch of the bullet holes where the tissue was knitting back together. The first of the two slugs suddenly fell from under his shirt as his body squeezed it out. It bounced off the scuffed checkerboard linoleum with hardly a sound. The second slug was probably not far behind. Gabe had no idea if the kid had seen, but it underscored that it was long past time for him to be elsewhere. Someone could easily have heard shots and dialled 911. Gabe couldn't afford to be around if the police arrived.

"Mate, I hate to do this, but I'm going to have to insist you do me a favour…"

Moments later, Gabe slipped from the shop in the clerk's jacket, t-shirt and jeans, carrying his own rolled-up and bloody clothes in a grocery bag. Thankfully it was February, and late. The cold, dark and icy street outside was all but deserted. Gabe tugged his beanie down, dropped his head and got moving.

No one would believe the young clerk or the sketchy stick-up guy's accounts. No one takes two shots at point-blank range and just walks away. Even if in all the drama their stories matched, it would sound crazy, impossible, and people preferred not to believe the world was crazy.

It was only later Gabe realised the store would have CCTV.

# Chapter Four

Carson Grave was a psychopath.

This diagnosis had not been reached in some powerful moment of self-discovery but through an extensive and sober battery of tests. The military psychologist who had profiled him was openly fascinated, and had explained to Grave what the news meant, which was helpful because until that moment Grave had known only that he wasn't like most people.

He learned that being a psychopath didn't mean he was automatically inclined to murder folk in cold blood and store their body parts in his freezer. In his case, it simply meant his capacity to empathise with others was significantly impaired. The psychologist said brain surgeons commonly scored notably higher on the psychopathic personality scale than the general population. In certain professions and situations, psychopathic tendencies could be an asset.

Scoring highly on the psychopathic personality scale didn't mean Grave felt driven to kill, but it did mean he didn't feel too bad about it on those occasions when he had to. To many, taken in isolation, this was a statement that might sound shocking, but Grave had spent most of his life as a soldier, and if killing folk was a red line never to be crossed then soldiering was, without doubt, a poor career choice.

The source of his condition, he was told, was physical rather than behavioural, a consequence of nature rather than nurture. From a physiological point of view, it boiled down to this: his amygdala was fucked. This small nugget of grey matter was the part of his brain that dealt with emotions, in particular fear, the so-called 'flight or fight' response.

This explained much. Grave didn't experience fear as most people seemed to, and found it hard to read the emotion in others. In a position of command, it turned out this was often advantageous. It allowed him to focus on the objective, rather than waste time fretting that those under his command might be ready to shit their pants.

Being able to remain calm and think logically in a fast-moving, dangerous and hostile situation was good. It made him an excellent soldier, and had almost certainly helped him scale the career ladder, to becoming a member of the US's legendary elite 75$^{th}$ Rangers Regiment, and from there to being recruited into a US army black ops regiment that had no official name and technically didn't exist. It had likely been just as useful when he had elected to leave soldiering for the state to work for a private military contractor, and from there to becoming a ghost and entering the world of the mercenary.

On the record, Carson Grave was dead.

He had been burnt to an unrecognisable corpse in an unfortunate accident. The DNA evidence confirmed the remains were his, or so the coroner's report said. Intimidation and a financial incentive could arrange much. His death certificate was filed. A charred corpse was buried.

Eventually, he had moved from being a gun for hire to assembling a unit of his own. Each and every man he recruited became a ghost too.

Grave's unit solved problems, for those who could afford it. He didn't pick sides or concern himself with the ethics of his chosen career. There were no good guys or bad guys. There were just clients, and people his clients wanted out of the way.

The way Grave saw it, when he had worked for the US military the morality of his actions, be it to capture, destroy, rescue or execute, was determined by others. That was the deal; he took orders from his superiors. His superiors were directed by politicians. But only a sucker believed the politicians were really in control. The world was run by money.

Politicians earned and kept their jobs by serving those more powerful and wealthy than themselves.

So given this was the case, why the hell not just cut out all the fucking monkeys, and work for the organ grinders directly?

For the last three years his squad had been on an exclusive and phenomenally lucrative retainer, hunting down a series of items for one such organ grinder.

The first of these items, what his client called fragments, had been discovered by accident and brought to his attention. The group who had found it were clever enough to know they had stumbled upon something remarkable and mysterious, and needed a partner with the resources and inclination to study it properly. Their intention was to secure an ally. In partnering with Grave's client, they had simply handed their candy to a big kid to take care of.

Grave had executed the clean-up. Every individual with knowledge of the discovery and the item's existence had fallen prey to a fatal, yet entirely plausible, accident. Thankfully, while dumb enough to share their discovery with someone who immediately decided to take it for himself, they had been smart enough not to share it more widely. No one had linked the eleven deaths.

His client assumed sole ownership of the fragment, and everyone subsequently brought in to study it had been inducted in such a way as to ensure that, should they abruptly vanish, they would never be easily linked to Grave's client.

The fruits of this team's labours had allowed them to locate the second fragment. Grave didn't understand the science, aside from it involving some sort of low-frequency signature. The fragment sang, and his client had set about searching for its song far and wide. Thousands of bodies across the world with the necessary equipment had been unwittingly recruited to perform scans for its special song. They didn't know why, but they were happy to take additional funding for their efforts. Eventually, one had hit paydirt.

A squad from Grave's unit had gone to collect, and almost failed.

Grave wasn't about to pretend that losing nearly half his men had been part of the plan. The woman who owned it had surprised them. They had no reason to assume she presented a threat, and would be so… resilient. It had not stopped them from acquiring the fragment, but the woman had escaped.

When they had located and gone after the third fragment, things had gone closer to plan. They now had reason to anticipate its owner would have a tough hide, and this time they expected a fight. They were correct on both counts. Grave had lost just one of his squad in retrieving the fragment, but they had dealt with its owner and left with what they came for.

A fourth fragment was now in their sights.

The way Grave saw it, when it came to executing an op, there were usually two paths. Go sneaky, quietly peel away your target's armour to leave them naked and ready for you to pop up and kick their ass, or land on them like a sledgehammer. Shock and fucking awe, hit them so hard they don't know Monday from Sunday.

On this occasion, Grave was doing both.

The building they were set to hit had some seriously stiff security, solid as an anvil, protected by the best tech money could buy. Thing was, the best tech wasn't always on the shop shelf. His client's people had hacked the shit out of the security system weeks ago.

An extensive series of drone sweeps had built a comprehensive picture of the exterior, and seismic scans carried out under the cover of minor road works had provided a detailed structural map of the interior. Some good old-fashioned surveillance had exposed behavioural habits they could exploit.

The digital attack dogs had found identities for two of the three individuals they would be dealing with: not the identities they currently went by, but their real ones.

The white guy, a Brit, was former special forces. This was a turn-up. Special Air Service. The woman was his wife, an Australian national, and a scientist, molecular biology. Both had vanished eight years ago. Now they were living large in the city that never slept, busily pretending to be someone different. The third individual stubbornly remained a mystery. Looked east Asian, aged somewhere in his mid-twenties.

Given their experience with the previous targets, they had to entertain the possibility they were potentially facing three like them this time. Grave was taking no chances. More than two dozen of his best, seasoned, handpicked, hard as granite, armed-to-the-teeth motherfuckers were prepped and ready to take what the trio had, and take them out at the same time.

Unlike the Norway op, the surrounding area on this strike was densely populated; they had taken measures to divert the authorities' attention elsewhere. Two carefully executed traffic accidents would choke the main roads into the area, and a little electronic monkey business with the region's traffic lights would strategically gum up key surrounding junctions. Toss in a couple of harmless but dramatic-looking building roof fires and a bomb hoax across town, and his team would be afforded an adequate window of time to get business done and be gone before anyone knew shit about shit.

Three teams would hit from different directions at once, one infiltrating the apartment building via the elevator, one via the stairwell from the street, and the third from the roof, having employed gas-propelled grappling hooks and power ascenders to rapidly scale the rear of the building. Once they secured the fragment they would create a kill box, herd the targets into it and eliminate them.

Two fake ambulances, quietly or full sirens and lights if needed, would transport Grave and his men to a switch-over point with fresh vehicles, and a short trip to the extraction point, where they would be airlifted out to The Shell.

The timing was crucial. Surveillance had indicated the saferoom where the item was kept was checked morning and evening. While the power to the saferoom was hackable, it couldn't be done remotely. The entry code and biometrics were local. The goal was to hit them hard during a check, while the saferoom was already open, circumvent the headache of cracking it on site.

The brief was simple. Secure the fragment. Kill its owners.

Grave's men would get the job done. They knew success was lucrative, and failure was a veeeery bad look.

# Chapter Five

Gabe stepped from the private lift into the penthouse suite and an expansive, open plan lounge and kitchen area.

The space was broken only by five polished concrete pillars, which the architect Holly had hired to remodel the place had called a 'harmonic design complement, evocative of the building's warehouse origins.' A purely aesthetic flourish rather than a structural necessity. The bloke obviously had a thing for the hard and grey stuff: the kitchen featured great polished slabs of it serving as work surfaces, including two piano-sized blocks as islands.

The centremost of the pillars in the living space was three times the size of the rest. The architect had protested against the 'asymmetry', but the client was king, and he had bent to the request, and the instruction to make it hollow. A different contractor had installed the secret vault that filled the void, where they kept the grail.

Gabe would miss the Brooklyn apartment. They were flying out at the end of the month, and the instant they departed a team of cleaners would move in and erase all trace of them. The apartment would be remodelled and let through a shell company, which was owned by another shell company, owned by yet another.

Since neither Holly nor Jin was present, he took an educated guess at where they might be and headed for the staircase and the floor below.

When they arrived in Tokyo, it would be under new identities. Time for them all to get used to new surnames again. Gabe could have worn the Big

Apple for longer. He liked it here, perhaps even more so than he had Berlin, but they were agreed: it was time to leave New York, and embarrassingly, it was his fault.

The bodega incident last month had been the impetus behind the move. He had messed up. He could have chosen to do nothing, risk letting the kid get shot, but who was he kidding? Standing by had never been his strong suit. Instead, he had got involved and drawn attention to himself, the cardinal sin. Security lay in secrecy. It was the grail's best protection.

Becoming the star of a viral video, which had escaped the internet to make it onto the state news, was hardly keeping a low profile.

*MAN TAKES TWO BULLETS, GETS RIGHT BACK UP, DISARMS WOULD-BE ROBBER AND TIES HIM UP READY FOR THE POLICE!*

It was a punchy headline, and one minute and two seconds of equally compelling footage. He was thankful for small blessings; it was cold and he had been wearing a beanie. The beard, too, had been a fortunate accident, and had quickly been shown the razor. Holly had been lobbying for him to shave it off anyway. She liked how it looked, hated how scratchy it felt.

The video covering the kiosk caught all the salient parts of the incident. The tussle, the discharge of the two shots, Gabe going down and obliterating a stand full of potato chips, then getting back up. It even caught the clerk peeling off his clothes and Gabe hastily pulling them on.

He, Holly and Jin had studied the video carefully. Thankfully the camera's vantage point failed to offer a definitively clear angle on his face, nothing a facial recognition algorithm could work with. Holly had taken the precaution of running it through the current industry-leading ones to check, and all had complained about not being able to compile sufficient data for a reasonable statistical match.

Even so, seeing the clip on the evening news and racking up hundreds of thousands of views on YouTube was uncomfortable, to say the least, and he hadn't even walked away with his chocolate digestives for his trouble.

The video meant thousands of people now knew about him, or they knew a bearded, beanie-hatted, apparently bulletproof guy was roaming around a New York neighbourhood. It was time to relocate again, go somewhere else, become someone else.

He found Holly and Jin where he had guessed they'd be, training in the gym. The space occupied most of the sub-penthouse floor and featured a bespoke and unusual combination of equipment. Free weights and resistance machines were complemented by a plethora of cardio options, a treadmill, a cross-trainer, a rowing machine, and a motorised climbing wall. To the back of the gym lay a firing range, including a space with reconfigurable walls for live-fire exercises.

His wife and his friend presently occupied the centre of the space, though, which featured a large matted area.

They were sparring, pensively circling each other, barefoot in white vests and white Gi bottoms.

Jin was wearing his charcoal grey eye patch, but not the charcoal glove which commonly accompanied it. His left arm and hand were exposed; the skin from his triceps down to his fist was extensively scarred, puckered and pale, shot through with streaks of livid pink. He had earned the burns eight years ago, in the course of defeating Reynaud and the Hashshashin.

In the years since, the scars had not healed. The grail's gift was not comprehensive. There were limits. It could patch up and fix a lot, flesh wounds, but that didn't extend to regrowing a limb or an organ if most of it had been destroyed, and it notably struggled with damage by fire. Jin believed it might take many centuries for his burn scars to vanish.

This aside, he was in phenomenal shape.

Gabe watched his wife orbiting Jin, carefully placing her feet, and conceded the same thing could be said of her. As long as they had known each other, Holly had always kept fit and healthy, but the physical specimen she represented these days was the product of years of real commitment. This Holly was leaner and harder than the one he had first met, her slim six-foot frame more muscular. In regular clothes, it was not so apparent, but in the Gi and vest, warmed up and ready to fight, it was a great deal more apparent. Holly looked like a fighter.

Eight years ago, Jin had saved both his and Holly's lives, literally.

Badly wounded and stranded in desolate Scottish moorland, had Jin not escaped with the grail and extended the same bargain he had made with Nicholas five centuries earlier, they would have died.

The deal? Immortality, and a pledge to help him keep the grail safe and secret, protected from those who might seek to use it for ill.

The bargain had fundamentally changed them both; scarcely more than half a decade later Gabe struggled to recall the simple human frailties he had once been subject to. The change went beyond healing rapidly when injured. He never got sick, not a single cough or cold in eight years. He and Holly had soon realised they no longer suffered from fatigue unless pushed to extremes.

Holly, still a scientist to her marrow, had her theories as to why. Something to do with improved ATP synthesis, acids interfering with the calcium release from something or other, the disturbance of excitation-contraction coupling…

The science was over Gabe's head. All he knew was, should the mood take him, he could choose to run a marathon every morning and another in the evening, and do it all over again the next day. No burning thighs, no aches and pains. Everything just worked better, more efficiently. One more perk afforded by the grail's gift.

For a year or two, she had continued to study the grail, test and analyse the changes in herself, but gradually her attention waned. The answers, the ones she truly wanted, were as distant as ever. She had found clues as to how the grail's gift did what it did, but not why, or how they were possible in a device over a thousand years old.

The grail.

They still called it the grail, even though none of them believed that was what it really was. The Templars, the council of nine, had found something miraculous, something which defied comprehension, and had made it comprehensible by grafting their beliefs upon it. They had taken its gift, protected it and kept it hidden until almost all of them were destroyed, and only Nicholas remained to shoulder the responsibility alone. In time he had enlisted Jin to share the burden.

In the confrontation with Reynaud and his Hashshashin, Jin had lost Nicholas and had similarly enlisted Holly and Gabe.

The woman through the window, sparring in the gym, had taken her vow seriously.

Gabe, once a member of the British army's Special Air Service, the SAS, already possessed the many skills for the job, but Holly's expertise had been in molecular biology. She was a scientist, not a soldier. To remedy this, she had conscripted Jin as her tutor.

Rather than feeling slighted, Gabe had been relieved. If she had asked him, he, of course, would have agreed, but at the same time he knew that if Holly wanted to become a warrior that meant learning to fight, and Gabe and didn't relish trading blows with her. Even now their bruises healed in seconds, he didn't want to be the one causing them.

Jin cared for Holly, too, but in a different way, which meant he could train her in the way she wanted, to test her as she would need testing, like he was doing right now in the large, square matted sparring area. Jin the tutor was about to make Holly run a gauntlet. Gabe had watched them at work enough times over the years to know this meant they were close to finishing up.

A high-density rubber mannequin torso lay at each corner of the sparring area. On each outside edge between was positioned a stand, bearing weaponry. The nearest held a rifle, the next a pair of wooden practice katana, the third throwing knives, and the last a pistol.

On the sparring mat, Holly moved in. Jin allowed himself to be taken down. Holly pinned him.

Jin spent maybe two seconds pressed faced down into the rubber-coated matting, his arm wrenched high behind him up to his shoulder blade, before slipping free to whip Holly onto her flank in a flash.

In the blink of an eye, she was pinned down exactly as he had been a moment before.

They exchanged words, lost to Gabe behind the armoured window. Jin released his hold, and they rolled back onto their feet, resumed their circling, each crouched, coiled like springs, but with hands loose and ready. After a bout of close quarters wresting Holly again had Jin pinned, face down, arm up behind his back, only this time she was a little further over his body and had set her legs wider.

Jin tried the flip again, but Holly seemed to have him locked down. Through the glass, Gabe detected the ghost of a smile on her face – about a second before Jin slipped from under her in the opposite direction to the one he'd taken before. A deft movement resulted in Holly again finding her face crushed against the mat. It wasn't that she wasn't skilled, just that her opponent was exceptionally skilled. To be fair he had around five centuries of experience over her.

Jin released her again and they rolled to their feet once more. Jin said something; Holly nodded and retreated to the edge of the mat.

Jin walked to the katana stand and plucked the topmost wooden practice sword from its notches, tipped his head, and spun to bear down on Holly who had taken the cue to come for him. He swung the katana. Holly tumbled and rolled, popped up beside the stand and seized the second practice blade.

Both adopted a stance that saw their legs set wide, arms crossed high aside their faces, and swords pointing straight out ahead. Holly was first to take the offensive. She threw a half dozen strikes. Jin deflected them all. Now he pressed her, three high strikes and a lunge. She parried the trio of strikes and sidestepped the lunge, dropping and spinning to sweep Jin's legs.

He deftly stepped over the sweep, as it seemed Holly had anticipated he would. She twisted and struck the back of his leg with the hilt of her katana. Jin buckled to one knee. Gabe was sure he caught him crack a smile too.

Jin rolled forward and back onto his feet. He shouted something, prompting Holly to discard the katana. She slid it clear of the mat and sprinted to the stand where the rifle lay. She grabbed it, set the stock to her shoulder, aligned her eye to the sight and down the long barrel. Gabe heard the muted thump of three shots in quick succession and glanced to the target across the gym, where three holes had now appeared.

Jin shouted something else and moved upon her. Holly slid the rifle away with time to spare to fend off his incoming brace of punches and kicks. She countered, landing a solid blow to Jin's ribs, but didn't pull back fast enough and took an elbow to the face.

She staggered and backpedalled. Jin continued to press her. She was fortunate to dodge a lethal-looking front kick. Jin followed up, advanced until she recovered enough to land another blow on him, at which point he shouted again.

Holly sprinted for the pistol, a Glock 19, rolled to face the rear of the gym, and emptied an entire clip. The three holes from the rifle were joined by another eighteen.

Again, Jin shouted and Holly slid away the pistol and sprinted to the last of the stands holding the throwing knives.

She grabbed one and took aim at the mannequin to her left. Gabe noted hesitation. Holly threw the first knife. The mannequin ended up with the blade in its hip, but barely. She plucked the second knife from the stand and aimed for the mannequin to her right. It missed the dummy entirely, hitting the gym floor half a dozen metres away and skidding off. The third and fourth throwing knives hit their marks, not bullseyes by any means, but sufficiently centre mass.

Clearly unhappy with the result, Holly turned and executed a sharp bow.

Jin returned it with his own, then moved to meet her. He began speaking, no doubt offering constructive criticism, but tempered with encouragement. Holly was getting faster and more skilled all the time. The grail's gift had made her fearless.

Gabe had to admit, it was kinda sexy.

The gym doors swung open and Holly and Jin emerged, Holly still berating herself. She spotted Gabe and headed over to meet him. Jin kept walking, raised a hand in greeting and left them alone.

"I looked for you earlier. Where have you been?"

"Just grabbing some air, enjoying the city, since we might not be back for a while."

"Ah, we have the whole world and no ticking clock. Who knows, you might like Tokyo even better."

"If you're there, I'll like it well enough," He pulled her to him, kissed her. When he broke away, they both surveyed the big splotch of sweat the clinch had left on his shirt.

"Wow," Holly said. "I am a mobile puddle of sweat." She sniffed under one armpit. "And potentially lethal body odour... Have you checked on it yet?"

"Not yet."

"Okay, well, how about you take care of that while I take a shower... and we can get back to you telling me how much you like me?"

"Honey, you had me at 'mobile puddle of sweat and potentially lethal body odour.'"

—

When Gabe reached the living area, he found Jin across the room in the kitchen area, drinking a glass of juice in front of an open fridge. Jin saw him.

"Want some?"

"No, I'm good. I'm just about to do the check."

Jin nodded, drained the glass and wandered over.

They approached the centremost pillar in the living area. At approximately a metre wide on each side it was larger than the others. Each of its faces featured an inset mosaic frieze. One had something the others didn't. Ten of its tiles were disguised buttons that formed a keypad. Punch in the correct sequence, which Gabe did, and the frieze rolled into the floor, revealing a steel panel with a black plate at its centre.

Gabe put his hand to it. The steel panel joined the frieze in rolling into the floor.

The cavity exposed a plain steel dais upon which stood an object whose purpose seemed to defy adequate description. Whatever words Gabe reached for, they inevitably felt insufficient to encompass what he saw.

In the most prosaic terms, the grail was a squat, slightly asymmetrical vase-shaped object with an opening at the foot on one side, through which it was possible to see a collection of shallow indentations. These contours were a perfect fit for a human hand. On the inner walls of the grail lay a multitude of razor-sharp semi-circular blades. It was seamless and made of an impossibly smooth metal covered in finely etched markings, wild sweeping arcs which converged at points, forming dense pockets of intricate detail.

While this was all accurate, it was woefully inadequate, like describing the universe as large, or love as a pleasant emotion.

For some things, words don't quite cut it.

"Will there ever be a day when it looks ordinary?"

From behind him, Jin replied, "Five centuries, and I have yet to reach it."

If what the grail looked like defied description, what it did was no less troublesome to explain. Holly had once been part of a secret team assembled by Nicholas and Jin to study it, and find some answers. What she discovered, and what Nicholas and Jin already knew, amounted to this: if someone jammed their hand into that barrel and permitted the razor-sharp teeth inside the wall to slice through their flesh, the grail imparted a gift, introduced something Holly called nanotech, which wrought changes at the most fundamental level, altered the building blocks of who that someone was, made them more than human, close to immortal.

The object was a miracle and a mystery. What it did was astonishing. It was natural to crave answers, but eight years ago, the search for them had led Nicholas Blake's former friend and latterly enemy, Raynaud Caldecott, to his door.

Reynaud wanted to use the grail to assemble an army of immortals, zealots who would have dragged what he saw as a godless world back onto the true path, but what in practice would have amounted to a dark age. Any who refused to kneel would face slaughter. They had stopped him, but the history of the world was littered with people like Reynaud. Their beliefs might differ, but if they got hold of the grail their plans would look very similar.

The three of them had discussed destroying the grail. It was the one sure way to prevent it from falling into the wrong hands, but destroying a miracle, a mystery, something so powerful and beautiful is not easy. The solution appeared simple, but also an easy one to defer, a move reserved for a day when the risk grew too great, or the truth was finally revealed about what it was they intended to obliterate. If they only knew what the grail truly was, perhaps the decision would become simple, even if the act remained challenging.

With Jin's blessing, two years ago, Holly had performed a small but significant test. The diamond-impregnated drill bit set to its surface failed to leave the faintest scratch. There existed the very real possibility the grail might be indestructible.

So, they did what the Templar council of nine had done, and Nicholas and Jin after them. They watched over the grail, kept it secret, kept it safe, until they knew what better to do.

# Chapter Six

The Brooklyn Heights building faced the Manhattan skyline across the East River, where an iconic skyline consumed the last sliver of a blazing orange sun.

Night time was about to claim the city, towers of concrete and steel set to undergo their daily metamorphosis, changing from monoliths of masonry and metal into pillars of light.

On a rooftop across the street, the woman saw Gabriel Roberts return. Gabriel Roberts wasn't his real name, of course. Gabriel Roberts was a figment, however credible his digital footprint and documentation might appear. It was a fake identity, constructed with great skill, but the seams were there if one knew where to look.

The woman had discovered his real name was Gabriel Reilly. He'd been a soldier in Britain's special forces, then for a time he was a bodyguard, then he vanished.

Now he was something else.

After ten days of surveillance his blunt, not entirely unattractive features were by now familiar. As were the subtle nuances of his body language and behaviour. He was considerably more aware and watchful of his surroundings than casual observation indicated. Early on she had been caught more than once in the sweep of his gaze while following him, and had quickly learned to keep her distance.

His car, a Fine Automotive Synapse GT electric sports convertible, glided down the block, reached the building, and turned into the ramp to the building's basement garage. The electric vehicle was effectively silent. Sports cars that roared were fast becoming a rarity, consigned to history.

Another technological paradigm had arrived, to slay an old one.

In the last three decades, it seemed the pace of technological progress had accelerated exponentially. Perhaps her unique perspective allowed her to see it more clearly. The journey to the future was moving at breakneck speed, and few seemed concerned about what might lie at the destination.

The car vanished from sight into the basement.

All three of the building's residents were now at home.

The man, the Asian gentleman and a blonde woman.

Atana had procrastinated for long enough.

They possessed something ancient and dangerous. She was going to have to do something about that.

She drew confidence from the fact that she was ancient and dangerous, too.

# Chapter Seven

Holly had just begun to peel off her vest and Gi when something captured her attention outside the window. She stopped and crossed the room, peering down the block.

A fire fizzled orange on the roof of a building in the distance. Thick smoke roiled from it, a pillar of darkness canting into the night sky. Then she spotted a second fire a moment later, on another rooftop a few blocks over, before her attention was drawn to flashing lights below.

Two Fire Department of New York ambulances raced to stop in front of their building. No sirens.

And then the lights in the apartment went out, and Holly suddenly found herself plunged into darkness.

Her first thought was a power outage.

Her second thought was that power outages weren't supposed to happen: the building wasn't exclusively reliant on the grid. It had a backup generator that was supposed to kick in if the external supply failed.

Holly didn't like it. Something…

—

…wasn't right.

The apartment lights had just died, all of them. Gabe waited for the generator to kick in. It didn't.

Was it just the lights or all the power?

He turned and saw from Jin's expression in the meagre street light bleeding through the windows across the room that he was thinking the same thing.

Gabe immediately backed out of the pillar vault and struck the switch to seal it back up. When nothing happened, they both knew that *something wasn't right* had just escalated to *something was wrong*.

Gabe heard the lift door open behind them, across the room.

He turned and saw a group of shadows slipping out, their movements tight and practised. *Something was wrong* suddenly sprouted a clutch of thick hairy legs.

One of the figures cut across a meagre swatch of street light. Gabe glimpsed insect-like stalks of night vision goggles flipped down in front of a helmet.

Somehow the apartment's formidable security management system had been compromised, not just knocked out but hacked. The functioning lift provided ample testament the building still had power and was operational, but only where it was desired.

Gabe and Jin were caught empty-handed, standing in front of the pillar vault, facing a brace of intruders with automatic rifles raised and swinging arcs for targets. The grail was standing on its dais, there for all to see.

Jin, already facing the lift, reacted faster to what emerged.

Gabe barely had time to register what he had seen before his friend had seized his shirt with both hands and thrown them both to one side as the rattle of suppressed gunfire rang out. Gabe felt a bullet tear through his elbow as Jin staggered into him, pummelled forward by the impact of gunfire smashing into his back.

Gabe did his best to back-pedal and swing them both behind one of the polished concrete pillars as gunfire carved up everything in their vicinity, chewing chunks of flooring and plaster. The windows were hosed with fire too. Bullet resistant, they didn't shatter, instead becoming a canvas for a string of cloudy impact points.

Jin was somehow still on his feet, but Gabe wasn't confident how mobile he would prove to be. The grail's gift made them resilient, but only within bounds. Jin had just soaked up a solid burst of automatic gunfire, and while the grail's gift would be working furiously to repair the damage, Gabe was in no doubt there would be a lot of that damage to repair.

The grail still sat exposed in the open vault, but if they were to secure it and survive, they needed to keep moving, with purpose. The wrong move would be their last move.

An armed squad had somehow breached the building's security.

They had gained access to the security and building management system.

All of it, or part? Could they have just hijacked a few sub systems? If so, some of the more exotic parts might still be active and accessible. It was time to find out.

The security system was part of the building management system, and both could be fully voice-operated. Most instructions it carried out this way were trivial but handy environmental functions, turning lights on or off, adjusting the thermostat, controlling appliances… The instruction Gabe prepared himself to yell from behind the concrete pillar was more singular, so uncommon it was hoped they would never have to issue it: an emergency lockdown and eliminate code.

When delivered, the following sequence was meant to unfold: The entire apartment would lock down, become hermetically sealed, and a fast-acting and lethal gas would be discharged. Lethal to any regular mortal, that is, but merely very unpleasant for the three people who lived in the building. A quarter of an hour later the machinery would kick into reverse and begin to vent the gas slowly and harmlessly from the roof. Gabe, Jin and Holly could then pick through the resulting garbage to see who these invaders were.

Gabe shouted the eight code words as loudly and clearly as he could, "Golf-Alpha-Mike-Echo-Oscar-Victor-Echo-Romeo!"

And waited.

Nothing happened.

Actually, this was not strictly accurate, another barrage of gunfire pummelled the pillar shielding them. A large chunk sheared dramatically off and thumped to the floor.

It was no place to hang around.

Gabe girded himself, got the best grip on Jin he could manage with one arm, gave himself a three count and propelled them towards one of the kitchen's two large granite islands. Gunfire erupted once more. Bullets tore up the apartment floor in their wake. Gabe hurled them into a dive and they landed in a bundle, sliding inelegantly behind cover.

Gabe scrambled to his hands and knees and tried to get a picture of Jin's condition. His friend was ominously still, barely responsive, vest and Gi more dark than white now. He tipped him forward and saw his back was a mess of tattered fabric and flesh. Worse, while what he could see wasn't pretty, he knew the internal damage, which he couldn't, might be worse still.

He fumbled for Jin's neck, searched for a pulse. At first, he struggled, then located a beat, stronger than he had expected. Good. Jin would heal, not fast, certainly not as quickly as the situation called for, but given the chance, he would mend. They just needed some way to buy time—

There was a blast and a crash to Gabe's left.

He peeked over the countertop and saw a weak rectangle of light cutting through the apartment door from the stairwell, which was now hanging from one hinge. More silhouettes scuttled into the apartment and vanished into deep shadow.

*Something was very wrong* suddenly gained two dozen pounds of rippling muscle and grew fangs.

By Gabe's estimation, they were now facing at least seven or eight armed invaders. Jin was out of service and vulnerable. Gabe was armed with just one fist, both feet and an unlimited supply of foul language.

Or perhaps not.

He had glimpsed something when he peeked over the counter top: the magnetised steel block which held a paring knife, a utility knife, a bread knife, a boning knife, a carving knife, and a razor-sharp Japanese chef knife.

Gabe reached above the counter and pawed for the block. His fingers found the handle of the chef's knife and plucked it from its slot. The move invited the rattle of more suppressed gunfire. He yanked back his hand as the countertop came under fire.

He eyed the chef knife. It was hardly a fair match for an automatic rifle, but big and sharp, and better than nothing.

Gabe tested the state of his wounded elbow, attempted to flex his right hand. The fingers responded, curled a little, but nothing he could pretend was in danger of forming a grip. He wasn't as confident with his left hand, but it would have to do. He wasn't looking to perform surgery, he just needed to get close and deliver sufficient force to any strike.

They were being attacked, by a heavily armed and presumably well-trained group. Their building's security had been hacked, thoroughly skewered. The invaders had cut the lights, taken control of the lift, disabled the emergency lockdown and eliminate system, and strolled in as if they owned the place.

It was impossible the incursion was just an armed robbery. They had wealth, plenty, Nicholas and Jin having accrued a sizable fortune over the centuries, but little of it was kept here. There were no suitcases full of cash or priceless jewellery or works of art that someone could walk away with, not sufficient to justify this sort of operation.

They were after the grail.

And they had known he, Holly and Jin were capable of putting up a stiff fight, given the chance.

If there were any lingering doubt it was put to rest when one of the shadowy figures barked, "Ghost Two, pin those targets down! Five, secure the fragment!"

The fragment? That had to mean the grail.

Gabe checked Jin. His ravaged back looked improved, but still bad. It was going to be a while yet before he was ready to move under his own steam, let alone fight. Gabe knew the invaders were unlikely to spin their wheels and let that happen.

He took a quick peek around the kitchen island, and just as quickly pulled back as he was rewarded with more automatic fire. The oak fronted kitchen cabinets were almost chewed to splinters.

The group didn't seem to be advancing, though, which meant the plan was to keep him pinned down while they collected the grail. Once they had secured it, Gabe had no doubt the plan would change.

Getting the grail was surely only half the job.

Eliminating its previous owners would be the other half.

—

Seconds after the lights had died, bursts of gunfire had sounded inside the apartment. Not naked rounds, Holly noted, but suppressed.

It was an indication of how much she and her world had changed in the last eight years that not only could she know this fact, but guess the model of weapon and ammunition. She had fired enough varieties on the range for the characteristic flat clatter of the suppressed rounds of an M4 carbine to be familiar.

She moved quickly to the bedroom door.

The gunfire sounded like it was coming from the main living space, where Gabe had gone to perform the twice-daily ritual of checking the grail was safe and sound in its vault.

Her first instinct, shrill and urgent, was to head there as fast as possible. It belonged to the old Holly and was immediately overruled by a surer, calmer voice, shaped from years of training under Gabe and Jin. To join a gunfight, she needed a gun. Crashing in empty-handed wasn't just rash and risky; depending on the situation it might even make her a liability rather than an asset. The armoury was close, just down in the gym, less than a minute away if she moved fast...

She pushed open the door and peered through. The hallway was dark but empty. She slipped through and hurried for the staircase that lay near the far end. One flight led down to the gym; the other up to the roof. As she drew near, a loud boom came from the upper flight as the roof door crashed open.

Holly froze as moonlight spilt through, followed by the thump of boots. She dived into the alcove beneath the staircase and threw herself flat against the wall.

Four figures in black combat gear headed down the staircase, automatic rifles up and ready to fire.

—

Gabe edged towards the other end of the kitchen island. He needed another peek to afford him the lie of the land, and a change of position might just prevent him from getting his head ripped apart by heavy automatic gunfire...

He was just closing in on the corner when he found himself staring up into the muzzle of an M4 Carbine.

It was obvious the figure shouldering it had been hoping to creep up on him, and seemed equally surprised to find himself face to face with his prey.

He was likely yet more surprised when Gabe lunged, swatted the M4's muzzle aside and stuck him with eight inches of Japanese chef's knife. The spot was well chosen, right in the armpit where his Kevlar plate afforded no protection. The blade, which infomercial-style would have cut cleanly through a car tyre, went in all the way to the handle.

The man screamed, but only briefly. Gabe tugged him down behind the island, relieved him of his M4, and silenced him by bringing the butt down on his face.

Unfortunately, the man had not advanced on Gabe and Jin alone.

Fortunately, the last few seconds had improved Gabe's means and the condition of his right elbow. His right hand was weak, but back in action.

When the second figure in black appeared around the opposite corner, he was more prepared and better armed. He let the invader have it with a burst from the M4. The guy was knocked clean off his feet.

Gabe wasted no time before plundering both men's vest pouches for magazines, stuffing as many as he could fit into his pockets.

—

Holly had spotted the armed intruders, but thankfully they hadn't yet seen her.

Decked out in military gear, they had night vision goggles affixed to their helmets and were busy sweeping their enhanced gazes left and right, seeking out targets.

Two peeled off and headed down the far hallway. One hung back, halfway up the stairs. The last of the group turned and moved in her direction.

She knew he would pass her in a moment or two. She also knew, thanks to the night vision goggles he was wearing, that the darkness wasn't about to hide her. One glance below the staircase would see her exposed, pressed into the alcove, her back literally against the wall.

Something stopped the figure in his tracks, noise and movement from the stairs to the roof. His squad mate who had been hovering there suddenly lurched forward, something jutting rudely from his abdomen. The moonlight caught the slick, wet tip of a stout sword. Whoever had put it there was busy propelling the man down the rest of the steps into the hallway.

Their advance revealed the sword's owner, a woman. She manoeuvred her victim onward, employing him as cover. His cries attracted the attention of his companions further down the corridor, who must have turned back, assessed the situation and promptly opened fire.

Holly had no idea who the woman washed in moonlight was, but her actions suggested she was no friend of the group who had entered ahead of her.

While she was also dressed head to toe in black, it was in stark contrast to the others' military apparel, her garments being of the civilian variety: a leather racing style bike jacket, slim black jeans and buckled biker boots.

She yanked her short sword free, slotting it deftly into a scabbard at her hip, but continued to frogmarch her wounded captive forward. An MP7 submachine pistol appeared over the man's shoulder, from which she commenced to fire in retort. Her meat shield made it a further three steps before she kicked him towards his companions and spun left to take cover behind the corner of the hallway.

She appeared unaware of the fourth invader close by Holly, who had already turned around, raised his M4 and was about to take her down.

Holly eyed his outline, saw the two holsters strapped to his thighs in the gloom, willing to bet one held a sidearm and the other a blade. What she didn't know was which side held which.

It came down to this: the one on the right was closer.

She made her move.

She darted from the alcove, unsnapped the stud on the holster, and reached in. Her fingers closed on the handle of a dagger. She snatched it out, seized the man's chin and delivered a strike to the back of his leg which buckled him to one knee. She knew what had to come next.

Despite this, she hesitated.

In movies, a neat sweep of a blade across the bad guy's throat resulted in a quick, silent and surprisingly clean death. In reality, cutting a man's throat open was generally messier work. She recalled Gabe's instruction on executing the manoeuvre, basic but, he assured her, the surest way to get the job done: get in close, get a firm grip, and get sawing. It was an ugly, violent way to take a life, no doubt, but if you were going to do it that was the recipe.

At her own insistence, she had spent the years since acquiring the grail's gift being trained to defend, to incapacitate, to kill, knowing that one day the situation might call for just those skills. Today was that day. Now was the moment. These men had invaded their home, armed and prepared. She had to do what needed to be done. Kill the man, now.

And maybe, in another half-second, she would have, had he not been sharper than she anticipated. Her instant of hesitation had been an instant too long. When she had driven her captive to one knee, she should have applied the blade, because while she dithered, he had ditched his rifle. While she failed to cut, he had planted one hand firmly on the floor and reached over his shoulder with the other.

And seized her wrist.

Realising her mistake, Holly immediately pulled the blade towards his throat, and, without the element of surprise, met considerable resistance.

When it came to leverage, theoretically Holly had the advantage; she was above and behind tugging back, he was already in a clinch and pushing away. The crucial difference amounted to approximately thirty pounds of muscle. Holly's adversary was simply bigger and stronger than she was, and not wanting for adequate motivation. He had a dagger inches from his carotid artery and didn't need a multi-media presentation to grasp what Holly planned to do with it.

His meaty hand exerted a formidable grip and backed by a thick clump of triceps it was doing an admirable job of keeping the blade from reaching into his throat.

Holly was steadily being overpowered. Her would-be victim was forcing her wrist away like... Well, like his life depended on it.

And if it came down to brute strength, she was going to lose.

Holly switched tack to ensure it didn't.

She quit fighting to wrench the blade back, and instead redirected her opponent's considerable muscle to her advantage, suddenly driving the dagger forward instead. The man found himself lurching forward, overbalancing. Holly took a whip-sharp step to the side, pulled back, broke his grip on her wrist and replaced it for one on his. She wrenched his arm up behind him and slammed the heel of her palm into his shoulder. She felt the ball of his humerus pop out of the glenohumeral joint as his face smashed into the floor.

Before he could do anything else, a burst of gunfire ended his life.

Holly looked up and locked eyes with the woman behind the corner of the hallway who had fired it. A brief exchange, but meaningful. An instant later the woman ejected the magazine from her MP7, slotted in a fresh one, and pivoted out of cover to re-engage with the soldiers ahead.

Holly collected the dead man's weapon, her hands as much as her vision identifying it as a fully automatic M4A1 carbine in the darkness. Personally, Holly favoured the Heckler and Koch 416, it stayed cooler with use, but she wasn't about to grumble. Beggars couldn't be choosers.

In the main living space, the fierce rattle of suppressed gunfire ruining expensive interior design resumed.

Holly went after the mystery woman, to join the fray.

—

Gabe leant from behind the kitchen island and returned fire, scanning for movement in the shadows. The magazine in the M4A1 was now easily a third spent, and his next magazine was his last.

This was no kind of plan. As it stood, he was scarcely holding his attackers at bay, and doing even less to stop them from stealing the grail. Even this inadequate state of affairs would only last as long as his ammunition did, and he was in no doubt they were as aware of that fact as he was.

To make matters worse still, he was taking pot shots at shadows, whereas they could see him clear as night-vision-enhanced day. They were just playing things out until he was back to fruity language and a chef's knife.

Beside him, Jin was improving with every second that passed, but was still in bad shape, and needed considerably more time than Gabe reckoned they had. Had he been alone, Gabe would have ditched his position and used mobility to improve his odds, but he wasn't alone. If he left Jin, their adversaries would soon move in and finish his friend off.

Gabe was literally between a rock and a hard place: a lump of polished granite and a squad of armed soldiers.

It was just as he came to this depressing conclusion that, across the room to his left, past the concrete pillars at the head of the hallway leading to the bedrooms, Gabe saw a burst of muzzle flash and heard gunfire.

—

Holly rounded the corner just as the mystery woman reached the head of the hallway onto the main living area. Two bodies lay in her wake.

The mystery woman had lifted one of the men's helmets and was now wearing it, night vision googles flipped down. Holly took the other dead man's helmet and followed suit.

The mystery woman was hunkered down at the corner, pressed tight to the wall. She leant out and let rip with a sustained burst from her MP7.

Holly hurried forward and took up a position on her opposite side, far enough back to provide cover, but close enough to earn a view into the main living space. Through the night vision googles, the scene was transformed, rendered in a greenish-blue hue. The dimensions felt a little off as a result of her viewing a camera feed, everything seeming ever so slightly magnified, but the veil of darkness was lifted.

She immediately located two aggressors positioned behind a pillar across the room. Then her gaze found Gabe and Jin. Her husband was tucked behind the far edge of the granite kitchen island, and her friend was slumped against the cabinets, his vest and Gi bottoms drenched dark with blood.

The mystery woman fired on some of the invaders on the right side of the room. Holly opened fire too, on the two figures she had spied behind the pillar to the left side.

They made good on their element of surprise; the mystery woman nailed one of the soldiers on the right. He staggered and crumpled. The two Holly fired on shifted position.

Gabe must have seen, because a second later he popped from cover, fired and nailed one of them. His target dropped his weapon, clutched his arm and shrank back behind the pillar, injured.

Soon after, one of the men yelled something, unintelligible from Holly's position, but the meaning soon became evident.

It was an order to commence a retreat.

A canister suddenly arced through the air, bounced into the centre of the room, and began to spew thick smoke. In seconds the entire room was choked with it. Several figures darted through the fug towards the door to the stairwell. Holly fired on them blindly. She had no idea of the outcome. It was already close to impossible to see a thing through the dense smoke.

Opposite her, the mystery woman abandoned her position and went in pursuit.

Holly was right on her heels.

—

When gunfire came from the hallway, Gabe thought he'd been flanked, about to face yet more aggressors moving in, but it soon became evident that wasn't the case.

He and Jin were not the targets.

Whoever had appeared fired on the soldiers across the room. He just had time to glimpse one struck and topple from behind his cover when movement in the two to his right offered an opportunity. He gave himself space and scored a hit. His target dropped his weapon, grabbed his arm and turtled up.

Gabe peered back towards the hallway.

It could only be one person, surely? He hadn't allowed himself to linger on the question of where Holly was until now. He had simply prayed she was safe and focused his attention on the immediate business of staying alive. This seemed to suggest she was not only safe, but had made it to the armoury.

He tried to pick her out in the shadows of the hallway and was surprised to identify what appeared to be two shapes lurking in the darkness.

Then came the smoke canister, and he had more immediate concerns.

It sailed across the room, tumbled into the centre of the lounge, and began to discharge thick white smoke. Someone back there yelled, and a collection of dark shapes suddenly scurried for the door.

It would have been nice to welcome their exit, but it wasn't that simple.

He again checked on Jin; the smoke had already reduced visibility to less than an arm's reach. He found Jin fighting to sit up. Fighting, but not quite succeeding. He wasn't going anywhere without help, not quite yet. Gabe ran to the central pillar, fumbled inside, peered through cloying dense smoke.

He knew what to expect, but the reality of the empty steel dais hit him hard all the same. The grail was gone.

He sprinted for the door and into the stairwell, snapped the M4 over the rail. The smoke was still rolling around his legs making its way down, sparse enough to spot two abandoned helmets and two figures a level down ahead of him. The woman foremost was dressed in black and her identity was a complete mystery. The second woman was considerably more familiar; she was his wife.

Holly was alive and well. She was also carrying a borrowed M4, and a stride, maybe two behind the mystery woman leading the pursuit.

Their quarry was a further two levels below them, the remainder of the soldiers who had attacked them. The rearmost of the group was covering his companions' exit, sweeping his rifle up through the stairwell and issuing intermittent bursts of gunfire which smashed into the railing and the ceilings.

Gabe veered to the outer edge as several rounds punched into the wall above his head.

He cleared another two floors when the firing ceased. A peep over the rail confirmed the invaders had exited into the street. He saw the mystery woman and Holly hit ground level too.

He picked up his pace, and spilt out onto the street sooner after, in time to see the first of two FDNY ambulances screech away into the night. A glimpse through the ambulance's rear doors before them slamming closed revealed a clutch of black combat gear suited figures.

The mystery woman paused in the middle of the road, but only for a beat. She was soon on the move again, sprinting across the street toward a parked motorcycle. Gabe raised his M4A1 and peppered the ambulances with the balance of its magazine, but in seconds both vehicles were squealing around the corner of the block. He looked for Holly, but she was nowhere to be seen.

Across the way, the mystery woman had straddled the bike. He heard the growl of its engine firing up, and a squeal of rubber as she rolled on the throttle and tore off after the ambulances.

He needed to get after them too. With no obvious transport to hand, he found himself looked around for a car to jack, but the nearest thing was a sliver sedan down the street, which quickly peeled right and vanished down a side road. The sight of a man standing in the street who had just fired on a departing ambulance probably played a part in the driver's hasty diversion.

The grail was getting further away with each passing moment...

A screech of tyres on tarmac caused Gabe to spin round. Something rocketed from the ramp leading to the bowels of the building behind and swung sharply to a stop in front of him. It was his Fine Synapse GT convertible, and Holly was at the wheel. She had taken one look at the group piling into their fake ambulances and immediately doubled back for the basement level garage.

# Chapter Eight

Gabe didn't wait for a gilt-edged invitation. He vaulted over the door and dropped into the passenger seat.

His backside hardly touched the seat leather before he was thrust back as the electric sports car's engine silently propelled them from 0 to 60 miles per hour in less than 1.7 seconds. Silent, but for the shriek of rubber on asphalt.

They tore down the block and around the junction just in time to catch the mystery woman's motorbike cutting across a junction two blocks further ahead, barely missing a white SUV, taking the turn so tight her roadside knee almost grazed the tarmac.

Holly put her foot to the floor. Buildings blurred past on both sides.

Gabe turned to her. "Okay… and she is?"

Holly eyes never left the road. "On our side?"

It was late evening and streets were relatively quiet, but this was still Brooklyn. Holly was required to execute a tight series of manoeuvres to negotiate slower traffic before they arrived at the same junction the woman on the bike had recently vanished behind. Hardly slowing, Holly slid the GT around it at nearly ninety degrees, and earned them another brief glimpse of both the mystery woman's motorbike and the ambulances ahead, before one by one they each cleared the next turning and once again disappeared from view.

Fortunately, Holly knew the surrounding streets well, and was able to anticipate their turns and earn them ground. When the GT screamed through the intersection at Middagh and Cadman Plaza, and once again regained sight of bike and ambulances, the gap between them had narrowed substantially. The ensuing straight allowed Holly to close the distance further. They were catching up fast.

The driver of the lead ambulance suddenly fired up his sirens and lights, then the one behind it too. Traffic ahead began to pull aside to make way for the emergency vehicles to speed through, but not all the vehicles ahead had somewhere to go.

Reaching an impasse, the lead ambulance took the measure of weaving into the oncoming lane to overtake a bus, forcing an oncoming Chevrolet to slam on its brakes and prompting it to blare its horn. A mini-van behind rear-ended the Chevrolet a second later. The ambulance behind missed both vehicles by inches.

The mystery woman and Gabe and Holly in the GT took advantage of the path carved out for them to gain yet more ground.

The combined two ambulance, a car and a bike breakneck convoy met a hard right at Prospect Street. One after another the ambulances plunged beneath the Brooklyn bridge. Holly cut across the oncoming lane to narrow the gap, and the bridge swallowed them too. They were now right on the tail of the mystery woman's bike, close enough to see her pull out her MP7 and begin firing on the rearmost ambulance.

Its back doors swung open seconds later, revealing two prone, black-combat-gear-clad men lying on its deck, automatic rifles braced to their shoulders. They responded in kind, with the added benefit of double the firepower and a steadier aim.

The mystery woman holstered the MP7 and peeled hard to the right, bent low over the handlebars and mounted the sidewalk. She surged forward, pulling almost level with the ambulance's cab, clear of the rear gunners' fire line.

The underpass at Clumber corner was fast approaching, and soon upon them, funnelling them all together. The ambulances, the mystery woman on her bike, and Holly and Gabe in the GT suddenly found themselves at tight quarters.

The rearmost ambulance driver spied an opportunity and seized it. He swung the emergency vehicle hard to the right, seeking to crush the mystery woman and her motorbike against the underpass wall.

The woman saw him coming, bent even lower over her handlebars, juiced the gas and pulled ahead, scarcely escaping the gap as it shrank to nothing. The ambulance collided with the wall, its metal flank scudding the concrete and spewing a shower of livid sparks before the wall fell away and it skidded onto Adams Street and then slalomed crazily into Sands.

The soldiers in the back were given little choice but to grab something solid and hold tight or face being bounced out into the road or thrown around the back of the vehicle. One door of the rear doors whipped and slammed closed while the other swung free, a slave to the caprice of velocity and momentum.

Holly glanced over at Gabe. He was climbing up out of his seat and bracing himself against the windshield frame to set the M4 to his shoulder. He gave her a nod and she took his cue, flooring the accelerator to draw tight with the trailing ambulance. He trained his fire through the open back door and scored a hit. One of the soldiers inside went down and showed no sign of getting back up.

They raced down Adams, plunging under the Manhattan bridge and the Queens expressway what seemed like mere heartbeats later.

The mystery woman, a short distance ahead, abruptly peeled away, cut a hard right, across the sidewalk and onto the turf at the head of Trinity Park, where she vanished between the trees.

One after another the speeding ambulances skated around the corner of Sands and Gold Street. Holly took the apex tighter, the GT's superior handling and speed again earning them ground. Gabe tossed his spent magazine into the footwell and slotted in a fresh one, his last.

The dark shape that came sailing overhead seemed to come from nowhere. Gabe and Holly looked up to see the undercarriage of a motorbike, appearing for a moment to be suspended in mid-air. In truth, it was simply travelling as quickly as the GT was eating asphalt.

Gravity shattered the illusion. The mystery woman's bike dropped from the fifteen-foot-high apex of Trinity Park to thump down, back wheel first, front wheel on the road ahead, dead level with the leading ambulance. The MP7 was in her hand an instant later, peppering the passenger side door with bullets and shattering the window.

The soldier riding shotgun attempted to return fire. His M4 rifle appeared over the sill, but not soon enough.

The mystery woman's aerial shortcut had won her the element of surprise and she didn't squander it. As soon as the passenger side ambulance window had shattered, she had cut closer. Gabe and Holly watched as she slammed her bike against the door, smashing the soldier's forearm and rifle against the frame, seized the lip of the window, abandoned her ride, and started to climb in.

Driverless, her bike toppled, hit the road, flipped, tumbled and crumpled, before sliding to an ungainly stop. The latter ambulance was forced to swerve violently to avoid it, which had the knock-on effect of forcing Holly behind the wheel of the Synapse GT to swerve violently too.

The mystery woman and the passenger were grappling through the ambulance's passenger side window. She had the soldier's tactical vest with her left fist and was vigorously pummelling his face with her right. He was jammed up against the open window, his ability to fight back limited. The woman took a break in thumping him to reach down. A second later he was facing the muzzle of her MP7.

Before she could pull the trigger, either by accident or design, the door between them flew open. If the soldier on the other side was responsible, it looked like he hadn't thought the finer details of his plan through, as he seemed every bit as surprised as she was when the driver beside him swerved around a car ahead and they both swung out. He suddenly found himself dangling on the inner side as the door flapped free, his boots scraping on the road, while the woman clung to the other side. She made something closer to lemonade out of the situation and set about climbing around the door and over the dangling soldier to access the cab.

Not oblivious to recent events, the driver of the ambulance had other ideas.

Three shots came from inside the cab, and the mystery woman fell from the ambulance to the road, but not empty-handed. She yanked the dangling soldier free too. They both hit the asphalt hard and rolled to an ungainly stop.

Driving expertly at speed while shooting expertly at speed takes an uncommon degree of skill, which, it turned out, the ambulance driver lacked. The result of his multitasking failure came in the form of the approaching intersection with Concord Street, and the eighteen-wheeler rig currently crossing it.

He wrenched the steering wheel to avoid a collision. The ambulance turned, sharply, so sharply it nearly tipped over. It teetered on two wheels, and would most likely have ended up on its side, but found its equilibrium with the assistance of a bright purple Volkswagen Beetle.

The ambulance swiped the car a glancing blow, which simultaneously righted it, and shunted the purple bug onto the sidewalk. The turn was uglier than a birthday cake sliced with a hatchet, but a turn nonetheless. The ambulance cleared the corner and continued down Nassau, quickly picking up speed.

The driver of the second ambulance, behind which Holly and Gabe snaked, had seen the one ahead careen towards the Beetle and taken evasive manoeuvres of his own. He pumped his brakes hard and cut sharply around both vehicles.

A rear-end collision between the GT and a truck wouldn't be much of a contest. The GT would crumple like tinfoil next to the hulking FDNY ambulance. Holly had no choice but to cut wider still.

The pedestrians ahead seemed to come out of nowhere, a young man and a woman, both sprinting to escape the ambulance racing towards them.

Then they saw the speeding GT heading for them too, realised they weren't going to be able to outpace it and froze, rabbits caught in headlights.

There was nowhere left for Holly to go. She steered hard, went wider to avoid the couple and collided with the first of a string of parked cars.

The impact threw both her and Gabe into the dash and triggered the airbags. The GT jack-knifed hard, spun out, and came to rest facing the opposite direction.

When they climbed from the ruined sports car, dazed, indeterminate moments later, the ambulances were long gone, their sirens not even in the air.

But that didn't mean they were alone.

Back down the street behind them, the mystery woman was hunched over the body of the soldier she had dragged from the ambulance with her. She had the scruff of his tactical vest in one hand. In the other, she wielded her short sword, out of its scabbard with its point pressed to his throat.

Even from where Gabe stood it was easy to see the goon was in grim shape. His high-speed tête-à-tête with the road had torn a large flap of skin from his face; a hint of cheekbone winked through the blood which sheeted down his jaw and neck. His left leg was bent sideways at the knee in a manner that would have been fine for a child's action figure, but less so for a real human being.

If the man was sharing anything, Gabe wanted to hear it. He and Holly hurried over. As they closed in, they caught the man's groans and the gist of the woman's questioning.

She wanted to know where the rest of the man's group were going.

The soldier stared into her face but said nothing. There was some question as to whether he wouldn't talk, or couldn't. The mystery was solved a moment later when he quit groaning and stopped breathing.

The woman relinquished her grip on his vest. His limp body flopped back onto the road.

Rising to her feet, the woman turned to meet Gabe and Holly. She winced as she got up; two bullet holes ventilated her leather racing jacket, and a nasty gash cut across her brow with a patch of road rash below. The last traces of both vanished as they reached her, leaving only a track of drying blood.

The fake or stolen FDNY ambulances and their sirens were long gone, but others would soon take their place, real ones, along with police cars and sirens too.

Gabe stared at the mystery woman, but before he could say anything, she did.

"We need to talk."

Gabe shared a look with Holly. "Too right we do, but first I think we might want to get our arses as far away from here as possible."

The mystery woman nodded. Gabe started back in the direction of Trinity Park. The woman followed his lead, but Holly stopped them short.

"Wait." She turned back, knelt beside the dead soldier, and set about tugging one of the man's boots free. She wiped its heel across his bloody jaw, then peeled off one of his gloves and pressed his hand to the other side of the boot, "Gabe. Got your phone?"

He nodded.

"Good. Then while we're on the move see if you can contact Jin. Tell him before he abandons the apartment, I need him to strip the dead, get their prints, applied to a ceramic cup will do, toss their clothes and anything else they have into polythene refuse bags, and take them with him."

# Chapter Nine

The battered and thoroughly fake FDNY ambulances drew to a halt inside the warehouse, and the huge roller door rumbled shut behind them. Six utterly unremarkable mid-range family cars awaited them, with an equally mundane change of clothes for those who would drive away in them.

The nearly seven-foot-tall, muscular frame of Carson Grave jumped from the rear of the first ambulance into the dank and cavernous building, swearing like a trucker who had once been a sailor and had just hit his thumb with a hammer. He removed his helmet and mask. Close-shaven head, bull-necked, his face wore the expression of a man not best pleased.

Seven of his men were dead. Each operative's body armour was fitted with a GPS tag and a heart rate monitor. One of the fallen still lay in the rear of the ambulance, one was somewhere a few blocks back, and the rest were back in the Brooklyn apartment.

Dead wasn't good, but Grave liked it better than captured. Dead men didn't talk. While the people he recruited weren't the sort who cracked easily, and each one of them knew what betrayal would mean, everyone had their limits. Grave had first-hand experience. Despite what the liberals and academics said, pain did loosen lips.

As ops went, this had not been the pinnacle of Grave's career, but really, who the hell could have predicted the bitch who had gotten away from them would come out of the fucking woodwork to throw a spanner in the works half a world away tonight?

She had transformed what should have been a well-executed strike into a shitshow. He had lost men, failed to eliminate the three targets, and failed, again, to kill the bitch herself, despite being offered a second bite of the cherry.

All less than ideal.

They had secured the fragment, though. So, not quite a total shit show.

Still, how had the woman known to be there?

A question for later.

Right now, they had to rendezvous with the aircraft that would transport them and it back to The Shell. In their absence, both vehicles and every scrap of clothing, arms and equipment would be taken care of. Hank, one of the two men from the unit tasked with the clean-up, was done locking down the warehouse door and approached.

"You get it?" he asked.

Grave nodded, then looked toward the ambulances.

"Make sure it's done right, Hank. Not a trace."

"You got it."

Grave nodded again.

Another of his men climbed from the second ambulance, carrying the object they had been sent to acquire. "Boss."

Grave took it from him.

While the rest of his men were stripping down and throwing their kit into the back of the ambulances ready for destruction, Grave intended to take a minute or two.

He wanted a look at what they'd got. And he wanted it in private.

# Chapter Ten

Minutes after midnight, the wheels of a private jet lifted off a private airfield off the 180 just past Ridgefield Park, carrying four passengers, Gabe, Holly, Jin and the mystery woman. Jin had chosen the destination. Somewhere safe and secret, and a continent away from recent events.

They had found Jin alive and well back at the Brooklyn building, only shredded, bloody gym attire and dented pride evidence of how close he had come to that perilous boundary where even the grail's gift reached its limits.

He had answered when Gabe had called him, listened attentively and moved quickly. As per Holly's instructions, he had collected the requested material while making arrangements for their departure. This part was relatively simple. They planned for contingencies. There was always somewhere, in fact, many somewheres, ready to head for at a moment's notice should they need to vanish.

They had people on retainer, prepared to transport them and to have things ready for their arrival. It was part of the apparatus of survival and security Nicholas Blake and Jin had carefully built and maintained, paid for by wealth amassed over centuries, old money, extensive, sober and resilient, in currency, in stocks, in gold and precious stones, in land and property.

But it had not made them invulnerable.

The shock of their failure had left them dazed. Jin had been guardian to the grail for nearly five centuries and had seen it plucked from his grasp in less than fifteen minutes.

It was a lot to absorb.

Someone had found out about the grail. They had sent a force to take it, and that force had been successful, but Gabe would have bet good money that had only been half the job. There was no doubt he, Holly and Jin were supposed to have been eliminated too. The mystery woman who had appeared from nowhere had evened the odds. It seemed she possessed the grail's gift, too. Gabe had seen it with his own eyes, seen her walk away from the fall from a speeding vehicle, watched the gash and the scrape on her face heal, seen no sign of wounds from the bullet holes in her jacket.

Now she was here, joining them in their exodus, an extra passenger in the eleven-seat luxury cabin of a Gulfstream G650ER. Leaving had been hectic. There hadn't been much time for discussion, but she had answers, she promised. Gabe, like Jin and Holly, was keen to hear them.

Was Holly correct in assuming their mysterious guest was on their side? Just because she had fought the group who had invaded their Brooklyn building didn't mean she was automatically their ally, and yet without her appearance there was every chance they would have been outgunned and overwhelmed.

The pilot announced they were at cruising altitude.

The mystery woman found her three fellow passengers looking at her. Holly asked the question.

"So... Fancy telling us who you are?"

"My name is Atana."

"How old are you?"

Holly was making the same assumption Gabe was. If this woman had the grail's gift that meant at some point in the past she had used the grail, and probably sometime before the Templars discovered it, over a thousand years ago.

"The truth?" she asked, and watched as all three nodded. "I don't know, but... Somewhere around three and a half thousand years? Possibly more. It is difficult to know for certain. My first memory is of having no memory. After that, they are of Crete, although it was known by a different name then."

Gabe couldn't help himself, "Three and a half thousand years..."

"You've walked among man for over three and a half thousand years?" echoed Jin.

The woman, Atana, shook her head, "I have *existed* for at least three and a half thousand years, but there are gaps, stretches where I sought respite in hibernation." Atana gathered from their reactions this too was news. "Our gift affords us this mercy," she added, before continuing. "You want answers, and I will offer illumination where I can, but the answers you desire most are almost certainly those I cannot give you. They are ones I would like myself. What I can offer you is my assistance, to try to help you recover the treasure taken from you today, in the hope I may also recover the one stolen from me. The treasure stolen from you? It is not one of a kind. There are others."

"More grails?" Gabe asked.

"More of whatever they are. I was attacked, like you. The one I possessed taken from me by force, like yours. I narrowly escaped with my life, like your friend here. With no idea how I had been found, how had the group learned about the treasure.

"I sought out an old friend, to warn him, and seek his assistance in recovering it. Torsten was the keeper of what we both believed to be the only other example of the treasure in existence. I reached his home to find it razed to the ground. I believe these men were responsible, and I fear Torsten did not escape with his life. If he had done, there is nothing on earth that would have stopped him coming to warn me too." Atana's face was sad, but her voice carried anger, "Someone found out about us, about what we had, and wanted them for himself."

"How did you find out about us?" Holly asked.

"Ever since meeting Torsten and learning my treasure was not unique, I have been watching for signs of others like us. In recent times this has become much easier. I have been able to apply technology to the task, custom software dedicated to sifting the torrents of digital information each day brings. It looks for items that fit the treasures' description, and for evidence of individuals who show signs of being more than human. This was how I stumbled upon you."

Gabe guessed before she had to say it. "The Bodega video?"

*Man takes two bullets, gets right back up...*

Atana nodded.

"You suspected I might have the grail's gift?"

"Yes, if the grail is the name you choose to give the treasure. Torsten knew it as Mjolnir. For the longest time, I simply knew it as my bracelet, and it had been with me from the beginning. I only learned I could remove it, that it took different forms, after meeting Torsten. His people discovered there was more to the treasure than met the eye."

"You don't know what it truly is, then?" Holly corrected herself, giving the woman the benefit of the doubt, for now. "What they are?"

"No, although I may know a little more than you. What we can surely agree on is that whatever these treasures truly are, they are astonishing and dangerous in the wrong hands. Anyone prepared to obtain them in the manner they have seen fit to... I fear someone like that controlling just one, let alone three."

A momentary silence was confirmation she was not alone.

"You said your first memory was of having no memory," said Holly.

"That I did."

"Would you care to elaborate?"

The sky outside the jet was still dark.

Atana nodded and began to talk, and Gabe, Holly and Jin listened.

"Perhaps I should begin with what I was told by the man who found me…"

# Chapter Eleven

Kitanetos heard the woman before he saw her.

He had assumed she was an animal, an uncommonly bold or careless one, ploughing through the brush and vegetation, snapping twigs loudly, stumbling into branches and trampling leaves underfoot.

He raised his bow and nocked an arrow.

The rugged hills which fringed the settlement were lush and teeming with life. Kitanetos anticipated the bitter meat of a wild goat or a boar, slowed his breath and steadied his aim to deliver what he intended to be a killing blow. No hunter relished the prospect of chasing down an injured and enraged boar, or worse a wild cat. A killing shot behind the shoulder was what he sought, and when upwind, undetected and prepared, he was usually able to deliver one.

Finding himself in the path of a beast, rather than having carefully stalked it, with only a few moments warning to compose himself, this shot would rest on circumstance as much as skill.

The creature's passage brought it closer.

Kitanetos spied a shape through the foliage and steadied his aim. The lean and ropy muscles in his arms and shoulders bunched, marshalling their strength, pulled back on the bowstring, ready to transfer the energy from weapon to arrow.

In his later accounts, he was careful with his words, too kind to say what he truly thought of the creature that stumbled through the leaves and branches, although others from the settlement were sometimes more candid.

When she first broke through the vegetation, Kitanetos struggled to digest the idea that he faced something human. For a split second, part of him was tempted to let his arrow fly, to cut down the wretched thing shambling toward him.

What blundered forward was a naked, pale, hairless assemblage of bone and sinew, skin stretched taut over a starved frame, emaciated, gazing from eyes which were dull and milky.

His arrow remained nocked in his bow.

The wretch raised its head in his direction and crumpled.

—

Beyond the realisation he had found a woman, the thing that invited most interest was the bracelet she wore. It ran from her elbow to her wrist. The fit was so precise, removing it would have meant removing her hand. She was otherwise utterly naked.

Kitanetos saw a soul clinging to life by the thinnest of threads. He put his goatskin water-bag to the woman's cracked lips and she drank.

He wondered how the woman had been reduced to such a pitiful condition. Had she been taken and held captive, trapped in darkness and almost starved? Bandits were rare around his settlement, but not unheard of. Was she the victim of a kidnapping, in the hope of extracting a ransom, the daughter or partner of someone of means? The bracelet she wore lent weight to the theory. It was an uncommon treasure, of that there was no doubt. The island's people were famed for their artisans, but even in the larger settlements where intense commerce and industry took place, Kitanetos had never seen anything close to its like.

The metal featured not one scratch of wear. Not a dent or pockmark. Whatever casting or beating had produced it was flawless, and the smooth surface was etched with fine patterns, sweeping lines and beguiling clusters of impossible detail. It was a mystery equal to the woman who wore it.

For her to have survived thus far was a marvel.

He gently scooped the woman up. She weighed almost nothing.

When he reached his settlement, he delivered her into the hands of the elders, trusting they would know what to do with her.

—

She was given shelter, nursed, fed a diet of food mashed into a paste and mixed with water, as one would feed to an infant.

Given her condition, those who cared for her were not confident she would respond, but to the surprise of all, the pitiful husk Kitanetos brought home not only survived, but thrived.

In the days that followed, she began to awaken to the world around her, to acknowledge those who brought her food and drink. She seemed to grasp they were trying to communicate with her. She heard their words but received them as though they were nonsense, so they coupled them with gestures that were more instinctively grasped. A primitive communication followed. She was able to ask basic things of them, and they of her, although not those things they wished most to learn.

The elders debated her fate. What did the bracelet reveal about this woman who did not appear to speak their language, or indeed any language, or seemed to lack any experience of how people behaved? She appeared almost feral to them, not violent, but like a small child who must be patiently taught even the simplest of things.

Larger settlements elsewhere boasted more learned men and women, and spiritual leaders too, the priestesses, but the elders knew attracting their attention was not always wise. Their advice could be inexplicable, and their intervention not always benign.

The island had experienced a series of tremors recently. They shook the ground and prompted many of the priestesses to preach of ill portents and angry gods. Who knew what they would make of the arrival of a stranger, wearing an equally strange bracelet? While Kitanetos's people dealt with the larger settlements to conduct trade, they were otherwise eager to run their own affairs.

Perhaps, for the time being, it was best to keep the woman's appearance a secret. Since she had been taken into their fold, by one of their own, it was decided she would continue to receive their care and protection until they knew more about her.

It was a state of affairs under which she progressively flourished. She came to learn their ways, and grew stronger, more rapidly than anyone had anticipated. She began to grasp their language. Complex and exasperated gestures were steadily supplanted by a growing lexicon of words.

If the elders had hoped language would unlock the answers to their questions, they were left disappointed. The woman assured them she would have shared her memories freely had she possessed any, but the truth was she remembered nothing of the time before finding herself among them.

In the absence of one, she took a name, chosen from many suggested by her growing pool of friends: Atana. In the people's tongue, it meant 'something found'.

Stronger now, she wished to contribute, to repay the kindness of those who had taken her in, and was duly allotted tasks.

And yet, while never raised in her presence, the questions persisted.

Who was she?

Where had she come from?

What did the bracelet she wore signify?

At the same time, life went on. Work, craft and trade, the passing of seasons. Friendships grew and deepened. Atana joined her new family in their celebrations, the blessing of births and unions, and the mourning of the old ones who passed and were returned to the earth.

Kitanetos visited her often. He brought her fine cuts of meat, which he insisted would help her grow stronger, long after she was strong enough, and other gifts too.

It was a friend who finally explained to her that Kitanetos's interest might extend beyond the responsibility he felt as her finder. Men in the settlement did not commonly lavish favours on every woman they knew or pay them such rapt attention.

Since her arrival as a husk, Atana had changed greatly. Her once bald scalp had grown hair. Her skin was no longer deathly pale but was tanned to a deep brown from collecting olives and figs from the trees in the sun. It was no longer stretched tight over knobs of bone and stringy sinew, but over long, finely muscled limbs.

By the time the warmer days of spring surrendered to scorching days of summer, and the cool and chill days of autumn and winter had come and gone, Atana was known by all in the village. She did not feel like an outsider. She felt like one of them. News of her never reached the wise men and women in the larger settlements, or the caves where the priestesses and their disciples worshipped.

Kitanetos became her lover. During her second winter in the settlement, the two were formally united.

In the process, Atana unwittingly made her first enemy.

Another woman believed Kitanetos to be hers, and was not pleased to find she was mistaken. She did not celebrate Kitanetos and Atana's union, but she did not forget it, either, nor accept it.

For Kitanetos and Atana, and almost everyone else, questions about her origins faded in importance with every passing day. Her bracelet, no matter how dazzling and mysterious, became familiar, simply part of her, a part of Atana, who had become part of them. The world would always be full of mystery, and yet life moves on.

After her union with Kitanetos, Atana grew to discover her true talent. After assisting him in skinning and cleaning the kills he brought home, she learnt how to set traps for smaller game. She was shown how to repair and maintain his bow and arrow, and blades, and soon petitioned to be taught how to handle them. Since denying her anything proved a test of his will, Atana got her way. What harm was there, after all? When her rapid mastery of these weapons became impossible to ignore, she told him she wished to accompany him when scouting and tracking game. His resistance was short-lived.

Atana joined her lover in the hunt.

His confidence grew with her own, and soon they simply chose to ignore she was the more skilled, the stronger, faster and stealthier, the more tireless and in possession of the better aim. Thankfully her man was man enough to take all this in his stride, as did their people. The island's folk did not care to divide men and women in the way Atana would see in most cultures she would later encounter.

It was easy for her to remember those brief years as idyllic.

She was dazzled by the world. It was beautiful and new, brimming with warmth and people she cared for as much as they cared for her. Her days were rich with work and play.

Their settlement lay on the coast. The ocean provided food and offered mariners access to trade. In the evenings she and Kitanetos would often walk down to the sea and sit on the beach. They would watch the sky change from blue to indigo and to orange and red, contemplate the ships further down the coast moored in the harbours. or cutting through the water, sailing toward the horizon. They were proof positive of a wider world, distant places and peoples, but for Atana they commanded no allure. As tiny as her world was, it was perfectly formed, and held everything she desired.

She loved her people and she loved Kitanetos. Their union was strong, strong enough to hold a secret.

They had discovered something they choose to keep from everyone else, fearing that unlike the bracelet, it would stir questions that would not rest unanswered.

—

The accident happened while hunting boar.

They had been tracking a group of the beasts, deep into the woods.

Atana and Kitanetos hunted the region often and knew it well, enough to know the boar they trailed were wandering into a glade fringed by steep and rocky hills. A spring birthed a stream that cut through the rock and fed a pool of water in the belly of the glade. Animals often drank there. It was to a hunter's advantage that the glade only offered creatures bereft of wings one path out.

The boars were approaching the neck of the pass. Soon they would meet the pool and stop, and that is when the couple would each select a target and strike.

They parted to flank their prey. Kitanetos assumed a position on one crest of the glade and Atana the rocky outcrop opposite. In doing so, they lost track of their quarry momentarily, but regained sight of them a few moments later, wallowing in the mud at the edge of the pond under the midday shadow of the hill.

Only their number was too few.

One was missing.

Atana never heard the animal rush her, but she did feel its tusks spear her back. She must have cried out, because as the beast tossed her up into the air she glimpsed Kitanetos racing toward her, bow raised, arrow drawn. A moment later she heard the boar squeal. And seconds after that her lover's face appeared over her, taut with fear.

She cried out as he moved her to view her injuries. The wounds felt deep, the pain equally so, and very real. Although this was not what scared her most. What dwarfed even the pain in her wounds was the total absence of sensation elsewhere. Her legs were numb, as surely as if they had vanished. She attempted to move them, and neither obeyed. She put a hand to her side and back and felt the wounds there for herself, horrifyingly deep and wide. The hand returned wet with blood.

Kitanetos was becoming frantic. The other boars had been alerted. They stood fixed in their soup of mud, alive to the sounds around them. Kitanetos did not wait to see if they would investigate. He scooped Atana up in his arms and hurried her away from the clearing.

She felt his heart beating in his chest, heard the hot, ragged breaths escaping him, the desperate engine of his panic and fear. She tried to find words to quiet him, but they would not come. She was afraid, too. She did not want to die. She was not ready.

When at last he finally set her down, what she felt was not pain; strangely, her wound was not the monstrous thing it had been only moments earlier, but had simmered to a dull ache, accompanied by a fierce itch. The sensation was returning to her legs, too. Perhaps she had not been as badly injured as she feared.

Kitanetos was examining her wounds again.

She felt him freeze. Once frantic and busy, his hands ceased to move, and then left her back. The pain there was almost gone now, the itching intensifying in its wake. She moved her own hand to her back again, tentatively at first, wary of reawakening the pain by blundering about there, but what she found was... nothing. The torn skin and flesh were now intact, as if they had never been damaged at all.

The only evidence the boar had struck what should have been a killing blow was drying blood and torn clothing.

Kitanetos could have responded in so many ways. What had just happened was impossible. She was impossible.

But Kitanetos was not apprehensive, repelled, or horrified, and it was easy enough to understand why.

He loved her, and was happy to embrace any miracle which spared her life.

# Chapter Twelve

It was the following autumn that their small settlement received emissaries from the island's largest one. The party came with a purpose. They came for Atana.

The settlement from where the emissaries had journeyed was, on the surface, governed collectively, but in truth, everyone knew that one man's voice there carried more weight than the rest, and the priestesses were never far from his ear.

It was this man who had dispatched the party, an ill-disguised collection of sellswords, to Atana and Kitanetos's settlement. They carried a message. Their master begged an audience with the stranger who had been taken in, the woman who had arrived half-starved and near death, wearing only a curious bracelet.

While neither this man, nor the place he obliquely governed, possessed a shred of authority over the one Atana and Kitanetos called home, it was not a simple invitation to decline. One glimpse of the collection of battle-scarred, hard-faced messengers, who carried their swords outside their garments, hands casually on their pommels, made this clear.

Some requests are what they appear, a plea one can choose to accept or ignore. Others, as the village elders were well aware, are not requests at all. They are the polite precursor to a demand.

Atana saw unease and fear in the people who had cared for her, fed and clothed her, taught her to talk and craft and hunt and love and live… She believed they would have stood by her if she chose to refuse the 'invitation'. She loved them for it, which is why she could never have made them.

Only one among them felt differently. This one did not look afraid. While she tried to hide her pleasure, her effort was wanting. Atana knew the woman travelled with her father each season to conduct trade at the settlement the visitors belonged to, and that she had never got over wanting Kitanetos for her own, never forgotten or forgiven.

Perhaps she believed she might get Kitanetos yet if Atana were to vanish.

Atana saw no choice but to agree to travel and see the man who had summoned her.

The decision was not without obstacle: when Atana stated her intention, Kitanetos refused to let her leave, as she knew he would. After considerable argument, he relented under one condition: he would be at her side. Whatever lay ahead, they would face it together. Of course, she agreed. They would go together.

This was the first and only lie Atana told her husband.

Her greatest fear, far greater than surrendering herself into the custody of these sellswords and walking into the domain of their master, was that once beyond their settlement, the men would simply kill Kitanetos and take her captive. She informed the leader of the group she would accompany them alone, without the knowledge of her husband, and they made plans to this effect.

While Kitanctos understood them to be departing the following day, the moment he was asleep Atana slipped from beneath his arm, collected her things and crept through the darkness to join the visitors at their camp in the nearby hills. As agreed, they were ready to leave the moment she arrived. They travelled through the night, with only short breaks to rest, and reached their settlement the following evening.

Atana had not known what to expect, and was astonished by what she saw.

Her settlement, up until now her world, numbered many people, many families, but what she encountered here was one hundred times its scale, in all respects. This settlement's edifices were huge. They towered above her as she was guided through streets and alleyways. She saw floors stacked one on top of another until they were tall as the oldest of forest trees. These buildings were adorned with richly decorated walls and blazing red pillars. Elaborately paved walkways and stone staircases twisted and climbed among them. She passed a courtyard that alone dwarfed the footprint of her settlement.

Markets offered a hive of commerce, conducted among exotic inhabitants. Vibrant and colourful clothes and jewellery spoke of wealth. She had no concept of class until that moment but grasped it in an instant.

Perhaps because she was compliant, those she passed would never have taken her for a captive of her escorts, even though by now she was certain that was what she was. Not one moment of the journey had she been left unattended. The men guided her up a series of staircases, and finally into a room whose windows looked out over the streets and people below.

The opulence she had witnessed outside was far exceeded by that she found within. An ornately dressed man with hooded eyes and silver-grey hair received her with naked curiosity and invited her to take a seat. A woman, dressed in far simpler garments, stood silently at his shoulder. Atana was reminded of one of the elders who occasionally performed for the children at times of celebration. He had figures carved from wood, with comically large eyes and noses, whose arms and mouths moved, worked by hidden fingers. The elder, a serene and unassuming soul, stood almost impassive, as the effigies he animated acted out stories, spoke in funny voices, waved their arms and flapped their jaws. It was great fun, but even the children knew who was really in control.

So it was with Atana, this man and the woman at his side.

The man wasted no time with his questions.

He asked where she had come from.

She answered that he already knew; his men had found her there.

Before she had been found, then?

She said she did not know, could not remember.

This earned her pursed lips and a glance at his silent companion.

He asked to see the bracelet she wore.

She drew back the sleeve of her garment and showed it to him.

He asked her to tell him about how she had been found, and so she did, as earnestly and fully as she could. Perhaps if he and the woman believed her, this would be where it ended. The man would be faced with the same mystery she was, and perhaps see the futility of asking questions for which she had no answers.

She might return to her home, to the life she loved.

It was a beautiful daydream.

She was a creature snared in a trap. As a hunter, she knew better than any what often came next.

Atana was surprised when the woman spoke for herself, and asked if she might examine the bracelet.

Atana nodded and the woman crossed the room. She looked at the bracelet for a moment, and then reached out, hesitantly, excitement producing a tremor in her hands. She gently turned Atana's arm and wrist, and the bracelet with them, so she could gaze upon the lines and patterns decorating its surface. The light from the lamps in each of the room's four corners slipped across the strange metal. The woman studied Atana, too. The assessment was unashamedly naked.

Their eyes met, and the woman seemed to stare deep into Atana's.

"You know nothing of your past," she said at last.

It was not a question, more the acknowledgement of a fact, an acceptance Atana had told the truth.

"You have my thanks for coming here, and for showing me the treasure you wear," the woman continued. "Now if you will let me, I have something I wish to show you in return. Journey with me, into the white mountains, see it with your own eyes, and I will share a story passed down by ones who are now bones and dust, who lived on this island long ago."

Atana was aware of two things at that moment.

The first was that she had misread the tremor in the woman's hands. The woman had been more anxious about meeting Atana than Atana of meeting her. It was not excitement betrayed by her nerves, but fear.

The second was that every time Atana had told herself it was of no concern where she had come from, she had simply repeated a lie she desperately wanted to believe.

They set out early the next day, a small party with Atana and the woman at the head, and commenced the trek towards the mountains. Their path took them across the island, by the second day into higher and ever more barren terrain. Elevation unravelled the island below them, stretching off to the coast. The ships Atana had sat and watched with Kitanetos were but specks on a brilliant blue sea.

Every step took Atana further from her home, too. The woman, a priestess, and her followers were respectful, but their stolen glances accumulated. Each one lay on Atana like a pebble, until eventually she feared becoming buried beneath their weight. More than once she pressed the priestess to disclose something of what she knew, of what it was they were travelling to see, but the woman's response was unwavering. Atana should witness it with her own eyes first, then listen. After this, the priestess would answer whatever questions she could.

Finally, after three days, in the fading glow of a burnished orange and purple sunset, the small party arrived at their destination, a mouth of a cave hidden in the belly of a gorge.

Atana saw torchlight flickering from within.

The priestess left her people to set up camp outside the caves and assemble shelter before nightfall. She took Atana's hand and guided her into the mouth of the mountain. They passed a handful of armed men situated within the cave's throat, a standing guard, it seemed. One of them handed a torch to the priestess, which she used to lead Atana down through a fissure in the rock. The flickering light revealed that parts of the cave beyond had been worked, tunnelled wider to offer easier access. They met steps, rough-hewn, and descended into the cool darkness, until eventually the passage widened and climbed sharply, becoming the roof of a cavity that stretched far above their heads.

A half-circle of wooden seats had been fashioned in the chamber. They faced a fresco, as tall as the two women stood, and as wide again. At the foot of the fresco rested a larnax, a stone burial chest. Together they indicated a sacred place, a site of worship.

The priestess lifted the torch, so its light spilt across the fresco, transforming a collection of indistinct shapes into a series of figures and an object.

A ring of men and women were depicted. The men were rendered in red, the women painted a chalky white. All were tall and dark-haired, naked save for a short and simple kilt, and each wore something familiar on their right arm. The jewellery stretched from elbow to wrist. The artist had attempted to capture the lines and patterns which decorated the bracelet's surface, a futile endeavour if ever there were one.

The ring of figures surrounded a woman, similar to those in the ring, but larger in scale. An object lay at her feet. It resembled a vase, only with an opening at the base.

Atana walked to meet the figures, felt drawn to them, almost as if they conspired to lure her forward, and as she walked she experienced a stirring.... Familiarity? She reached out and pressed her hand to the plaster, on the chest of one of the female figures. The stone was cold beneath her touch.

She studied the figure, examined her profile, her dark eyes and hair, her bone-white skin. Like the men, she wore a simple kilt, and like them, she was naked above the waist, her breasts exposed. Atana followed their swell, moved her fingers down the sweep of the figure's arm to the bracelet there. She couldn't help but compare it to the one which encircled her right arm.

The priestess waited for her to take it all in.

"What do you know of what lies before us? Of these people?" Atana asked.

"I know what the story tells me," The priestess replied. "The one written upon the tablets held in the larnax at your feet. Transcribed by the old ones, it is a tale from our island's forgotten past, which tells of others, gods, perhaps, who came long ago, and a champion who saved our ancestors from their greed and might. It is warning, perhaps, in case these strangers or deities should choose to visit us again."

Atana turned then, saw the priestess under the light of her torch. Did she want to hear the tale? She was suddenly afraid it would change everything. As things stood, she might yet flee, return to her village. She and Kitanetos could run away, escape her past, leave these figures with their bracelets and their strange object, the stone chest and the story stored in its belly, board one of those ships at the harbour laden with goods, disappear into the world beyond this island...

Hide.

But from whom?

From herself, who she was, where she had come from? In coming here, seeing this, these questions had been nourished. They would not be easily quelled. They would travel with her, no matter how far she ran.

To pretend otherwise was a delusion.

She could not run, and so she would stay, and listen.

When the events of any life are reflected upon, some moments seem too cruelly capricious to pass for chance. They are the moments that lead men to invent gods, so perfectly and precisely do they alter one's fate.

Atana would have listened to the story, and asked her questions, but something else happened.

She was still staring, her face twisted towards the priestess, her hand pressed to the figure in the fresco, when she felt a tremor travel up through her feet and across the plaster. The priestess felt it too. Her eyes looked from the floor to the ceiling as a shower of grit fell upon them.

There was little time to do anything more before the tremor became a rumble, a violent judder that shook the ground beneath their feet and caused the cave to crumble. The priestess fought to keep her balance as all around them the mountain heaved with increasing vigour.

A deep and thunderous grinding escalated to a deafening roar as suddenly debris began to crash around Atana's feet. The priestess was struck by a falling sheet of stone and brutally dashed to the ground. The torch escaped her grip, fell and was close to extinguished. The chamber was plunged into near-total darkness.

Rocks large and small crashed down as Atana scrambled for the torch's guttering orange light. When she reached it, she also encountered the ruined body of the priestess beside it, lifeless, broken and bloody. She retrieved the dying flame and held it aloft where it regained some vitality. She was able to locate the entrance to the cave ahead, half-collapsed.

Atana hurried towards it and commenced scaling the razor-sharp rubble to squeeze through the gap, fighting to keep her wits as all around her threatened to disintegrate.

She scrambled, repeatedly struck by stone and rock. During one desperate lunge, she lost her torch. Immediately buried and snuffed out, she abandoned it, pushing on through the darkness, pawing with her hands for the walls, trusting the incline to guide her to the surface.

She climbed blindly, to escape being crushed by the mountain or buried alive, with no assurance she was even heading in the right direction.

Then came a draught of air. She followed it to arrive at a meagre grey light and the hope of escape.

She climbed onward and, eventually, her efforts earned her a thin shaft of moonlight, piercing through a wall of fallen rock. She heaved the rubble away, one rock after another and another and another until, finally, she had earned a large enough opening to climb through to freedom.

The relief she felt upon emerging was momentary.

Beyond the cave, she was faced with yet more destruction.

Night had fallen, but the full moon produced ample light to grasp the scale of the catastrophe. Between the walls of the gorge, cleaving the deep indigo sky like a finger of doom, coiled a gigantic column of black smoke. It poured upwards, swallowing the stars. At its feet seethed a livid orange glow.

In the belly of the gorge, all was panic. A shelf of rock had broken away from the head of the ravine, shearing off to bury a group of the party camped beneath it. Their tent had fallen into the fire built before it and was now ablaze. The flames had already leapt to nearby trees and bushes.

Atana saw similar fires peppering the landscape below.

Her only thoughts now were for her people.

She began to run and did not stop.

—

Her breathless sprint took her down the mountain. She sought a route as the crow flies for the coast. She knew from there, if she followed the shore, eventually she could not fail to reach her settlement.

It was a path littered with destruction. The tiny smudges of fire she had observed high up on the mountain were settlements which had caught ablaze, where cooking fires or night torches had been scattered and their flame spread, consuming dwellings and nearby vegetation.

As if this were not dire enough, dawn revealed a new and different variety of catastrophe as she neared the coast. The ground beneath her feet grew sodden and then transformed into ankle-sucking mud. The ocean had risen up, reached in and clawed the shoreline, smashed all in its path and raked the remains far and wide in its retreat. In low-lying areas, great pools of water still lay trapped. She passed trees that had been uprooted and swept inland like twigs. Animal corpses lay rotting in the sun, painted with a layer of silt. Fields of crops were buried under stinking sludge.

Eventually, Atana was able to discern landmarks she recognised from her hunts, the skeletons of rocks and hills, their features stripped and deposited in splinters and heaps of filthy sand and dirt. She passed a ship, upturned, and smashed in two as though it had fallen straight from the sky.

It was in this way she arrived at her settlement before realising it, simply because the dwellings where her people lived and worked had been erased, or survived only in the broken stumps or nubs of foundations that reached through the wreckage.

Rubble and broken timber had replaced the home she knew.

Dead and broken bodies had replaced the people she loved.

They were everywhere, many half-buried, some tangled in branches of trees, bent and broken.

She examined every body she passed for signs of life, but found none.

As she turned corpse after corpse, cataloguing the dead in her mind, cleared muck from their faces and hauled them from the filth, she of course looked for one above all others. She imagined eventually her labours would cause her to grow numb, but she was wrong. Instead, she discovered a capacity for pain and grief greater than she would ever have believed. She carried the dead and laid them together, men and women, the old and the young, children and infants.

Atana did not find Kitanetos, not then and not later. Many of those taken had been swept back into the sea when the water retreated, sucked into its depths, either to be consumed by its teeming life or washed up on distant shores to be picked at by the carrion eaters, insects and grubs.

She did find survivors. Thankfully, some had escaped with their lives. As darkness fell, she saw the glow of a fire in the nearby hills. When she reached it, she found a handful of men and women, wretched and traumatized.

They shared what they had witnessed.

They described a thunderous clap, whereupon the earth began to shake like an angry beast seeking to shrug all from its back, as she had experienced from deep within the cave in the mountains. Many of the settlement's dwellings crumbled there, the survivors said, causing fires as timbers collapsed upon hearths and braziers. At the same time, while they struggled to deal with these fires, a steady rumble in the distance slowly grew to an ominous roar.

One woman described watching the ocean inhale, seeing the water recede from the shore to strand crabs and fish beneath the glare of the sun. Many of the settlement's people were drawn to watch, fascinated and mesmerised by the spectacle.

They saw the wave cresting on the horizon too late to do anything but blindly flee.

Then the ocean was upon them, crashing through the settlement, towering and utterly savage. Everything in the wave's path was cast asunder, those caught in its path were swallowed by the surge, to be drowned or battered against rock and trees.

When the water retreated, the scattered few who chance had spared sought each other out and headed for higher ground, lest the water return and claim what it had missed, but also to escape the dead they could not yet comprehend were gone.

In the days and weeks following, stragglers from other settlements along the coast joined their number. They spoke of the cataclysm in other regions. While one shore of their own had borne the brunt of the catastrophe, an entire neighbouring island had been all but destroyed, claimed by the sea.

The portents the priestesses spoke of were real, the disaster they predicted had come to pass. The occasional tremors which visited the island before Atana's arrival and since had been the whispered warnings of a reckoning to be visited upon them by the gods.

In the aftermath, Atana remained on the island longer than she should.

She stayed to help those of her own who had survived. They buried their dead, sent them to the afterlife as custom dictated, and rebuilt dwellings. She taught those who were capable how to hunt. The rest tried to sow crops, but it was difficult and harvests were lean. The cataclysm which had devastated the neighbouring island and wounded their own had darkened the skies, heralding a winter that ate all seasons, and bringing rains that sickened the crops as much as they nourished them.

Despite this, life went on. The settlement grew, as more survivors were received, accepted as though they were the settlement's own, but Atana had lost her appetite for company. For her, these new faces remained strangers. The new community that developed no longer felt like her home, or its inhabitants her people. Their lives rarely touched her own. The place she once loved seemed only to stand as a monument to what she had lost.

The island's fleet of ships was slowly rebuilt, and began to approach its former strength. New vessels replaced those smashed on the shores, and once again protected the island and transported what its people produced for sale, returning with raw materials they did not possess.

Once Atana had cared little about where these vessels went, the lands they carried their goods to, but now she found she could think of nothing else.

She dreamed of what these new lands promised, but also of what they did not.

She yearned to be anywhere but where she was.

# Chapter Thirteen

Atana negotiated passage on a ship destined for Egypt, setting her tireless arms to its oars to earn her seat.

A stranger in strange lands, she adopted the life of an adventurer and a sellsword, albeit she would only take on causes of which she approved. She achieved fame, infamy and power. In various guises, she commanded armies, became a living Mycenaean myth, and the foundation for an ancient Greek one. She bore witness to events that would later be romanticised in Homeric epics, although the truth and the stories bore scant resemblance to one another.

She watched mighty kingdoms flourish, flounder and fall; mighty civilisations tumble into a dark age from which many did not recover. Eventually, she left these crumbling giants behind her, and ventured into wild and distant lands of ice and snow.

She had long since learned she was different from those among whom she moved.

She was resilient – she and Kitanetos had discovered this together – but the dawning awareness that she did not age as others aged was grasped by her alone. The passage of time itself revealed the secret.

The nomadic life she led allowed enlightenment to escape her for far longer than it should have done. When it finally arrived, it was a shock. A journey back to see an old acquaintance after many years laid it bare. The trip was considerable, across an ocean. A woman greeted her at the man's home, and when

Atana enquired after him, explaining she was an old friend, the woman invited her in.

She found her old friend was now an old man.

The woman was not his wife, nor even his daughter.

Atana's voice caught in her throat when the woman roused her grandfather from his nap.

The old man shifted in his chair, craned a stringy, fragile neck to take his visitor in. The startling blue eyes she remembered had been stolen by cataracts, misty pupils instead staring blindly in her direction.

A ghost of the youthful face Atana recalled was all that remained. Its features were familiar, but more sloppily drawn. What had been firm and smooth was now loose and peppered with liver spots, cut with deep wrinkles. The strong jaw had softened to baggy jowls, thick curls of corn blonde hair reduced to spare wisps of white clinging to a balding pate.

The meeting was a strange one; the man remembered her, and brightened greatly as she introduced herself, but naturally assumed she too was in her winter years. They talked, but Atana could not have said about what. Old times, she imagined. Her mind was elsewhere, racing to count seasons, places…

She did not stay long, and a confusing exchange surely took place in the wake of her visit, in which the old man and his granddaughter attempted to reconcile the impossible. The vibrant young woman who visited, and the fragile old lady the sightless old man assumed he had spent time with.

How had she failed to see? On some level she understood men aged, children were born and became youths, youths became adults and adults grew old and infirm, the old and infirm perished, but her constant roaming had detached this cycle from her personal experience.

She returned to other places where she had spent time, where she had made friends, acquaintances and assorted alliances, only now she was more discreet. What she saw, who she saw, what she heard from people who remembered the names she enquired about, confirmed what she already knew to be true.

She looked no different than she had done the day she had first stared at her reflection in a pool of water. While others lived their lives in seasons, the birth and blossoming of spring and summer, the wane and wither of winter, a beginning and an inescapable end, she lived an eternal summer.

She was alone.

Apart.

An immortal tourist among mortals.

She learned it was unwise to remain anywhere for a significant length of time, lest it become evident, but transience spared her heartache, too. For a time, she couldn't escape the thought that any person she grew fond of was in every passing moment closer to the grave, to know every instant shared came from a finite allotment. To be in their company was to watch time relentlessly gnaw at them.

Every relationship she dared to forge was fleeting, and breaking away before her secret became apparent was painful. But nevertheless, forge them she did, again and again. How could she not?

Eternity is long, solitude is testing, companionship becomes an alluring balm.

She endeavoured to keep her relationships purely platonic or strictly erotic. To mix the two, flirt with romance, with that shade of intimacy, was dangerous, but there were times sense and restraint failed her.

Kitanetos was not the only man Atana grew to love, or even to wed.

A handful of times throughout those centuries, the connection between her and another grew too strong to sever. They would either discover her secret, or she would share it with them. When the time came for her to move on, these partners would travel with her and make a life somewhere new.

Each one thought they understood what she was, that they would tackle whatever came to pass day by day, but the outcome always left both parties wounded. The mortal half would either grow to resent losing their vigour while Atana continued unchanged, or they would grow insecure, suspicious of imagined suitors, in itself a sure and fatal poison to any union.

The precious few she truly shared a life with cut her most deeply, because ultimately the life they shared was always the life of the other.

Losing these partners, who were young and vital when she had first shared their beds, and old and feeble when death came for them, was torture. Each time she swore she would never let such a thing happen again.

But eternity is long, solitude is testing, and companionship becomes an alluring balm.

Then she met one like herself, another who did not age.

# Chapter Fourteen

Atana was a citizen of Florence in the spring of 1348, playing the role of a wealthy socialite to divert herself from a malaise she seemed unable to escape. Had she not met him, it was a period she would otherwise surely have associated only with decadence and death. A plague was busy feasting on mankind, the Black Death. It would consume half of Europe's population before its appetite was sated.

She had no reason to fear it. Common mortal sickness was not something she had experience of. The malady she suffered afflicted the soul.

Existence had thickened to a mire that sucked at her limbs. Time and experience had congealed and wore her down. She moved among mankind but felt disconnected from it. She had grown numb, and almost envied the men and women who surrounded her. The spectre of death lent their lives, already brief and fragile, a value and lustre beyond her reach.

She did not want to die, exactly; she merely struggled to muster a reason to live.

She was tired.

She also happened to be wealthy, and wealth at least afforded opportunity for distraction, and the freedom to move in whichever circles she fancied. Even in the midst of such an age, where bodies were daily heaped by the dozen to be buried in trenches rather than graveyards, there will exist an appetite for pleasure. As adrift as she was, she threw herself upon them all, seeking the richest of all things, the finest wines, the finest foods, the most dazzling of garments, the grandest dwellings, the loveliest and most supple of bodies, in an increasingly vain effort to taste anything at all.

She moved among high society and slums alike. She was a strange creature and had grown less careful to blend in. The people who crossed her path seemed to sense she was different, and found her alluring and unsettling in equal measure.

She was careless, often courted danger, sometimes unconsciously and sometimes by design.

The night she encountered another like herself, she had attended the wedding festivities of a prominent Florentine family, and grown bored long before the evening grew old. She had drunk heavily, and when she departed, elected to eschew a carriage and walk the streets instead, allowing her feet free rein to carry her wherever they desired.

They desired, it emerged, a poorer quarter of the city.

A lady dressed in finery, strolling alone, was always going to attract attention.

The brute who accosted her demanded money, or at least, this was his foul-mouthed opening entreaty. She softly replied that if he removed himself in short order, she might yet decide to spare his life.

His retort was to produce a knife.

In lieu of a florin, she gifted him a fat lip.

He staggered back at the blow, shaking his head like a dog stung on the nose. Had the agitation stirred mental sediment sufficient to wake some measure of common sense the encounter might have ended there. It would have pleased Atana merely to see the thief chastened. She would have let him take his leave, allowed him the opportunity to repent his decision before resuming the ugly life had he chosen.

He did not.

She sidestepped his blade, thrust at her face, and struck him a second blow. A broken nose now complemented his fat lip. She waited while he collected himself. His next few attempts to cut a path through her with his blade were equally simple to avoid, even drunk as she was. Enraged, he barrelled towards her. She evaded him, turning swiftly enough to deliver a boot to his rear.

He went over, but scrambled quickly to his feet and rushed her again, his blade high above his head in his fist, falling as he closed the distance.

To this day she did not know why she chose not to move, why she allowed him to drive the blade deep into her chest.

He seemed surprised he had succeeded in landing the blow, although not as surprised as when her own blade entered his flank and carved a path along the lower shelf of his ribs. His eyes, staring into hers, widened, and his hand left the handle of his knife.

It remained buried in her breast as he stumbled back and sank to his knees, his innards tumbling onto the cobbles before him. He gazed up. Their eyes locked. His widened as she reached for his knife and tugged it from her breast, casting it into the darkness.

Then he fell back, and his eyes saw no more.

The man who had watched all this from the shadows finally spoke.

She had known he was there. His eyes had scarcely left her from the moment she had arrived at the festivities, and he had followed her when she left, trailed her through the streets and alleyways. He had done so with a skill worthy of note, but insufficient to escape her detection.

Most interesting of all?

She believed he knew she was aware of his presence the entire time.

It was not the first time they had crossed paths. She had seen him before, at other society gatherings. A tall red-haired gentleman, handsome, in the manner a bleak and inhospitable landscape might be called handsome. He did not seem the least bit surprised by what he had just witnessed.

"Is it your habit to kill men for sport?" he asked, in Italian, but laced with a deeper-rooted accent she could not place.

"Only if they seek to kill me first, or be of sufficiently ill character they would commit such an act with little encouragement."

"Shall we wait a moment for your wound to heal?"

And there it was. In an instant, she was truly alive once more.

After so many centuries, she felt the frisson of something new enter her world.

"Who are you?" she asked.

"I am Torsten. I have been watching you, although I suspect you already know this."

"I do."

"The bracelet you wear, do you know what it is?"

"What do you know of it?"

—

Torsten's people had been Vikings, who took to the sea and raided coastal villages and monasteries. The monasteries were a favoured target. Riches were common and the monks who inhabited them rarely a test in battle.

The clan had been scouting a village to plunder when they had seen a pair of boats laden with provisions sailing towards a cluster of rocks off their coast, hardly large enough to be called an island.

They had grown curious. What lay on the broken tooth of rock worthy of the trip? When the boats departed, they went to investigate and discovered something they would otherwise almost certainly have missed. The small island hid a cove at its heart. In this cove, between two fingers of cliff face, an edifice had been cut into the rock, fronted by two ornately carved, formidable doors, a secret monastery. The clan was not the only one of their kind, and some victims had learned to hide their valuables more carefully.

Arne, the clan's leader, was at once convinced that something of great value must lie inside. Why would anyone build such a fortress otherwise? Many monasteries they stripped of valuables scarcely had protection at all.

The party gathered driftwood and kindling and built a fire before its huge crustacean studded doors, waited patiently until the flames had weakened them, and then rammed them until they crumbled. Beyond the threshold, they found a handful of monks, suffocated by the smoke, and deeper, a cluster of caves made into rooms.

They searched them all and found nothing, merely straw beds, simple provisions. The treasures Arne had anticipated were nowhere to be found.

Then came renewed hope.

They had almost missed it, a door artfully concealed, that opened to reveal a stone seal, too heavy for one man to move, but with levers and ropes, the party finally managed to topple it back to reveal a small chamber.

Here they found the treasures they sought. Jewellery and precious stones, surrounding a stone coffin. There were pots also, which when smashed oozed honey and distilled liquids.

Arne commanded his men to heave the stone lid of the coffin aside, to see if other valuables had been buried with whatever remains lay inside.

The body that was exposed was not what they expected; the remains appeared not years or decades perished but mere days. Thin and white, the corpse was naked but for one piece of incredible jewellery, a bracelet that stretched from elbow to wrist, decorated with fine markings. This was a treasure to render everything else they had seen here pale in comparison. Neither Arne nor any of the men he led had ever seen anything of its like.

One of them reached to take it from the corpse. He was a man admired and famed for his courage, but it was not courage enough to prevent him from crying out and stumbling back when the corpse opened its eyes, fixed him with its milky gaze, and began to climb from its coffin.

The assembled men retreated, repelled and dumbfounded by what they saw. The cadaver ran its skeletal fingers over the jewellery which encased its withered arm and the bracelet transformed before their eyes, its metal swimming to close over the ghoul's fist.

Finally, one of the raiders recovered sufficient wits and will to move upon the creature. He brought his sword down, but the creature's emaciated limb shot up. The sword glanced off the treasure. The sword clanged harmlessly off the stone coffin, and before he could ready a second blow, the creature struck him in the chest. Its fist, enclosed in the bracelet, struck with an impact that seemed impossible given the force with which it was delivered. The man was smashed off his feet, sent hurtling back into those clustered tightly behind him in the cramped chamber, knocking them all off their feet in turn.

From the floor of the ice-cold stone bed of the tomb, they watched the creature clamber from its grave.

Arne, first to regain his feet after being toppled, yelled and swung his axe. It met the creature's skull and cleaved it in two. The horror sank back into his stone coffin.

Arne collected himself, took his prize from the cadaver's arm, and watched the treasure change once more. Its polished metallic surface swam, as did the strange lines and markings finely etched into it. It contracted, the metal rolling and curling until it was a bracelet no more. When it had finally reached a state of rest, it now resembled a strange vase with a mouth at its foot.

The party gathered their plunder and returned to their ship, and home.

As for the object, they tried to understand it as men often try to make sense of mysteries, by creating myths, or grafting the ones they already believe onto them.

They reasoned the treasure they had acquired must have been stolen from the gods, and the creature they had slain an ancient warrior.

They grew to believe the treasure was the hammer of Thor, Mjolnir itself.

It had to be woken for battle – they had seen as much with their own eyes – and they set themselves to the task of unlocking the secret of its transformation.

For years the clan failed to return Mjolnir to its true form, but that did not prevent them from discovering its other secret.

Mjolnir at rest appeared, through its sheer form, to offer a challenge.

The indentations which lay at its base begged a hand to sit within them.

The blades that lay within its core waited to slice deep into any man who tried to do so. The contradiction was an irresistible test to men who prized courage to the point of foolhardiness.

Soon the clan discovered the gift that courage conferred, and all availed themselves of it. They called it Odin's Blood, the gift of strength, resilience and agelessness.

They also discovered something that Atana could never have been certain of on her own. It made their women barren, and their men unable to father. The clan could not die, but unless they welcomed outsiders, neither could it grow.

With the passage of time no longer of consequence, their leader, Arne, became increasingly obsessed with solving the puzzle of how to transform Mjolnir into its true form. He yearned to take the weapon into battle, and became a recluse. He spent years tracing paths across its surface as he had seen the creature from the crypt trace them, and finally, after many mortal life spans, he succeeded. The bracelet was his, and in time, too, he had mastered the gestures to make and unmake the weapon he craved.

Arne's labours, hours, days, weeks, years of endlessly tracing patterns, exacted a toll, infecting his mind with a madness. He saw patterns everywhere he looked, warnings written in the landscape and the skies. He grew prone to unpredictable bouts of fury and beheaded without warning those he suspected of conspiring against him, until even his second in command was accused of plotting to kill him, plotting to take Mjolnir and usurp his place as the clan's leader.

The man was captured and beheaded.

As was the man who took his place…

Arne's actions only served to nourish the very sedition he feared.

The clan turned on itself, divided among those who remained loyal and those who refused to be led by a madman. Torsten belonged to the second faction. The conflict was bloody and brutal, ravaging the clan until only two of them remained, and then one alone.

Torsten was the sole custodian of Mjolnir.

He taught Atana the gestures, the different forms her bracelet could take, and how she could remove it.

When she saw it at rest, the fresco in the cave immediately entered her mind's eye, the object at the feet of the central woman surrounded by the ring of men and women, all bathed in the priestess's torchlight.

Torsten and Atana became friends and companions. Eventually, he showed her how he stored his own treasure, always somewhere secret and near impossible for a mortal to reach. He believed it was dangerous to wear the bracelet. Those who saw it invariably coveted it, some enough to seek to take it. It also might identify them to others like themselves. It was, after all, the way he had identified her. He knew the bracelet she wore was more than mere ornamentation. Like Torsten, she selected secure and secret places, where she could feel confident the object was safer than on her person. For the first time in over two millennia, she could choose to walk into the world without it, naked, but also liberated.

The weight lifted was indescribable.

Kinship became friendship, friendship something deeper.

She and Torsten became lovers.

They left Florence behind them, and then humanity.

Torsten knew the remedy for her malaise.

They embarked into the wild lands of northern Europe, threw themselves like dull blades on the whetstone of its raw environment. For two decades they lived that way, stripped to their truest essence, animals not merely in the sense that they were savage, but in that they were creatures who bent to nature's shape, rather than seeking to bend it to theirs, which is the way of man. His greatest power and blindest weakness.

They lived in caves or crude transient dwellings, more basic even than those she had known in her earliest memories of Crete. As she had done then, she foraged and hunted daily for food. Drank from springs and streams.

They were nomads, always moving, steering clear of people when their path crossed them. Atana grew to love Torsten, perhaps more even than she had once loved Kitanetos. For the first time since those days, she did not feel alone. Torsten understood her, would have given his life for hers as she would have given hers for him.

Torsten had taken to the wilds before, so that he would be able to return to humanity and civilisation with fresh eyes, he explained. After stripping himself to his basic and most essential self, he was required to learn how to live among men once more.

When this failed him, he hibernated.

Time had given him ample opportunity to revisit the day his clan had acquired Mjolnir. The crypt and the creature were a puzzle. He recalled the pots of honey that did not spoil with age, and similarly the sealed pots of distilled spirits, which might have rested, untouched, for centuries. He thought about the creature that had climbed from the coffin, resilient, ageless…

After his second century alone following the decimation of his clan, he fell to despair. To live had become an effort, and so he journeyed into the wilds. He found a fissure which led to a cave, and deaf to the pleas of hunger and thirst he ceased to eat or drink. Instead, he stacked rocks against the entrance and lay in the cold and the dark until delirium took him, and he was swallowed in dreams and oblivion.

Until, one day, he awoke, roused by whatever magic it was that ran through his veins, yet another secret of Odin's blood.

He woke Mjolnir to clear the opening, one blow unsealed the cave, and crawled into the daylight, all but a husk, a creature driven by base instinct, a twin of the creature who had climbed from the coffin to face his clan's raiding party. His thirst guided him to water and he drank; his appetite steered him to vegetation and he ate. Slowly he returned to the world of the living, grew sturdy enough to think, to hunt and search out mankind.

For over two centuries he had slept. The world he had abandoned had changed, and he found his desire to explore and experience it renewed.

Their self-imposed exile in the wilds having proven sufficient, Torsten and Atana returned to civilization to find much changed, and her spiritual ailment appeased.

The plague which had consumed one-half of an entire continent's men, women and children had exhausted itself. The price exacted had been immense, but had brought an unexpected dividend. The half taken had increased the value of those who survived two-fold.

Before the plague, common men and women had been little more than a wealthy man's property, forced to work his land in exchange for food and shelter. Malnutrition was common, their lives hard and short. Now, these same men and women found themselves in much-increased demand. Many whose masters had perished of the sickness moved to other estates, which, after losing half or more of their workers, were motivated to offer their replacements greatly improved conditions and higher pay. It became possible for the commonest of men to accrue wealth, eat better, work less, prosper in body and spirit.

The division between classes faced erosion, and the age of decadence Atana left seemed to have passed. New ways of thinking and living emerged; the Florence she and Torsten had abandoned had become a crucible for art and creativity. These new artists looked to the old world of Greece and Rome for inspiration, the inherent beauty of humanity and nature. New modes of thinking also grew out of this changed stage, in science and literature.

Atana and Torsten were together for almost three centuries until they parted ways. The eventual parting was not easy. They still loved each other, but, it seemed, not enough to constantly be in each other's company. They resolved to part, with the promise it would not be forever.

To this end they swore to preserve a way to locate each other. Each had their secret places and emergency boltholes, sanctuaries which were hard to reach and harder to breach, unless one knew how. When their journeys brought them close to these places, they would leave a letter, written in cypher. It would summarise their recent movements, how they were faring, their thoughts on the world surrounding them.

Often, when found, these missives were decades old, and commonly out of chronological order. In some, the Torsten who wrote to Atana would be invigorated by some new event or movement, inspired by an artist, philosopher, scientific discovery or invention; in others he seemed ready to seek the wilds or hibernation, exhausted by experience.

Atana imagined that the letters she wrote made for an equally erratic narrative, given Torsten too was likely to find them as much as centuries apart and out of sequence.

Twice during this time, they each found a letter that enabled them to locate the other and subsequently shared many years together. Like many estranged lovers whose paths again converge, they would recall much about the other that they still adored, only for time to eventually remind them of those things that had pushed them apart. When they inevitably agreed to go their separate ways, to negotiate the world alone once more, they did so happier. It was a comfort to know the other was out there somewhere, another soul who understood, an enduring friend should they need one.

In time reunions became markedly easier, and their letters unnecessary. Coded messages, sent by telegram, could be deposited at multiple locations as frequently as each wished from all over the world.

Atana could often locate Torsten in a matter of months if she wished to.

And in 1858, she did.

She was living in Paris and had grown weary. The malaise that had ailed her half a millennium ago in Florence had returned, deeper and more potent than ever.

She yearned for oblivion, but sought out Torsten first. He travelled to spend time with her, but his presence had little impact.

He offered to join her if she wished to take to the wilds, but she had not the energy or the inclination, with or without him. She did not want to die, but marshalling the energy to live was beginning to feel beyond her.

She told him she wanted to do what he had once done. She wanted to hibernate, to sleep and perhaps reawaken with a desire for existence she had lost.

Once he was convinced this was truly what she wanted, and perhaps needed, he agreed to help her make preparations. They would require a suitable tomb. There was a place he knew; one he had held in mind should he ever seek the same remedy. It was located near one of his more remote dwellings, uninviting to potential settlers. He had discovered the cave while climbing in the mountains. It was difficult to reach, in the mountains of northeast Greenland.

They made the journey, scaled the mountain, made a camp close to it, and began to prepare it for her long sleep.

They stocked the cave with provisions, a small quantity of gold, clothing, wood, kindling and matches, jars of honey and whisky, both of which would serve as sustenance when she eventually emerged from her slumber. They would comprise a strange breakfast, but one which would survive centuries unspoilt. They sealed these things in a chest, beside a sarcophagus Torsten lovingly built, carved and lined with his own hands, in which she would rest.

When everything was complete, Torsten and Atana spent a final day together. They ate, made love, and she began her fast.

Torsten stayed at her side, and when the time was right, he carried her to the cave, and placed her in the sarcophagus…

# Chapter Fifteen

"I awoke in 1993," said Atana, in her impossible accent, a blend of continents, countries and ages, over the hum of the private jet's engines, "to a world greatly different from the one I had left. A world of machinery, drastically more populated than I could believe.

"In little more than a century, the number of humans populating the planet had multiplied sevenfold, and their impact upon it was almost impossible to escape. I had gazed in wonder at towering edifices of the ancient world, the cathedrals of the old world too, but the skyscrapers of this new age dwarfed both by orders of magnitude. They speared from sprawling metropolises, super-cities connected by impossibly dense networks of roads and railways. Horseless carriages sped through streets day and night. Flying machines passed overhead, transporting people from one continent to another in a matter of hours.

"Technology, the like of which I could never have imagined, was commonplace.

"I slumbered through the invention of the internal combustion engine, radio, the phonograph, the telephone, the lightbulb, the motor car, the moving picture, the aeroplane, the television, penicillin, the transistor, the microcomputer, satellites, the microchip, the cell phone, the internet... Man had reached and walked on the moon, and captured pictures of distant galaxies...

"I had also, of course, slept through the creation of the tank, the Gatling gun, mustard gas, napalm, and the atomic bomb... used in two conflicts of such magnitude they beggared belief, with more than one hundred million lives lost.

"The world had known darkness while I lay in oblivion's womb, but ultimately a tyrant had been defeated, and a cold war had ended. A wall that had divided a captured capital for over four decades was torn down, the collapse of an oppressive regime seemingly crumbling with it. There was a palpable feeling of optimism in the air, and I embraced it. I wanted to be a part of the world again, rejuvenated not just from my sleep, but by what I saw around me.

"Naturally, I sought out Torsten. We shared our customary honeymoon period, found our unique connection intact. We discussed all I had missed, debated its meaning, ate, drank, made love, and parted while it still produced a wrench, after almost a decade, judiciously before either of us grew tired of the other's company. Torsten had maintained several of my homes, and I moved among them, sampling what this new age had to offer. Beguiled by its new technology, I applied myself to understanding and mastering it.

"For the first time in millennia, I thirsted for answers again. I wanted to know what the treasure I possessed was, whether mine and Torsten's were the only two in existence, or whether there were more. Perhaps there were others like us, who had once used it, whose lives measured not in years, but in centuries."

Atana paused, her eyes finding each of them, Gabe, Holly and Jin.

"Then one day my home was attacked, my treasure stolen, and my oldest friend killed," she said, "and then I found you."

# Chapter Sixteen

*Iceland. The Westfjords.*

The Fine Innovation Facility, or The Shell, as it was more commonly known, was perched on the edge of a cliff, on a rugged peninsula in the remote north-western region of Iceland.

From an aerial perspective it was easy to see how the facility had earned its nickname. From above, the facility resembled a huge fanned sea shell. The similarity was compounded by the roof, a latticework of glass and steel. The eight segmented bands started with glass and were progressively checkerboarded with purple-blue photovoltaic panels which stretched out toward cliff face and sea. The gradual mosaic-like transition, fading from translucent to pale blue to deep indigo at the outer edge, completed the sea shell-like comparison.

Beneath The Shell's enormous roof lay a high-tech village, expansive gardens, luxurious living quarters, recreational facilities, including two tennis courts, three gyms, an Olympic sized swimming pool, running track, a cinema, five world-class restaurants, and of course, offices, and a complex of AAA spec laboratories where Fine Technologies' engineers attempted to, and frequently did, break technological boundaries.

The facility had also been Professor Mervin Pickering's home for three years.

Three years, in which he had not gone beyond the immediate locality. For starters, The Shell was all but inaccessible outside of the summer months, save by helicopter. While his contract stipulated 30 days' leave from the site each year, he was yet to take a single one. Benedict Fine prized and rewarded focus and passion; any staff who remained on-site all year through saw a 100% bonus added to their salary. In Mervin's tenure, he had only known three incumbents who had chosen to sacrifice it, and it was telling that in each instance their need to leave had proven strong enough that, on reflection, they had elected not to return.

For most, the financial incentive wasn't even necessary. Departure during contract was rare for a more straightforward reason: The Shell was the nearest thing to a dream working environment a career-focused individual could imagine. Dissatisfaction over budgets or red tape were so rare as to be exotic. If equipment was requested it appeared, however unusual or expensive. It was the same with materials, requests for samples, external data or expertise.

There were no standard working hours at The Shell. There were simply goals, and if the people chasing them were only motivated by industry-leading wages and benefits, they were probably not in the right place, the right job or the right field.

While the environment outside The Shell was frequently harsh, it was never less than stunning. The Westfjords' ancient landscapes were almost untouched and could be explored. Supervised hikes into the wilds beyond the facility, the mountains, valleys, hot springs and waterfalls were available when conditions permitted. After all, The Shell's personnel were valuable assets. It would not do for one to get lost in the wilds and perish of exposure or starvation, or fall and break their neck, or drown in a river…

For his part, Mervin was content to enjoy the environs' splendour from behind toughened glass in the facility's comfortable climate controlled, 68% self-sustaining biodome campus, an area large enough to feel more like a village than a workplace.

Socialising was encouraged, but the strictest confidentiality was observed where work was concerned. As a result, Mervin hadn't the foggiest idea what projects The Shell's other residents worked on, and was equally confident they were completely in the dark about his. However, he found it hard to believe they were engaged in anything nearly as exciting.

His project was one he could scarcely have imagined being blessed enough to be involved with, let alone lead, and Benedict Fine's estimable resources in the pursuit of results had allowed for astonishing progress. Rare artefacts were loaned or purchased outright, seemingly with the same readiness as liquid soap for the bathroom sink dispensers or blueberry muffins for The Shell's coffee shops. Items that couldn't be obtained for study on-site were scanned in situ, high-resolution 3D mapped, 3D printed, precision weighed, and analysed in exhausting detail, and, Mervin suspected, at considerable cost.

Without a doubt, every penny had been worth it.

It was fair to say Mervin's team was conducting the most ground-breaking study into early human civilisation anywhere on the globe, making discoveries destined to redefine man's understanding of his ancestors, and perhaps his place in Earth's history.

Mervin's work would one day be recognised as monumental, his vindication beyond argument.

How very different things had been on that day three years ago when Benedict Fine had invited him to discuss his work on the fragments. He well remembered his state of mind on leaving the lecture hall. Walking from the university into a scorching Arizona afternoon, he had been fighting the encroaching fear he was drifting ever further from who he thought he was, and where he had imagined he would be. A bold theory had slowly transformed him from a respected expert into a pseudoscience carnival barker. He had felt like a man in quicksand, sinking, the sludge lapping at his neck. When Fine's people had intercepted him in the university car park he had almost been tempted to flee.

Fortunately, he hadn't. Benedict Fine was about to throw him a rope.

Mervin had spent ten minutes in the back of a Fine electric limo, and from there to the back of a chopper. Less than half an hour later the aircraft landed beside a stylish building perched on the edge of a plateau facing a terracotta vista of buttes and mesas.

He had been steered under slowing rotor blades across the private helipad into a blessedly air-conditioned interior, to a huge room offering the same spectacular views without the baking heat.

A large oil painting Mervin recognised hung on a slate wall partially dividing a lounge area from a kitchen and dining area. His first thought was that the painting was a reproduction, but then he remembered who he was here to meet, and reconsidered. While no expert in fine art, Mervin had some knowledge and an appreciation, and in this case the subject matter was close to his passions.

A short, surprisingly burly fellow in the flesh, Benedict Fine was dressed casually, in jeans, boots and a plaid shirt, with the sleeves rolled up, capping a pair of lean, muscular forearms. He didn't look like an eccentric billionaire genius businessman whose personal wealth rivalled the GDP of many countries. Tanned and good looking, he appeared remarkably down to earth, like an ex-college athlete who ran a bar.

"Professor Pickering!" he began. "So grateful you agreed to meet with me. I've been a keen follower of your work."

A small part of Mervin still feared that he was subject to some sort of bizarre practical joke. It seemed unlikely Fine got his jollies transporting history academics to his home for lunch by helicopter only to pull the rug out from under them for cheap laughs, but one never knew. He erred on the side of caution.

"Thank you."

Mervin had to ask about the painting; the subject matter was too close to his heart.

"Excuse me, but would I be correct in assuming that—"

"Is Tiziano Vecelli's The Rape of Europa?"

"I understood it was held at—"

"It was, I acquired it from them last year. Magnificent, isn't it?"

Mervin took in the creamy skinned figure of Europa, one hand clinging to the horn of a white bull, a crimson scarf clutched in the other, gazing back at her home.

Inspired by a story from Ovid's Metamorphoses, it depicted the Princess Europa's abduction by Zeus, who had concealed his identity in the guise of a bull. Once lured onto his back, he carried Europa to Crete, where they were wed and produced three children, one of whom became Minos, King of

Crete, and established the Minoans, the first European civilisation.

"I've developed an interest in the Minoans," Fine said, "as have you, Professor Pic—" Fine paused, smiling. "May I call you Mervin?"

"Erm, yes, of course."

"Mervin, let's say I was putting together a team of experts to study a find of substantial historic significance, something that might have ties to our shared interest here, and I wanted you to lead it? How would that sound to you?"

"Mr Fine, I—"

"Ben. Please."

"Ben… I'd say it would sound incredibly exciting, and like quite an offer."

"It is, incredibly exciting," Fine agreed, "and quite an offer. I assure you the financial package would be more than generous, but we both know that's not what drives men like us, correct? It's the work. I need someone able to think freely, explore possibilities others might be too conservative to pursue. What I have… It's fascinating, but it's a real square peg; I've no interest in seeing a bunch of dullards struggle to bang it into a round hole. I've studied your work on what you refer to as your 'fragments'. This find needs to be approached with an equally open mind."

"I see…" said Mervin, realising, as the words left his mouth, that he wasn't really sure he did see, but very much wanted to.

"There'd be a few conditions. I want the team's work to be conducted in total secrecy, the strictest adherence to security and confidentiality, until the time is right. I doubt I need to tell you how people often respond when their established ideas and boundaries are pushed. As I see it, the only way to counter that sort of response is to leave no room for debate or argument. When the time comes to share the find with the world, the team's conclusions must be robust, the evidence to support them rock solid."

It was true; Mervin's own experiences had demonstrated Fine's point thoroughly and painfully.

"If you choose to come on board, it will mean non-disclosure agreements, and a relocation, albeit to a very pleasant and comfortable setting, to conduct your work. If you chose to leave the team before any findings are released, you would be legally bound not to disclose anything you saw, heard or learned of the project. In perpetuity."

"I see," Mervin said again, only marginally more truthfully than before.

"Any of that sound like a deal-breaker, Mervin?"

Mervin took a moment to consider whether it was. He was a single man. His parents had passed away many years ago, his mother from ovarian cancer, and his father from complications arising from cirrhosis of the liver, and a life-long drinking habit that had not improved with the years, and had only been exacerbated by the loss of his wife.

Mervin's only romantic relationship had lasted sixteen months, in university, and had ended with a fizzle rather than fireworks. Mervin still wasn't sure quite what he had done wrong.

In summary, Mervin had no one to miss, and few people to miss him. He had dedicated himself to the pursuit of knowledge, to his work. It had been a satisfactory arrangement, until recent years when his work had come to be seen as a joke.

An offer to lead a team of experts, funded by a billionaire, to study a find of *substantial historic significance…*

"Not that I can think of, Mr Fi— Ben."

He had accepted Benedict Fine's offer, signed his NDAs, moved to live under a dome of glass and steel in the middle of nowhere, and was yet to experience one moment of regret.

Benedict Fine had indeed secured an astonishing find, still as yet secret from the world at large, including Mervin's peers. Mervin now knew secrets of human history that were shared by fewer than two dozen people.

Among other items, the find included sixteen tablets, intact, all but one written in Linear A. With a relatively limited extant corpus, somewhere in the region of just 1400 examples, they were already special, particularly given their remarkable condition, but one of the tablets made the collection priceless.

Its immense value lay in the fact that the content of the tablets should have been an utter mystery. Linear A was a lost language. It had thwarted scholars' attempts to translate it for more than a century since its discovery by the English archaeologist Sir Arthur Evans.

Between 1900 and 1905 Evans had conducted excavations on the island of Crete and found evidence of a civilization. The archaeologist believed the ancient Greeks' mythology was rooted in this earlier civilisation and looked to it when naming them.

In Greek myth, King Minos was a son of Zeus, born to a mortal mother, who came to marry Pasiphae, daughter of the sun-god Helios. According to the myth, Minos appealed to the sea god, Poseidon, to send a white bull as proof of his divine authority as King of Crete.

The sea god acquiesced, but Minos made the mistake of ignoring the promise he had made in return, that he would soon after sacrifice the creature to Poseidon. As punishment, the sea god caused Minos's bride to fall in love with the bull. Their union resulted in a monstrous half-breed beast: The Minotaur, which Minos hid away in the Labyrinth, an intricate maze beneath his palace.

Due to the prevalent imagery of bulls in the decorative ruins he had unearthed, Evans dubbed the island race he discovered the Minoans.

The ruins indicated a civilisation rich in culture and technology, capable of building elaborate palaces up to four stories high, with sophisticated plumbing systems and vibrant artistry, pottery, frescos, jewellery and clothing. Its people engaged in an immense network of trade, and had flourished from the early bronze age, around 3000 BC to 1100 BC.

The Minoans were recognised as the first advanced civilisation in Europe.

Evans published a paper about several clay tablets he had unearthed. They bore scripts that differed from any discovered up to that point. The oldest were pictographs, which he referred to as Cretan Hieroglyphs, and another group he dubbed Linea, as their characters were organised in lines and possessed characteristics suggestive of a syllabic writing system. Both scripts were believed to have developed around 1700 BC.

In the time since Evans' discovery, both scripts had stubbornly resisted translation. Whatever secrets they carried remained impenetrable.

Functional comparisons, the most common route to translation, were sorely lacking. What became known as Linear B, the deciphered script for the Mycenaean language, had not proved a fruitful comparison. Unlike, for example, Egyptian hieroglyphs, which were deciphered through the surviving written and spoken language of Coptic, and the later discovery of the Rosetta Stone, a bilingual, triscriptual text which included Greek names transcribed into hieroglyphs, Linear A enjoyed no such bridging link.

Until the find that had come into Fine's possession. Along with the Linear A, one tablet held passages inscribed in Linear B, clearly from a later age, dating from around 1450 BC, when some knowledge of the dying language must still have survived. Common decorative elements strongly suggested the tablet's Linear B passages repeated the content of one of the Linear A ones.

This was the key.

After much work, and after as many as 3800 years in which no one on earth had been able to decode it, Mervin's team had deciphered Linear A, and the story the tablets held, a story that not only supported Mervin's work but expanded its horizons further than he could have ever imagined.

# Chapter Seventeen

Gabe, Holly, Jin and Atana touched down in England and arrived at the manor house, a huge Georgian building surrounded by gardens, fields and woodland, as the sun was rising.

Jin collected the keys from the hidden security lockbox where the estate manager had left them nearby, and escorted Atana to a guest room. They had changed clothes after collecting Jin from near the Brooklyn building, but the sweat and grime of their encounter still lay underneath.

"You coming?" Holly asked from halfway up the staircase, on her way to clean up too, when she realised Gabe was still standing in the huge entrance hall.

"You go on up. Be with you in a minute or two."

Holly nodded, climbed the stairs.

Years had melted away in an instant. The manor house was just as Gabe remembered it, save for a few small details. In the last few hours, the place must have been a hive of activity. The estate manager hadn't been given much time to prepare for their sudden arrival. Dust sheets had been hastily removed, and furniture brought out of storage. The short notice was evident in the fact that not everything had been reinstated. The oak-panelled walls remained bare, their decorative tapestries and paintings still wrapped and stored in the attic where the light couldn't bleach them.

The suit of armour Gabe recalled from his very first visit was present though, again standing sentry in the entrance hall, inviting memories of the house's former owner, and one-time Templar, Nicholas Blake, Jin's mentor and friend.

The manor house was one of many such properties across the globe, ready to become home at a moment's notice. They would find suitable clothes hanging in their closets, favoured food on the shelves, transport in the garages. Accruing wealth when you live for centuries is a good deal easier than in a single lifetime. Nicholas and Jin had used the centuries to build security and flexibility, but this house was different from all the others.

It was the one Gabe had arrived at eight years ago, in the wake of seeing Holly abducted.

Holly had been on the run, with the grail, and had come to him for help. They had been attacked. He had seen Jin injured, and then miraculously heal right before his own eyes. Jin had convinced him if he wanted to get Holly back alive, they should work together.

Jin had taken him to Nicholas Blake.

Beyond the entrance hall was the study where he and Blake waited for the information that would tell them where Holly was, allow them to attempt to recover both her and the stolen grail. In one of the twin wingback armchairs flanking the huge fireplace, he had listened to Blake's story, a life measured in centuries.

It encompassed the birth of the Knights Templar and that order's secret Council of Nine. It was a tale of loss, brotherhood and betrayal. Blake and Jin were close to immortal, and so too were the men who had taken Holly.

Together with Jin and Blake, he had rescued her and recovered the grail. The men they fought had not survived the confrontation. He, Holly and Jin had barely escaped with their lives. Nicholas Blake had not been so lucky.

One man and a thousand years of history, of memories, had been lost.

What would Blake have made of Atana's tale? Would he have been surprised that three and a half thousand more years of history left the grail, now grails, no less a mystery, but perhaps an even greater one?

—

Showered and in fresh clothes, Gabe and Holly convened with Jin, walking together through the gardens.

"The island, the people in her story, she was talking about the Minoans," said Jin.

Holly nodded.

"The who?" Gabe asked.

"The ancient people native to the island of Crete. Perhaps Europe's earliest civilisation," said Holly. "The Minoans predate the Mycenaeans, the first Greeks."

Jin nodded, "If true, that would indeed make her over three and a half thousand years old. The cataclysm she described was the eruption on Thera, an island to the north of Crete. The volcano devastated Thera, submerged most of it. Archaeologists believe the neighbouring coast of Crete would have faced quakes and a tsunami too, been blighted by ash clouds, seen harsh winters for years.

"Some scholars believe the event survives in ancient Greek literature a thousand years later, in the form of Atlantis." Holly added. "The Minoans, too.

Homer speaks of a rich and lovely, densely populated land. There's poetry which alludes to an island and a people even the ancient Greeks had almost forgotten, who survived only in the form of myth."

Holly found Gabe's gaze on her, and a small smile.

"Okay," she said, "I thought of Minoa too, and maybe spent a little time on Google. If we believe Atana," Holly said, "it means the bracelet she wore, the grail in another form, was ancient long before the Templars discovered it."

"Do we believe her?" asked Jin.

Gabe shrugged. "Mate, I thought you were crazy when you first told me you were nearly five hundred years old," he said, "and when Nicholas claimed to be a thousand, but neither of you was lying. Yeah, I think I believe her."

"Me too," said Holly.

Jin nodded.

"We want our grail back. She wants hers. She's clearly smart and formidable..."

Holly nodded. "And let's acknowledge something before we begin to kid ourselves otherwise: if she hadn't turned up and thrown a spanner in our attackers' works, would we still be here to have this discussion? If she was only worried about recovering her own grail, bracelet, whatever... She could have opted to hang back, opted to track the men who hit us back to where they were going. She chose not to. Don't we stand a better chance of getting the grail back with her help?"

"Before we can get them back, we need to get some idea of who took them," said Gabe. "I think I might know where to start. That outfit was mercs, no doubt about it. Experienced and professional.

There can't be too many groups at that level for hire."

"It would help to know where they came from. I have a few ideas there," Holly added, looking to Jin. "There's a chance the answer might lie in the items I asked you to collect..."

—

Holly claimed one of the east wing's rooms and compiled a list of equipment, which she and Jin set about procuring as fast as possible.

Gabe contacted an old friend: Lance Hewitt.

He got lucky. His call found Lance both in the country and with spare time to meet up. Lance had been his captain for a time when they were both in the Special Air Service, and had then retired to start a private security firm, LHS Security Ltd. When Gabe also left the regiment several years later, Lance recruited him.

LHS Security Ltd kept on the clean side of the private security game, but given the nature of the business, any big firm that operated internationally occasionally veered close to murky, dirtier waters.

In more volatile and dangerous parts of the world, a firm like Lance's often found itself working alongside other armed outfits, including PMCs, and armed mercenary groups who operated outside of the law. It was these groups Gabe wanted to quiz Lance about, ones you couldn't find on Google, ones hired via word of mouth or the dark web.

The group that had hit them was experienced and professional. Highly skilled operatives like that were expensive. Hitting a building with top-flight security somewhere as public as Brooklyn, with orders to steal and execute, wasn't a job for clowns. This group had disrupted the surrounding area with diversionary fires and staged traffic accidents. The price tag for an operation like that had to be significant. Someone had hired the best who specialised in doing the worst.

If that was something you offered, you gained some degree of notoriety, even if only in limited circles. To have clients, you had to be known by the right people, even if only in rumours and whispers. Someone like Lance might hear those same whispers and rumours.

It wasn't a conversation to have over the phone, so Gabe suggested an afternoon pint or two at wherever Lance now considered his local.

It turned out Lance's local was now the village coffee shop. Gabe learned his old friend had given up booze and was taking a more disciplined approach to his diet. Less red meat and red wine, less bacon, sausage, fried egg, black pudding and baked beans, and more red beans, green beans and brown rice. On paper, Lance was just nine years older than Gabe, but while Gabe had seen eight years pass without physically degrading one bit, the same couldn't be said for Lance. From a biological standpoint, Lance was now seventeen years Gabe's senior.

It wasn't that his old friend was decrepit. Not at all: Lance was in good shape for a man approaching sixty years of age, but he *was* still a man approaching sixty years of age. Lance had moved into his autumn years, whereas Gabe now existed in perpetual summer.

The discrepancy didn't escape Lance.

As Gabe poured milk into the mug of earl grey tea beside Lance's skinny latte, his erstwhile captain and employer shook his head, "I swear you don't look one day older than the last time I saw you. It's like being mates with bloody Tom Cruise."

"I'd tell you my secret, but you wouldn't believe me."

"Try me."

For a crazy second, Gabe was tempted to.

It was good to see Lance. It had been too long. He was one of his oldest and closest friends, yet outside the occasional phone call, they barely spoke, and hadn't met face to face in four years. Seeing Lance had aged in that time shouldn't have come as a shock, but it did. Gabe found himself wondering whether he had already begun to measure his years differently.

Another thought: how much longer could he meet Lance without it becoming brutally apparent he genuinely wasn't growing older? At what point would he be unable to meet his friend like this? How long before Lance was a frail and doddery old man who struggled to recall his name? How long before Lance wasn't around to meet or speak to at all? How many years before all the people he knew before accepting the grail's gift were distant memories, names in records, someone's great, great, great, great, someone on a family tree?

When you agreed to forever, could you truly know what you were agreeing to?

He wished he could have been honest, but then sanity returned.

"How do I maintain my youthful visage? Moisturiser, mate, the foundation of any robust beauty regime."

"You're right," Lance said, deadpan, "I don't believe you. It would take some face cream to make that ugly mug beautiful."

Gabe laughed, and steered them into a little small talk.

Soon enough, they fell into the old rhythms. Each asking how the other's missus was, and in Lance's case his girls, tweens when Gabe last saw them, both now grown women. Just two old mates catching up, fondly taking the piss out of one another. Gabe wished he had done it sooner, regretted the existence of an ulterior motive for the meeting, one he couldn't set aside any longer.

When Gabe asked Lance what he knew about mercenary outfits, currently active top-flight ones, his friend naturally asked why he wanted to know. When Gabe said he would rather not say, Lance nodded slowly. Gabe knew him well enough to know this was not to be taken as a sign he had let the question go.

"How about this? Let's shelve the bollocks for a moment," he said. "I don't know what went down eight years ago, except you suddenly up and vanished, and then reappeared a couple of months later, Holly on your arm. I was relieved to see you alive and well, and pleased to see you looked happy again. When you told me about your unexpected inheritance... It was a surprise. As far as I was aware your only remaining family was your aunt who, from the way you spoke, wouldn't have given you the free toy out of her cereal box, let alone name you the beneficiary of her estate. And your plan to retire from the security business and travel around the world? Why not, I thought? One life to live, live it to the fullest, right?

"I never tackled you then, nor since, but truth be told I don't believe you inherited any money from your aunt, not tuppenny ha'penny or a bundle. I don't know what happened to iron things out between you and Holly either, but I'm glad you managed to." Lance stirred his skinny latte. "Truth be told, I was too glad to see you were your old self again. Hell, I didn't even begrudge having to find someone to replace you at work.

"But now you're here asking about mercenary outfits, you can't blame me for wondering why. Has the 'inheritance' money run out? Tell me that's not how you made a fast bundle back then, and, if it was, you're not thinking about working for any of these scumbag outfits again, something dark and dirty that pays insanely well to maintain this globetrotting life of yours?"

"Come on, Lance, you know me better than that. I don't need money, and I'm no merc."

"Not the Gabe I knew, but people change, mate."

"You honestly think I'd do that?"

Lance studied him, sighed. "No, I guess not. So why then?"

"I swear, you of all people I would tell if I could, but the situation is… complicated."

"Complicated, eh?"

"Okay…" Lance didn't deserve to be lied to, or at least no more than necessary, and Gabe wanted to keep as close to the truth as possible. "Let's say I have a friend. A very old, very wealthy friend. A couple of days ago this friend was hit by a team of around two dozen highly trained soldiers. They robbed him of something crazy valuable. They were highly skilled, able to disable his building's security system and swagger in like they owned the place. Whoever sent them wasn't afraid to create a little local mayhem to get what he wanted, either. My friend was lucky to get out alive. Now he wants to get back what they took."

"So, you're working for this guy?"

"Not exactly. I'm helping him. As I said, it's complicated."

"Yep, you did."

"I think they were a private mercenary outfit, and a damn good one. One of the best is my bet. If I can find out who the best is right now, I might be able to work out which one it was, and then maybe who hired them."

"And then what?"

"That's a problem for later."

"So, what top tier mercenary outfits are currently the go-to for someone with deep pockets and no issues causing mayhem to get what they want?" Lance mused. "There are a few names I've heard, but you need to understand how it is. Some of them might not even exist, or they may have, but not anymore. The way I hear it, most of these outfits fall apart sooner or later. Soldiers who wind up on the fringe like this, they're well… What's the technical term? Nut jobs?" Lance sipped his skinny latte, chewed it over. "Let me ask around. I have a contact who might know more than I do."

"I'd really appreciate that. Thanks, mate. The sooner you can get back to me the better."

"Your friend's keen to get his gear back?"

"Very."

Gabe left Lance reluctantly, again wishing he had caught up sooner and under different circumstances. Gabe told Lance to say hi to his wife Mary and his kids who were now old enough to have children of their own. Lance could be a grandad… The thought, the reality, was unsettling.

"Say hi to Holly from me too." Lance replied, "I'll do my best to get back to you with something soon, yeah?"

"Cheers Lance, I owe you one."

# Chapter Eighteen

Holly's makeshift lab was coming together. She had built a polythene-sheet-lined clean room and begun to go through the bags containing the gear and fingerprints harvested from their felled assailants back in Brooklyn.

Atana had asked Holly if she could use an assistant. Together they had donned disposable aprons and gloves and set about collecting and clipping sample material. Holly was determined to tease out any secrets they might hold.

No one was a ghost, no matter how hard they tried. People left traces and trails, even she, Gabe and Jin, with their enviable resources, included. How else had someone been able to find them and the grail?

Findings trickled in, and additional analysis was conducted. Holly and Atana chatted while they worked, more comfortably than Holly expected given the strange circumstances.

Holly knew she should be more cautious, but was struggling to mistrust Atana. She had helped them, maybe saved their lives, and answered their questions. She and they had been attacked by the same aggressors and thieves. They shared a common foe, and were equally eager to find out who this foe was so they could set about getting back what had been taken.

Perhaps it was the methodical quality of laboriously selecting, clipping and bagging samples, processing and analysing, but they quickly relaxed into something approaching simple conversation.

"Gabriel is your partner?" Atana asked.

"My husband."

"And Jin?"

"Jin is..." Holly smiled. "Jin is... our friend, our mentor? Gabe and I are still relatively new to this whole immortal thing..."

"How long?"

"Nearly eight years now."

"And Jin?"

"Closer to five hundred. His mentor Nicholas Blake was approaching a thousand. Once, Blake was a Templar. He believed, or used to believe, the object stolen from us was the holy grail..." And so it went.

Holly told Atana what had brought her to Nicholas and Jin, how she had been recruited into a secret project team assembled to study an object the two owned. She talked about how the team had learned the mysterious object was actually a piece of technology, nanotechnology, underpinned by science so advanced it shouldn't exist.

She talked about how she had eventually learned the greater truth, that the object wasn't new, but very, very old, and so were its keepers.

Nicholas had first encountered the object during the Crusades. Its discovery had resulted in the founding of the Knights Templar, and the order's clandestine heart, the Council of Nine. Both would eventually be destroyed, betrayed by one of their own who stole the grail for himself. The traitor, Reynaud, believed the order and the council had lost their way. He sought to use the grail to assemble an army of immortals, wage a holy war against Christendom's enemies and retake the holy lands.

Nicholas narrowly escaped the Templar purge and eventually tracked Reynaud to feudal Japan. He recruited an ally there, Jin, and with his assistance had wrestled the grail back. He would regret his failure to eliminate Reynaud. Half a millennium later his nemesis would track him down and come for the grail again.

Holly and Gabe had helped Jin and Nicholas emerge as victors in the following and final confrontation. Reynaud and his party were defeated and lost their lives, but Nicholas perished, too. Jin had survived by the skin of his teeth, in time to find Gabe and Holly, teetering between life and death. He had used the grail to save their lives, in exchange for a promise. They would take Nicholas's place, dedicate themselves to keeping the grail safe and secret from the world, protect it from men like Reynaud.

"The Holy Grail… Mjolnir…" Atana said, once Holly was done. "Why are men compelled to graft myths onto mysteries? I scarcely know more than you what the treasures we held are, but would wager they explain the myths more than the myths explain them."

"Doesn't it drive you crazy? The not knowing what they are after thousands of years?"

Atana smiled. It was world-weary but warm. "A little, but I remind myself the universe is bursting with mysteries for which I have no answers. I have lived with these for thousands of years, too. Maybe one day the truth of all things will be revealed, but at this time, I simply seek to recover what belongs to me, confident it is safest in my care."

# Chapter Nineteen

It was past midnight when Holly summoned them all to the manor house's generous library. After four days she was confident she had something worth sharing, not the whole picture, but enough to offer a path forward.

Gabe had news of his own. Lance had called that morning, after which he sent a link to an encrypted file, together with the clue to the password to unlock it, the punchline to an old regiment joke they used to share in tense situations. So bad, it only got funnier the more Lance told it, and the more dangerous the situation he told it in.

The question:

How does a soldier unlock his car?

The password:

He uses his Khakis…

Gabe immediately retrieved the file and pored over what it contained.

He headed downstairs to the library early, but still wasn't the first to get there. He found Jin staring into the darkening grounds beyond the library's huge sash windows. Gabe crossed the room to join him, past those twin wingback armchairs flanking the library's massive granite fireplace, which for as long as they lived there would evoke a tale of crusades, friendship, zealotry and betrayal.

Jin had chosen to bring them here. Of all the many places across the world he could have picked, this was the one they had fled to. If Blake's ghost lingered here for Gabe, how could it fail to for Jin? Perhaps that was *why* Jin had brought them here.

Gabe knew Jin still felt Blake's absence keenly. Blake had been more than his mentor. Their relationship had smacked of something closer to father and son.

Jin pulled his eyes from the window. Gabe knew his approach had been detected long before he entered the room. Jin was not an easy person to sneak up on.

"Gabriel. Are you well?"

"Still finding it a bit strange, being back here. Seems like a lifetime since we last were... and then just yesterday."

Jin nodded, "I've been thinking."

"About?"

"Choices," said Jin, "Maybe being here is part of it... Or makes certain things I've felt for a long time impossible to ignore. My mind keeps returning to the night we fought Reynaud and the Hashshashin, to one moment in particular, again and again. There was a moment, after they were defeated, when it seemed everyone was dead, and I was trying to escape the castle, the fire... when I believed, finally, that I was going to die too, and the grail along with me.

"The castle was ablaze. I was literally clinging by my fingertips as everything crumbled around me. My other hand was around the handle of the case holding the grail. Then the ledge I was clinging to suddenly broke away. I started to fall, down towards the flames, and I knew, *knew* this was it... the end." Jin paused. "Do you know what I felt in that moment?"

Gabe shook his head.

"Relieved. Glad. It was *over*, done. The world would be saner, make more sense, even if I would never know it. It would contain no impossible immortals, no inexplicable treasures that offered impossible gifts…

"And then, instead of plunging into the inferno, my clawing fingers grasped something solid. I saved myself, escaped, albeit with these burns and less one eye, but alive and still in possession of the grail. I found you and Holly outside, both mortally injured. I knew if I did nothing you would perish.

"So, I offered you the same bargain Nicholas had offered me when I found myself in the same position centuries before. I did it without thinking. I did it because you didn't deserve to die, and I didn't want you to. I did it because you had helped recover the grail. I did it because I had grown to like you both, and I did it because finding you had escaped too, and that the grail was right there in my hands… It felt… like fate, like something preordained. I allowed the notion to steer my judgement, or that's what I have chosen to tell myself. Maybe all of that is wilful self-obfuscation, and there is a deeper truth.

"What if I saved you not out of compassion, or to aid in protecting the grail, but out of cowardice? What if I didn't want to shoulder the burden of keeping it alone? What if I simply couldn't face the prospect of sharing eternity with it as my only company?"

"You don't believe that."

"Gabriel, I'm less sure what I believe these days. Nicholas was always so… self-assured. I was content to bow to his greater experience and wisdom. But perhaps that was cowardice too? I chose to trust he knew best. It made our existence easier, lent us purpose, but even had he survived, it was untenable. The world has changed. How can people like us not call attention to ourselves sooner or later?"

Inside, Gabe winced. The bodega incident.

"Jin, I know—"

Jin held up a hand to quiet him, "Gabriel, I am not affixing blame, quite the opposite. For centuries Nicholas and I kept the grail safe and secret, then three times in the last decade, if we include Atana, we have been found.

"The world as it is today is more connected, more recorded, more populated, secrecy a greater challenge to maintain. I keep arriving at the same conclusion: we should have destroyed the grail while we had the chance. It was inevitable the day would come, eventually, when someone would learn about the grail, covet it, come for it, and advancing technology improve their odds of success with every incremental innovation. What I am, what *we* are, once made us formidable opponents; the armaments of our modern age mean this is no longer so.

"The warriors of my youth carried swords, knives and arrows. Then came those first, cumbersome, unreliable, clumsy and inaccurate muskets. In the last century or so the repeating rifle, now? Now? The men who attacked us carried weapons that fire hundreds of rounds a minute. They hunted us with vision that allowed them to see us in the dark. They breached our walls not with iron or steel, cannons or battering rams, but computer code and silicon.

"We have been rendered fragile. Had you not been there, had Atana not intervened, had Holly not helped us all, I would not be here now. It was folly to believe we could continue to keep the grail safe and secret as we have done for so long."

"What are you saying?"

"I am saying that if by some miracle we can recover the grail, we must destroy it."

"But Jin, if what Atana says is true, ours isn't the only one. What about hers? What about the one her friend had?"

Jin seemed about to answer, and then abruptly stayed his tongue. Gabe realised why moments later when Holly and Atana arrived, directly, it seemed, from Holly's makeshift lab.

Holly had loaned Atana some of her clothes. Out of the black leather and boots, sans sword at her hip, she no longer looked like something out of a Hollywood action movie, or a three-and-a-half-thousand-year-old Minoan huntress. Dressed in jeans and an olive sweater, she looked as ordinary as anyone else. Well, at just over six feet tall and looking the way she did, maybe not *ordinary*, but at least not so obviously extraordinary.

Jin caught Gabe's eye. His glance made it clear he would prefer the discussion they had just had remain between the two of them for the time being.

—

"Okay, here's what I got," Holly began. She had hooked a laptop up to a compact DLP projector, which right now beamed a map onto the library wall, the world painted in splotches of colour.

"Okay, so I analysed and profiled traces of soil harvested from the boots we collected. What you can see here is a global FAO-UNESCO soil map of the globe, which I compared the results against," she said. "The plant materials and organic matter all point to northern Europe. Helpful in narrowing things down, but a long way from X marks the spot. However, when we include analysis of pollen grains found in the sample things get more interesting.

Two species of Cryptogams, and one Monocotyledon are present. The latter is a from a plant species indigenous to Iceland, one rarely found outside the region."

Gabe frowned. "Our attackers came from Iceland?"

"The dirt on their boots says they do," Holly replied, before moving on. "That's not all. We have another interesting finding from their kit, specifically the body armour they were wearing. It's an exotic Kevlar derivative. Very nice, lighter, stronger, and… not a commercially available product. I tracked down a patent that matches an aromatic polyimide; it was approved eighteen months ago. The company that filed it has all the characteristics of a shell.

"Next, we got DNA, several profiles. If we were able to run them through a bunch of private and national databases, we might get a hit. That's beyond my talents, which brings us to…"

"I have a home in Paris." Atana said, "The set-up I have there should be sufficient to gain access to the DNA databases we need. I can run the profiles, but I can also try to determine the parent of the shell company who owns the patent on the body armour material."

Gabe joined the dots, "If the DNA nets us a name, that could narrow the field when it comes to identifying the outfit that hit us. Thanks to Lance, I have some potential culprits regarding armed mercenary groups active during the last few years. The backbone of these units usually lies in one military force or another. If we can find out which one a dead attacker once served in…"

# Chapter Twenty

*Paris, Le Marais.*

Holly clung to the back of the motorcycle as Atana wove expertly through congested traffic.

When Atana had said she had arranged transport from the private Le Bourget airfield to their destination, Holly had, not unreasonably, expected something with four wheels. What they had collected was a sleek black Japanese motorcycle.

As they approached the capital and cruised past queues of congested traffic, she conceded it was perhaps not just her companion's predilection for speedy two-wheeled locomotion that lay behind the choice. The bike sliced past the cars, snaked down tree-lined boulevards populated with hotels, bakeries and boutiques, ornate stone facades, full of Juliet balconied windows and garret roofs.

The streets narrowed as they entered the old heart of Paris, the medieval streets of the city, eventually slowing before a six-story building with grand wooden doors. Atana steered the bike through an arch into a central courtyard and deployed the kickstand.

She retrieved an old, bronze, patinated key from beneath a nearby plant pot, and opened an equally old lock in an equally elderly looking door.

A second considerably more modern and substantial interior door blocked their path through the vaulted entry room beyond. Atana tilted her face upwards. Holly spotted the beady nub of a tiny camera's eye above the decorative stone lintel. An artfully concealed panel in the wall retracted, revealing a keypad, into which Atana tapped in a code. An instant later the heavy door rattled open. Atana pushed it wide and crossed the threshold into a modern, elegantly furnished, lived-in looking lounge. She judged this was the last place Atana had lived before heading to New York.

Atana led them on through to a birdcage elevator. They climbed inside and she pulled the concertina door shut. They ascended five floors and disembarked at a garret room with a window that framed the rooftops of a city two thousand years old.

While the room and the building belonged to a distant century, the tech across the room were rooted firmly in the here and now. A cluster of monitors and a bank of workstations were flanked by shelving filled with cables and a plethora of other techy looking hardware that looked well used.

Atana began to power up the workstations and monitors and fetched out the USB drive containing the data they had harvested from Holly's forensic blitz, and the info Lance had provided Gabe.

The garret room felt like a considerably more personal space. Art adorned the walls, sculptures and framed sketches. Holly's eyes grazed a picture in a silver frame and were immediately drawn back to it.

It was a portrait of a couple. The outer edge of the image was dull and tarnished, in sharp contrast to the man and woman at the centre, who were brilliant and striking. Holly realised it was a framed daguerreotype. She moved closer, and, without thinking, picked it up.

Atana gazed out of it; she looked much as she did across the room, not a day older, only in the picture her hair was up, tightly plaited and pinned. The man next to her was equally arresting. Even captured in silver-plated copper his complexion was icy pale next to Atana's Mediterranean colouring, and where her features were subtle and fine, his were strong and broad. He looked hewn more from marble than flesh.

The daguerreotype's unearthly mirror-like surface seemed the perfect medium for such an otherworldly pair. Holly tilted the picture under the light spilling through the window, seeking a clearer view. When it reached a certain angle the image flipped negative and positive, shadows reversed to blazing whites as the bare silver plate caught the sun's gaze.

Atana had turned from her array of monitors and caught Holly studying the portrait. Holly felt suddenly embarrassed; aware she had not asked before handling such an obviously personal item.

"Sorry. I couldn't seem to help myself."

"It's fine. I don't mind, really."

"This man? Is he the one you told us about, Torsten?"

"He is. If spending eternity with one person was possible, for me that person would have been Torsten."

"You don't think it's possible?"

Atana seemed to think about it, and said, "Forever is a long time for any union to endure. A thousand years is a long time, even a century is. Torsten and I were fortunate enough to spend longer than this together. We never stopped loving each other, but progressively other wants and needs intruded. It was enough for us to know the other was out there, to know we would one day see each other again. What is the expression? Absence makes the heart grow fonder? Perhaps in this way we might truly have shared eternity."

Atana smiled, but all Holly saw was sadness.

"You think they killed him?" she said.

"I know they killed him. Had he escaped, the first thing he would have done is to have warned me we were in danger."

# Chapter Twenty-One

*The Westfjords, Iceland, 129 miles north of Reykjavik.*

The helicopter skimmed over rugged mountains and moss-carpeted hills.

Its solitary passenger, Benedict Fine, watched the facility grow from a speck in the distance to the point at which it began to exhibit the characteristics behind its nickname.

The facility did indeed look reminiscent of a sea shell perched on a cliff edge. From a distance, surrounded by the vast and isolated natural landscape, its dimensions were deceptive. As the aircraft closed in, though, its true scope was impossible to ignore.

One could see the many fully-grown trees beneath the transparent span of its roof, transplanted at great expense, populating the huge indoor garden. One could see the walking paths dotted with people, and the electric carts parked near the entrance, designed to accommodate two passengers, scooting around the site.

The chopper slowed, dropping towards the helipad just outside The Shell's walls, and soon enough its skids touched down. Fine disembarked to find Oblonsky, the head of the fragment team, awaiting him.

Pale and perpetually wet-lipped, the scientist lurked outside the climate-lock entrance gate. When Fine reached him, Oblonsky reached out a hand, which Fine reluctantly shook. For some reason Fine always wanted to wipe his hand on his pants after such a greeting. Oblonsky had an unsettling quality about him.

"I have a cart waiting. I can drive, unless you would prefer—" Oblonsky asked in his quiet, Russian accented voice.

"Nope," Fine replied. "Happy to ride shotgun."

Oblonsky nodded and led them toward the atrium's verdant and manicured gardens and the small electric vehicle.

More than three hundred people lived and worked under The Shell's roof. Most were split among various research projects, with the remaining number providing support, hospitality, maintenance and security. The last of these were seen more as service personnel. The facility was light on overt security. The site was not fenced off; there were merely simple signs around the perimeter that made it clear it was private property, and that to progress further constituted trespass.

The Shell had uniformed security staff, just enough to provide comfort, but few enough to easily ignore. The real steel was obscured.

A bare handful of people were aware The Shell was home to a troop of highly skilled and well-equipped soldiers, Carson Grave's men. They were hidden in plain sight. They occupied a residential block over in the west section, and as far as other residents were concerned, they were a QA team comprised of extreme sports veterans; their purpose was to put potential Fine Tec outdoors recreational and military gear through its paces.

The most common security threat in the tech development world came as often from within as from without, as Fine knew only too well. Fine Tec had been the victim of industrial espionage in the early years of its success. Competitors succeeded in acquiring valuable information on the company's revolutionary battery technology, not enough to circumvent the company's patents, but enough to muddy the commercial landscape with similar-sounding but inferior solutions.

In the aftermath, Fine had questioned the wisdom of locating the firm's R&D efforts in a place surrounded by competitors. When the time came to expand and invest in new headquarters, he elected to leave Silicon Valley behind, far behind, a whole continent behind. Fine Tec's new R&D facility would be situated in the remote Westfjords of Iceland. The decision to spend two point eight billion dollars constructing a facility in such an isolated location was made precisely because it would be difficult to reach, and difficult to leave. Like the kings and chieftains of old, Fine conscripted geography and nature as his allies.

It was a challenge to visit or depart The Shell without being seen. While there were no fences, concealed cameras covering the approach from the half-mile perimeter and a pressure-sensitive array detected anything which strayed within the same radius. The rear of the facility was a sheer cliff face, obstacle enough all on its own.

To further diminish the risk of internal leaks, security inside its walls adopted a similarly practical, tech-lite approach. Psychology over surveillance.

While keen to secure the best talent, the recruitment process filtered out those inclined to respond negatively to confinement and isolation. A positive bias was afforded to natural loners, workaholics and the socially challenged. People like Oblonsky.

Treachery was further discouraged by stringent contracts, encouraged with industry-leading salaries and healthy bonuses, and lastly by fostering a culture of mild paranoia mixed with just a soupçon of Stockholm syndrome.

The area had no local post boxes to stroll to, no mobile phone masts. All contact with the world outside was conducted via The Shell's infrastructure, physical or digital. Anyone hoping to share company secrets had their work cut out.

Building the facility in the middle of nowhere had raised questions, but far fewer than it should have done. From the outset, Fine was vocal about the project. He actively courted coverage for the facility's development and construction. He loudly trumpeted the environmental benefits the design and construction would herald. He enthused about how energy efficient the site would be, practically carbon-neutral, and how it would serve as a testbed for cutting edge technology destined to make its way into the homes of the future.

Initial media interest was strong. Benedict Fine was not usually so accessible, and, when he did give interviews, he was generally an engaging and entertaining subject. Articles about the new Fine R&D headquarters became the polar opposite of an exclusive.

In the ensuing pieces, Fine's strategy was to be as enthusiastic about the new facility as possible, while being as dull as possible. The information he shared was plentiful, but painfully dry and technical. Interviewers found themselves with a subject akin to the boring enthusiast no one wants to be sat next to at a dinner party: eager to talk in exhaustive and tedious detail about his hobby to any audience unfortunate enough to fall into his clutches. On the topic of The Shell, the media soon learned to excuse themselves and grab a different seat, and coverage quickly dwindled.

Unfortunately, certain environmental groups hadn't tired quite so quickly. Fine had anticipated their objections and been equally clever in finding ways to smother them. The Shell would be a blot on the landscape, they argued, 'an incongruous modern carbuncle scarring an ancient region of natural beauty' as one lobby group put it, but, when complete, the design had been praised by mainstream voices. As one prominent critic, incentivised by his editor on Fine's behalf, conceded, "during its construction, even the Eiffel Tower had been labelled *a mast of iron gymnasium apparatus, incomplete, confused and deformed.*"

What most incensed the environmental groups was the manner in which Fine had secured permission to construct it in the largely unspoilt Westfjords at all. An agreement to operate a fixed percentage of the Fine Tec empire from the site meant a significant tax benefit to the larger Icelandic economy. Post relocation, Fine technologies accounted for nearly four per cent of the country's GDP. While a transparent bribe to many, it was rarely presented as such in the media.

Fine had always been careful to manage his and his company's image, limiting scrutiny of its more unsavoury endeavours, such as its military contracts. Projects which threatened to result in unfavourable optics were buried deep in subsidiaries, pushed far enough away they couldn't sully the Fine Technologies brand, or Benedict Fine's personal reputation.

Fine's three-pronged strategy for image control was:

Be loud when news was good.

Make sure bad news was starved of oxygen.

Make sure all news, whether positive or negative, prompted some degree of scepticism.

The third prong he achieved by deliberately cultivating a reputation for eccentricity, casting himself to some degree as Silicon Valley's Willy Wonka.

It wasn't difficult. The occasional outlandish response during interviews, like boasting about having teams working on atomic matter transportation or hard light holograms (or other technologies likely to remain science fiction for generations, if they ever came to fruition at all) did the job nicely.

Such claims were not an outright lie. He did have teams working on these unlikely projects, just in case anyone ever asked for proof. Although, 'teams' usually meant two or three people, who covered a range of speculative projects. Their efforts generally amounted to writing papers and discussing theoretical approaches. The budgets supporting them were negligible.

Being able to assert in one breath that his electric cars were the future, and in the next that even these would soon be made redundant by the Star Trek-style particle transportation his 'teams' were developing, ensured everything he said was perhaps best digested with a grain of salt. On the other hand, as someone who had genuinely pioneered cutting-edge battery technology, and become one of the wealthiest men on the planet as a result, people could never easily dismiss what he said, either.

The contradiction allowed him to maintain credibility, and make strange decisions without attracting undue attention.

For instance, if someone heard he had hired Mervin Pickering, the author of 'THOSE WHO CAME BEFORE' and a team of historians, linguists, and archaeologists for some project, they might reasonably assume it was either A: untrue, or B: true, but some wacky endeavour sparked by a billionaire's whim.

Oblonsky steered the electric cart through the gardens, eventually rounding a clutch of bushes where the lab block swung into view.

Fine reflected upon his companion. Despite being strangely repellent, Oblonsky was undeniably brilliant. His work on the fragments had surpassed even Fine's wildest expectations. Oblonsky's first triumph had been the discovery of the resonance array emitted by the fragments, something he called macrowaves, a type of ELF wave. This 'song', as one of Oblonsky's more imaginative and romantic subordinates dubbed it, was what had enabled them to locate the second and subsequent fragments.

Complex, but repetitious, like a beacon, the song's 90,000-kilometre frequency wave shared similarities with those generated by lightning and natural disturbances in the earth's magnetic field. The slow but powerful waves were able to penetrate seawater, diffract around large obstacles like mountain ranges and travel huge distances around the curvature of the planet.

They had set about searching for other sources, and, when found, Fine had charged Carson Grave and his operatives with obtaining them.

Oblonsky had also identified nanotech as being the fragments' foundational paradigm.

Fine had plenty of opportunities to invest in nascent nanotech start-ups and passed each time.

He had studied the research papers, and was perfectly aware of the technology's potential. Nanotech promised to revolutionise every aspect of human life. Nanobots would construct entire buildings atom by atom, taking whatever detritus they were provided, breaking it down into raw atomic particles, reassembling it into whatever molecules they were programmed to, and repurposing the resulting substance.

Nanotech would explode possibilities in molecular medicine, too. It would open the door to synthetically produced or modified microorganisms designed to support or replace natural healing functions. These nanomachines would offer rapid diagnosis followed by immediate therapy, cell surgery... The technology would push the envelope of human evolution in the field of genetics, going so far as to rewrite unwanted or unhelpful portions of DNA. It might even conquer the biggest cause of death and illness, the ageing process, might retard it, might even reverse it...

He did not doubt that one day, nanotech's potential would be realised, but no day soon.

Instinct had told him it was not a technology on the near horizon, and Benedict Fine never ignored his gut. This above all things was the secret of his success.

He had made his fortune identifying 'black swan' tech. Technology that appeared deeply speculative, but once realised was quickly viewed as inevitable and commonplace. The battery technology that made his fortune was the most obvious example. He had since made shrewd investments in several technologies which had broken new ground, and rapidly become part of the fabric of everyday life.

Developing new technology always requires a leap of imagination, but distinguishing the impossible from the improbable was the trick. He had been correct often enough to make millions, and turn those millions into billions.

When it came to nanotechnology, the fragment did nothing to prove him wrong.

They weren't dealing with near-future tech.

They were deciphering ancient secrets.

And once they unpicked and replicated them, the potential of nanotechnology would be freed, and herald a technological shift of such magnitude it was unimaginable.

Fine would be crowned the father of a new age.

The transition would be disruptive, changes wrought by radical leaps in technology always were, but Fine saw that as no excuse to be timid. It wasn't a matter of morality, but destiny. Wasn't this man's story?

From flint and kindling to make fire, the bronze age to the silicon age, the drive to create new technology wasn't just something Homo sapiens did, it was his defining characteristic. It was what set him apart from every other living creature on the planet. Man's thirst to solve problems, to shape his world to fit him better, to learn the secrets that governed his universe and use them to his benefit, wasn't a choice. As long as man existed, if something *could* be discovered or invented, it *would* be.

Knowledge was merely a buried fossil. Science just exposed more of what lay covered with every passing day. The pace of excavation might accelerate or diminish but in time the anatomy of the beast, magnificent or monstrous, would inevitably be exposed.

The only variable was time, and the acceptance that not every discovery could be beneficial, or at least, not immediately or directly so.

For every Alexander Fleming, Johann Gutenberg, Edward Jenner, James Watt, Thomas Edison, Alexander Graham Bell, Albert Einstein, Orville and Wilbur Wright, Jack Kilby, Robert Noyce, or Tim Berners-Lee, the journey would inevitably include a Thomas Midgley.

Midgley was famously, or infamously, the father of Chlorofluorocarbons, a compound that would go on to decimate the ozone layer for decades. Before this, the man had discovered that adding lead to gasoline prevented car engines from knocking. Both innovations would be the source of worldwide environmental and public health catastrophes.

While Fine would never argue Thomas Midgely's contribution to science and technology was positive, he would insist that had Midgely not created Chlorofluorocarbons, or added lead to gasoline, it was highly likely someone else would have done. The bone of the fossil was under the soil. Someone would find it.

The same could be said of Penicillin, the printing press, vaccines, the steam engine, the light bulb, the telephone, the theory of relativity, the aeroplane, the microchip and the internet…

As long as mankind flourished, so would creation and discovery, and the impact would be assimilated and adapted to. CFCs had been largely banned from the eighties onwards, and lead was now rarely added to gasoline. However, its negative impact on the environment did contribute to the search for cleaner fuels and alternative energies, creating a fertile market for Fine's own markedly more environmentally-friendly electric vehicles.

The technology found in the fragments was astonishing, but it wasn't magic. It operated subject to physical laws, mechanisms that could ultimately be understood, and then exploited. Fine's contribution would simply be to circumvent the tedious fumbling incremental breakthroughs along the way.

The future would arrive a little sooner, that was all, which was fine with Fine. As with all visionaries, he wanted the future today.

Oblonsky pulled the cart to a stop. They had arrived at the lab blocks.

They climbed out and crossed the wide plaza to meet a wall of undulating glass, behind which lay a warren of labs, all busy developing something. Some projects would come to nothing; some would go on to become products sold by Fine Technologies or one of its subsidiaries.

Two labs were different.

One housed Mervin Pickering and his team, the other Oblonsky and his.

They made their way down to Oblonsky's lab. Oblonsky swiped his card at the door. Fine followed him inside, and onward, to the fragments.

Fine marvelled. The fragments practically demanded fascination and awe. His eyes were drawn from the opening to the contours inside the base, which seemed to invite a hand to rest within them. A step closer and a peek down the core revealed the blades that promised to carve deep into the arm that hand belonged to if it tried. He had pondered the paradoxical arrangement again and again, imagining how it might feel to press his fingers into those indentations, to feel the blades slicing deep into the soft tissue of his forearm…

The logic was seductive and simple, but left plenty of scope for two plus two to equal five. True, the individuals they had recovered the fragments from were resilient, but were they resilient *because* they had used their fragment? Or had they been able to wear the fragment *because* they were already resilient through some other means?

The multitude of tests Oblonsky's team had carried out, and was still carrying out, offered clues, but also dangers…

Several primates had been employed as test subjects. Fine had seen the videos and read the reports. All had perished within twenty-four hours. Victims of massive, catastrophic systemic haemorrhaging. A deeply unpleasant way to meet an end. Oblonsky had gently pushed for a human test subject, and he said it was too soon. For now, those contours and blades would wait.

They were learning more about the fragments every day. It was not as if they had hit a dead end; in fact, it was quite the opposite. He was about to witness the most recent development first-hand.

Each of the four fragments before them was suspended in a rig with eight multijointed robotic arms, next to a workstation. Oblonsky's team had dubbed the devices 'Kraken'.

Seven of the arms were dedicated to the task of holding, tilting and rotating the fragment 360 degrees on any axis. The eighth arm was larger, had an even greater degree of articulation and terminated in a flexible carbon fibre-studded tip.

Oblonsky led them to the first of the Kraken. An image filled its workstation's screen, a three-dimensional render of the fragment. The rendered fragment was overlaid with an animated path, pulsing blue nodes marching like ants across the surface in a series of zigzagging and looping arcs.

Fine had seen the first Kraken prototype at work a few months ago. The team had developed it in the wake of the Norway acquisition.

Grave and his team had seen the Norway target transform the fragment with a gesture, from a bracelet into a weapon. When they took it from him it transformed a final time, to its current form. Kraken was built to find the gesture that presumably transformed the fragment back into a bracelet. The device was doing more than just brute-forcing the task, blindly testing an infinity of random gestures across the fragments' markings.

Grave's operatives were fitted with hi-resolution, high frame rate capture body cams. The footage had been downloaded and studied by Oblonsky's team, and of course Fine had seen it too. The footage, frenetic though it was, offered multiple viewpoints of the Norway target performing his gesture. Each frame had been collated, analysed, correlated, then recreated within a four-dimensional volume. This data was the foundation for the machine-learning AI in the Kraken. The resulting software would hopefully reduce an infinite number of potential gestures to mere hundreds of thousands.

For twenty-four hours, seven days a week, all four Krakens had been executing gestures upon all four fragments. One Kraken had succeeded in its task late the previous evening. Fine had been called and was ready to see the results for himself.

Oblonsky tapped away at the workstation, then turned to Fine.

"Ready?"

Fine nodded.

The dormant Kraken awoke, its robotic arms pivoting and tilting the fragment in its grasp, as the one with the carbon fibre tip traced the crawling pattern on the monitor across the fragment's surface.

The fragment suddenly began to shift, liquify and transform, taking the shape of a long bracelet.

# Chapter Twenty-Two

The connection was secure, scrambled and unscrambled several times and bounced around the globe. On the centremost monitor in the garret room of Atana's Parisian dwelling, a webcam feed of Gabe and Jin appeared. A second and a half lag served as testament to the feed's tortuous journey.

A webcam feed of Atana and Holly would similarly be filling a computer screen in the manor house across the channel. They began to share what they had discovered.

"Okay," Holly said, "The shell company who holds the patent for our exotic Kevlar derivative? It's a subsidiary of Fine Technologies."

"As in everyone's favourite billionaire, Benedict Fine?"

"Yep."

"Okay, but I'm guessing Fine Technologies must have a lot of subsidiaries?"

"Almost certainly, and each of them no doubt file patents for all sorts of things under their names to prevent their competition getting an idea of what they're working on. I bet they cook up a lot of promising developments in Fine Tech's fancy R&D labs."

Holly turned to Atana, "Remind me again, where is Fine Tech's R&D facility located?"

Atana provided the answer, "Iceland."

The one and a half-second delay on the feed caught up, and Holly was rewarded with the expression on Gabe and Jin's faces as they saw the connection. "Iceland," Gabe said. "Like the soil and pollen harvested from the samples? That's one hell of a coincidence."

"Isn't it, though?" Holly agreed. "Want another? We got a hit on one of our DNA profiles. It was on CODIS, the national US DNA database. We have a match for a Carlos Ortiz. That's interesting for two reasons, firstly because we collected this sample mere days ago, and yet according to his death certificate, Ortiz has been dead for more than eight years. Secondly, he was a retired Army Ranger, with a criminal record. Attempted armed robbery. He got two years, and a dishonourable discharge. We ran his name against the regiment. Ortiz served under a Carson Grave."

The name was familiar.

"Carson Grave heads one of the groups on Lance's list," Gabe said. "An outfit known as The Ghosts. Every operative is a dead man, or that's what any records will show. So Carlos Ortiz was recruited by Grave, his death faked, so he could vanish off the grid and become a ghost?"

"Looks that way."

Gabe laid it out, "We have connective tissue between Fine and a prototype Kevlar derivative worn by the soldiers who attacked us. We have connective tissue between Fine and Iceland via his R&D facility. We have connective tissue between Iceland and the soldiers who attacked us via the soil on their boots. We have connective tissue between Ortiz and an elite mercenary group called The Ghosts. If he became aware of such things, who might have the desire and means to hire a very expensive elite mercenary group to collect mysterious treasures utilising beyond cutting-edge technology?"

Holly completed the thesis. "Maybe Benedict

Fine, Mr Beyond-Cutting-Edge-Technology himself?"

# Chapter Twenty-Three

Holly and Atana had remained in Paris and made good use of Atana's set-up. They had returned with the fruits of nearly two weeks of solid research into Fine, his company and his facility in Iceland, and a casket full of hi-tec equipment.

"Okay, a left turn here brings us to..." Gabe progressed along the brutally spartan corridor until they met a door, flat-shaded polygons making up an origami-esque virtual environment. Holly was at his side, similarly represented in the form of a crude low polygonal human model. She wasn't animated; neither of them was. If Gabe looked down, he would see his own feet skating over the floor just as Virtual Holly's were.

Ironically, when it came to Fine Tec's Iceland facility, nicknamed The Shell, one of the richest sources of information had been Benedict Fine himself. He had given a TED talk after the facility's three-year construction was completed, in which he talked at length about the site, the philosophy behind its design and construction, if not the motive. Although the motive wasn't hard to work out. Fine Tec had been the victim of leaks, industrial espionage, which had evidently proven costly, both in lost competitive advantage and the bottom line. Fine's response had been to abandon Silicon Valley and shift his operation to an environment where he held greater dominion.

They reached a door. Gabe hit a button on his controller. A panel suddenly popped up in front of him, with a short list of items. He selected the virtual hacking device and deployed it. In the simulation, the gadget was represented as a simple rectangular red box sporting a jpeg hourglass texture on each face.

He held it to the virtual door and the hourglass texture started to blink to show it was active. The software in the virtual device met the code securing the virtual door.

Real-world NFC signals and proximity parameters aside, it was, on a software level, the same transaction as would have taken place if Gabe had been attempting to hack the door in real life. Atana had cracked the manufacturers' keycode algorithm and identified a vulnerability she was exploiting to feed the lock interface thousands of potential codes a second. The math said gaining access should take no more than seven minutes per door, and once acquired the code would remain stored in the device's memory to re-open the same door instantaneously.

The VR simulation was Atana's handiwork.

She had hacked the architectural firm behind The Shell's design and acquired digital blueprints for the facility, and employed architectural visualisation software to create a walk-through simulation of the site.

The actual rooms and corridors wouldn't look like the simple virtual environment they were negotiating, but their overall layout should be identical. It lent them a huge advantage against going in blind or even an extensive study of the site's two-dimensional blueprints. The simulation built an on-the-ground mental map, allowing them to search the facility's lab blocks more efficiently, and to get out more briskly if they were successful in finding what they were there for.

The virtual door turned from white to green, the visual flag confirming the code had been accepted and their avatars were now able to pass through it. Like their crude, gliding models, Atana had not wasted time coding fancy door-opening animations.

It took a further four minutes five seconds to reach the virtual exfil point.

Gabe set his controllers down and prised off the headset. He blinked, his eyes readjusting to the real world, an actual focal distance rather than the one they had just been tricked into. At least the mild nausea his early runs had brought on had vanished. He had since earned what Atana called his 'VR legs'.

Atana looked to Jin, "We're up."

Jin nodded and collected the headset from Gabe. It was Gabe and Holly's turn to observe the 2D feeds from the headsets on the monitors.

It had been an intense half dozen weeks, with a lot to arrange and procure, but most of the pieces were now in place. They needed every advantage they could earn. As with any op, the old British Forces maxim of the seven Ps maintained: Proper Planning and Preparation Prevents Piss Poor Performance.

They were preparing to enter the lion's den.

## Chapter Twenty-Four

Gabe had woken early, before sunrise, and climbed quietly out of their bed, leaving Holly sleeping, or so he had thought. Today was the day.

In approximately eight hours two planes would be flying out of a private airfield, one carrying Jin and Atana, a direct flight destined for Iceland, and the other Gabe and Holly to Germany, where another aircraft would be waiting for them to complete their journey.

They were going to hit Fine's facility and attempt to recover the grails, but it wasn't just this on his mind. He had found himself thinking more and more about what came next, if they were successful.

He set the kettle to boil in the house's huge kitchen, tossing a tea bag into a mug. He was just taking his first sip when Holly appeared at the door; a towelling robe wrapped around her.

"Can't sleep?"

"Busy mind."

She nodded.

He looked to the recently boiled kettle, "Want one?"

"Please."

He made a second cup of tea, set it next to his at the table.

"Do you think there's a chance what we've been doing was a mistake from the start?"

"What do you mean?"

"Helping Jin protect the grail, to keep it secret. To what end?"

Holly frowned a little, cast a glance through the kitchen door before answering. "Preventing someone like Reynaud getting hold of it? Someone even worse?"

"If safety is the intention, wouldn't we have been better off trying to find a way to destroy it these past eight years? Stop anyone using it, once and for all?"

"We made Jin a promise. That means something to me, and to you too. I know it does."

Gabe considered telling Holly about his recent conversation with Jin, that it was Jin himself who was questioning their actions these past eight years. Only Jin had expressly asked him not to. What Holly said next was perhaps why.

"I'm not sure I could bring myself to destroy it," she continued. "Not without knowing the truth. The same questions Blake and Jin wanted answered, the questions that brought me to them in the first place, the need to learn what it is, how it can exist, why it does what it does… I'd still like those answers myself. I suppose I think one day we might get them, find tools which will allow us to learn more, understand more… Don't you think that's possible?"

"That sounds a lot like Blake's feelings the night he was killed by Reynaud, the night Jin was scarred, and we almost died. We walked away in the end, and we recovered the grail, but eight years on here we are, fighting to get it back again."

## Chapter Twenty-Five

Jin snapped the carabiner over the steel cable and the loop closed around the rock, creating a secondary anchor point sufficient to hold the submersible in place.

He began to swim back, fins kicking through the dark and icy water, following the cable to its point of origin. The 2500 lumen glare of his diving torch carved a cone of visibility through the gloom, into which the midget sub now loomed.

He thumped the hull and waited. A few moments later the lockout chamber door slid back and Atana swam out to join him. They collected two handheld sea-scooters from the belly of the sub, checked their bearings, fired them up and headed for the cliff face.

As they neared, the water grew turbulent, the upwards crash and resulting downward churn from the waves hitting the rocks and smashing down creating unpredictable currents that pushed and pulled at them. They met the cliff and abandoned the sea scooters.

Jin pulled himself from the ocean first. The waves tried their best to tear him off the rock, but soon he had climbed clear of their reach and looked down into the spume, to see Atana break through the frothing surface. She quickly caught up with him and they began to scale the rockface in earnest. She had assured him she was a proficient climber, and she had not exaggerated.

Within minutes, the roiling Greenland Sea lay over a hundred feet beneath them.

They were equipped primarily for stealth: to recover the grails without a fight was the ideal outcome, using nothing more than their coms and Atanas' security door-cracking equipment, but if combat ensued, they had brought firepower too. They each carried an FN P90 and sufficient ammunition for a skirmish. Jin carried a silenced Glock 19 as his sidearm, while Atana trusted in her short sword.

If everything went their way, they would be long gone before anyone knew the grails had been lifted. This was the ideal, plan A, but they were realistic enough to acknowledge they had to allow for a messier Plan B. Holly's forensic detective work indicated Grave and his ghosts might be operating from out of the facility.

The Westfjords were remote, and the facility took clever advantage of the available topography, utilising nature as soundly as any stronghold of old. Perched on the elevated crest of a peninsula, the outer edge spilling over the edge of the cliff, The Shell could be reached over land from the north, east and south, but each of those options meant a hike across rugged terrain, or negotiating a single-track road in a suitably solid four-wheel-drive vehicle, with nothing available to cover the approach. If a visitor wasn't seen, he would still be detected. A network of motion-sensitive cameras and a pressure-sensitive array monitored the half-mile perimeter. Anything on legs or wheels over 30kg would be brought swiftly to the attention of the security station within the facility.

Getting near The Shell from any of these cardinal points was a nonstarter.

Reaching it from the west meant negotiating an icy sea and a couple of hundred feet of sheer cliff face. Who was going to attempt something like that?

Fine had created a fortress.

Jin wondered whether it ever crossed the minds of those working in The Shell that they were effectively prisoners. How did someone like Benedict Fine encourage the best and brightest to live in virtual captivity? The right financial incentive and the promise of working on envelope-pushing projects backed with industry-leading budgets... Or by creating the most luxurious prison possible?

Surrounded by a landscape of blistering natural beauty, strolling under the toughened glass and steel matrix articulated canopy roof in an expansive seventeen-acre, climate-controlled garden, afforded a high spec employee apartment with maid service, gymnasiums, an Olympic sized swimming pool, a running track, squash and tennis courts, a cinema and several restaurants a short walk or electric buggy ride away, Jin supposed it might be easy to forget one was walled in.

Secure in the knowledge nothing was getting in or out without getting past him first, Fine was able to deepen the illusion of non-confinement by making security inside the Shell appear astonishingly light, almost invisible. Even in the working areas, in the R&D labs which comprised the west-facing side of the Shell, access to areas was restricted by the use of simple pass cards.

There were two entrance points into the laboratory block from the plaza inside The Shell, and a third that wasn't meant to be a route in at all. It existed to provide access to the maintenance platform on the cliffside face.

Their vertiginous climb finally brought them to the crisscrossed metal grating of the access platform. They climbed up and over, progressing along the slim platform until they reached the door, whereupon they unshouldered their kit and peeled off the more cumbersome parts of their diving gear.

Atana took out the device that they hoped would get them through the maintenance door into the labs. Jin kept abreast of technology, but since waking from her hibernation, Atana had clearly discovered a passion and a natural aptitude for the new tools of the age that surpassed anything he could follow.

Jin checked the time again.

If everything was on track, they would hear from Gabe any moment now.

—

Cruising at high altitude, the clouds far beneath its enormous body, the Hercules cargo plane carried just two people in its whale-belly hold.

Now they moved from the head to the rear. It was time. The huge door began to fall open and Gabe and Holly walked down it. Soon, the tail of the aircraft was yawning onto a night sky and the muffled roar of the plane's engines became a full-throated bellow mixed with the white noise shriek of the air vortex the lowered ramp created.

Terry, the ex-RAF pilot in the Hercules's cockpit, was a friend of Lance's. He ran a freight business that serviced PMCs. Lance had assured Gabe that if he was looking for someone who wouldn't ask questions, or answer them if things got messy, Terry was his guy.

Gabe and Holly adjusted their oxygen masks. They had both been breathing pure oxygen for the last hour, flushing nitrogen from their bloodstreams to counter the effects of the low pressure of high altitude. An unnecessary precaution. Atana assured them they were highly resistant to hypoxia, and the bends. Gabe believed her, but felt this was not the best occasion to test out their gift's parameters.

They each wore a generously loaded tactical vest. Fixed securely among the pouches and webbing were a combat knife, night vision goggles, an FN P90, and as many 50 round 5.7x28 magazines as they felt they could carry and remain agile. Sidearms nestled snuggly in thigh holsters. Holly favoured a Glock 19, and Gabe a trusty Sig P226.

Gabe was also laden with a front-hanging rucksack, home to a hand-operated, ten-ton lifting capacity hydraulic toe jack, and 60 metres of static rope and descending gear.

He checked the GPS coordinates: they were close. He tapped a message on the satellite phone: *Jin. Okay if we drop in?*

He hit send.

Jin's response arrived a moment later.

*Ready when you are.*

Gabe sent a second message: *See you in 30,000 feet.*

Gabe shot Holly a glance.

She nodded and leant in. They exchanged a gentle bump of helmets, and then both flipped down their night vision attachments.

They watched the desired GPS coordinates narrow.

Terry had got them close as dammit to bullseye.

Three strides took them to the edge of the ramp, a fourth launched them over the precipice. They tumbled into the void, a black canvas of twinkling stars above and a dirty carpet of grey below.

They plunged cloudward, slowing from the Hercules's 400mph cruising speed to their terminal velocity in the region of 120mph in seconds. Gabe glanced to his left and saw Holly had already achieved freefall position. If not for the air rushing past and tugging at her gear, she might have looked as if she were floating, suspended in space.

They hit the cloud layer, were swallowed briefly and then emerged, earning their first glimpse of The Shell below. The luminous structure was lit up like a Christmas tree in night vision. Most landscapes surrounding such a large structure would have made for a busy canvas, studded with businesses, homes, streets and neighbourhoods sketched in threads and clusters of light.

The Westfjords were almost blank.

Gabe thought maybe, just maybe, he could discern the distant fizz of Reykjavik to the south.

The Shell expanded and gained definition. The spotlights surrounding the facility marked out its footprint and the subdued lighting inside was enough to define the glazing of the huge glass and steel roof.

Gabe fanned his arms and legs, cut himself into a foil against the rushing air and adjusted his trajectory to steer himself more surely on target. Holly followed his lead. The goal was to land on the photovoltaic panelled section of the roof, but close enough to the glazed half to spare them a hike.

If they missed the roof entirely and landed anywhere else, even a few metres from the facility, then Gabe might as well be hammering on the front door while Holly screamed 'howdy' through a bullhorn. The half-mile band arcing around the facility from cliff edge to cliff edge was lousy with cameras and a pressure sensor array. There was simply no way to approach at ground level without being detected.

The HALO jump had been Gabe's solution. Passing over at high altitude the Hercules would look no more suspicious than any other bog-standard commercial jet. They were two dark specks on a dark sky, even on radar they would almost certainly pass undetected.

They hurtled like invisible spears toward the drop zone, dead on target, the facility ballooning rapidly beneath them with every passing second. Gabe's impression was of a giant hi-tech, modern snow globe village dropped in the wilds of Iceland.

At 1,250 feet above ground level Gabe heard a beep in his helmet. Holly would be hearing the same thing in hers. They had reached the optimum altitude to deploy chutes. Holly released her chute and suddenly vanished above his head as her descent slowed from approximately one hundred and twenty miles per hour to under twenty.

He paused a further three seconds to gain a safe lead – any later and the only landing he'd be making would be in the style of Wile E Coyote – and then deployed his chute.

It flared and similarly throttled his speed.

He pulled sharp and long on his grips to decelerate further as the roof of The Shell rushed to meet him, and touched down with the barest thump.

Holly landed just a dozen feet away seconds later, almost as lightly as he had, a testament to the two hundred plus freefall jumps she had completed during the past half a dozen years. Unlike close-quarters combat, skydiving had been something Gabe had been more than happy to tutor her in.

He unclipped his front hanging rucksack and they briskly gathered up their chutes. The HALO jump had been executed to perfection, and Gabe was confident no one had seen them coming or knew they were here.

They walked to the lip of the glass roof. Getting on-site unseen and undetected was one thing. Now they had to get inside unseen and undetected too.

Gabe dragged the rucksack across the roof until he was standing at the edge of one of the atrium garden's massive trees and selected one of the toughened glass panels nearby. The unit was ajar, the sophisticated climate control system busy either venting warm air or catching cool drafts to regulate the temperature inside.

Gabe sprayed the hinge side of the panel with insulating foam. In seconds it swelled and began to harden, which would serve to muffle the noise of what was to follow. He removed and readied the jack, positioning its teeth and foot into the gap between panel and frame, screwed in the lever, and began to work it back and forth.

The teeth and foot inched further apart, until finally the mechanism which secured and adjusted the unit surrendered to the ten-ton persuasion of the jack, and the panel broke free. The insulating foam did its work, the resulting crack was audible, but over the whistle of the wind and the white noise grumble of the sea beyond the peninsula's edge, only just. Hopefully, it wouldn't have carried too much more below.

Gabe flipped the panel up and over and stared down to the garden below.

Holly reached into the rucksack and pulled out what they needed next. Working quickly, he set an anchor point and reeved the length of rope through. He attached his belay device to the rope and moved to park his backside on the lip of the opening.

He looked at Holly.

She kissed him, and said, "Here we go."

A push and a twist, and he dropped slick and steady downwards, coming to rest on the atrium garden's perfectly manicured lawn. Holly slid down after him. They retrieved the rope, coiled it, and dropped it at the foot of the tree.

The atrium gardens had featured prominently in Fine's TED talk, and were used heavily in available media. Artfully landscaped to obscure sightlines and complemented with large sculptures and foliage, they created the illusion the gardens were even larger than their already generous seventeen acres. The space was climate and humidity controlled, heated and cooled to simulate an environment considerably more temperate than that outside.

Gabe messaged Jin, and they got moving, creeping through the darkness, hugging the ground until they reached a path fringed by bushes and trees which steered them toward the lab blocks.

# Chapter Twenty-Six

Jin read the message Gabe had just sent.

*Taking a gentle stroll through some gardens. You?*

Jin looked to Atana at the maintenance door into the facility. She was holding her hacking gadget to the card reader while it invisibly generated and spewed out codes. Theory was one thing, boots-on-the-ground reality quite another. Jin hoped the ancient Minoan's confidence in her device wasn't misplaced.

A moment later the reader's LED flashed green, and Atana pushed the door open, proving it wasn't.

Jin tapped a message back.

*We're in.*

It was the dead of night, but this was no promise the corridors and labs would be deserted. For all they knew, Fine's R&D staff worked idiosyncratic hours, and even if they didn't, some sort of security oversight was to be expected.

Jin took point, and they advanced through the lab block. The plan was to systematically cover the ground as efficiently as possible. Jin observed the corridors in the VR simulation they had grown familiar with were only slightly more spartan than their real-world counterparts. Hard white surfaces, glass and matt steel were abundant. The bigger difference would be found in what lay behind the doors. The VR rendition was featureless; one of these, they hoped, was home to the grails.

They just needed to find out which one.

Gabe and Holly continued down a paved trail in the direction of the lab blocks. The path they were following was one of a number that cut through the gardens, expressly designed to give the impression of seclusion. As such, they were able to move almost entirely under the cover of surrounding trees and bushes. Gabe checked their bearings. The lab blocks were a little further to the west. Eventually, they were forced to abandon the path, and scurry over open ground.

At last, they arrived at their destination, a plaza fronting a striking wall of undulating glass, like a vertical wave frozen in time. The wall had two entrances, one on each side.

There were no cameras visible, as the intelligence they had collected indicated, but setting foot on the plaza would see them exposed. Unfortunately, there was no other option.

They stowed their night vision kit and fetched out Atana's card reader gizmo. On the count of three, they broke from the bushes and hurried to the entrance on the left-hand side. The plan was to get in and systematically sweep the upper level. Jin and Atana, entering from the maintenance point on the cliff face, would be doing the same thing on the level below them.

They weren't here for a fight. They were here for the grails. Reprisals or dealing with Benedict Fine was something to tackle later. Get what they came for, regroup and exfil from where Jin and Atana had entered, that was the plan.

Gabe set Atana's gadget to the task. Holly watched their backs. At worst they faced being stuck exposed at the door for approximately seven minutes, and Gabe was relieved when they lucked out. The LED flashed green in under a minute.

He pushed the entrance door open and they slipped through.

—

Jin and Atana advanced along yet another corridor. They had accessed and eliminated two labs thus far. Their path ended in a junction. P90 raised, Jin swung around one side, as Atana mirrored the action on the opposing side.

All clear.

The time they had dedicated to their VR walkthroughs had been time well spent. Despite being simple untextured representations, the layout was as expected and felt eerily familiar. They moved on, briskly and efficiently checking a further two labs. These too showed no evidence of what they were looking for.

The labs and corridors were largely windowless. Until entry, what each room contained was a mystery to Atana and Jin, and probably between different R&D groups. In an effort to alleviate the claustrophobic feel all these closed spaces invited, decorative hi-resolution panels had been installed where windows might naturally have been located. The screens presented a series of congruent looping panoramic landscapes.

One showed a vista of rolling hills under a night sky, another the shore of a lake with a weathered timber jetty where a solitary row boat bobbed nearby, tethered by a length of rope. Water lapped at the lake's edge. Jin wondered if the video was synced to the time of day. The illusion was impressive; Jin even imagined he heard the faint tap of the boat against the jetty, but only for a moment.

He quickly realised the tapping wasn't imagined.

It was real, the faint tread of footsteps, and they were getting closer.

Someone was approaching.

—

Gabe and Holly moved silently through the upper level of the lab block, checking labs as they went. The facility felt deserted. Maybe R&D staff were encouraged to keep to regular hours?

They set Atana's gadget loose on their fifth lab door. It took a couple of minutes before the LED blinked green. As with the four previous entries they got ready to swing in, FN P90s tucked into their shoulders, eye to the sight, fingers on the trigger ready for trouble.

The door opened.

The sound of music split out, Queen's *Radio Ga Ga*...

This lab was not deserted.

—

Atana and Jin were ready to strike; the footsteps closed in, almost on top of them now.

When the figure behind them rounded the corner, Jin was ready. A blow to the man's sternum knocked the wind out of him and sent the two recyclable coffee cups he had been holding flying. Jin moved in. A second later the man was in a choke hold. From the first strike to trussed, Atana had her P90 on the man, but there was never any danger of her having to use it.

The struggle that followed was feeble and short-lived. Jin's technique compressed both carotid arteries rather than the man's airway. It took less than twenty seconds for him to be rendered unconscious.

Jin let go and performed a brisk search.

The man was unarmed and wearing a lab coat. Jin pulled two sturdy zip ties from his webbing, and set about binding the man's hands and feet and taping over his mouth, but not before relieving him of his key card and tugging off his lab coat and trousers.

He lobbed them to Atana, who used them to mop up the contents of the two vending machine coffees the man had been carrying, which were now across the floor. The clean-up job would pass casual scrutiny.

This done, Atana and Jin each grabbed one of the man's ankles and briskly dragged him back to the lab they had recently exited. With its code already stored, the device got them straight in. They pulled the man inside and looked him over again. He was sort of doughy looking. Almost certainly one of Fine's R&D staff.

Atana looked to Jin. "He was going that way, with two drinks."

Jin nodded.

They followed the man's bearing and reached two lab doors, one on either side of the corridor.

Atana waved the man's key card over the left-hand side door.

Jin readied his P90. The LED blinked red. Wrong key card, wrong lab.

Door number two it was, then.

Atana waved the pass over the reader. The LED winked green and the door retracted.

They swung inside; weapons raised.

Gabe stared down the sights of his P90. A man was seated behind a wooden desk, with his back to them. Several books lay open before him. The desk was one of a collection, arranged in a horseshoe shape. The man had grey wiry hair, and the overhead lights shone off the balding pate where it had thinned.

Something, a change in the atmosphere, perhaps the ambient light coming from the open door, or maybe that indefinable sixth sense that tells one living being another is near caused the man to lift his head from his studies.

As he turned, the makeup of the rest of the room started to filter into Gabe's awareness.

The lab had a starkly different feel to the others they had encountered. Less like a hi-tech workspace and more like a study room. The hard metal and sterile panelling of the walls were softened by the presence of other natural materials, items made from stone, paper and clay, furniture made from wood and fabric rather than steel and plastic. Gabe saw prints of old yellowed maps fixed to walls, shelves filled with books, furniture more befitting a venerable library. Ancient looking artefacts populated the shelves, rather than technology and scientific paraphernalia. The workspace felt warmer, more cluttered and human.

Then there was what stood seemingly in pride of place in the centre of the room.

A big metal frame, glazed front and back, held the remains of a fresco. While plainly ancient, its colours were still astonishingly vibrant. There were four pieces in total, perched on metal pegs between the glass. Together they formed a huge plaster jigsaw.

Below them, in a second glass box, rested a stone chest and two rows of clay tablets.

When the man twisted around far enough for his eyes to reach Gabe and Holly, the resulting shock almost caused him to fall off his chair. For an instant, he seemed on the verge of crying out, but the weapons pointed in his direction counselled silence. His Adam's apple bobbed in his neck. There was no cry. Instead, he slowly raised his hands in the air.

Gabe's eyes flicked to Holly and then the fresco.

They both knew what they were looking at.

The figures were just as Atana had described them. The ring of men and women painted in blood red and bone white, tall, slim and dark-haired, wearing simple kilts, ornately decorated bracelets on their right arms. The figure they surrounded was as she had described, too, larger, although the size seemed to denote importance rather than scale, as was the case with the familiar object at her feet.

# Chapter Twenty-Seven

Atana and Jin crossed the threshold, sweeping their weapons to cover the lab as they advanced. It was a full twice the size of the others they had searched. Atana judged it had once been two. The dividing wall had been removed so both spaces could be combined. Even so, it looked busy, a stark, hard-edged hi-tech wonderland, littered with an abundance of sophisticated-looking equipment, electron microscopes, racks of servers, monitors and cabinets.

It also appeared deserted. Maybe the man currently trussed up in a lab behind them was working alone, had intended to drink both beverages, earn a double dose of caffeine?

They advanced. A row of devices with slim, multijointed and dexterous looking robotic arms lay ahead. Each station had a monitor. Three were inactive, black-screened, but one was alive.

Its screen showed a three-dimensional render of the bracelet Atana had worn for over three thousand years. The model was skinned with a crawling trail, indicating a gesture. She knew the gesture well. It was as ingrained as a signature. Torsten had long ago shown her how to execute it. She had since performed it more times than she could recall.

There was no doubt.

This is where Fine was keeping the treasures, where he was intent upon learning their secrets. It seemed he was succeeding. What's more, there were four machines. Did this mean Fine had found a fourth treasure, too?

A door at the far side of the lab suddenly opened, and a man in a lab coat casually strode through. He must have glimpsed he was not alone because he started to speak.

"'I was beginning to think you'd got lost—"

When he saw it was not his colleague he shared the room with, his words died on his lips and he froze. They watched him notice their weapons, and that they were now trained upon him.

Jin beckoned him over, and he dutifully obeyed.

Atana pointed to the stations with the robotic arms, the monitor with the depiction of the bracelet, and fixed the man with her eyes. She saw fear in his. Good.

"Where are the treasures?"

The man's eyes twitched to the door.

"There's no coffee on the way," Jin said.

The man swallowed. with a heavy French accent he said, "They're not here. They've been moved."

Atana looked to Jin, saw her own scepticism reflected.

"They're not here, I swear it!" the man repeated.

If that was true, Atana thought, why did he suddenly seem so worked up at the prospect of her poking around?

She cast her eyes across the room, towards the door through which the man had recently emerged.

"What were you doing when we came in?"

The man didn't answer, and Atana didn't bother making him.

Instead, she reached out and snapped the lanyard from the man's neck. The key card clipped to it dangled from her fist.

Atana set the stock of the P90 to her shoulder and began to head towards the back of the lab where the door lay. Jin tapped the man on the arm with his own weapon, and they followed a pace behind.

She waved the pass over the door's reader.

It slid open.

The room beyond was dimly lit, and not at all what she had expected. She had imagined another technology-laden lab space. This room was brutally spartan and contained a cell at the far end. Light from the door picked out bars running the length of the partition.

As her eyes adjusted to the gloom, she saw the cell wasn't empty. A figure hovered beyond the bars, a man, with his back to her. He was rocking slightly, shifting from one foot to the other. His broad-shouldered frame was hunched. As she took a step forward, the room's automated lights responded. The space was suddenly laid bare, and the figure too.

Atana stepped forward; hope strained at trepidation's leash.

*"Hello?"*

The man didn't move, seemed not to hear her, continued idly rocking, staring into the corner of his cell. It had to be him. Even unkempt, his hair, the deep fiery red of dying embers, was unmistakable.

She took another step, raised her voice, *"Torsten?* It's me, Atana."

The prisoner behind the bars began to respond, albeit sluggishly, as though surfacing from a powerful daydream. He shuffled his feet and turned to face her.

It *was* Torsten.

At first, he appeared to be cradling his right arm, but as he turned more fully, the truth was exposed. Half the arm was gone, amputated below the elbow. His left hand pawed the stump idly, as though he had somehow simply misplaced the missing limb and was trying to recall where he had left it.

The loss of his limb was a shock, but less than the impact of seeing his face. His expression was blank, his gaze dull and vacant. It passed over her as though she wasn't even there, or of no more interest to him than the bars between them. A string of drool dangled from his carelessly shaven chin. The thread spooled to his chest and fed a large discoloured stain down to his shirt.

She called again, hoping to rouse him from his stupor, "Torsten?"

But his gaze had moved on, wandered to the floor.

She realised Jin and the man were behind her and turned.

"What have you done to him?"

"The patient is—"

"I know who he *is*," Atana said slowly, each word dry and combustible kindling. "What have you *done* to him?"

The man licked his lips, swallowed deeply, "He was a danger. We worked to sedate him, would have preferred to, but he proved highly resistant... He has a remarkable metabolism... Quite incredible... but we needed him compliant, docile..."

Atana whirled. In an instant the man found himself flung up against the wall, the muzzle of her P90 buried in the soft flesh of his cheek.

"Tell me *exactly* what you have done," she hissed.

The man cringed, and the words spilt out, "We had no choice but to take a surgical approach, cauterise several connective white matter sites between temporal and frontal lobes and the thalamus and limbic system..."

On and on he went, but Atana had already heard enough. She felt stunned, winded, as surely as if had she been struck. What this monster in a lab coat had said was correct: Torsten, she, Jin, Holly and Gabriel, none of them could be sedated, intoxicated, poisoned even. Their gift prevented it. They had needed their captive compliant... docile... to examine him, to test him. *He was a danger.* She didn't doubt it. The Torsten she knew would have made a battle of every attempt to study him. Her imagination conjured a multitude of painful vignettes: batons and cattle prods, tasers and tear gas, even bullets and blades.

Every fight would have taught them more, until at some stage they had discovered that fire damaged, and did not heal as other wounds did.

So, eventually, when they determined their prisoner would never comply, never talk, never be broken, once they realised the only secrets they could extract lay in his flesh, blood and bones, they had devised a permanent solution to spare them a fight. To pacify him, once and forever, they had learned it was useless to cut. The lobotomy that had destroyed his mind had not employed a blade.

They had *cauterised*, burned away the part of his mind that made him who he was.

She hurled the man in Jin's direction. He lost his footing and fell at Jin's feet.

"Get him away from me. *Please Jin.*"

Jin's eyes flicked to Torsten. He nodded and dragged the man back into the lab.

The door closed behind them.

Atana walked deeper to the room, to the cell, and held out the key card. The barred door released its locks and rolled back.

She walked inside.

The cell was bare, just walls, floor and ceiling, seamless, near featureless. Not one scrap of comfort had been provided. There was not even a mattress for its prisoner to sleep on. A drain in one corner and a hose fixed to the wall outside the cell spoke volumes. How often had he been hosed down like an animal?

"Torsten?"

She reached out, afraid to touch him but needing to. When her fingers made contact with his flesh, he was roused again momentarily from his stupor, the stimulus enough to cause him to shuffle around and look in her direction once more.

The eyes that met hers through a struggle of matted blood-red hair looked like Torsten's, but she saw not one flicker of recognition or reflection in them. The man she knew had been excised, hollowed out. Centuries of memories had been wantonly immolated, the wonders he had seen, the measure of so many lifetimes of places and people, the years they had shared…

All so they could study him without fear, perform tests on him like a lab animal, peck at his flesh and bone for clues to what made him remarkable, when the most remarkable part was what they had already destroyed.

The man she loved was gone, burned away.

What remained was an affront to him.

She took the mindless husk of Torsten into her arms, kissed its face. She breathed in the scent of him it still carried and then drew it down so they were both kneeling. The husk did not resist.

*We needed him compliant, docile…*

When she stood back up, the husk hardly noticed. It remained on its knees, staring absently at the floor.

Atana reached over her shoulder and drew the short sword from its scabbard.

It was believed by Torsten's people that when a great warrior met his end, an afterlife awaited, with two possible destinations. Half the warriors the goddess Freyja would claim, to join her in the heavenly meadow of Folkvangr. The other half were carried on Valkyries' wings to a great hall of heroes called Valhalla, where Odin himself welcomed the warrior home, to feast every night beside his equals.

For a warrior such as Torsten, perhaps death was not the end.

Atana's strike was swift and decisive.

When she returned to the lab where Jin and the man waited, her friend's blood peppering her skin, her sword was back in its scabbard and the silenced Glock 19 was in her hand.

She pointed it at the man in the lab coat.

"If our treasures are not here, then where are they? Understand, I will not ask again. I give you one slim chance to save yourself."

The man took it. He spoke. If he was lying, it was with impressive fluidity and detail. He and two others were all that remained of the team studying the objects; the rest had departed weeks ago…

When Atana's questions were exhausted, the man fell silent. Waited to see what his answers had bought him.

The Glock's silenced 9mm round passed through the front of his head and took a generous chunk of the back as it exited. He began to slide down, then toppled from his chair.

Atana turned to Jin. If he was surprised, he showed no sign of it.

"There's nothing more here for us," she said. "We know where they are, and where Fine is. We're going to get our treasures back and then I'm going to kill Benedict Fine."

## Chapter Twenty-Eight

Hank waved his key card at the lab door. It slid into the wall like something out of Star Trek.

The facility was full of stuff like this, fancy shit that got geeks stiff. Call him old school, but doors that pushed open and swung closed still worked for Hank.

He strolled through into the lab, cast a casual glance around, backed out and walked along the corridor to the next one, waved his key card…

Tediously patrolling fucking hallways. It was mall cop bullshit, beneath him. He'd led covert ops in Afghanistan, Iraq, Libya, Syria, and some real crazy shit in recent years under Carson Grave as a 'ghost'.

The only thing that made swallowing the mall cop shit bearable was the paycheck. The retainer and bonuses deal Grave had negotiated with Fine were insane.

So… He was doing the rounds, a glorified night-watchman. Walk the corridors, check on the labs, smile nicely at any fucking geeks he found working the early hours, although few did. Technically, the labs were in operation 24/7, but most of Fine's people kept to sociable hours. They were encouraged to, so at this time it was usually quiet as bingo night at a graveyard.

There had been one or two habitual night owls, like Oblonsky, the creepy little Russian fucker who headed the team studying the 'fragments' and the asset they'd dragged back from Norway, but those guys had shipped out nearly a month ago. Oblonsky worked almost exclusively during the night, with some poor subordinate asshole who Hank got the impression had been handed the short straw, like him being saddled with this rinky-dink crap while most of the unit was already soaking up the sun in their off-hours on a big ship in the Med.

The Russki, Oblonsky, always made Hank think of a kid who used to live back on his neighbourhood block. The little weirdo used to catch rats and mice in traps he bought from the local hardware store with his allowance. He'd shake them out, starved and feeble but still alive, into a big mason jar with holes punched in the lid. He'd pour lighter fuel in, douse them, and finally drop in a match, watching them squeal and ricochet around, scrabbling at the jar's slippery glass walls.

Hank had done some harsh shit in his time, tortured intel out of folk when necessary, but he'd never got off on it. It was a means to an end. He wasn't a sadist.

What Oblonsky's team had done to the Norway asset, that was something else… Hank had been there when they'd taken the huge red-haired fucker down, lost a couple of colleagues in the process. The guy had heart.

No warrior deserved a fate like that.

Hell, no living creature at all deserved a fate like that.

Hank waved his key card at the lab door. It slid open and he strolled through, casting a quick look around. He was about to leave when he thought he heard something. He walked deeper in, circled one of the benches…

A guy was on the floor, trussed up, tape over his mouth, hands and feet zip-tied, wearing a sweater, underpants and brogues. His trousers and lab coat, stained brown, lay in a damp and crumpled ball nearby.

When he clapped eyes on Hank, he got real excited.

Hank looked around with considerably more attentiveness and pulled out his radio.

"Boss, I think we got ourselves a problem."

—

Gabe pulled out his sat phone, began to tap out a message, then thought, 'screw it' and opted for voice coms. Before he could make contact, Jin's voice came in through his earpiece and beat him to it.

"Gabriel? The grail, ours and the others, they're gone. They were here, but they've been moved. We have the location. It's time to leave. Head for the maintenance point. We'll join you there."

"Hold on. We found something. I think Atana will want to see it."

Before Jin could respond, a voice issued from a tannoy system, calm, officious and pre-recorded.

*"Due to a security or maintenance issue, the lab areas must be evacuated. In the interests of safety, we direct all personnel to calmly leave their stations. Follow the walkway lighting to a designated exit point where you will be assisted out of the lab block. Thank you."*

Gabe looked at Holly, and then at the timid-looking man sitting at the desk.

"Jin? I'm guessing you heard that too?"

His friend's voice came back a moment later. "We did."

"Okay, we'll meet you at the exfil point. We'll be bringing a plus-one to the party."

"What? Who?"

"I have no idea, but I'm confident he's going to have plenty worth hearing."

Gabe looked at the fresco, ensuring his body cam captured at least another half-minute of clear and stable footage before turning back to the man seated at the desk.

"You," he said. "what's your name?"

"Mervin."

Gabe grasped the man's arm and pulled him from his seat. He didn't resist. He guided him toward the door. "Okay Mervin, do as you're told and we can all stay friends. Understand?'

Mervin nodded, but there was no mistaking the fact he was afraid.

The lab door retracted and they were back in the corridor, which now sported slowly throbbing LEDs, indicating a path toward the nearest designated exit.

Mervin glanced at Holly. He had the look of a man trying to gauge exactly how dire his situation was. It was probably futile, but Holly tried to reassure him. 'Mervin, we don't want to hurt you. We just need to know everything you know about what you have back there. Unfortunately, I don't think we're going to be able to do that here, so we need to get to somewhere we can talk."

Gabe ignored the LEDs. They were heading for a different exit entirely. He took point and led them in the opposite direction. Holly followed close behind, shepherding Mervin onward.

Overall, things were not going well.

The grails weren't here. It seemed someone was alert to the fact The Shell had uninvited visitors, and now they had a captive to deal with. They were almost at the end of the corridor. A few more to go and they would meet the staircase that would get them to the lower level, not far from the maintenance and exfil point—

Gabe raised an arm to bring them to a halt.

He saw Holly had heard it too, the squeak of boots on the plastic-coated flooring, not just someone, but a number of someones heading their way. She put a hard eye on Mervin and a finger to her lips, and shifted the P90's selector from safe to fully auto.

Gabe made a brisk rewind hand gesture and they began to back up.

The only objective now was to get out, and there were alternative routes available.

—

Carson Grave didn't believe in coincidences and hated loose ends like a pig hates pork.

He spun around the apex of the corridor, sweeping his weighty firearm, an M249 SAW, right to left.

He was flanked by Halsey and Blatch, two of his ghosts, covering his three to nine.

The path ahead was clear.

They moved forward.

The fully automatic, belt-fed machine gun in his arms weighed over twenty-two pounds, and the two hundred rounds 'nutsacks' ammunition drums in the side pouches of his tac vest contributed another fourteen. Light and nimble the SAW wasn't, capable of firing a solid and sustained fifteen rounds a second it was. For Grave, the stopping power was worth the heft. He wasn't out to penetrate or poke holes. He was looking to devastate and dismantle.

Grave had a powerful hunch regarding who had come to visit. He had no idea how the crazy bitch had worked out how to find them, but the same thing could have been said for how she had learned about and located the targets in Brooklyn.

If he was correct, she had come looking to take her shit back. The fact she was still alive to try didn't reflect well on him. He had failed to kill her twice now. That wasn't good, not one bit. It raised questions of customer satisfaction. Coming up short wasn't sound business. He had a reputation to maintain.

The men he recruited weren't dumb, either. They followed his commands for two reasons: because the pay was right, and because they trusted he was smart enough to not get them killed.

Except he *had* lost men to the woman, the first time they had tangled with her *and* the second. Not his fault, he would argue, no one in his boots could have done a better job, but excuses were for fuckups. There was no escaping the fact that her kills and her continued existence didn't reflect well.

Ending the woman wouldn't just dot the I's and cross the T's with Fine and quash any doubts over his competence among his men. He'd enjoy putting the bitch down.

He imagined her inside the facility, skulking around, scouring the labs looking for her stolen whatnot. Even if she searched top to bottom, she was going to be disappointed. All four 'fragments' had been transported to Fine's research ship stationed off the coast of Crete five days earlier, together with all but a few of the team studying them, and three-quarters of his men. He and the remaining quarter were set to fly out and join them in just six or seven hours.

He had every intention of making the flight.

There were only three routes back out of the lab block. His men were now divided between them.

They would close in, and like a rat in a maze, sooner or later they would flush the woman out.

Grave reached the next intersection and swung the SAW around it.

Three figures were backing away up the corridor.

—

Gabe, Holly and Mervin had almost retreated to the last corner they had turned when Gabe saw the hulking figure swing around the one ahead, flanked a second later by two armed companions.

Built like a brick outhouse, the man was cradling a belt-fed machine gun with a two hundred round ammo drum fastened to it. His torso was bare, but for the tac-vest he wore. Tall, more than a head taller than the two men alongside him, and broad in a way that had nothing to do with flab, head shaved down to stubble, he looked fit to audition for an eighties straight-to-video action flick. Two thickly muscled arms carried the weapon.

He saw them, and seemed to frown in confusion over the machine gun's barrel before he directed the machine gun on their position.

The corner was close. Gabe shoved Holly and Mervin towards it.

As he threw himself after them, the last thing he saw was the brute's legs stiffen and his shoulders tense against the butt of the stock, his finger squeezing the trigger.

The light machine gun's muzzle erupted and the corridor was abruptly filled with the full-throated roar of sustained 223 calibre automatic gunfire.

Gabe hit the floor and looked up at the corner just as a huge chunk of it was crudely erased. The wall was shredded into chunks of plaster and plastic cladding, great ragged holes blasted into particles.

He scrambled up and they kept moving, Holly just ahead, propelling Mervin in front of the smoke now rolling down the corridor as the man burned through dozens of rounds in little more than seconds. By the time the assault paused, the corridor behind them had been transformed. It looked like a giant chainsaw had been swung through it. They skidded right and turned into another corridor.

The din ceased. Had the brute burned through an entire two hundred round drum already? Gabe thought maybe he had, in which case he was almost certainly busy attaching a fresh one, offering a window to counter…

It was too much of a risk. The grails weren't here, and Jin had said they knew where they had been moved to. They had Mervin, which he felt sure meant more answers if they had the chance to question him. Stay and go up against four hundred more rounds of steel encased lead capable of cutting them to gory confetti, or get the hell out?

The smart move was just to reach the exfil point as fast as they could.

Gabe drove them onward, making sure to keep himself mentally oriented. They needed an alternative route. It was then he saw the door ahead and realised what lay behind it. In his head, it was the huge split level grey box he knew from the VR simulation. The actual lab was sure to be very different in appearance, but one thing the real lab and its VR counterpart would have in common was the door on the lower level which opened onto a string of corridors close to the maintenance door at the cliff face. The problem was that this was not a lab they had yet entered. Atana's gadget would need to get them through, which might take anywhere from one second to seven minutes.

It was a gamble, a big one.

He pulled them up short as they reached the door, and looked to Holly as he removed the gadget and set it running. He saw from her expression she had also identified the route beyond.

"We just need to hold them off, make sure they're not keen to round that corner back there."

Holly nodded. He knew she would already be performing the rudimentary math, auditing what their vests held, how many rounds, and the widest window: seven minutes. Like Gabe, she knew that long was too long. They were leaning hard on luck. If they ran out of ammo, they would need to take a longer, more complicated route, with useless firearms.

Gabe perched the gadget near the door, took up a kneeling position next to Holly, and like her shouldered his P90 and aimed down the corridor behind them to where a big guy with a big gun and plenty of ammo was itching to come and put an end to them. A P90 mag held 50 rounds of pistol ammo, capable of penetrating body armour. The SAW carried a 200-round drum of ammo that could punch holes in cinder-block.

They saw something peek around the corner. The nose of the SAW.

Both of them loosed a burst of fire on the corner. A statement of intent, a warning to anyone on the other side it would be wise to stay where they were.

From here they took turns firing bursts. Gabe ran dry first, ejecting the spent P90 magazine and smacking a fresh one in. Holly ran dry seconds later, as he let loose his next burst. They both counted agonising second after second as the gizmo generated and chewed through codes.

They were eking out their ammo, spacing out their fire, trying to balance deterrent and potential opportunity to move on them, but all too soon they had burned through half of what they carried. It had bought them perhaps two and a half minutes.

Unless the big guy was a total dummy, which was unlikely, he would have worked out they were stalling. He would also have guessed they weren't carrying an unlimited supply of ammunition. He had, Gabe realised, decided to let them burn through it.

Four minutes and Atana's gadget rolled on without a hit. They had to be close…

The dry click of Holly's final magazine having discharged all 50 rounds came far too soon. Gabe had just slotted in his last.

Holly pulled out her Glock and went to single shots. The pistol held fifteen rounds.

Holly had discharged twelve when Gabe tapped out the P90 magazine and reached for his Sig. He fired his first shot just as the small green LED on the door reader lit up, Atana's gizmo finally having spit out the correct door code.

The lab door slid open and he herded Holly and Mervin through.

He should have just followed. Immediately. He had nothing to gain by glancing back down the corridor. It was a mistake.

Their switch to handguns had been noted. The brute with the SAW had decided to make his move.

The weapon's barrel swung around the corner of the corridor, already firing.

And Gabe was in its path.

# Chapter Twenty-Nine

Jin and Atana were closing in on the exfil point.

Atana hadn't uttered a word since they had spoken to Gabe. Jin had seen what they had done to her friend, and could only imagine what he would be feeling if the same thing had been visited on Holly or Gabe…

Somewhere in the distance, the sound of gunfire reverberated through the lab block.

Gabe and Holly.

He stopped running, and so did Atana.

He didn't even need to say the words; as he turned and headed in the opposite direction Atana was right beside him.

His friends were in trouble.

—

Hank heard the not-so-distant roar of gunfire, Grave's SAW. Hank was carrying the same weapon. Like Grave, he knew from experience what they could be up against. It wasn't enough to put these assholes down, you had to make sure the damage was big enough they simply couldn't get back up.

The M249 wasn't the most versatile weapon in close quarters, which was why Kollar, another ghost accompanying him, was equipped with an M4. It only had to slow the woman down. The SAW would finish the job.

Hank waved his card at the lab door. Cutting through it would save them the more circuitous corridor route.

The door slid open and Hank's partner took point and stepped through.

Hank saw a thin slash of silver, followed by an awful lot of red.

Kollar dropped to his knees and toppled forward. Not flat on his face, because his face was still on the front of his head, and that had just bounced off the floor and rolled out of view.

Hank raised the heavy M249.

A burst of fire hit him square in the chest, and that was that.

The last thing he saw was two figures appear in the doorway, one of them with a sword still in her hand.

—

Holly saw Gabe fall back and then spotted the blood pouring from his face.

She yanked him clear of the doorway as the corridor across the threshold was hosed with lead and steel. The door slid closed. A second or two later the screaming din outside stopped.

Holly glimpsed the wound in her husband's head. She didn't want to accept what she was looking at: a small portion of Gabe's scalp and skull above his left ear was ripped away, offering a dark, wet view of fragile grey matter. She stared into his face, shaking him. Nothing.

Mervin was still beside her, looking as shell-shocked as she felt.

Holly seized Gabe's vest and started to drag him across and deeper into the lab. She screamed at Mervin, who seemed frozen. "Help me!"

For a moment Mervin looked uncertain, then came and grabbed Gabe's vest too. They pulled her husband's dead weight past three rows of solid-looking work benches and behind the fourth.

Holly took in the lab. Behind them lay the lower level, beyond a huge wall of glass with a frosted Fine Technology logo. A split staircase offered paths down into it on the left and right. Through the glass, she saw a collage of robotic arms and mechanical and electrical engineering kit, and past these the door that would get them tantalisingly close to the exfil point.

She looked back toward the door they had just entered, keenly aware their adversaries would already be advancing on them. Mervin was looking at it too, and had long since realised their pursuers seemed unconcerned about collateral damage.

Holly reached into Gabe's vest, removed Atana's gizmo, and thrust it at Mervin. She pointed to the button that activated the hacking sequence and fixed Mervin with a stare equal parts desperate and determined.

"Take this, go get that door open down there, and take him with you. Understand?"

Mervin nodded, received the device, looked at the man lying in a fast-pooling puddle of blood, swallowed and nodded again.

Holly bent down and kissed Gabe, relieved him of his side arm, then looked back to Mervin. "Hurry!"

Mervin obeyed. Taking hold of Gabe's vest again, he began to drag him towards the stairs. A thick trail of blood charted their progress. Soon they reached the stairs and fell out of sight, as Mervin negotiated the steps to the lab level below.

Holly checked her inventory. Two empty P90s, her Glock 19 with a few rounds remaining, Gabe's

Sig P226, with an almost full mag, and a combat knife.

Versus? A hulking lump with two hundred plus rounds of heavy automatic fire, and two pals to chip in. Holding them at bay had ceased to be an option. She was going to have to make what she had count. She held one card: from their standpoint, she could be anywhere in the room, but they had to enter through the doorway.

When the door slid open, she was ready.

A figure flashed across the frame. It was a textbook doorway sweep. Executed in one fluid motion, the figure moved through three carefully practised steps, his gun acting as his pivot point, its barrel swinging counter to his body so its firing line swept nearly one-sixty degrees of the lab.

At least, that was the plan.

It was a manoeuvre Gabe had versed Holly in. She had practised it until it was stored deep in her muscle memory. She knew it well, and how to exploit its predictability. In a fraction of a second, for a fraction of a second, the figure would stand square in the doorway.

She emptied the balance of the Glock into the doorway and nailed him. One of the shots found his throat and sent him down. He clutched at the wound, blood spurting through his fingers, kicked for a few seconds, and fell still.

A moment later the body was yanked clear.

One down. Holly ditched the empty Glock and reached for Gabe's Sig, trying not to think about the hole in her husband's head, trying to put her faith in the Grail's gift...

She remained where she was, the Sig steady in a two-handed grip, levelled just above the crystal white workbench.

Given the manner in which she had dispatched the first attempted entry, she wasn't surprised by what followed.

The barrel of the hulking lump's M249 swung around the doorway and opened fire. By the time its owner pivoted to fill the doorway, Holly had no choice but to duck beneath the bench to take refuge from the unrelenting stream of devastation sweeping across the lab. The barrage of fire pummelled everything in its path.

In most circumstances, twenty seconds is almost nothing, a moment. A person might daydream for three, four or five times as long and hardly notice time had passed.

When each second is punctuated by the ear-ripping, matter-smashing din of multiple projectiles hammering into that person's immediate surroundings it can feel like a very, very long time indeed.

When the assault paused, Holly opened her eyes to behold something akin to a magic trick: the once crisp and sterile R&D lab had been transformed into the site of a cataclysm. The air was thick with smoke and dancing particles. Crisp white designer lab benches had been stripped to their carcasses, and the cinema-screen-sized curved window separating the upper and lower floor had been thoroughly destroyed, now existing only in dunes of shattered glass.

Holly had to move. She would have bet good money the goon was busy swapping out the white-hot barrel of the spent drum on his machine gun for a fresh one, and the little substance that stood between them now wouldn't offer the same protection a second time, brutally Swiss-cheesed as it now was.

Holly scurried across the aisle for the next block of workbenches a row back, barely finding cover before a burst of fire slammed into them.

She peeked out and saw the lump's surviving cohort. The man was heading for the left side of the room, discharging bursts from his M4 carbine on her position as he went. She reached over the bench and blind-fired with the Sig before risking another peek, and glimpsed him reach the far corner of the room and vanish into cover.

A shorter burst of fire from the doorway punched into the already raddled benches ahead. They were trying to limit her movement and then flush her out.

She needed to move before that was allowed to happen. She dashed back another row. The man in the corner shadowed her across the room, her path attracting more fire from his M4. She pulled behind a fresh bench and fired back, two shots—

And then a trigger squeeze to nothing.

The Sig was empty.

Maybe the man knew it, maybe he was just crazy, or maybe he was simply ready to push his luck, but an instant later he emerged from cover and advanced on her position, discharging further short bursts as he came to pin her down.

Out of ammo she might have been, but unarmed she was not. The moment she realised the Sig was spent, she had reached into her other leg holster…

She waited for the next short burst from the M4 and the subsequent pause, and slid the empty Glock into the aisle, a move expressly designed to bemuse and disarm.

She hoped it would buy her the moment of confusion she needed.

Emerging from cover, she found her adversary directly ahead, ready to fire his M4, and from its position, pinched between thumb and forefinger, she sent her last hope flying.

The dagger spun through the air, a steel pinwheel, and buried itself deep in the man's left eye.

He convulsed, waved a hand vaguely in the direction of his nose and promptly dropped dead.

The M4 clattered to the floor at his side…

Holly scrambled for it.

Unfortunately, the dead man was not her only opposition. The lump was done readying his next assault; the SAW's exhausted two hundred round ammo drum had now been replaced with a fresh one: a monstrous fury of sustained automatic gunfire once again ripped into the lab.

Holly threw herself onto the ground, and crawled on her elbows and knees across the wreckage-strewn floor, through chewed up fragments of work benches, lab apparatus and glass, her eyes on the prize. The orphaned M4 carbine.

The SAW's stream of lead battered the lab. Holly crawled onward, half anticipating the breach, waiting for the matter between her and the barrage to surrender and for the bullets to pound her body, rip her flesh apart and shatter her bones…

Instead, after just seconds, the firing ceased, too soon.

The question was, why?

She was unarmed. He had a good idea where she was. All that was called for was for him to aim, jam his finger on the trigger for a quarter of a minute and let whatever lay in the SAW's path be reduced to ruins, Holly included.

Why stop now, unless…

She got to her knees and peeked around the bench. Amid the smoke and whirl of particles, she saw the big guy wrestling with the drum. The SAW had jammed.

And the M4 was still laying there, just ahead.

She went for broke, scrambled and lunged for it, snatched it up, stood, pivoted and swung it around.

To find a huge shape bearing down on her—

A huge fist smashed into her face, sent her flying back. She saw stars and caught a glimpse of the M4 carbine. It now lay between her and the big guy.

They both raced for it.

Holly had the lead; she was about to snatch it up and the big guy knew it. He didn't bother reaching down; instead, he simply swung his boot and sent the M4 flying. It skated across the floor, under the benches and Holly heard it tumble over the lip and clatter to the floor below, out of sight and now impossibly out of reach.

All the race to acquire it had achieved was bring her almost face to face with the hulking steroid advert who was trying to kill her. Robbed of the M4, Holly resorted to basics and took a swing.

It was a good one. The blow landed hard at his temple, and it staggered him. She moved to follow it with a strike to his throat, which he evaded, leaving her knuckles to graze off his shoulder. He shoved her back, hard. She crashed against a bench, losing her balance and any advantage she had earned. She was David facing Goliath, and she was all out of stones.

A meaty right cross looped in and broke her nose.

The hook followed, knocking her off her feet and to the ground.

The vicious boot shattered ribs and ruptured something.

White-hot agony exploded in her gut.

And then he was on her.

Nearly seven foot tall, and at least twice her weight, in an instant, he had one of her arms pinned beneath each of his stocky, muscular legs and was crushing her chest. Then his arms and fists set to work. A string of blows slammed into her face and head. She lost count of how many. She was too busy barely clinging to consciousness.

The beating was relentless. When it stopped, she was amazed to find herself still in a position to be aware it had. She tried to open her eyes. Both were swollen shut.

As her body strived to heal broken cartilage, tissue and bone, to stem the damage and repair whatever organ or organs had surrendered to his vicious boot, the bruising around her eyes receded, some semblance of vision returned and he came into focus above her. He spoke, sounding almost reverent.

"Goddam, goddam…" he said, with dark and delighted awe. "What those things do is something else, right? And… makes it more fucking work than I can be bothered with to kill you bare handed. Take a rest."

She felt the huge weight of him climb off her, and tried to roll onto her side and get up. The attempt invited a fresh explosion of pain in her torso, and she flopped back down.

The man watched her. Satisfied she posed no threat, for a short while at least, he strolled towards his dead companion nearby.

Holly tried again, fought through the pain, rolled over, and started to crawl for the ledge that separated the upper lab from the lower portion, striving to reach the drift of shattered glass that had once been a glass diving wall. She looked back, saw her hulking foe reach down and tug the dagger from his dead companion's eye, and nimbly flip it into an underhand SEAL-style grip.

He turned back in time to see her heave herself over the edge. As she tumbled off, the last thing she saw was him stomping toward her.

The drop was easily ten to twelve feet and she landed hard in a shower of shattered glass. Her bruised and beaten body soaked up yet more punishment. She had to keep moving, buy time…

The same glass crunched under the man's boots as he jumped down.

Crawling was too slow. Holly tried again to get up. Everything, literally every single square inch of her hurt, but beneath the pain, she felt something else building: the familiar itch of the grail's gift at work.

She only needed time. Just one or two minutes…

The glass crunched behind her with each of the giant's steps. She tried to get up again, raised herself from a crawl to an ungainly, bent over shuffle. The boot that slammed into her butt sent her sprawling face-first back to the floor. She rolled over to see her killer looming over her, dagger in hand.

The first burst of fire ripped a hole clean through his arm, causing the dagger to fall to the ground a bare inch from her head.

The second burst, as he turned to see where the first had come from, hit him centre mass and sent him careering backwards and past where Holly lay. He went down and didn't get up.

Holly shifted her gaze across the room. Through still swollen eyes she saw Gabe standing there holding the M4 carbine that had been kicked from the upper level. Mervin was behind him, close to the door, peeking out from behind a tower of servers.

Her husband looked as dazed as she felt.

"Hol? Where the—"

She read the confusion on his face. He seemed lost. His head was still a mess, but the wound looked to have closed.

"Gabe, honey, we need to get out of here. You're going to have to trust me, okay?"

A frown, followed by a nod.

Time to get moving.

Holly struggled to her feet and crossed the room to join them. Mervin stood holding Atana's device by the door.

"It's done?"

"It is."

Mervin had followed her instructions. Sure enough, as she put it to the door, the stored code worked its magic. The door slid open immediately. She peered through. All clear.

The maintenance door exfil point was only a short distance away. Unarmed, and, for a few minutes more, in less than showroom condition, she knew they couldn't afford another encounter.

Gabe was keeping pace but disoriented. He recognised her, but seemed unsure what was going on. There would be time to worry about that later. Once they were safe.

She drove Mervin and Gabe onward.

They hit the end of a corridor.

Holly peeked around it, to check it was clear.

It wasn't.

Two figures stood at the far end, coming their way.

They stopped and raised their weapons. Then, just as quickly, lowered them.

Jin and Atana were one hell of a sight for Holly's sore eyes.

# Chapter Thirty

Both Holly and Gabe looked in bad shape. Both would heal, given the chance, and that was exactly what Jin intended to give them.

He reached the maintenance door and thrust Atana's gizmo toward it. It slid open and they were immediately blasted with cold air and the scent of the ocean. Holly guided Gabe and Mervin onto the narrow metal walkway bolted to the cliff face. A look down through the grille offered a sheer drop beneath their feet, and an ice-cold ocean, churning against the rocks a couple of hundred feet below.

Jin unzipped the bags he and Atana had stowed close by and began to distribute diving gear. Gabe and Holly were already wearing the same lightweight wetsuits he and Atana wore, they just needed goggles, face hoods, their masks, and the lightweight carbon cylinders and regulators that locked onto them. The compact mini dive rigs were good for twenty minutes. Jin and Atana had anchored the mini-sub close enough to reach in half that time.

Jin helped Gabe into his gear. He still looked disoriented, unsure of the situation, but he was with it enough to not need urging to put his diving kit on. Jin saw his own concern reflected in Holly's face. Instead of putting any kit on, Holly was busy peeling her wetsuit off. She handed it to the terrified-looking man they had brought with them.

"Mervin," she said, "Get your clothes off."

"Excuse me?"

"Trust me. You won't enjoy jumping into that water wearing corduroy slacks and a knitted sweater."

Mervin looked down through the walkway's grating at the ocean roiling below.

"I can assure you I won't enjoy jumping into that water no matter what I have on."

When he continued to dither, she barked, "Now!"

He began to undress.

The mini-sub was only minutes away, but when the water temperature was below zero, minutes was more than Mervin might last. Jin was sure Holly didn't relish the prospect, but she also knew their gift would make it uncomfortable rather than hazardous. The man was soon down to his Y-fronts and awkwardly squeezing himself into the wetsuit.

"I'll assist our friend here. You'll stick with Gabriel?"

Jin nodded.

Mervin stared out of the goggles with the eyes of a man caught in a nightmare. Holly checked his mini dive kit regulator, and said, "Once we're in the water, I'll be needing this occasionally too, okay? You ready?"

"Not even slightly."

"You'll be fine. I promise."

Atana had kitted up while covering the doorway, and now she suddenly started firing through it, with someone else firing back.

She shouted back, "Go! I'll be right behind you."

Jin and Gabe straddled the rail.

Holly helped Mervin over the rail too, and Jin heard her say, "We're going to need to jump, get some distance from the rocks. One, two—"

He removed the regulator, "Wait. I'm not sure I can—"

More gunfire battered the doorway.

Holly stuck the regulator back into Mervin's mouth, and said, "Three!"

# Chapter Thirty-One

In the wreckage and ruin of the lab, an equally ruined Carson Grave lay in a pool of his blood and shattered glass, his chest and arm riddled with bullets.

The initial shock had long since worn off, leaving pain to take its place.

Had he the strength to cry out, perhaps he would have done so. It was as though his agony was too large and required every drop of his remaining energy to further torment him, until there was nothing left to draw upon. His body was giving out on him.

After all the close calls, all the hostile situations and hot zones, could this be it, the day he died?

Credit where it was due, they had nailed him good.

Hit with nearly a full magazine at close range, the plates in his tac vest hadn't stood a chance. He had gone down, and stayed down, the rounds that had torn through his body armour having also torn him up inside. Above him, the ceiling, a collection of neatly fixed power cables, fat air-con piping and fluorescent lights melted into one unfocused blur.

Then came the itch. His mind crafted an image of fire ants, chewing at his wounded arm and chest, thousands of tiny mandibles feasting on his insides.

The pain began to ebb away.

His lungs, whose operation had fallen to erratic and feeble at best, suddenly sucked in a deep gasping breath. Grave first inhaled and then aspirated a chest full of blood. A fit of coughing followed.

He rolled onto his side and eventually raised himself onto one knee. He assessed his shredded tac-vest and his arm. The wounds in his arm shrank as he watched. He rotated his forearm and brought it closer in time to see a bullet pop from the pale belly of flesh. It hit the floor, and before he had time to look up it was followed by another, and another…

It had worked. He hadn't been sure it would, hadn't been sure how far the trick extended.

During the last year or so, Grave had seen some crazy shit. In his obsessive hunt for the fragments, Benedict Fine had been forced to reveal increasingly more information about what they were, and what they did. Some revelations they had learnt together.

By the time Grave led his unit to capture the fragment in Brooklyn, he knew quite a lot.

He knew the owner of the first fragment he had been sent to obtain was not easy to kill; a brace of bullet wounds certainly hadn't been enough to get the job done.

He knew from capturing the second fragment the same went for *its* owner too, and the freaky things changed shape. It could be transformed from the vaselike object they were expecting to a bracelet, to a dangerous melee weapon capable of smashing one of his men clear across a room with enough force to kill him, and back again when removed.

By the time Fine located the one in Brooklyn, Grave felt confident enough to demand fuller disclosure. That was when he learned about the historian, the fresco and tablets, and the story those tablets told.

Aside from Fine himself, Grave probably had a fuller picture of what was going on than anyone. It was clear Fine had siloed off different parts of the venture for as long as possible. Up until a few months ago, Oblonsky hadn't known about the historian, and the historian still knew nothing about Oblonsky.

He knew about the experiments Oblonsky had performed on the Norway asset, locked away in his cell, and what those experiments revealed.

He had held three out of four of the freaky, and seemingly ancient, objects in his hands before either Fine or Oblonsky had the chance to study them up close, and conclude that what Fine called their 'resting' form was something between a puzzle and a test.

The vaselike objects presented a challenge. They seemed to dare an observer to slide his hand down the barrel and press his palm flat to the bottom, to let his fingers rest neatly in the ridges awaiting them; at the same time, the brace of blades promised to slice his wrist to ribbons if he did.

It made no sense, unless…

You were someone whose body might heal that sort of injury in moments.

Fine wasn't an idiot. He had to see the same thing.

All the targets they took fragments from had been the same. They were hardy bastards, healed fast. The question was, were they owners of the fragments because they possessed this ability through some prior means, or had they gained it from the fragments to begin with?

Egg, chicken, chicken egg…

Oblonsky's tests on the Norway asset had hoped to determine which it was. They had peered long and hard at the guy's DNA. The conclusion they arrived at was that technically, the Norway asset wasn't truly human. Close, but different enough. Around as different as man and the closest of the primates. If the object was behind the difference, it seemed Fine wasn't in a rush to have his DNA blindly rewritten, and was too cautious to let someone else become superhuman, if superhumanity was on the table.

Fine needed more reassurance, a bigger safety net before he could muster the stones to jam his own hand into a tunnel of razor-sharp blades. Trusting in hard science had made him a billionaire.

Grave respected science, but the thing that had kept him alive when danger was a frequent companion was instinct and nerve. He was used to walking the highwire without a net.

When he took his men to New York to capture the fourth fragment, he already knew what he was going to do once he had it. Just a couple of minutes alone with the object in the back of the fake ambulance had been enough. The blades in the fragment's barrel had cut, and cut deep, but the fragment had gifted him something that healed them right back up. He had stepped out of the back of the ambulance without a scratch, and more than human.

The pain was almost gone, and the itching too.

He climbed shakily to his feet, feeling stronger by the second.

# Chapter Thirty-Two

Mervin felt small in a large leather armchair, facing the impressive oak-panelled library.

Showered, and dressed in clean clothes, albeit loaned and hence a little large for him, he was, nevertheless, warm and comfortable. He tried to look on the bright side: his kidnappers were at least treating him with impeccable courtesy and care. He could just as easily be in some basement chained to a radiator.

His captors, hosts… sat facing him. The blonde woman was closest, on the other side of the fireplace in the wing-backed armchair identical to his own. The man he believed was her partner was perched on one side of the library's reading table, the East Asian looking man on the other. The dark-haired Mediterranean woman sat apart, further back, in a chair by the window.

The blonde woman had introduced them all, forenames only. Her name was Holly, her partner's, Gabe, the other man was Jin, and the woman by the window was called Atana. It was all very cordial.

The last ten hours had been nothing short of dizzying. They had hopped from vehicle to vehicle, a submersible, to something with wheels, to something else with wheels, to an aircraft, to another aircraft, and finally back to something with wheels. He had been blind to each transition from one vehicle to another, not because a burlap sack had been roughly thrown over his head, but because a temporary but firm hand had been held over his eyes. He had been handled respectfully and provided with food and drink.

His nerves were undoubtedly jangled, but he imagined they would have been in any case. Oddly, given the previous night's events, he felt almost comfortable in the company of these people, perhaps more than he would have been in the hands of Fine's security force back at The Shell. He had no idea such a force existed at the facility, a bunch of lunatics who seemed at ease obliterating anything in their path and taking stock later.

On one of the legs of the journey, a small aircraft, he had even slept, admittedly more due to exhaustion than relaxation.

Mervin wasn't about to kid himself he wasn't scared, but that fear had a potent counterweight. He was fiercely curious.

He had seen the man sitting at the library's reading table receive a monstrous injury to his head; part of his skull had been blown away. He had also seen the same wound heal minutes later. Likewise, he had observed serious lacerations and the most horrific bruising acquired by the blonde woman, Holly, vanish just as quickly.

While counter to the realities of science and human biology as he knew them to function, he had seen these things with his own two eyes. Even for a man who fancied himself open to startling possibilities and radical departures to established thinking, a quality which had damn near ruined his career, recent events were testing his boundaries.

When considered in the context of what the tablets carried, the implications were wilder yet…

'We want to talk to you, that's all,' this Holly had insisted.

Strangely, he believed her. He had seen the look on her face, and her partner's face as they took in the fresco. He was certain they had known what it was, or what it depicted.

Mervin wanted to know how that was possible. So he followed their instructions and behaved himself. Even if he had possessed the sort of courage an escape attempt called for – and he suspected he did not – he would not have tried.

Let them ask their questions, and maybe he would get to ask some of his own.

"You've been working for Benedict Fine?" asked Holly.

"Yes."

"The nature of your work?"

"Studying perhaps the most significant archaeological find in human history. I... We, my team, believe it offers the most compelling evidence yet that our understanding of the past is woefully incomplete. The find supports my long-held hypothesis that another species of human likely predated, or for a time existed concurrently with Homo sapiens, and into a far later era than our brief overlap with Homo neanderthalensis."

Jin reached behind him and picked up a Kindle e-reader. He held the screen up to display the cover of Mervin's book, replete with its slightly embarrassing science-fiction style illustration.

"As you claim in your book?"

"Yes," replied Mervin, more defiantly than he had intended.

"Tell us about the fresco," said Holly.

"It's early Minoan, as much as four and a half to five thousand years old. It was discovered in a cave system on Crete, together with a larnax, a clay chest, containing a cache of clay tablets, inscribed mostly in Linear A, although, crucially, not all. The chest and all the tablets belong to a later period than that of the fresco, somewhere around 1800 BCE, but one tablet comes from a later period still, we estimate around 1450 BCE. It bears two scripts, the old Minoan, Linear A, and the Mycenaean script that supplanted it, Linear B. The texts appear to be the work of someone who still had command of both, and, in a similar fashion to the Rosetta Stone, we believe both texts carry the same content. This, plus a great deal of work and some wondrously sophisticated computer AI, have enabled us to finally decipher the previously impenetrable Linear A, and unlock what the cache contained."

"And what was that?"

"A story."

"A story about what?"

Mervin swallowed, marshalled the nerve to ask a question of his own.

"Why do you want to know?"

He expected Holly to answer, but the tall dark-haired woman sitting near the window further back spoke first. What came out of her mouth caught Mervin off guard, less by what she asked, but how she asked it. She repeated his question, only not in English, but flawless Attic Greek. *Ancient* Greek.

"*Why do I want to know?*"

She clearly hadn't meant him to answer because she now answered the question herself, and Mervin was again required to translate her words. This time, though, it took a little longer, because what she had said was spoken in a still earlier variety of ancient Greek.

"*Because it is my due, scholar.*"

The dark-haired beauty leant forward. Her next words were in yet another language. One which sent a shiver through Mervin. He had only heard it vocalised synthetically, by a computer attempting to recreate a phonetic interpretation based on his team's work. They were words of ancient Minoan, and if he was correct, they translated roughly to:

*"Promised to me long ago."*

Curiosity and fear no longer teetered on the scales. With these words, fear became a downy feather, and curiosity developed the heft of a concrete elephant.

—

"The tablets," Mervin explained, "describe an encounter between the early Minoans and emissaries of a civilisation lost to memory and record. The events themselves would predate written language in the region. The story would have been passed down through oral tradition and recorded many generations later.

"My team's translation is, as with any translation, subject to debate, nuance and some interpretation, but I believe it is as coherent as one could hope for after over five thousand years.

"The story begins with the arrival of a vessel at the shore of what we assume is Crete. Seven mariners emerge. They encounter one of the island's tribes, among the most ancient and earliest Minoans, and are received cautiously. Given the visitors are few, and unarmed, they invite much interest.

"The visitors are each clad in a simple garment of immaculately woven fabric, and wear a finely crafted bracelet which makes the work of the island's skilled craftsmen look crude in comparison.

"The mariners assure the tribe's elders they wish only to study their island's flora and fauna. Hoping to build a relationship, and perhaps form an alliance for trade with their guests, the islanders make them welcome. To begin with, their hosts are dazzled, excitement and curiosity quieting any other concerns.

"However, as time passes, unease builds about the visitors. The number who visit by day, returning to their vessel at night, steadily diminishes. Soon, only one of their number remains a constant, a woman. While the rest of the mariners withdraw, she spends increasingly more time in the tribe's company. She shows their healers how to better treat their injured and sick, their craftspeople how to refine their tools, and takes pleasure in listening to the tribe's myths and legends passed down from their ancestors.

"Despite the woman's presence, concerns surrounding the rest of her companions grow. The vessel at their shore bears an ominous presence. The mariners' refusal to invite any of the islanders aboard it, claiming such a thing would be a breach of their customs, exacerbates the tribe's mistrust with each passing day.

"One night the woman appears after nightfall, unexpectedly and bearing a warning. She seeks out the tribe's elders and confirms they are justified in their concerns. Her people are not their friends. Her cohorts aboard the vessel have reached a decision, and it is the one she had feared. They intend to take the islanders' home for themselves, scouring all inhabitants from its surface until none remain. Inside the belly of their vessel lies the means to do so, with ease.

"She confesses her kind are sorcerers, capable of magic beyond the islanders' understanding. She proves her words by removing her bracelet, whereupon it changes shape and becomes another treasure entirely. She goes further, drawing a blade across her flesh, so the elders might see how her people's wounds close almost at once, and without a trace of injury.

"She confesses something else: in the short time she had known them, she has come to care for the tribe's people above her own. Her kind is cold. They place no value in tenderness or any other emotion. Living among the tribe has shown her that before she met them, she was hardly alive at all. She will not stand idle while her people destroy the islanders and steal their home.

"The elders pledge their strongest to fight at her side, but the woman refuses. In a pitched battle, they will be defeated, but alone, with stealth and surprise as her allies, she might yet deliver a fatal strike, destroying their vessel and all within it.

"The tribe waits for her return. Those who cannot sleep keep one another company.

"When the sun rises, the vessel is gone.

"The islanders continue to await their saviour's return, but it never comes.

"They craft shrines in her honour. The island's artisans paint frescos and carve effigies of their would-be destroyers and their champion. These shrines serve another purpose, too: they stand as a warning, lest the vessel and its people ever return. In time, the story, passed from ear to tongue from generation to generation, survives as something closer to legend, and is eventually recorded on tablets so the people's descendants might never forget it."

For a moment the library was silent, then Jin said, "You believe these objects are the relics of a lost people?"

"I do, one vastly more advanced than our own, a race who may have existed for tens of thousands of years before us, which built wonders while we were still huddled in caves."

"Would we not have found some other evidence? Ruins or artefacts?"

"We might easily not," Mervin answered. "The first thing to consider is the timescales involved. We have evidence of ancient human civilisations, but the older they are the more fragmentary and sparser that evidence is. Wooden structures, ones featuring mud and primitive types of cement, do not fare well pitted against millennia, or even centuries.

"The oldest ruins we have are ten, eleven thousand years old. These have survived primarily because they were built from stone, and stone is resilient. The mighty pyramids at Giza were built four and a half thousand years ago, and indeed still stand, but much has been lost. The giant slabs of granite remain, but the fine white polished smooth limestone is long gone. Stripped for reuse or worn away.

"Without constant maintenance, the sophisticated edifices of our modern age would fail to survive hundreds of years, much less thousands. Unattended to, the most iconic and mighty structural icons of our time, such as The Empire State Building would crumble in mere centuries. If mankind was wiped out tomorrow, it's highly doubtful any ruins would still stand to prove we existed in as little as ten thousand years."

"As *little* as ten thousand years?" repeated Gabe.

"You think this is a long time?" Mervin replied. "By any measure other than human history, it is nothing.

"Homo sapiens, modern humans like you and I, have existed for *two hundred thousand years*. Twelve thousand years ago we find evidence of fixed settlements, of rudimentary farming. Five thousand years ago we have the first city-state emerge in Sumer in Mesopotamia, the first example of what one would consider a complex advanced civilisation.

"Just five thousand years out of *two hundred thousand*. Think about that. And then ask yourself whether there's any reason it couldn't have happened long before that. A complex, highly sophisticated civilisation that flourished and then crumbled? Perhaps one hundred and seventy thousand years ago, perhaps just ninety thousand? Perhaps closer still, sixty thousand? Given another fifty-five thousand years, would even the pyramids at Giza still be there for us to find?

"And this is if we only consider mankind, if we believe only Homo sapiens capable of forming civilisations and advanced technology.

"Homo erectus utilised fire around one million years ago.

"Hominids existed three hundred thousand years ago.

"Life on earth reaches back six hundred *million* years... For a moment let's set aside our monstrous egos and entertain other possibilities: some other kind of mammalian race perhaps, or one derived from fish or birds, amphibians or reptiles... Would this be evident in the fossil record?

"Not necessarily. To form a fossil, conditions need to be quite specific. An organism has to be rapidly buried in the right composition of sediment, sufficient to harden and protect its skeleton, and subsequently turn its bones into rock over millions of years. The overwhelming majority of animals to roam this earth will not have been fossilised. We know only about those we have found, and from even this paltry collection much is incomplete, subject to speculation and theory. Not so long ago we believed the dinosaurs were 'terrible lizards', now we recognise they are more closely related to birds.

"So, there would be no way of knowing if an advanced civilisation came before us?" asked Jin.

"The Silurian Hypothesis agues there should be," countered Holly. "Albeit indirectly."

"Ah," said Mervin, "Yes, The Silurian Hypothesis..."

"And that is?" asked Gabe.

"An unfortunate title for a reasonably robust theory," said Mervin.

Gabe interjected, "Unfortunate, why?"

Holly answered, "The Silurians are a race of fictional lizard people, in Doctor Who. The name was attached to a theory put forward by a pair of astrobiologists, to try to answer your question: if an advanced civilization predated mankind, hundreds of thousands, perhaps millions of years ago, how could we know?"

"The hypothesis presents the sort of clues we should seek as evidence. We would be looking for molecules," Mervin added, "plastic polymers and rare earth metals. Evidence of mass consumption of fossil fuel in the form of heavy carbon isotopes, specifically a marked shift in the Carbon-12 ratio in rock strata."

"And do we see that?" Jin asked.

"As it happens... we do," said Holly, "around fifty-six million years ago, but... the rise occurs over hundreds of thousands of years. We would be searching for evidence of the same rise occurring in just a few centuries. The change in climate and Carbon-12 ratio for the previous example were almost certainly a natural occurrence."

"Indeed," said Mervin, "However there are those, like myself, who believe the Silurian hypothesis is fundamentally flawed, predicated on assumptions that may be rather shaky.

"The hypothesis assumes once civilisation emerges it will spread exponentially, and similar civilisations will soon proliferate. It assumes this growth will inevitably become global in scale, but there's no reason that should be the case. Many species, and perhaps civilisations, remain localised, sometimes for geographical reasons, mountain ranges, deserts, oceans that deter expansion. They may remain limited for biological reasons too: extensive rearing periods for their young, low reproductive capacity. Maybe they develop technology that negates the pressure to seek resources from further afield…

"The central flaw with the Silurian hypothesis is it assumes any past advanced civilisation would inevitably share similarities with our own, but it need not. How can we know when currently we have just one isolated example of a creature capable of such advanced civilizations, ourselves?

"It may have taken Homo sapiens two hundred thousand years to progress from cave dwellers to city-states, five thousand to go from those first city-states to space exploration, two and a half thousand to move from the iron age to the silicon age, but how confident are we that another species couldn't have got there far sooner? Why not ten thousand years from cave to city? Why not five hundred years from iron to silicon, why not a further brief twenty to go from the silicon age to technologies beyond anything we can imagine?

"Progress does not adhere to a predictable linear curve. Environment, culture, resources, chance discoveries and unforeseen breakthroughs accelerate and retard. Even today primitive tribes survive in Brazil, West Papua, Peru.

"If we were to somehow divide the world down the middle, make it impossible for one side to interact with the other, in a century would both sides have access to precisely the same technology? All the evidence we have points to the rate of technological advancement being exponential, so that a small breakthrough on one side of the divide could result in civilisations that appear centuries apart in the space of mere decades, and millennia apart in centuries. In time, the gulf between one half and the other might grow large enough that were they suddenly reunited, the more primitive side would face technology they couldn't comprehend, and found miraculous to behold.

"I believe this is what occurred. An advanced civilisation took root and developed rapidly, but some other factor prevented its expansion, biological, geographical, cultural, or technological… And then something happened which brought about their destruction.

"Perhaps they suffered a cataclysm only a fraction of their species survived. These survivors were left among ruins, left with technology they knew how to use, but not how to recreate. This too seems a characteristic of exponential technological progress: technology outpaces the mass's ability to fully understand how it functions. Knowledge becomes the preserve of the specialist. We see this ourselves, today. How many devices does the average person use in his day-to-day life that he could create for himself?

"We could all utilise friction to create fire, fashion a cutting tool, craft clothing to protect us from the elements, but what percentage of us understand the workings of a tool as ubiquitous as the smartphone? How many of us possess the knowledge to build one from scratch?

"Perhaps the remnants of this advanced civilisation were left with no choice but to look outwards, were driven to make contact with emerging civilisations they had either seen fit to ignore or actively avoided?"

Mervin paused, for a moment, conscious that he had been speaking for a long while with little interruption, and aware that he had slipped seamlessly back into the manner of a lecturer addressing his students. But these people were not bored, were not mocking him, were gripped by his every word.

"I don't know who you people are," he continued, "or what your connection to all this is, and I have no idea of whether I should be afraid – although trust me, I am – but I've also spent a significant portion of my life searching to find evidence for something I grew convinced was true. The quest ruined my reputation, reduced me to a joke among my peers, and saw me ostracised. I arrived at a point where no respected expert with a desire to preserve his credibility wanted to be seen collaborating with me.

"Then, out of nowhere, Benedict Fine approached me. He told me he wanted to fund my work, but this was not all, he believed he had the hardest evidence thus far I was on the right track."

"The fresco and tablets," Holly said.

Mervin nodded. "They bore the oldest representation of the fragments I had yet found, five and a half thousand years old, and seemingly a depiction of the people they belonged to.

"I believe that these items, fragments of a lost people, survived and were passed down, won or stolen throughout human history. Representations of them occur again and again. They are real, and if one was found it would offer incontrovertible proof of a people more ancient and advanced than ourselves. I'm not an idiot, I know such an item would also be unimaginably attractive to a man like Benedict Fine for other reasons, too. What technologist wouldn't want to possess technologies which might still surpass our own? He wanted to find one." Mervin paused, studied each of the four people facing him, and asked the question he could hardly dare to imagine. "Did he? Is that what you were searching for at The Shell?"

Holly looked to Jin and Gabe. If they had hoped to confer, they were set to be disappointed. Atana dispensed with any debate.

"He didn't find one," she said. "He found four. You were working corridors from where they were once kept, in a neighbouring lab."

Holly saw at once that Mervin had had no idea. The others must have read this from his face, too. Atana had delivered her answer so bluntly precisely because she had wanted to gauge his reaction.

"Fine found... *four?*"

"No," Atana replied. "He may well have found one, but the other three he stole, from me, from them, and one other. The treasures are ancient and are indeed made from technology beyond anything we have today. They are also, without any shadow of a doubt, extremely dangerous in the wrong hands. Fine sent an armed mercenary force to take them by force and then kill us. This is the man you've been working for, Mervin."

"And right now," Holly added, sharing what Atana and Jin had learned, "he's on a hydrographic research vessel in the Mediterranean, off the coast of Crete. Above a section of the Hellenic trench, parts of which reach over five thousand metres deep. He's taken the fragments there, and he's looking for something in those depths. Do you have any idea what it is he expects to find?"

"Something that may," Mervin suggested, "have been lying at the bottom for a very, very long time?"

# Chapter Thirty-Three

Mervin had been invited to return to his room, and the door locked.

"Okay, so what the hell do we make of all that?" Gabe asked.

"It explains Fine's sudden interest in what might be at the bottom of the ocean off the coast of Crete," replied Jin.

"He's hoping to find something?" Holly said.

"Or he's already found something," added Gabe.

"If the story is true," Atana said, "and this *champion* sank her people's vessel, what's to say it isn't still there, waiting to be found?"

"A vessel that held something that could *wipe out a whole island full of people, scour them from its surface, with ease.*"

"Is it true, though?" Jin countered. "Can we trust a story that's at least three and a half thousand years old?"

"It's a question worth contemplating," Atana replied. "Are we to believe none of it, some of it, all of it? Especially given the original events and tale are far older. The cataclysm wrought by the Thera eruption, which places my time on the island, is commonly held to have occurred around 1600 BCE. Our professor upstairs believes the twin scripts on the tablets place their creation to between 1900 and 1750 BCE. The issue is it seems the tablets were not contemporary to the events.

"What casts most doubt is not the age of the tale, however, but the medium. Both the fresco and the tablets were relics back when I first encountered them, and the story Mervin relates has all the characteristics of one passed down through oral tradition. It features a hero with uncommon powers, the threat comes from 'others', who are initially exotic and strange, but ultimately hostile, they possess magical powers, the threat they pose is apocalyptic…"

"The story becomes legend, its details exaggerated and distorted," added Holly.

"And yet, the treasures the tale describes are real enough," said Jin. "They change shape as described. *We* are real. Beings whose wounds heal almost at once without trace of injury. What is sorcery to a simple people, but a word to describe something they cannot understand?"

"The real question is," Gabe said, "can we afford not to take the story seriously? If something is down there under the sea, buried, long forgotten, are we happy to let Fine find it? It seems to me there might be more at stake now than recovering the grails," he turned to look at Atana, "or revenge."

# Chapter Thirty-Four

Sunrise.

A burnished orange glow kissed the skeletal remains of a ruined city, its surviving stone walls and walkways, staircases and buildings. Many edifices were assembled from perfectly rectangular sandstone blocks, hewn into precise dimensions and slotted neatly together. Some walls even clung to patches of richly painted frescos, and the pillars traces of rusty red paint. Testaments to their former grandeur.

Benedict Fine watched the sun creep higher until it became a blazing glare, challenging him to squint to maintain his view. Finally, when it broke free of the horizon, he abandoned his seat on a low wall and began to stroll among the ancient ruins of Knossos.

It was tranquil, only the chirp of crickets disturbing the silence. The site was officially closed to visitors. The tourists were still another hour or two away from meandering the paths, reading the historical information plaques, visiting the gift shop to purchase souvenir fridge magnets and tea towels before filing back onto the coaches that brought them. He had been able to arrange a more dignified visit.

Aboard the Oculus they were still receiving and installing equipment, some shipped directly from The Shell, some new, obtained specifically for the task at hand. Oblonsky and Grave's man Feeney, a former Navy Seal, were busy preparing the ROV for the first exploratory mission to the site of the ELF signal, or 'song' two hundred metres below the sea.

Pacing around on the ship had become intolerable. To alleviate his growing agitation, Fine devised a distraction, a trip to watch the dawn break over the heart of the Minoan civilisation. What better place to contemplate the past and the future?

The ancient ruins around him had once been lost under a flower-covered hill, and a layer of dirt just a handful of metres deep. Their discovery had written a new page in man's antiquity.

Kalokairinos and Evans, the two men most responsible for exposing them, might not have unearthed Daedalus's labyrinth, or the bones of King Minos's monstrous half-man-half-bull minotaur son, but they had handed the world incontrovertible proof of an impressively sophisticated civilisation, and forged a clear link between the myths of the ancient Greeks and tangible history.

Threads of truth lay in the old tales of gods and kings.

Together with the fragments, the story deciphered by Mervin Pickering, recorded in the tablets found with the fresco, hinted at truths and discoveries more astonishing still.

The discovery of another ELF, or 'song', by a scientific hydrographic survey vessel had initially seemed to point to the existence of a fifth fragment. To set about retrieving it, Fine had promptly acquired a company that specialised in deep-sea mining support. The purchase came with two fully crewed and operational world-class Dive Support Vessels.

He had yanked the largest of the ships, the Oculus, from a ten-month contract in the Gulf of Mexico and immediately instructed the crew to head directly for the Mediterranean where the ELF had been located.

Oblonsky and the core of the fragment team had decamped from The Shell to the ship. Once on-site, surveys carried out from the surface pointed to more than just the existence of a fifth fragment. They showed the source covered a wider area.

It was enough for Fine to begin to relocate the rest of the fragment team and the four existing fragments to the ship, along with most of Grave's men. Grave himself and the remainder of his men would join them before the end of the day. The Oculus was the project's new base of operations.

Something was down there in the depths, something larger even than the hulking Dive Support Vessel floating above it. Perhaps more ruins, of immeasurably greater importance and value than those surrounding him.

A polite cough begged his attention. Benedict turned to find his chopper pilot waiting.

"I just received word from the Oculus, sir. They're ready."

—

The Oculus was not difficult to spot. Its hull was a vibrant fire engine red, against an expanse of glimmering brilliant blue sea. The massive 120-metre-long vessel had three decks: main, tween, forecastle and shelter, and the bridge was topped with a helicopter platform at the head, approximately 70 metres above the water.

Distributed across its decks were facilities to support over two hundred people, crew, technicians, and divers. There were bedrooms, toilets, laundries, rec rooms, dining areas, kitchens, and then the business end of operations, engine rooms and maintenance, control rooms, both navigation and dive support, laboratories, habitats for saturation dives.

Perhaps as few as a fifth of those on board had any real idea of why they were there; the vessel's crew simply knew they had been re-contracted at a considerably more generous rate and were surveying and supporting the exploration of a site along the Hellenic trench. The fragments were now housed in the largest of the vessel's two laboratories, under armed guard by Grave's men.

The chopper's skids set down on the helipad and Fine climbed out into what promised to be a blazing Mediterranean day. He crossed briskly to the ladder and descended to the bridge. Another set of steps took him to the shelter deck. More steps down finally saw him in the dive control room, where he found Oblonsky sitting next to the ex-SEAL, Feeney, at the ROV console.

Feeney was in charge of dive operations. He had the technical experience, and it dispensed with the need to bring in anyone new. Grave's men already knew about the fragments.

The ROV control console featured a cluster of monitors. Right now, he was directing the group readying the ROV on deck. The ROV had been fitted with a special modification, a sensor specifically designed to track the ELF of the fragment's 'song'.

"Okay," Feeney announced. "Let's get this lady wet."

An on-deck camera showed the group lowering the ROV, while simultaneously the ROV cameras captured the horizon, and then water briefly lapping over their lenses, followed by the deep blue of the ocean.

"Let her go."

The ROV's clamps were released and Feeney began to guide the submersible toward the depths. The ocean was teeming with life. A shoal of lurid fish broke apart to make way for the ROV as it moved towards them. Steadily the water shifted from a bright cyan to a deep royal blue, and then eventually blackness, broken by cones of blue where the ROV's lights reached out to illuminate the way.

Feeney pushed the submersible deeper.

Down.

Down.

Down.

The submersible was now approaching a depth of two hundred and seventy-five metres.

Sections of the trench reached five thousand metres deep.

The ROV's camera picked out a patch of sandy shale studded with sporadic clusters of rock. It had reached a stretch of the sea bed.

The ELF tracker on the ROV fed a number to the monitors, scaling the closer the sensor got to the source. On the journey down, the number had grown quickly, but now it had slowed. Feeney used the figure to guide his way, steering towards the direction which most encouraged it to climb.

The ROV met a rock formation, that abruptly terminated in a drop-off. The submersible glided off the edge and once again plunged downwards. The number on the monitor climbed quickly until it met a shelf.

Feeney directed the ROV to its edge and again sent it over and down further into the abyss.

The number on the monitor immediately began to fall.

He brought the ROV around and doubled back. The source was located somewhere in the area above. After some to and fro surveying of the surrounding geography, something became apparent. A section of the uppermost lip of the trench had collapsed. The debris now formed a slope on the shelf.

The source of the ELF appeared to be somewhere within the sloping section of rock. Feeney began scouting the area more methodically, using the tracker to find the closest point he could reach—

"Hold on," said Fine. "Back up."

Feeney decelerated the ROV, "What did you— No, yeah, I see it. Hold on."

He brought the ROV around and moved in closer. A deep cleft in the rock exposed something which looked starkly at odds with the area around it. The ROV inched closer; they were working in tight quarters, but Feeney was skilled and navigated the fissure well enough to get a good view.

The ROV's lights spilt over a material that was smooth and sheer, entirely free of the crustaceans which liberally studded the surrounding rock. He guided the ROV sideways, tracking the seam of pristine material, until it was swallowed under rocks, but not before the ROV's beam illuminated something even more interesting: a collection of sweeping arcs etched into the material. They converged at points, weaving complex clusters of detail.

All three men had seen similar markings before. They would be recognisable to anyone who had seen the fragments up close.

A rap on the dive room door broke the spell.

Another of Grave's men entered, his face tight.

"There's been an… incident at The Shell."

Fine frowned, "What sort of incident?"

# Chapter Thirty-Five

Grave had not long touched down at Heracklion airport, and was on his way to the chopper that would take him the final leg to Fine's ship when the video call came. He had expected as much as soon as a secure line of communication became available.

He accepted the video call from the tarmac, beside the chopper.

As expected, Fine hadn't taken the news well.

Given the sensitive nature of what and who were involved, he had hoped to discuss the incident in person, and said so.

"Incident?" Fine barked, "Sounds to me like 'incident' is underselling it some. From what I can gather half the lab block had been destroyed! Pickering has been abducted, the Norway asset fucking beheaded and dead... If I'm missing anything, Grave, please, feel free to contribute."

Carson Grave let Fine vent. His insanely wealthy client was free to curse up a storm, so long as he remained respectful. Grave was aware of the concept of catharsis, but his tolerance for disrespect was limited. When Fine seemed done ranting, he responded.

"I'd ask you to remember what my men and I were up against, and how many of us were there to address the incursion. Most of my unit was with you on the ship, protecting you, protecting your people, protecting the fragments they and I obtained for you, from people who, trust me, are very difficult to kill. Also, remember that on those previous occasions we engaged with the element of surprise. This time they did."

"I don't pay for excuses, Grave."

Now, this was pushing it.

Working for Fine had been extremely lucrative, and Grave had a reputation to maintain, but no gig was essential. If he was honest, what he had gained from the fragment rendered Fine's money trivial. Curiosity, more than money, was the main thing keeping him compliant at the moment. He wanted to know what the fragments were, too, and what Feeney had found down there under the sea. Moreover, either Fine was dumb, or he must have realised the power dynamic had long since shifted. Maybe he was, and it was time to make it clear.

"If you'd prefer to terminate our relationship, Benedict," Grave's flagrant familiarity and choice of the other man's forename was no accident, "we can close out our retainer agreement, settle my bonus payments, and part ways. That's your prerogative. Just say the word. My men and I can be out of here in a matter of hours—"

Grave was gratified to see his suggestion had the anticipated effect. Even over the video feed Grave saw Fine blanch. He'd have expected a billionaire businessman to have a better poker face. They both knew the gig was never meant to involve Grave becoming such an integral presence. His unit had been hired to acquire an item, illegally, with murderous intent, through force, and the discovery that its owner was more than human and not so easy to kill was a surprise to all. The mission to acquire the second fragment saw them better prepared; the bonus acquisition of the Norway asset attested to this and involved them further.

By the time they went after the fragment in New York, Grave knew far too much to cleanly cut loose, and had proven himself invaluable. Another outfit would be equally risky from a secrecy standpoint, and perhaps less operationally effective to boot. It would not be easy for Fine to terminate their relationship, and they both knew it.

"No, no, of course, that won't be necessary. It's just... a very delicate time right now. This latest find could change everything."

Grave simply nodded.

"Perhaps, on balance, things aren't too dire. Thankfully there's little Pickering can divulge that can upset things here. As for his work, there are others on his team who can take his place. If he surfaces and starts to shoot his mouth off, who's going to listen? There's nothing to connect him to me. The loss of the Norway asset is regrettable, but we have samples and a lot of data.

"One of the two resident fragment team members? Could they have disclosed anything? Oblonsky insists they weren't told where the rest of the team were going, but one of their colleagues may have let something slip."

Grave reasoned the white coats left behind were naturally the least vital. Why else had they been selected to remain at The Shell and babysit the Norway asset when the rest of their team had been relocated to the Oculus to study and investigate the anomaly?

"The surviving one I spoke with, the one who'd been tied up and gagged, didn't know anything. The other... We can't know for sure what he might have shared before he was shot in the head. Probably nothing, but I'll give the word to step up security here, just in case."

In truth, this was easier said than done. He had a limited number of men, a full four less than he'd had just forty-eight hours ago. Recruitment was delicate and took time; they wouldn't be replaced any day soon. To make matters trickier, unlike the Shell, the ship they were on had not been designed with security foremost in mind. The cold truth was, they were a lot more vulnerable here should four superhumans succeed in finding them, looking to take back their possessions.

But there was no benefit in telling all this to Fine.

There was a knock on the cabin's heavy steel door behind Fine. Fine called whoever was on the other side in. It was Feeney.

"Our fancy suits have arrived. Want to come lookie-see?"

# Chapter Thirty-Six

*Crete.*

They had moved quickly, ensconcing themselves in a residence close to the coast, outside the port of Kokkinos Pirgos near Tymbaki.

The question of what to do with Mervin Pickering had involved some debate. The result was that Pickering was now a guest at the Kelvin Arms Hotel, a rather lovely rural luxury spa retreat.

His room was booked and paid for a six month stay, and Gabe had left Mervin a holdall with enough ready cash to comfortably cover expenses for a similar duration.

Ultimately the crucial factor was how risky was it to let the professor loose? In theory, he could have immediately rushed to contact the authorities, but what exactly would he say?

No one knew he had been working for Fine. It was a secret, to the extent he would find it hard to prove he had even met the billionaire tech mogul, let alone been on his payroll. Fine wanted his work to stay secret until the time was right, and would have taken measures to make sure of it.

His story would sound like the ravings of a madman. Maybe if his work at the Shell had reached the world at large his reputation would be more robust, redeemed, but it had not. As things stood, he was still viewed by many as a kook peddling pseudo-scientific theories about ancient advanced races.

Seeking to connect himself to Fine could be seriously unwise. Gabe reminded Mervin, although he probably didn't need to, that Fine had a bunch of trigger-happy thugs on his payroll, who would have reported seeing Mervin escape The Shell with the two men and two women who had infiltrated it. Fine might suspect him of duplicity, of working with them to facilitate the incursion.

If all this wasn't stick-like enough to keep Mervin quiet and concealed for a few months, Gabe dangled a carrot, too. Once they had taken care of more immediate concerns, they would be back and arrange a surer footing for his continued safety.

It was not difficult to identify Fine's ship. Even before arriving on Crete Atana had gathered a decent amount of information. A Dive Support Vessel named The Oculus had arrived recently, with permission to conduct hydrographic research. The company that operated the DSV had been newly acquired by… a subsidiary of FineTec.

Hacking into the local port's IT systems confirmed cargo was still being transported to the ship, several loads each day. While the relocation of Fine's people seemed complete, transfer of much of the specialised equipment and materials they required was still ongoing.

Gabe and Holly were up at dawn, sitting in a hired van observing one such delivery. A cargo boat was moored at the dock. The awaited truck arrived on time and parked under the long shadow of the crane that would lift the load of the latter to the former.

Two other men loitered on the dockside. The truck driver engaged in a brief exchange with one, a hard-looking man, whose body language screamed military, or former military.

Holly said it before Gabe could.

"Fine's mercs."

"One hundred per cent."

The man performed a perfunctory, clearly disinterested, check of the cargo, before stepping away to let the boat's captain direct the load's switch.

"Just as sloppy as the last time. You get the feeling these guys think they're above checking deliveries?"

It took less than ten minutes for the two small shipping containers and several tarp-covered pallets to go from the truck's flatbed to the boat.

Gabe and Holly watched the two men climb aboard and the boat subsequently sail off in the direction of the Oculus.

A second load of cargo was scheduled to be collected from the dock and transported aboard the DSV later that evening.

If all went to plan this one would be carrying more than Fine anticipated.

# Chapter Thirty-Seven

The ADS rigs were installed and ready for use in the dive room.

To date, the work carried out to clear rock and install the Kraken at the site of the anomaly had been undertaken by a team of saturation divers, orchestrated by Feeney. It was standard deep dive engineering work, the sort of operation teams throughout the commercial offshore gas and oil industry carried out twenty-four hours a day, three hundred and sixty-five days a year.

There were eight divers, rotating between the pressurised habitats in the dive room suite. They descended in one of the Oculus's two diving bells in two shifts of six hours apiece before ascending in the pressurised diving bell to return to the similarly pressurised habitat in the ship's dive room. When their run was complete, they would need to complete approximately one day of decompression for every thirty meters below the ocean they had ventured. An unglamorous nine days in a cramped habitat that smelt aggressively of armpit.

Given Fine's wants this was a workable, if undesirable, state of affairs. Fortunately, there was a solution.

Approximately eighteen months earlier, Fine's revolutionary battery tech and developments in ultrahigh molecular weight polyethylene had allowed a team in Houston, Texas to prototype an Exosuit Swimmable Atmospheric Diving Suit or EX-SADS. These suits allowed deep-sea dives to be more spontaneous and simpler, virtually eliminating the risk of decompression sickness, nitrogen narcosis or oxygen toxicity, and the need for divers to breathe Trimix. The wearer of an EX-SADS could breathe regular air at atmospheric pressure for up to eight hours, and would be able to walk around post-dive at surface pressure again in minutes rather than days.

The EX-SADS should have heralded a revolution in deep-sea diving operations, removing the demand for lengthy decompression stints, but in practice, they had struggled to gain commercial traction.

The reason the commercial offshore oil and gas industries didn't throw parties, pop corks or hang up bunting was a small matter of expense: the cost of an EX-SADS rig and the service contract each required was considerable. While cumbersome and laborious, running shifts of saturation dive teams simply remained more economical. Until costs could be driven down, the EX-SADS were destined to remain exotic specialist devices. So much so that the number of them presently assembled in the Oculus dive room was probably the largest collection to stand together outside the facility where they had been built.

What they most resembled were futuristic space suits, coloured a warm grey, with a tasteful yellow accent colour. Their helmet-style facemasks and propriety local coms technology allowed their wearers to speak freely, and to benefit from a 160-degree monocular field of view. While hardly lightweight, each EX-SADS weighed 150 pounds, the rig's motorised exoskeleton meant the perceptual weight was around 15 pounds. Once powered up, they felt lightweight, and if the wearer wished to trade operational duration for ease, there was an assisted mode that reduced this to zero and offered enhanced natural motion, with both speed and strength augmented.

Since Fine had decided he intended to be the first human being to step into the ruins of a lost civilisation and assess the wonders and promises it held, expense was a minor consideration. The nine suits before them were all they could get hold of, and as soon as more could be procured, they would be.

Feeney was obviously impressed with the new hardware, "Ain't they pretty?"

"When can we dive?" asked Fine.

"Give the word," Feeney replied, "and we can be ready by this evening. That's with four of our guys supporting you as saturation divers. You'll piggyback a ride to the bottom on the side of their diving bell. If you want more people on hand down there than that, we're looking at tomorrow afternoon."

"Four will be sufficient. We'll dive tonight."

# Chapter Thirty-Eight

The truck carrying the Oculus's evening delivery snaked through the twisting hills leading to Kokkinos Pirgos harbour. Some of the roads it had to take were old and perilously narrow. At one particular section, the road passed beneath a bridge immediately followed by a junction with a restricted view. Any sane driver, and without a doubt any professional one, was forced to inch to the neck to obtain a clear view, stop, and diligently check the coast was clear of traffic coming from both directions before carefully pulling out and executing a hard turn if they were heading in the direction of the harbour.

As he slowed and then stopped, the driver of the truck was oblivious to the two men and two women who leapt from the edge of the bridge onto the bed of the truck behind him.

Gabe, Holly, Jin and Atana slipped among the cargo until they reached one of the three 8x7 shipping containers. Gabe broke the lock and seal, and before the truck pulled away, they had squeezed inside. The morning delivery had received no more than a cursory glance before being moved from truck to ship. With luck, this one would be the same.

The truck turned sharply and rumbled down and along the twisting roads leading to the harbour. Eventually, it came to a stop.

From inside the container, the clank of activity accompanied cargo being hoisted aboard the boat, until they felt the jolt and lurch as their own container was lifted and swung over, before being lowered onto the deck. The boat's engines kicked up a short spell later, and they felt the chop of the ocean as the cargo boat charted its course for the Oculus.

The container experienced a second jolt and lurch when they were craned from the cargo boat onto the deck of the DSV. When the delivery was complete and they heard the engine of the cargo boat rumble into life and begin to fade into the distance, Jin crept forward, peeked out from the container, and confirmed the coast was clear.

They slipped out, emerging into a jumble of recently delivered cargo. There was a lot of it. The collection of containers, pallets wrapped in tarps, drums, boxes and cages of tanks and machinery provided plenty of cover.

The deck of the ship was enormous; from a distance the Oculus had looked big, up close it was a behemoth of a vessel.

Two tall cranes lay ahead, one on either side of the shelter deck. The smaller of the pair was the one that had lifted them aboard. The taller crane beyond serviced the forecastle deck, and the bridge decks. Towering above even this crane's head, extending over the front of the vessel, projected the ship's helicopter platform. Ahead of them were the interior spaces belonging to the shelter deck, below their feet main deck, then double bottom, where the dive rooms would be located. The general arrangement was common enough that even without technical specs, obtained once more by virtue of Atana's formidable hacking skills and reviewed by all, the basic geography of the ship would have been reasonably predictable.

The main deck, where the laboratory wing was sited, was their destination. The grails had been kept in the labs at The Shell, and it seemed reasonable to assume they would be here, too. Reaching the labs without any fuss was the goal.

Even if they had the numbers for a brazen assault on the ship, they had to acknowledge a good percentage of those aboard were innocents.

Fine and Carson Grave's Ghosts, however, deserved little mercy. Likewise, neither did those who had been studying the grails. Atana viewed anyone working in the lab where Torsten had been imprisoned and abused as worthy of extinction.

However, these were not the only people aboard the Oculus. A vessel the size of the DSV called for a correspondingly sizeable crew to operate it. There was little doubt these men and women were entirely ignorant of what they were involved with, and they didn't deserve to end up as collateral damage.

A stealthy approach offered the best chance of success. Recovering the grails and finding out the status of Fine's search was enough to bite off and chew on. As much as a more conclusive end to Benedict Fine's activities was needed, taking down Fine and his army for hire might be best attempted subsequently, a coup de grace delivered from a stronger position. Atana wanted Fine's head, possibly literally, but accepted a battle won was preferable to a war lost.

If they secured the grail and determined Fine was yet to locate anything that posed an immediate threat, their departure did not need to be elegant. Simply the opportunity to throw themselves overboard into the ocean would suffice.

Each of them was perfectly capable of swimming back to land, and could swim submerged intermittently for long enough to get a safe distance from the DSV. If things got dire, Atana was adamant the grail's gift meant they could not drown. She assured them they could make the whole trip back to land submerged if necessary. Gabe didn't doubt it was true, but equally doubted the experience would be a pleasant one.

The night would be upon them soon. The first pinpricks of stars were visible above, and already the fading light was throwing welcome pockets of shadow over the deck. From their present vantage point, things appeared quiet: Jin pointed out two figures on the bridge walkway, and another two below, at the doors leading to the interior rooms of the shelter deck.

"Sentries on the bridge and below, the doors to the main deck. Atana will take the bridge."

"Holly and I will deal with the other two," Gabe agreed. "Let's get this done."

He and Holly set off and cut left, negotiating the litter of cargo until only open deck lay ahead. They waited.

On the bridge walkway, Gabe glimpsed something slip over the rail and cleave to the wall where the shadows swallowed it. A moment later, Atana's silhouette appeared on the other side of the bridge. Gabe and Holly heard Jin's whisper over the coms.

"Ready?"

Atana's whispered response came back, "In one, two, three…"

With liquid grace, Jin's shadowy form slid forward and took his sentry down. There was a brief struggle as the man asphyxiated, and by the time Gabe's eyes had shifted to Atana on the starboard side of the bridge, the sentry there was gone, too.

Now it was their turn. Jin signalled and then provided a distraction, a tap on the rail above the two mercs flanking the main deck entrance doors inviting both men to look up. Gabe and Holly fired two silenced shots from their pistols.

Both mercs flanking the door crumpled.

He and Holly hurried forward and under the shadow of the walkway. Jin dropped down beside them, and Atana a moment later. All marks were relieved of their SMGs, and their bodies tossed overboard.

Sooner or later their absence would raise concerns, and one of those concerns would be correct: a hostile force had boarded the DSV.

The clock was ticking.

Gabe, Holly, Atana and Jin pushed through the doors to the ship's interior, P90s up and ready to do harm.

## Chapter Thirty-Nine

Gabriel took point on one side of the passage, with Holly close behind covering his back. Atana and Jin adopted the same formation on the opposite side. They moved quickly but cautiously. Compared to The Shell, the vessel's plans had been easy to obtain. They knew their bearings and charted a route that favoured the ship's less-frequented arteries. They were called upon to pause and hide just once as a couple of crew passed by, but otherwise encountered no one, arriving at a flight of steps leading down to main-deck unchallenged. If they were correct, the laboratories were just a little way ahead, beyond a short flight of steps.

It was then they heard an exchange down the passage below. Loud enough to identify two speakers, but far enough away for their words to be unintelligible. Jin moved level with Atana, shouldered his P90 and signalled his intention to descend first. She, Gabriel and Holly held their positions while Jin crept to the bottom and slipped quickly and quietly behind the shoulder of the stairwell.

His hushed voice reached their earpieces a moment later.

"I see two." He said, "Both men wearing body armour, carrying M4s. We need one alive; the one on the left will do, I'll leave it to you to deal with the other. On one, two, three—"

Jin spun out as Atana, Gabriel and Holly advanced down the stairs. Two shots to the leg took Jin's merc down. A succession of silenced pistol shots saw the other dispatched. Jin was on his man before he hit the ground, an arm around his neck and a hand clamped to his mouth. Atana turned her weapon on him. Gabriel and Holly did the same. The man's eyes showed he got it. He remained as silent as someone who had just taken two bullets to his left thigh could be.

Jin twisted the man toward a curved, inch thick, steel door fronting the laboratory wing. A simple card reader and keypad lay to one side. The captive shook his head. Jin nodded to Atana, who happily fired a third shot into the man's right thigh.

The captive convulsed and groaned behind Jin's hand, but quickly held his hand out before slowly reaching into his pocket to produce a key card. Gabriel took it from him.

"The code," Jin demanded.

The merc nodded and Jin removed his hand.

"Seven, two, four, eight."

Gabriel swiped the key card through the reader and punched in the code. The lab's curved door began to open. Atana fired a second shot, and Jin divested himself of his captive.

The door was fully retracted in seconds, offering a view of the room beyond. The hi-spec laboratory space was no surprise, but the number of people in it was. The lab was a good deal more populated than they had anticipated, crowded even.

The assembled were standing, facing an array of screens off to the right, the sides of which faced Atana, Jin, Gabriel and Holly.

Slowly, a few of the group nearest the door turned, their faces registering shock as they took in Atana and the other three figures standing there, weapons ready, fingers at the trigger. All thought better of shouting or screaming, but a chain reaction was already in motion and travelling through the room. As each of the assembled noticed his neighbour twist his head, they did too, until soon enough the entire group was looking into the doorway, watching the gatecrashers stride inside.

Atana grabbed one of the white-coated figures, drew her sword from its scabbard over her shoulder and brought the point to his throat. Meanwhile, Gabriel, Holly and Jin spread out to surround the group gathered at the centre of the open-plan lab.

"Where are they?" Atana demanded of the man she had at sword-point. His eyes flicked to a heavy metal pillar across the room, inelegantly welded to the floor and wall. It featured a panel, for security biometrics.

Atana marched the man over to it.

"Open it."

"I— I can't. I'm not… senior enough."

"Who is?"

The man pointed a shaky finger to another colleague across the room, who didn't look thrilled to have been singled out. He stepped forward, held his hands up, and then started over. She was willing to bet none of these people had been made aware of what had happened at the facility they had recently vacated.

The man pressed his palm to the reader and faced forward so the tiny bead of a camera lens could scan and identifying his face.

A pneumatic hiss and several deep clanking thumps followed; the metal pillar split apart and the doors rolled back to reveal four compartments arranged vertically. Each compartment held a treasure, in every detail identical.

She reached in and took one out, thrust her hand into it. She couldn't know if it was the same treasure she had worn and kept safe for over three thousand years; it was possible she never would. Perhaps it was the one Fine had first acquired, or the 'grail' that Jin and his mentor Blake had kept safe and secret for nearly a thousand years, or Torsten's clan's 'Mjolnir', plundered from the crypt over twelve hundred years ago…

If Mervin Pickering's translation was correct, and the fresco was to be believed, all were the legacy of a people long since lost to history.

She executed the gesture, and at once the treasure shrank and slipped around her wrist and forearm.

She took out a second one, and tossed it to Holly, a third, which she threw to Jin, and finally the last, which landed in Gabriel's hands.

—

Gabe caught the grail. Atana had wasted no time; hers was already wrapped snuggly around her arm. In all the years he had watched over the grail, he had never contemplated driving his hand into its mouth for a second time. Why would he, when he already had what it shared? Just to feel those razor-sharp edges carve into him, and feel the itch once he withdrew his hand and the wounds began to heal? How was he to know there was so much more to it than that, more secrets they hadn't known?

Now he knew better, he didn't hesitate to drive his hand in, and as Atana had promised, the blades didn't carve deep. The grail immediately recognised one of its own. The blades bit, but only for a moment before shrinking back, melting away.

He pressed his open palm to the base, slid his fingers into the indentations, and started to trace the gesture Atana had shown them, helped them practice, across the markings on that smooth yet somehow coarse surface. She had exactingly reproduced the markings, familiar to him after nearly a decade, but surely unforgettable to her after so much longer.

He felt the grail shift against his forearm, saw the unique metal it was comprised of liquefying, flowing to shrink and enclose his arm. When it settled and solidified, it resembled an archer's bracer which ran from beneath his elbow to his wrist, as Atana had described.

He looked up to find Holly and Jin were now wearing their fragments in the same way.

They had done it. They had recovered the grails, and now surely one of the people in this room would be able to tell them what if anything had been found in the deep below them. Then he realised that question might already be being answered. His new position meant the bank of monitors were now visible, and his eyes made sense of what they were showing. It also explained why so many people had gathered in the lab, why the room was crowded. What they were watching finally sank in.

The monitors were showing a live feed of a dive, streaming the feeds coming from the divers' cameras in multiple real-time perspectives. Each feed had a name attached and metrics overlaid. Gabe's attention fastened upon two names in particular: FINE, and GRAVE.

It was dark down where they were, torchlight slicing through the gloom, particles and sea life drifting through the beams. The diving party were on the sea bed, marching forward.

Fine himself, and the boss of the mercenary outfit he had enlisted, were personally diving to the bottom of the ocean. There was an additional metric displayed on the feed overlays: water depth, which currently read 875 feet. That was *deep*.

Saturation diving was technical and dangerous, mistakes could be fatal even for an experienced diver. As the group occasionally roved into each other's camera fields, it became evident while some of the divers were wearing regular diving gear, chunkier and designed for depth, others were wearing diving rigs that appeared significantly more exotic. This made more sense. Gabe was aware of the existence of compact swimmable ADS suits, enough to know they were rare and eye-wateringly expensive. It appeared Fine had got himself a bunch of them.

On several of the feeds, a rock formation loomed out of the darkness. More than one diver altered their gaze to stare up, and the formation's huge shadow attested to its scale. A moment later something else resolved from the murky depths. A machine was bolted into the seabed. Gabe had seen a device that looked remarkably similar, on Jin and Atana's cam recordings from their mission to The Shell. This machine's multijointed and dexterous looking robotic arms were larger and more robust, but otherwise, it was a close relative of the ones back at Fine's facility, the ones that had been designed to crack the gestures which caused the grail to transform. This one had been built to withstand pressures deep beneath the sea.

Gabe barely had time to ask himself what all this was for before the diving party's torches had illuminated the scene more fully, and the question was answered.

There was something buried beneath the rock, or within it. Part of it had been excavated, exposing a smooth metallic wall. The section closest to the machine bore markings, a cluster of delicate swooping lines etched with impossible precision, which collapsed at points into clusters of intricate detail, just like the ones on the grail.

The monitor feed bearing Fine's name showed him reaching the machine first; the others hanging back to let him.

He stood beside the machine for a time, then looked back to view the men behind him. Gabe counted eight divers in the fancy compact swimmable ADS suits, and four in more traditional, clunkier diving gear. Fine's head-mounted camera swung back around, hesitated for just a moment and reached out to hit the button on the machine's body.

The robotic arm awoke and performed a series of movements. Its finger traced over the marking on the metallic wall, graceful and fast. It seemed clear that these motions had been rehearsed and preprogrammed into the machine, given what happened next.

A small hole appeared in the wall and began to expand. Fine instinctively stepped back as the smooth metal material shrank back to form a perfectly circular entrance, behind which beckoned seamless darkness.

## Chapter Forty

Fine stood at the threshold of the flawlessly circular maw which had opened in the wall. Hours previously, he had watched as the same phenomenon unfolded on a monitor, but what had sparked only fascination and jubilance then now stirred something else.

He was about to step into the unknown.

Beyond the opening lay the remains of a civilisation lost to history. The fragments were astonishing, beyond anything mankind had yet created. What might lie inside a vessel crafted by the same minds?

One thing was certain, he had to be the first to see.

So why was taking the first step so difficult?

He hadn't got to where he now stood by being timid, but the longer he waited, unmoving, before the threshold, the more aware he became of Grave and his men behind him. The less confident he felt and appeared.

And Grave was already a concern.

He had been driven to share too much with an individual who was, by open admission and profession, a mercenary. Benedict was under no illusion Grave's loyalty was bought, and its foundation rested upon how lucrative that loyalty continued to be. At some point, once this site had been secured and its secrets extracted, something would have to be done about Grave and his men. Others provided similar services; perhaps he would enlist one or more to wipe out Grave's unit if he had to.

A problem for later.

Right now, all he had to do was take one great step for man.

Fine lifted a boot, and set it down, crossing the threshold into darkness.

Once inside, his torch illuminated the walls around and above him. He had entered a seemingly featureless chamber. He turned and beckoned Grave and his men to join him. One would remain outside to operate the Kraken.

As Grave and his coterie entered, their torch lights illuminated the chamber further and confirmed it was indeed utterly featureless, an unbroken sphere of the same metallic material of which the wall and the fragments were composed.

Suddenly, the aperture through which they had entered began to shrink.

This was anticipated; they had seen this, too, on the video feed, but that time, reflected Fine, it was not closing him in. In moments they were fully enclosed within the sphere.

Then another aperture opened, on the opposite side of the spherical chamber.

The water trapped within the chamber rushed out into a long passage, until they stood, seawater dripping from their diving suits.

## Chapter Forty-One

On the bank of monitor screens, the diving party advanced one by one through the maw in the smooth metallic wall. Only one remained outside.

A moment later the circular opening shrank and vanished completely, sealing the group inside.

All but one of the monitor feeds cut to black. The overlaid metrics froze and then vanished, replaced a second later by a simple message: CONNECTION LOST.

They all heard Atana's words. "I have to get down there."

She started toward the lab door. Gabe reached her at the threshold, caught her arm. She stopped, turned to face him. He maintained his grip. She turned her gaze on him. Something in her eyes... She was afraid.

"Okay, what aren't you telling us?"

"I've told you everything, everything I can be sure of... When I saw that thing open.... It's not memory, or maybe it is, but if it is, it's one I can't grasp and pull into the light. I know it, though. There's something down there, and I'm not going to stand idle while a fool like Fine and his bunch of hired guns blunder around until they find it."

She was right. If the grails were connected to what had been found beneath them, who knew what else might lie inside? He let go of her arm.

"The dive room will be down at double-bottom," he said, "I know you said we can't drown, but some diving kit wouldn't hurt, and the moonpool will offer us a route straight into the ocean."

# Chapter Forty-Two

Fine and Grave led the way.

Oblonsky scuttled in their wake, surrounded by the rest of Grave's men.

The ground was tilted slightly upwards, and a little to one side. Enclosed in the EX-SADS, with its extra weight, the gradient soon had him breathing hard. Oblonsky was not a man accustomed to physical exertion.

Why hadn't he just thought of a suitable excuse?

He should be hundreds of feet above, with his team, watching this venture on a bank of monitor screens in the laboratory.

He was in no doubt the wreck they were inside had been buried and forgotten since the earliest days of human civilisation, and was, like the fragments, clearly built by a race with technology far in advance of any created by modern man. But he was far too scared to be excited by this fact.

When Fine had said he thought Oblonsky should be among the party to first venture inside the anomaly, his instinctive reaction had been a violent 'no thank you', and technically he had never actually agreed to go. Fine had simply assumed he'd agreed. The problem was that Fine had put him in the position of having to explain why he shouldn't go, and before he knew it, enough time had passed while he struggled to think of a suitably convincing excuse that it seemed he had agreed, without ever having actually done so.

What made finding an excuse so difficult was that Fine obviously viewed the invitation as an honour.

Fine seemed eager to put himself hundreds of feet below the ocean and inside a complete enigma.

And if he had offered an excuse, what then?

Benedict Fine wasn't a man accustomed to being told no. Others in the team would be all too willing to take the lead... Brant, Kelly, Jiankui... Oblonsky wasn't about to let someone else usurp him and take credit for all they had achieved and might go on to achieve. When their breakthroughs were shared with the world, he wanted the recognition he was due, not someone else who had sneaked in and won Fine's favour at the eleventh hour.

Their torches cut a path through the gloom. He shone his torch on the wall beside him and noticed the material was different from the chamber. It was paler, with a mottled pink texture. The metallic grey metal of the shell and chamber was still evident, but was now only marbled through the new material, like capillaries or seams of ore. While the passage itself was broadly straight, its walls seemed to twist, spinning out, expanding and then converging. Oblonsky found himself thinking of the spiral patterns so prevalent in natural structures, plants, shells, weather formations, solar systems and galaxies...

Fine suddenly called to Grave to pause, then said, "Can everyone kill their lights, just for a second?"

Oblonsky obeyed, turned off his torch, followed, one by one, by the rest of the party until soon they stood in darkness, or what had appeared to be darkness. Slowly their eyes adjusted and it became apparent the corridor was still visible but lit now not by their torches but by some source of ambient illumination inherent to the pale material Oblonsky had just noted. With their lights off the material seemed to respond accordingly, the illumination increasing in intensity. It was dimmer than the torchlight, but offered a more complete view of their surroundings. The passage arced ahead, curving into a bend.

What became starker was how… unusual the environment was, how… Oblonsky resisted reaching for a particularly insistent word, but it proved impossible. The ruins felt *alien*.

He knew the theory Fine subscribed to, and the probability the thesis was correct. A race predating Man felt so much more likely than any of the alternatives… A sophisticated hominid who had evolved before, even independently of man, whose civilisation was ancient and perhaps collapsing when Man's was just emerging seemed an infinitely more reasonable proposition than visitors from the future, or ones from another dimension, or from across the galaxy, beings that were truly alien, extra-terrestrial…

Grave and Fine set off again, leading the rest of the party forward, but less than a minute later suddenly came to a halt as they negotiated the curve in the path ahead. Grave raised a hand to bring the party to a standstill.

Oblonsky peered into the gloom.

Something lay ahead, slumped against the wall of the corridor. Still, and long expired.

A body.

## Chapter Forty-Three

They had left the inhabitants of Fine's lab, suitably intimidated, face down on the floor, with the assurance that any alarm would invite the detonation of the explosive devices with which they had rigged the ship. It was an empty threat: there were no explosives, but Gabe felt the odds were good that none of the white-coated individuals would be in a hurry to test it. Not given the presence of the two dead mercs they had dragged into the room to offer the technicians something to think about.

Heading for the dive room, they had encountered just one more person so far. The man, obviously a crew member in his hard hat and orange safety vest, had rounded the corner to meet four strangers and an equal number of guns in his face. He had been swiftly subdued, bound with zip ties and gaffer tape and dragged out of sight. Gabe, Holly, Jin and Atana had continued apace, searching for the staircase or a set of ladders that would get them to double bottom, the location of the dive room.

Holly saw it first. "There!"

She pointed to the end of the corridor, towards a staircase. A flight up offered access to the deck above and another led down to the one below. Gabe and Jin covered their rear while Atana and Holly took point and started down the steps to double bottom.

Just as several figures rounded the staircase above.

These guys were not crew. The body armour, helmets and guns were something of a giveaway. The two mercs leading opened fire. Gabe and Jin fell back against the wall and fired back in return, backing down the corridor to seek cover.

For a split second Gabe locked eyes with Holly, her face still visible above the head of the stairs.

He had no idea whether she'd heard him yell 'GO!' over the din of exchanged semi-automatic gunfire before his retreat saw her vanish from view.

Jin got behind the shoulder of the passage. Gabe mirrored him on the opposite shoulder. He stole a second to get on the coms.

"Okay," he said, "I think it's fair to say this dog has figured out it has fleas. Holly, Atana, you keep heading to the dive room. Jin and I will join you in the water as soon as we can."

## Chapter Forty-Four

Holly and Atana threw the door to the dive room open, weapons at the ready, to find three crew members clad in orange vests monitoring the diving bell rig. Atana brought her P90 around and all three reached for the ceiling.

Holly swung the dive room's heavy steel door closed, locked it, and then did the same with the one on the far side of the room too.

Atana closed in on one of the dive crew, indicated towards Holly as she returned.

"Get her ready to dive. Deep. Just the essentials."

The man nodded and scrambled, collected up the necessary gear and helped Holly into it, a big helmet with a full face-plate, integrated regulator and a tank of Trimix. Soon after, Atana was equipped with the same set-up herself. They zip tied the crew and strode to the first of the dive room's moonpools.

A huge winch hung above it, to manage the thick umbilical cable carrying gas, power, coms and heat to the diving bell currently hundreds of feet below in which the saturation divers had made their descent. The cables would lead them to the diving bell, and close to the site of the wreck.

Holly and Atana exchanged a look, stepped off the edge, and plunged through the well into the ocean.

# Chapter Forty-Five

Gabe and Jin continued to return fire, but the situation didn't favour them. Trying to advance down a passage towards half a dozen armed and highly experienced mercs, the best money could buy, would be tantamount to suicide. They'd be shot to shreds. Fortunately, the dive room wasn't the only route to the ocean.

Jin said out loud what Gabe was thinking.

"The deck. We just need to reach open water."

*If* Atana was right, and they really couldn't drown, it was true. All they had to do was jump overboard and let the weight of their equipment and body armour carry them down to the bottom.

Gabe nodded.

They commenced a retreat towards the main deck. Gabe focused on issuing suppressing fire in their wake while Jin navigated, keeping a hawk's eye out for trouble ahead. The biggest danger was being trapped, meeting another group of mercs before they made it into the open. Gabe was sure they were scrambling into action, the presence of intruders having become the world's worst-kept secret, and the opposition knew the vessel's layout better than they did.

They navigated the same route they had taken to reach the lab, only in reverse and under fire. Gabe felt a rush of relief as he cast a glance back and recognised the doors to the main deck. Jin hurried forward and shouldered them open.

They slipped through into the alcove beyond and immediately came under fire from both sides.

They jerked back, hugging the small shoulder of cover the alcove offered.

Gabe took a breath, and popped out to return fire, and earn a lie of the land.

Grave's men had worked out where they were heading, and instead of trying to intercept them, had waited to ambush them when they emerged on deck. Gabe saw muzzle flash from multiple sources as he quickly ducked back into cover.

"We have to move, Gabriel. We have hostiles closing in behind."

"Agreed, return fire and then break for centre deck, get behind the base of that crane. See if we can find a route to the edge of the deck from there."

Gabe sprayed a wide arc of fire portside, and Jin starboard, then they emerged.

Gabe felt a round hit his body armour, like a crashing hook to the ribs, but remained on his feet and moving. The deck and steelwork seemed alive with the impact of bullets; they fell under the long shadow of the crane. It was almost dark. The plan had been to use the last of the light to aid their infiltration, and encroaching night to cover their escape. If the helicopter perched on the vessel's helipad was deployed to search the water, its task would be a great deal harder in the dark.

The base of the crane was an improvement on the doorway, but no closer to the edge of the deck, and Grave's Ghosts were almost certainly shifting to gain better positions to exploit where they were exposed.

Gabe looked further up the main deck, to a spot that would offer 360-degree cover: the shanty town of unsorted cargo, the same spot in which they had arrived. Still nowhere near the edge of the main deck, but more advantageous than their current position.

Gabe tapped Jin and gestured to the cargo dump. Jin nodded, joined Gabe in once again spraying their aggressors with enough fire to encourage them to take cover, and abandoned the shadow of the crane.

They sprinted like crazy until they plunged amid the steel containers, cages, rolls of steel and electrical cables and canvas-strapped tarpaulin pallets.

—

Holly and Atana sank quickly. The thick cable reaching down to the diving bell resting on the seabed ran alongside them, and stopped them drifting away as the water grew colder and darker, and the pressure increased.

The scientist in Holly wondered what her augmented biology was doing to counter the effects of the temperature and the pressure. Was her skin becoming denser? How exactly was her blood chemistry receiving assistance from the nanotech the grail had gifted her? Before the HALO jump Atana had assured them they couldn't get pressure sickness, or oxygen narcosis, and the bends were not something to concern themselves with. They couldn't even drown. Atana had evidently discovered both these things through personal and no doubt fraught experience. The science was, well, academic, and as far as survival went, moot.

For several years the science had still held Holly's interest, but eventually, even her work had ceased. The tools available to get her to the answers she needed were still too primitive. There was so much about how the grail changed them that they couldn't explain.

Was it possible that what lay beneath them might hold the answers?

Holly realised Atana was looking at her.

Their faces, bathed in the lights built into the diving helmet's faceplate, were now the only thing visible in the sea of darkness that surrounded them.

—

Gabe and Jin tried to gauge the extent of their opposition. The mercs had been waiting and ready for them, and had surely worked out they were trying to reach the ocean. They had taken up positions on both sides of the deck. If there was a weak spot that might allow Gabe and Jin to make a break and dive over the edge, right now, it wasn't an obvious one.

He and Jin were edged within the confines of the cargo dump taking occasional shots at the perimeter, but the instant they emerged from cover, return fire was not slow in coming, and seemingly from every direction. They were, it seemed, surrounded. They were eating ammunition just holding their foes at bay.

And things were only about to get worse.

The first burst of flame rolled across the deck like a belch of dragon's breath and illuminated the whole area as starkly as if someone had thrown on floodlights. A blast of intense heat accompanied the light show until the flames vanished and the night was filled with the acrid tang of napalm and gasoline.

Gabe shifted position behind a steel cargo box, peeked out, and located a silhouette of a man shouldering a huge tank and weapon tipped with a guttering flame.

He pulled back as a sheet of fire raced his way. Suddenly the cargo box was engulfed in flames. When they retreated, the cargo box was still ablaze, the napalm clinging to where it had landed.

A flame thrower!

Fire, their Achilles heel.

Jin was suddenly at his side.

Of course, Grave and his mercs would know; they had kept Atana's friend Torsten imprisoned and used him as a guinea pig for long enough to have conducted who knew how many 'tests', looking to winkle out the grails' secrets, and discover what made their former keepers so difficult to kill. They would have realised that not all wounds healed in seconds or minutes. Moreover, after their battle at The Shell, the mercenary group had taken steps to invest in weaponry to exploit their vulnerability.

They hadn't just allowed them to reach the open deck, they had *wanted* them to reach it, patiently herding them into a kill zone.

He and Jin couldn't afford to let Mr Flamethrower get comfortable. The guy was, without doubt, aware he was humping gallons of highly flammable liquid on his back. They needed him to grow more acutely aware of it.

Gabe leant out and poured half a P90's 50 round mag on the flame thrower's position, near the crane, and sure enough, the silhouette vanished as he quickly sought cover. Now Gabe just needed to keep him there until he and Jin came up with a way of not being roasted alive, or to death.

Jin saw what he was doing and began to move more widely among the varying cover afforded by the cargo litter to fire intermittently on the various positions from which they were surrounded.

Jin's voice was in his ear, over the coms.

"Gabriel, this is no good. They're too entrenched. We can't afford to stay here much longer," Jin was telling him. "Keep holding them off, I need a few moments to try something."

"Okay, but whatever it is, try to make it quick."

Gabe withdrew his focus on the goon with the toaster to fend off the rest of the mercs around them. It didn't take long for it to be noted.

Mr Flamethrower emerged from cover and unleashed a second, more sustained sheet of white-hot incendiary orange flame. Gabe and Jin crouched as it ripped over the cargo, and licked greedily around the edges. When it passed, more of the cargo was blackened and blazing.

Gabe threw a glance in Jin's direction: he was hunched down, in deep concentration, wholly focused on what he was doing. Gabe realised what he was up to, but wasn't sure how it would help them given their present predicament.

The third blast of flame ripped across the deck and licked at the cargo.

Gabe had no choice but to ignore the firepower on all other quarters to keep Mr Flamethrower in check. He blind fired around the steel crate he was behind, and the flames died, but both the gloves he was wearing, and his P90 were ablaze when he drew them back. He beat the flames down, peeled off his gloves, and got ready to fire another burst.

A fourth blast engulfed the cargo box. Their adversary felt closer now. Gabe was swallowed in a furnace heat that seemed to suck all the air from his lungs. His boot, closest to the edge, caught a splash of fuel and was instantly ablaze. He tried to beat these flames out, too, but the mixture wasn't easily extinguished.

Meanwhile, the barrage from other quarters continued.

Jin was right, things were going badly. They couldn't afford to stay there much longer, but escape was beginning to look impossible.

Gabe shifted to take cover behind a huge spool of power cable, and peeked out to fire on Mr Flamethrower again, only to find himself staring straight at him. This time he had not retreated back into cover. He was making his move. Any moment now a blast of gasoline and napalm was going to arc in their direction, and this time it wouldn't be straining to reach the centre of the littered cargo, it would fall right on top of it…

—

Down they sank, until a faint glow appeared beneath them. It grew in intensity until it took shape and the cable met with a diving bell, studded with lights. A few moments later they touched down on the sea bed beside it. A power cable snaked from the diving bell.

Holly and Atana followed the cable, like Theseus's ball of thread, towards the ruins. It led them from sandy seabed to a huge shelf of sea-life-encrusted rock, followed by an almost sheer drop.

They stepped off in unison and drifted down until they met solid ground again and continued to follow the cable until another pool of light appeared in the distance.

Atana's voice entered Holly's ear through the coms.

"There."

The light grew in intensity and clarity, became two distinct sources of illumination under the shadow of a huge sloping shoulder of rock.

A bank of floodlights illuminated the machine they had seen on the video feeds on the monitors in the lab. The wall of metal lay behind it, with the familiar markings they had also seen. A lone diver, one of Grave's mercs, stood guard at the wall, his back to them.

He saw them coming too late, and barely had time to get his dagger out as they closed in.

The fight was ended swiftly, as was the merc.

Atana's sword and Holly's dagger were returned to their sheaths and the merc's body was shoved clear. It drifted away and was soon lost in the darkness.

Holly stared at the markings on the metallic wall. There was no doubt they and the grails were of the same origin, shared the same creators. Holly cast her eyes toward Atana, who stared back, her expression hard to read.

Holly reached out, as they had seen Fine do, to strike the button that would wake the machine beside them, would activate the robotic arm that would perform the gesture upon the markings, which in turn would open a door into the ruins.

Open sesame.

Except before Holly's hand had reached the button, Atana's blocked its path.

The two of them once again locked eyes. Atana looked like she was struggling to remember something.

Holly lowered her hand and Atana reached out and began to perform a gesture with the tips of her fingers across the markings. At first, her movements were hesitant and slow, but soon and steadily became complex and fluid. Holly got the feeling she was watching something once so well-practised it had been second nature.

A tiny pinprick of a hole appeared in the wall. In seconds it was as large as a dinner plate, air bubbles spilling out of it, and soon large enough for both of them to step through, should they choose to.

"How—"

"I don't know." Atana looked to her again. "I swear."

Nothing in Atana's face indicated deceit, quite the opposite. She looked as though she wished she hadn't been able to do what she had just done.

"Ready?"

Atana nodded.

They stepped through the portal.

A moment later it closed behind them.

—

Gabe was pretty sure he knew what he would see if he peeked from behind the corner of the crate. The approaching figure of Mr Flamethrower, the tank of fuel on his back and the flickering flame waving from the end of the weapon's nose. This would be swiftly followed by the gun's nozzle spraying a jet of blazing fuel in his and Jin's direction, unless he was extremely lucky and was able to down the man first.

The odds were not on his side. He needed a dead shot. His adversary hardly needed to aim at all. He began to give himself a count. One, two…

Before he could get to three, something else entirely happened: an eight-foot by eight-foot square steel cargo box to his right shot across the deck as though it had been launched from a cannon.

It rocketed forward, collided with Mr Flamethrower and made a sandwich of him and his weapon with the assistance of the crane's base. With the sandwich filling containing well over the recommended daily amount of gasoline, the result was both inevitable and highly incendiary. The fireball and its resulting mushroom cloud of black smoke erupted on the deck. Gabe and Jin threw themselves to the ground behind a huge spool of power cable to shield from the blast.

When it retreated, Gabe looked to his side to find Jin staring at his hand, which was now enclosed in a snub-nosed point.

In all the chaos, Jin had remembered something Gabe hadn't: the second gesture Atana had tutored them in. The one which transformed the treasure not from the grail they knew into a bracelet, but from the bracelet into a weapon. The weapon Torsten and his clan had called Mjolnir.

Thor's hammer.

The mercs surrounding them had begun to recover from the shock of watching one of their own, perhaps believed to be their trump card, literally go up in flames, and following a short lull, Gabe and Jin were once more under heavy fire.

Now Mr Flamethrower was gone, Gabe leaned out of cover and fired back.

Jin struck a second piece of cargo.

A huge reel of power cable skated across the deck. Five foot tall and almost as wide, weighing maybe half a ton, it sped forward. Gabe had no doubt Holly would have a theory as to how it was possible, the science behind it, but all he knew was that the reel had shot across the deck like a bullet and sent the small group of mercs in its path running. Not all of them escaped it.

Jin was momentarily exposed, and the other mercs didn't miss their window. He staggered as return fire found its mark, and threw himself behind an identical reel that had been sitting beside the first.

Gabe saw Jin check himself. The shots had hit his body armour. His ribs would be smarting, and one or two might even be broken, but not for long. Another concerted barrage of fire from all quarters pummelled their position, reminding them they were still outgunned and surrounded. Taking out Mr Flamethrower had just bought them a little more time, and Jin could smack more items their way, but every item he threw at their adversaries ate away their cover.

Jin tugged at the cable on the reel he was behind and snapped the tail end free. He quickly began to unspool more cable, over a dozen feet of it, as more gunfire beat on their position.

"Gabriel, do you trust me?"

"You have to ask?"

Jin smiled. It was lean and tight, but a smile all the same. He bent and tied the cable he had just unspooled around his ankle and tugged it fast. Seconds later the remaining tail end was wrapped around Gabe's ankle.

Jin stood, drew back his arm, and proceeded to launch a textbook uppercut into the huge reel of cable.

Gabe had perhaps half a second to contemplate it shooting into the air, before the slack between the knot at Jin's ankle and the reel soaring skyward snapped taut. Jin was whipped off his feet and upwards, and an instant later Gabe had joined him.

He looked down to glimpse the deck falling away, and then it was just water beneath him. The weird fairground ride lurch in his stomach flipped polarity as gravity conquered velocity.

Everything switched places. Suddenly Jin and half a ton of power cable were no longer above him, but below. He could see the ocean rushing to embrace them. The reel punched the surface and vanished first. He snatched one hurried breath, and it took Jin and him in quick succession.

They were submerged and sinking fast.

# Chapter Forty-Six

Grave stopped, and raised an arm, bringing the rest of the party to a halt.

Then he looked to Fine.

The billionaire looked hesitant. After a moment he nodded, signalling that Grave should be the one to take a closer look. Grave wasn't surprised. Fine's brand of white-collar courage, boardroom bravado, hard-talking corporate conflict was all well and good, but it was an imitation of true bravery. It wasn't much use when the skin in the game was the skin you were wearing.

The body lay slumped against the wall of the passage. It was dead and looked to have been that way for a long time. What remained was mummified. Bones were visible where the skin and flesh had sunk and dried to a paper-thin layer.

The husk wore something Grave couldn't fail to recognise.

On one arm a fragment, in the bracelet configuration, encircled an emaciated, yellowed arm. The body had one other notable feature.

It was headless.

Grave bent and prodded the remains with the muzzle of his rifle.

He heard a voice over the coms in his diving helmet. It belonged to the weaselly head of Fine's tec team, the Russian, Oblonsky.

"It's human?"

Grave almost smiled. So, he hadn't been the only one questioning Fine's confidence in his historian's theory. Fine's conviction that the fragments were the product of a long-lost advanced civilisation of ancestors who predated man sounded perfectly reasonable. The work his team of historians had done to tie old myths to impossible technology and hard-as-hell to kill targets was perfectly reasonable too, but stepping through that wall of freaky metal...

Nothing here felt of this world. Grave would not have been shocked if on closer inspection the body had looked like a barfly from the *Star Wars* cantina. Ever since accepting this gig, shit had been crazy as fuck on a near-daily basis. The experience had bred liberal expectations and the most open of minds.

He got up and advanced a little further down the passage. He didn't have to walk far to find what he was looking for; he chipped it with his foot like a soccer ball. It rolled to a stop against the body it had once belonged to.

A human head, dehydrated skin wrapped around it like a mask.

He turned back to face the group and beckoned them on. "Who's ready to see what other surprises this place has for us?" he asked.

He raised his hand and waved them on, continuing down the passage.

Fine notably remained a pace or two behind.

They hadn't gone far when it suddenly narrowed, twisted and broke into three. He chose one and kept moving. A short way on the path branched again, and then again. As far as Grave could tell the passages were leading broadly in the same direction, sometimes the different paths so close to one another they simply converged again, or crisscrossed, seemingly for no purpose at all.

These passages felt more sculpted, felt almost grown rather than built. Again, he simply picked one at random. Given they were all leading one way, getting lost didn't seem likely. They could just turn one-eighty and eventually return to the chamber through which they had entered.

The silver-grey metal threaded through the walls did not appear randomly distributed. The thickest, richest seams flowed through some passages more than others, as though pointing the way to something.

As always, Grave trusted in instinct and let it chart his course.

# Chapter Forty-Seven

Holly and Atana had watched the aperture close behind them, sealing them in a spherical space momentarily before another aperture opened before them. Water rolled forwards until it became a puddle at their feet.

They stepped through into a passage.

Holly drew her fingertips across the wall, a pale material marbled with the metal of the chamber and the fragments. The new material was equally singular. It looked soft but was extremely solid, and smooth to the touch. Holly simply knew at once that, like the material the grail was made of, it was something the like of which she had never encountered before.

Like something from another world.

The grail had always felt alien, in the broad sense of the word, but it was also something you could hold in your hands. They were in the ruins of something a great deal larger, a vessel, but from where?

The Silurian hypothesis was all very well, more plausible, and Holly favoured cutting with Occam's razor... It was clear Professor Mervin Pickering *was* biased. He didn't want the visitors in the story or the object he found depicted in ancient images to be alien, or from another dimension, or the future, or anything else that smacked of science fiction, because he viewed people who made such claims about the construction of the pyramids, or the Nazca lines, or other supposed works of ancient alien visitors as crackpots and pseudoscientists.

Being lumped into their fold had come close to ruining his career, and had succeeded in demolishing his credibility.

Given what was knowable, the Silurian hypothesis was more plausible than the alternative.

But was the theory also more alluring because it was more comfortable?

Alien visitors. The phrase conjured images of black and white movie footage with spinning hubcaps hanging from catgut, of bad actors in bad suits, or more contemporary blockbusters rendered in overblown CGI. Alien visitors, chariots of the gods, little green men building ancient pyramids, grist for kooks and fantasists.

The odds of an advanced civilisation emerging on Earth and then becoming lost to all historical records was magnitudes more likely, because life inarguably exists on Earth, and has done for billions of years, with complex life having been around hundreds of millions. The dinosaurs were roaming around over two hundred million years ago.

The planet was abundant with life. That another variation might have achieved a level of sophistication equal to or beyond that of man was not outlandish at all. Man had evolved from one of the earliest known mammals, the morganucodontids, tiny shrew-sized creatures that lived among the dinosaurs over two million years ago, into a complex and sophisticated creature who had built wonders and unravelled innumerable secrets of how the universe he inhabited operated.

For life to have spontaneously occurred somewhere else in the cosmos was infinitely more questionable.

By current evidence, extremely limited though it was, life existed here on Earth and nowhere else.

One could consider the scale of the universe, how myopic mankind's view, how limited its reach, and argue life was abundant, had to be abundant, but ultimately the odds were unknown. The best evidence, positive or negative, lies beyond our reach.

The nearest star is over four light years away. If one were to take the trip at the speed of a rocket destined for the moon, at its peak, reaching the nearest star offers a journey lasting one hundred thousand years.

Life might be non-existent, rare, or abundant, and supposing it was abundant, there remained the question of its reaching Earth.

The odds of another being becoming advanced enough for interstellar travel, and being inclined to reach Earth among all the universe's other celestial bodies, and to coincide with mankind's inevitably brief tenure on it… Compared to another advanced species evolving and thriving for a time at home, Holly was prepared to admit, the odds did seem, well, astronomical.

But not impossible.

—

Atana paused in the passage, reaching for something inside her, maddeningly beyond her grasp, a shadow among shadows, something buried deep, buried for a very long time. She remembered this place, or had a feeling she did.

She touched the wall, and found something familiar in its strange, soft yet unyielding surface. She moved her fingers to one of the seams of silver-grey that shot through it like marble, half hoping and half fearing it might work as a catalyst, breaching the barrier between and her lost memories, where the truth lay.

It didn't, so she reached up and pulled her helmet free, allowing it to fall to the ground. Beside her, Holly looked ready to intervene, surprised at what she had done. They looked to each other as Atana drew in a deep breath, and then exhaled.

"It's fine. I can breathe. We can breathe."

Holly tentatively removed her helmet but held onto it as she too drew a series of deep breaths. With the helmet lights directed downwards, it was possible to see the passage ahead was not as dark as it had appeared. When Atana's helmet light automatically shut off, detecting it had been removed, the ambient light seemed to increase. When Holly's helmet light did the same, there was no doubt it had.

The passage wasn't dark; the pale material seemed to possess its own reactive, intrinsic form of illumination.

"We need to keep moving," Holly said.

Atana nodded, and they continued onward, hoping to intercept Fine and his group, to see what the ruins held, to find the truth, and prevent something terrible but unremembered from occurring.

They encountered the body first.

Holly knelt by it, studied the headless, mummified corpse and the severed mummified head resting against it.

Now a shadow broke from the shadows, the memory glinting from the gloom, vivid, but brief: Atana seized upon it, saw the sweep of a bronze sword, followed by an arc of blood as a head spun through the air, the body it once belonged to toppling…

To rest where they found it now.

The memory retreated back into the darkness. Atana found Holly staring up at her.

"What?"

"I was here," Atana answered, "I think I did this."

# Chapter Forty-Eight

Gabe and Jin were dragged into the depths, swallowed whole.

What little light there was soon died, and it was left to the pressure which pushed on them to speak to how deep they were plunging.

Gabe struggled to hold his breath, the fight to avoid drawing in a lungful of water warring with the urge to draw in a lungful of anything at all.

The darkness was so complete, so utter, that Jin, who was only a short distance below him, tethered to the very same trailing length of power cable, was invisible.

Eventually, after how long he couldn't have said, an age or just a few minutes, biological impulse defeated will and Gabe heaved in a chest full of cold seawater. His body swiftly made it clear it did not welcome the introduction, but he didn't drown.

The desperate urge to draw breath first diminished and then vanished entirely. His lungs tried a few testing breaths and went through the motions of inhaling and exhaling. The effort was laboured, and uncomfortable, but grew less so with every breath.

Gabe had no doubt the grail's gift was doing something remarkable, and like most of what it did, the mechanics were entirely beyond his understanding.

There was a tremor in the cable tied to his ankle, and slowly his feet hit something solid. They had reached the seabed. He peered into the darkness and saw the faintest of glows nearby.

He felt something graze him, then Jin's hand on his wrist. The hand was joined by another and they climbed down to his ankle. The power cable was loosed and Jin's hands climbed back up, to take hold of his wrist again.

They started to walk across the sea bed, heading for the pale light close by, which gained shape and grew brighter as they approached. Jin took shape beside him, too, until his friend felt confident enough to release his wrist.

They saw the illuminated body loom before them, a diver, drifting but otherwise motionless, one of Grave's men. Jin snagged him and examined what he could see. The man was dead. His torch was appropriated, and the rest of him pushed from their path. Another source of light lay ahead.

They kept going, closing in on it.

It resolved into a bank of lamps, installed to illuminate the thing they had seen on the video feeds in the lab.

A wall of rock lay ahead, and within it a seam exposing a smooth metallic wall. The markings they had seen were there too, as was the machine designed to decipher them and perform the gesture that opened the portal within.

Jin reached the machine first and hit the button on its control panel. Its robotic arm awoke and began to draw its carbon fibre finger over the markings on the wall. The moment the arm had completed its work, and before it even came to rest, the aperture appeared.

It expanded, became a perfect circle offering access to a pitch-black space beyond.

Gabe and Jin stepped over the threshold, and the wall closed.

And then a weak light appeared and ballooned in front of them. The water level fell until it covered only their feet, the rest of it rushing forward into whatever space lay ahead.

Surrounded once more by air, Gabe's body reacted accordingly. He breathed out, and immediately heaved, ejecting half a lungful of seawater. Beside him, Jin was doing the same thing. A few more heaves and a fit of coughing, and he and Jin were again breathing air.

The passage ahead was bright enough to discern a path.

They entered it.

Holly was in there somewhere, a reckless billionaire was in there, a bunch of conscienceless mercenaries was in there, and a mystery sealed up tight for perhaps over five thousand years.

–

Atana pushed onward, fuelled by a new sense of urgency.

There had been more flashes, more shadows rising from the gloom to tease, taunt, and confuse her. She remembered these passages, their labyrinthian weave, she glimpsed a moment of running through them, her heart pounding in her like a drum, carrying a raw, unvarnished, fear.

*She hates the feeling, despises it, wants nothing more than to never feel it or anything like it again. She is not alone in the passage. Others are here, and they are running too. A few lie dead in her wake, cut down.*

*The passage tilts and shifts as the vessel plunges down, down to the bottom of the ocean—*

"Atana?"

She paused, the shadows she had chased were bolder now, emerging into the light. Where once she had fought to grasp them, they now seemed ready to emerge. Like falling dominos, they rushed to spill in front of her. She almost wanted to laugh. She had been so desperate to remember. How did the phrase go? Be careful what you wish for?

Holly was sprinting beside her, fighting to keep up.

She had to explain. They couldn't allow Fine and his mercenaries to clumsily stumble around, it was too dangerous, far too dangerous…

"We have to hurry. They can't reach it before we do."

"Reach what?"

"The end of everything you know."

"I don't understand. Atana—"

They spilt from the passage into a huge cathedral-like space. If the passages were like arteries, this was the heart they led to. The spiralling architecture of the passages was more evident here. The winding arcs that formed their walls reached out and spoked into columns that climbed from floor to ceiling. Here they formed a latticework, almost a honeycomb of columns and beams, all bending around one focal point at the centre.

It was as though everything around it spoke to its importance, its singular place in the heart of everything. The silver-grey threads that wove through the pale mottled material converged and terminated here too, into one column, and the ominously pregnant bulge at its centre.

Atana felt drawn to it, a magnetic attraction that conversely seeped dread through her veins with every step she took towards it. As she approached the pillar it peeled open like a flower, the pregnant bulge folding outwards, exposing what lay within.

A metallic grey sphere small enough to hold in her hand and suspended by threads so fine that from anywhere but this distance, they might have appeared invisible.

The barrier dividing her from her past suddenly, and wholly, collapsed.

# Chapter Forty-Nine

Holly followed Atana to the centre of the chamber, just a pace or two behind, to the small metallic grey sphere at its heart.

The chamber gave the best glimpse yet of the nature of the ruins they were in, of the shared geometric motifs, complex but recursive, which formed the architecture. They had the hypnotic echoes of fractal patterns, the secret but fundamental code of nature, universal, observed in the largest and smallest of things, patterns viewed through electron microscopes and the Webb or Hubble telescope alike. She considered the technology the grail contained. She had once read a paper on nanotech that predicted a revolution in construction, how cities of the future could be built atom by atom from waste into towering metropolises, designed on the fly by AI utilising tried and mathematical procedures. She had wondered what something like that would look like. Perhaps she was looking at an example right now.

They reached the central column and the object at its heart.

"What is it?"

"An engine of destruction… and creation. The blueprint for a world ready for thieves."

"You remember?"

"More than I want to. The story in Mervin Pickering's tablets, the same one the priestess meant to share with me so long ago, it does not lie. The people who visited the ancient Minoans did mean to destroy them, but not just their people, or their island. They meant to destroy *everything*, scour this world clean, shred its surface to raw matter, and then, once every molecule had been undone, to reassemble it particle by particle, into an ecology compatible for its intended colonizers."

Holly's mind raced to marry Mervin's story, the tablets' story, with what surrounded her.

Visitors had arrived on the ancient Minoans' shore. They had taken a brief look at what they intended to erase, had catalogued it, perhaps... Except one had grown to care for the Minoans more than her own. She had appeared to save them, but vanished. Atana had stumbled into the path of an island hunter, emaciated and a blank slate over a thousand years later, wearing the bracelet.

"Colonizers... You mean from somewhere out there, another galaxy?" Holly shook her head, "But the remains we passed—"

"Were human? Not really. You said it to me yourself, your work with Jin and his companion Blake, your project team: the treasure alters one's DNA. Those of us who use it are no longer truly human, we are changed. 'Tweaks' is how you put it, but what if they're only tweaks if you happen to be human already?

"The ones who visited the ancient Minoans, their changes went beyond a few beneficial tweaks like resilience and agelessness. They may have appeared human, but that was only because of the environment they needed to explore. They had to bend to fit the place they had found before they could bend the place to fit themselves.

"What more efficient way to tolerate an alien environment, to breathe its air, to be attuned to its climate, to traverse its landscape, than to mimic the anatomy of a creature which has evolved over millions of years to meet its particular idiosyncrasies?

To select its apex predator, its most advanced organisms, and take on that creature's form."

Holly stared down at the bracelet wrapped around her forearm, "The grail is… an organic space suit?"

"The remains we passed looked human, but what you saw was a lie."

"What would the truth have looked like?"

Atana turned her eyes to face her, and they both knew what Holly had truly asked.

"You mean, what did I once look like?"

# Chapter Fifty

Atana didn't want to answer the question, didn't want to accept the truth of it.

She didn't want to relinquish her humanity.

Instead, she turned her eyes to the ball of silver-grey suspended before them.

The wall barring her from her past had crumbled, and the vista confronting her across the divide was almost too enormous to digest, the truths it revealed threatening to tear down everything, to call into question her very identity, the person she had believed herself to be.

She realised too, that she, or some essential, ancient, part of her, had helped build the wall, and maintained it all this time. It wasn't simply that she couldn't remember, it was that she had chosen not to.

Once the wall faltered, everything was there.

The truth of what she was lay in a gesture Torsten and his clan had never discovered, one that would not have done anything for them or to them if they had. It configured the treasure, or tool, for a new purpose: to change her back into what she had once been, a drone, a spore, a slave, a process to enable the theft of worlds...

She refused to accept that being as her true self.

Whatever she had been before, the creature who had emerged from this vessel to survey the life it planned to casually destroy had simply looked like Atana. Like those who stepped out with it, whose lungs also breathed the island's humid fragranced air, who left human-shaped footprints in the dirt, whose eyes drank in the contours and colours of a strange and distant world and heard its vibrations through the same ears, the wash of the ocean hissing against the shore and the birdsong in the trees, whose new skins felt the warm breeze, it was not honestly human. It was not human in the literal sense, but also because they were bereft of anything close to the figurative concept of humanity.

How had Mervin's translation put it? *Her kind are cold. They place no value in tenderness, or any other emotion.*

They were creatures of instinct and reason, and while life in the cosmos was not uncommon, the feelings warring in them now were. The intricate marriage of intellect and sensation was something new, and for all but a few, entirely abhorrent.

They were assaulted with a cacophony of unwanted stimulus, a maelstrom of fear, disgust, sadness and anxiety. It was a vile infection that ate into their bones and contaminated their flesh, a sickness they immediately craved to shed. The sooner their assessment of what existed was complete, the sooner the extant life could be erased and the seed released to prime the planet for a new population, perhaps in thousands of years, perhaps millions. The creatures of the future that their current work would give rise to would eventually join others, and Earth would be simply one more home for the inevitable expansion of an exponentially growing population. Beings who reproduced, but did not age, and rarely died.

For one of the visitors, the transformation was different. For her, it was like finding herself alive for the first time, intoxicating and exciting.

She loathed returning to their vessel, and instead spent as much time as she could with the beings who inhabited the island. She became beguiled by them, with the richness of their existence, the power of their bonds for one another, and the bonds she felt forming between herself and them.

As her companions raced to wipe all she saw from existence, she realised she could not allow their destruction to come to pass, and when the time came, she acted.

She sneaked back onto the vessel, undid it, and drove it deep into the ocean where it would never be reached, where the seed of destruction it carried would lie sealed away for eternity. She began to kill her companions one by one as they slept.

She dispatched some, but not all, before her betrayal could be discovered.

As the vessel plunged into the cold deep of the ocean she was forced to flee, and the survivors chased after her.

One lost their life to the blade of a bronze sword, a prized gift from her new friends on the island. Three escaped behind her as the vessel crashed into the side of the chasm on the sea bed where she had intended it to lie forgotten and unreachable.

The collision buried both pursuers and pursued under rock, and crushed them there, killing all but one.

She was trapped, alive but a prisoner, to slide into hibernation.

Together with the remains of the others, she was freed over a thousand years later, when the pre-shocks foreshadowing the eruption on Thera caused the rocks burying them to shift and tumble into the abyss nearby. All drifted into the ocean, to be washed up with their treasures on distant shores.

Atana, no longer crushed and broken but a husk nonetheless, washed up on the coast of Crete, and came to wander its forests, naked, bleach white, and close to skin and bone.

She had forgotten what she had been, but with a tribes' kindness and care had discovered who she truly was.

She looked at Holly standing beside her.

"I know what I have to do, but there's something I have to, want to, tell you first."

# Chapter Fifty-One

Truth be told, Grave couldn't quite believe his eyes. Credit where it was due: these assholes were as tenacious as they were tough.

The passage had widened onto a chamber. In it, he saw something that made him stop his group dead. Fine almost bumped into him before he saw them too.

*They* were here, or two of them, at least.

The women were standing before a column, obscuring something and talking. Neither was wearing breathing gear. From where he stood, his hearing hampered by the EX-SADS helmet, he couldn't make out any of what they were saying. It didn't matter. The important thing was that they were both distracted and it seemed he had the jump on them.

He was being offered another opportunity to do what he was keenly aware he had failed to do more than once now: to eliminate the previous owners of the fragments. The simple fact they could be here, have reached this depth into the wreck before them, was testament to the fact that as long as they lived, they would prove a threat and a complication.

Grave shouldered his rifle, got on the coms, "It's them."

"Who?" Fine asked.

"Two of the folks you had me steal your nice shiny fragments from."

"How the hell are they here?"

"Does it matter? I'm going to kill them. We can work out the how later."

Grave hissed instructions to his men, instructing them to fan out and creep deeper into the chamber, using the freaky columns twisting from ground to ceiling as cover until they got his word and were ready to strike. He kept one back to wait at the neck of the passage and babysit Fine and the Ruskie, Oblonsky.

Grave crept to a column which offered him a clear line of fire on the two women. He and the men to their left would target the dark-haired one, the rest on the right could deal with the blonde. If all went well, they could focus enough fire on both that it would be impossible to tell what colour hair each once had.

The blonde was animated; she gestured at the column in front of them. He couldn't get a good look, and then the dark-haired one shifted and he finally had a clear view.

There was a small grey ball in the middle of the column. At first, Grave thought it was hovering in mid-air, and then he saw it was held by a clutch of fine threads, no thicker than strands of hair.

There was something about that ball, or perhaps not the ball itself, but how this whole chamber, the whole vessel seemed to exist around it…

He pulled his mind and his concentration back to the task at hand, raised the rifle to his eye, and squinted down the sight until the dark-haired woman's head lined up just so…

Over the coms, he said, "On my word, three, two… one."

He squeezed his trigger finger.

—

Holly threw herself at Atana with such force they both crashed awkwardly to the ground as gunfire tore through the chamber, seemingly from all directions at once. Lumps of the column they had been standing in front of were smashed loose and shattered. The grey seams remained intact, seemingly impervious.

Holly had glimpsed movement, and in the half-second her gaze swept across the chamber saw multiple shapes low in the shadows, and the tip of a rifle muzzle. It was enough. They weren't alone.

She and Atana scrambled behind a nearby column and fired back.

Holly knew from the video feed in the lab that Fine's party had been thirteen strong. Discounting Fine, that allowed for as many as eleven armed mercenaries. Fire was coming from both flanks. They couldn't stay where they were, so they backed up into the chamber.

Then Holly saw one figure scuttle from behind one column to another deeper into the chamber, trying to get behind them. She brought her P90 up, drew a bead and hit her man. The burst hit him square in the chest, but failed to take him out. The fancy diving suit he wore was designed to withstand pressures hundreds of meters below the ocean, and it seemed to offer a surprising level of protection from gunfire too. The merc stumbled and his suit took a battering, but he didn't go down. He staggered in ungainly but ultimately successful fashion into cover. He wouldn't get his no-scratch deposit back, but he might live to return it to the dealer.

Multiple bursts of gunfire from different directions slammed into the column Holly and Atana were hunkered behind. Holly saw a second figure scurry forward, again trying to outmanoeuvre them.

As she watched, multiple figures on both sides did the same. From the corner of her eye Holly saw one on their left dart closer, and more than one on her right. She and Atana fired on them but the forest of columns between them favoured their foes rather than them.

They had been caught too far on the back foot, and if they stayed where they were, all too soon they would be surrounded.

Atana knew it, too.

She pointed deeper into the chamber, and back to back they abandoned the large central column and broke for the next nearest one behind them, firing as they went.

—

Benedict Fine watched Grave's men fan out across the floor, firing on the two women near the central column as they retreated deep into the chamber. They closed in, driving their prey deeper still.

The silver-grey sphere hung in the gossamer-thin latticework of the central column they had deserted.

He found he could scarcely take his eyes off it.

He had no idea what it was, but if they wanted it, he wanted it. Context alone was enough to attest to its value and importance. It was as though not just the chamber they were in, but the entire ruin they had negotiated were wrapped around it.

A simple silver-grey ball.

Except nothing about the fragments or these ruins was simple. So, while he had no idea what the sphere was, he had already decided he would not leave here without it.

He turned to Oblonsky crouched beside him, and adjusted his coms setting so that only the Russian would hear what he said next: a command.

"Get it. Now while we can. Trust me, Grave has found eliminating these people difficult enough. Grab that object and we can make our own way out of here, back to the diving bell, and the safety of the Oculus."

—

Oblonsky heard Fine clearly enough, but the request struck him as insane. Run out into a chamber filled with gunfire to grab the object. Him? Was Fine serious?

One look at his face behind the EX-SADS helmet's faceplate left no doubt.

Oblonsky wondered when the man had last been told no.

And yet, the promise of being gone from this place, the prospect of a swift return to the safety of the ship… This was very tempting indeed. How long would it take to sprint and pluck the small grey sphere from the column and sprint back, especially if he engaged the EX-SADS' enhanced mode? Twenty, thirty seconds? In half a minute they could be on their way to safety, leaving the fighting and the danger to those better suited to it. These men had once chosen battlegrounds as their workplace. He had never signed up for anything but the quiet confines of a laboratory.

There was the question of why Fine couldn't just dash and grab the object himself, of course, if he wanted it so badly, but Oblonsky already knew the answer.

Grave and his mercs continued to drive the two women deeper into the chamber, moving the battle further from the centre of the room where the sphere was.

Oblonsky swallowed, and chose to suspend all reflection over what he was about to do in the full knowledge it would lead him to abandon the attempt. He activated his EX-SADS' enhanced mode and instantly perceived the rig grow almost weightless as the motors delivered more power to its exoskeleton.

Then he broke from the cover where he and Fine were huddled.

With the EX-SADS in enhanced mode, it was as if his own muscles had suddenly doubled in strength and endurance. His sprint to the central column felt Olympian in pace. Before he knew it he was there in front of the silver-grey sphere. In just as brief a spell he could be back at Fine's side, and they could set about getting the hell out of these unnatural and unnerving ruins.

The silver-grey ball was right in front of him, no bigger than his hand. It was cast from the same material as the fragments, but utterly featureless, without marking or blemish. Somehow unremarkable and powerful at the same time.

He reached out and tore it free of the threads that held it in place…

# Chapter Fifty-Two

The mercs were closing in, and Atana and Holly were being herded into a spot where they could be surrounded and pinned down.

Atana saw one adversary emerge, snap his weapon to her position and fire, an instant after she did.

Her bullets pinged off the merc's suit, and he staggered, his barrage running wild. What she saw too late was his companion who spun from another position nearby. He fired too, on the heels of her burst. His fire caught her flank, and she experienced an explosion of pain.

He pressed on, bolder now she was wounded, aimed again.

The next burst of fire came an instant later, but it wasn't his. His helmet was drilled and didn't survive the assault. He dropped to the floor. The second merc behind cover came under fire as well. His suit was struck by several rounds, enough for him to turn and receive a second serving that put him down too.

Atana and Holly watched as Gabe and Jin advanced from the neck of a passage at the side of the chamber.

Their odds suddenly looked more favourable.

It was then Atana's gaze moved across the central column and stopped dead.

A figure was standing in front of it, and he was reaching out for the silver-grey sphere.

She heard herself scream 'NO!' as his fingers closed around it.

—

Oblonsky's gloved fingers closed around the sphere. He had it, right there in his hand, and pulled it towards him. The myriad silver threads holding it in place offered no resistance, seemed to almost melt and offer it willingly.

His first thought was that the sphere was hot.

A sharp sting of pain lit up his palm. He twisted his wrist to look.

The sphere was melting, sinking through his fingers. It had lost its definition and sheen, was now more like a clump of grey goo, and stuck fast to his glove.

Suddenly his hand was on fire.

He whipped his arm, attempting to shake the grey goop free, to little effect. It was then he realised that the stuff was eating through his glove, the tough but intricate joins of his EX-SADS offering no protection. The goo had already consumed them, and with utter horror, Oleg realised his hand was being eaten away too. The goo was like a small creature with needle-sharp teeth chewing on his hand.

He spun, staring back imploringly at Fine. Someone needed to help him, to get it off. The expression he found on Fine's face, framed by the EX-SADS helmet, was no comfort at all. Fine's shocked eyes were fastened to his hand.

Only, when he followed Fine's gaze down to his own hand, it wasn't technically true to say it was a hand at all any more.

Everything from the tips of his erstwhile fingers to just before his elbow was gone. The grey goo had consumed them, and seemed to have grown in size as a result. The mass was now moving apace up to his shoulder.

When he started to scream, it was not only into his helmet but over the coms into the rest of the group.

—

Oblonsky's screams held Fine in stunned paralysis. The grey goop had fastened onto Oblonsky, and now leapt to his shoulder and crept up his neck.

The gloved hand and armoured arm that had grasped the poisoned apple were already gone. Fine had glimpsed a knob of bone for a moment as the mass ate his elbow, and quickly moved to consume his upper arm.

That was when Oblonsky's eyes had turned on him.

Wide as saucepan lids, they ably communicated the man's sheer terror at what was happening to him. Then the goop climbed his neck and swam around the back of his head, and a half-second later the faceplate of his helmet was spattered with blood and Oblonsky's terrified gaze was obscured.

Fine saw blood rise inside the helmet, lapping inches from the top of the glass, before the goo folded around this, too.

In seconds the fragment project team lead had been reduced to a stumbling, armless, headless torso of grey goop.

What remained of the Russian managed two more steps before it collapsed and the legs were consumed too. The goo settled, becoming a pool of liquid, which began to expand.

Throughout all this Fine had been frozen.

As the mass settled into a lump and then a puddle, expanding accordingly, as it reached towards where he cowered, the terror that had held him in place seemed to flip and release him.

He stumbled back, keen to be away from the grey mass but wary of taking his eyes off it. The puddle seemed to sense him and suddenly lurch in his direction, spilling across the ground, cutting him off from the passage by which he had entered. He looked around, to the many other passages that connected to the chamber, hurried to the next closest and ran like hell.

—

Grave could spot a situation going south, and this one was, fast.

In the space of a minute, he had gone from having the women surrounded and on the back foot, finally ready to be dispatched for good, to having the other two Brooklyn targets appear from fucking nowhere and start firing on his men.

This was followed by the screams of Fine's scientist.

Grave had looked back to see why.

The idiot scientist was stumbling around, and seemed to have lost his arm. He had a weird grey mass stuck to him, which was rapidly on the move. As Grave watched, it swallowed his head, and his screams.

That was when he noticed that the column which had once held a small grey sphere at its centre now did not.

The stumbling mass had once been a scientist toppled over and melted into a puddle, which sank and consequently doubled in size as Grave watched.

He caught sight of Fine, as the billionaire tried to retreat into the passage, and saw the puddle shoot in his direction, cutting him off, and forcing him in another direction, towards another passage.

Fine vanished from sight.

It was enough for Grave. There wasn't a man alive or dead who had deep enough pockets to tackle shit this crazy. The puddle was spreading fast, and soon nowhere in the chamber would be safe.

He issued the command.

"Okay, Ghosts, we're pulling out. Now!"

—

The man Gabe was firing on suddenly abandoned his position and commenced a retreat. He slipped back through the forest of arcing columns, steering well clear of the pool of silver-grey muck which was creeping swiftly across the rear right-hand side of the chamber.

Gabe had borne witness to the same bizarre horror show they all had, seen the guy stumbling away from the central column consumed by who-knew-the-fuck-what until there was no guy left.

The other mercs were retreating too, and in moments their fire had petered out as they vanished across the chamber and into one of the passages leading back, presumably toward the entrance.

With them gone he was finally able to reach Holly.

She hurried to intercept him.

They looked across the chamber to see Atana and Jin heading over, too. Atana was clutching her side. She had taken damage.

Gabe looked at her, pointed to the spreading goo. "What is that stuff?" he asked.

"The end." It was not the most expansive description, but it seemed to cover the important details. She continued, "You all have to get out of here. I'll take care of it. There's no stopping it now, but it knows not to deconstruct anything that belongs here, including anyone wearing one of these." She twisted her arm, indicated her bracelet. "But if one speck of that stuff gets beyond the confines of this place…"

"What do you plan to do?" Holly asked.

"Finish what was started."

"We can stay and help—" Jin began.

Atana shook her head. "No, actually you can't, not now. Only I can do what needs to be done, and I'll find it easier knowing the three of you are safe."

Without another word, Atana broke away, striding across the chamber until she met the goop creeping steadily across the floor and up the walls. When she was close enough, something remarkable happened: it suddenly cut around her, leaving a perfect circle where she stood. She stayed that way for a moment, as if to reassure them it was safe, then beckoned them over.

Sure enough, when Gabe reached the edge of the goop it cut around him, then Jin and Holly, leaving an intersecting pattern of naked ground around each of their feet.

Atana headed for one of the passages ahead. They followed.

Once they were deep enough in, with the goop in their wake, but creeping relentlessly at their heels, she pointed to the bracelets they each wore.

"They can't leave here, not again, not ever," she said. "It's time humanity was free of them."

Gabe looked to Jin, and found his friend already executing the gesture that would remove the bracelet from his arm. It slipped off, and seconds later reverted to the object he had been custodian to for over five hundred years. He passed it to Atana, who tossed it to the ground.

Soon it was joined by two more.

Atana cast a glance behind her and saw the creeping grey material had caught them up. In less than a minute it would reach where they stood. If they were leaving, it was now or never.

Atana began to back away towards it. "Run!" she shouted.

"You'll try to get out too?" asked Holly.

"If I can."

Gabe heard the words, but nothing in Atana's face matched them.

He tugged Holly away.

They took Atana's advice and ran.

# Chapter Fifty-Three

Atana watched her friends depart into the passage, turned, and headed in the opposite direction, deeper into the ruins of the vessel.

With the wall between her and her past now broken, she knew what she had done. She knew what she was, what this place was, what had to be done, and how to do it.

She plunged back into the chamber, and the twisting intersecting passages on the other side, knowing they were less for navigation or access than to support the mechanisms surrounding them, until she reached another place.

This second chamber was not as large as the previous one, but no less distinct.

It too held a central column, only this one was comprised of the familiar grey metallic material, and covered in those equally familiar sweeping markings. A ring of devices encircled the column, save for a few gaps. The ring was incomplete, with some devices missing.

She knew what had to be done now, and how to make things right.

It was the only way to keep everything she had grown to love safe.

The seed built to scour a planet had been set loose and was striving to carry out its purpose, to find foreign matter, reduce it to the rawest of particles, and then replicate itself until everything was gone, at which point it would begin its next task.

All that raw matter would be reassembled, and slowly, over millions of years, would evolve a new home, to suit a different creature, who required a different ecology, a different atmosphere. Earth would become one of many such stolen worlds ready for a burgeoning population that lay light years away.

She performed the gesture on her bracelet.

It slipped from her forearm and returned to its resting state, the object Holly, Gabriel and Jin had called the grail, what Torsten's clan had called Mjolnir. She suspected it had gone by many names as it tumbled secretly through human history, mystifying and amazing those who crossed its path.

It was none of these things. It was simply a tool.

She spared a thought for her new friends, dearly hoping their flight from this place had been successful, that they had escaped before they became trapped. Her memories, once more her own, recalled her flight from the vessel five and a half thousand years ago with a stark and sudden stab of clarity. She recalled the panic and anger, the slaughtered bodies of her companions in her wake…

She held the tool in her hands, knelt before the column, and pushed it into one of the gaps in the cuff encircling the column.

It connected neatly, like lock and key.

Her gaze roved the others that comprised the ring. They were similar, but not identical. While the indentations on hers welcomed a human hand, these had wider bases, with indentations shaped to fit something very different, something with more and differently-shaped fingers, larger and longer, possessed of considerably more joints…

Atana stared down the tool's mouth, saw the glint of the blades that awaited, and thrust her hand into it.

This time the blades did not taste her familiar blood and withdraw. They were set for another task and bit deep, setting a chain reaction in motion. The technology that flowed through her veins and had rewritten her natural blueprint to turn her human, now received a new instruction to enact the opposite, to make her what she once had been.

The transition was painful.

Atana briefly heard her own screams, until either the mouth from which they issued or the ears which caught them vanished, all replaced by new organs, new senses. She was being unmade. Stripped cell by cell and rebuilt, torn apart and reassembled.

When the change was complete, the tool she had carried through six millennia was changed too. Now it was identical to those around it, the base and the indentations upon it befitting the anatomy which filled them.

The thing that was once Atana removed the appendage pressed into those crests and ridges.

The change was stark and extended far beyond anatomy.

A hollow now existed within it, a cold cavity where something precious had been excised.

Something unique and wonderful.

What some men would call a soul, or others humanity.

The enigmatic engine, where the rare alchemy of complex reason and complex sensation collided, which afforded men and women slack on the tether which enslaved most other creatures to simple instinct, which allowed them to transcend base drives like survival and reproduction, was gone.

The creature Atana had reverted to was of a different kind. Its race had no artists or philosophers, no religions, no concept of a soul. It lacked any sense of an essence that transcended matter, of something ethereally eternal.

There was a void at the heart of what Atana had become, an empty place where something treasured had lived, a chaotic cauldron where love, hate, passion, joy, despair, and desire bubbled…

All that lingered was the decaying memory of what it felt to be truly alive, and yet this ghost of humanity was potent, its shadow enough to prove it had lost something of inestimable value, to want it back so keenly she would do almost anything.

Thousands of years ago, it had been enough to fuel betrayal and murder.

As the thing that was Atana reflected on these events, the ghost of her humanity mourned its past, and mourned the knowledge that it would fade and be forgotten in time, and not even a shadow of it would remain.

Then the woman called Atana would truly be dead. What stood in her place would forget what it was that had made the messy, violent, wondrous, marvellous experience of humanity so worth saving.

But while it still survived, it had work to do. It strode to the markings covering the wall and set to work.

–

Gabe was running, as fast as his legs would carry him, and so were Holly and Jin beside him. The passages they plunged down bent and crisscrossed, but mostly seemed to run in the same direction.

When the ground suddenly lurched under his feet, he almost lost his footing. He looked to Holly and Jin, who had also had to fight to keep their balance. A second jolt followed the first, accompanied by an ominous growl that seemed to come from all around them.

The passage was shaking.

No, not the passage: the ruins, the whole thing.

The path ahead curved sharply and joined with another passage that ran almost parallel from the right.

A figure appeared on Gabe's flank, cutting into their passage from the connecting one. The man, intent, as they were on getting the hell out of the ruins, almost crashed into him.

Less than two seconds later it was evident he wasn't alone. The merc was joined by several others who spilt into the passage behind them.

Gabe had reached for his weapon and fired on the one closest on his heels.

The merc staggered backwards as the burst from the P90 hit him square in the chest. The suit he wore soaked up the damage but the impact was still enough to stagger him, and a sudden jolt beneath their feet slowed him further.

Unfortunately, return fire from the rest of the group wasn't slow in coming.

Gabe, Holly and Jin weaved to make themselves harder targets and intermittently fired back.

The passage suddenly lurched more violently, tilting markedly upwards, and both groups found themselves thrown off their feet to the ground.

For a moment they were all strewn across the floor of the passage, staring at one another, Gabe into the face of a hulking figure he was pretty sure should be dead, given he had emptied nearly a full M4 mag into him back at The Shell.

A digital readout, like a name tag below the glass faceplate of the helmet the man wore, identified him. The display carried his name, the same one that had been attached to his video feed in the lab. GRAVE. This was the leader of the mercenary unit Fine had hired, Carson Grave.

He looked over to Holly, "Are you seein—"

"I am."

They both knew what it meant, but were not in a position to give it a great deal of consideration.

One of the mercs was jabbing a finger behind him.

Then they all saw it.

The grey goo was racing up the passage. It had climbed from floor to ceiling to coat the entire passage wall and seemed to be moving a lot faster than it had been.

Unnervingly fast.

Both groups scrambled to their feet.

And both were soon running again, suddenly less concerned by one another than they were by the thing which seemed happy to indiscriminately consume any of them.

To Gabe's surprise, the mercs were keeping pace, one or two were even gaining on them. He, Holly and Jin might not be afflicted by fatigue due to the grail's gift, but in suits, these men should be fighting to maintain a healthy jog by now, not the sprint they were. It had to be the suits.

Letting them get ahead was too dangerous.

Gabe fired on one as he drew level, and nailed one of the merc's legs. The man stumbled and went over. Gabe knew he should focus on escaping, but couldn't seem to stop himself from glancing back. A couple of the fallen merc's companions were forced to hurdle over him as he tumbled into their path.

Like Gabe, they looked back and saw the grey goop snare him.

In an instant, it was slipping up his legs as he flailed. Now Gabe did tear his eyes away.

Head down he pumped his legs against the sharper incline of the path and hoped the exit chamber was close.

—

The floor rumbled and shook as the ruins commenced tearing themselves free from the shelf of rock and rubble that had encased them for thousands of years.

The thing that had once been Atana abandoned the markings. With this task initiated it advanced to the next. It had one more promise to keep to the woman it had once been.

She turned and headed back into the ruins, knowing time was short. The engine designed to devour worlds was racing through the ruins, in all directions.

She had to reach her quarry before it reached her.

—

The passages had started to converge, funnelling them all together like competitors in some sort of insane foot race. The convergence spoke to something else, too; they were closing in on the entrance chamber.

As if to confirm Gabe's assumption, out of the gloom the headless mummified body they had passed on the way in appeared in his path.

Like everyone else, he was pumping arms and legs with all he had, sprinting towards salvation. Gabe vaulted over the headless remains, certain now they were very close to the chamber.

The ground lurched violently.

As a group, they were all thrown up and crashed into the top of the passage.

Then crashed down as gravity snatched them back.

The litter of runners scrambled to their feet and resumed their dash to the exit, but the jolt hadn't interrupted the path of the grey goop. It was close now, dangerously close, and some at the tail end of the pack were too slow.

Gabe saw the goo reach them. He snapped his gaze back in the other direction. He didn't need to see more, not with the goop almost close enough to spit into.

Then there it was: the chamber.

The remaining runners bore down for a photo finish.

They spilt into the chamber, colliding with one another, some falling into the shallow puddle of water still trapped there. Gabe was hauled to his feet, saw Jin there, and Holly.

They looked back to see the grey goop hurtling toward them.

Then, just as the last of the trailing mercs cleared the threshold, the aperture began to shrink behind him. The stopper was in the bottle.

An instant later the one on the opposing side began to widen. The ocean slammed in, a vortex of freezing seawater which smashed Gabe and everyone else inside on their feet over like skittles, and spat them out into the depths.

Even submerged, they heard the thunderous bass rumble of the ruins shaking themselves free. Seeing much was more of a challenge; the huge floodlights installed outside the fissure had fallen, but still beamed light into the murky depths beyond.

Gabe was again inhaling seawater. The pressure had immediately squeezed the air from his lungs. Huge lumps of rock that had buried the ruins for thousands of years were tumbling and falling as the vessel ripped its way out of its prison.

Gabe saw a merc close by suddenly buried by a boulder the size of a small car.

A smaller chunk of rock grazed Gabe's shoulder, a glancing blow but enough to underscore the fact that this was no place to linger. He desperately scanned the floodlit area, saw Holly and then Jin just ahead, and swam to join them. The ruins took another huge lurch and shook more of their coat free. Another shower of rock bounced and tumbled around the group desperately swimming away.

The plate of rock that crashed down in Gabe's path was the size of a truck.

Jin and Holly were right underneath it.

An explosion of silt erupted, a dark cloud that swallowed any sight of their fate.

With more rock tumbling and landing all around him, Gabe kicked furiously and blindly into the murk.

# Chapter Fifty-Four

Another violent tremor threw Fine to the ground. He climbed to his feet as further ominous rumblings reverberated along the passage he hurried through.

He had screwed up. He had somehow wound up on the wrong side of whatever the hell had eaten Oblonsky, and spooked, had taken the first exit from the chamber he had seen, which he realised too late had taken him in the opposite direction to the one which had brought them into the chamber. Turning around was not an option; he had tried backtracking and seen the grey carpet of gunk creeping towards him. He had spun right around and hurried his pace.

Perhaps there was another way out, another chamber offering access to the outside of the ruins like the one they had used to get in?

Hope burgeoned when he stumbled from the passage into another chamber, smaller than the one before, but larger than the featureless one through which they had entered.

This chamber had a series of pits in the floor, arranged in a spiral formation. He edged forward and peered down into the one nearest, swallowed, and circled to view the others. A handful were empty, but many were not...

His eyes and mind struggled to digest what they held: there were the remains of something inside, mummified, like the human remains they had passed on their journey in.

Only there was nothing human about these things. These creatures looked like no animal he had ever encountered. He instinctively knew what he was looking at, and it was not of this world, no distant precursor to man.

The possibility had of course been raised when he had come into possession of the first fragment, but Pickering's work had seemed so much more plausible, comfortable… When he had brought in Oblonsky, the Russian had concurred. Scientifically, a terrestrial ancestor was all but assured.

These ruins were a vessel, of that Fine had no doubt, but it was not one that had crossed seas to reach the ancient Minoans.

The ground suddenly leapt and Fine was thrown, landing painfully as a rumbling built to another violent shudder. He struggled to his hands and knees, looked up and was confronted with something across the room.

A shape loomed from one of the passages leading into the chamber.

Grave! Grave had come back to rescue him!

Hope flared brightly: he was about to be saved from this madness!

As quickly as it had arrived, the elation Fine felt was extinguished.

What took shape as it emerged from the gloom was not Grave.

Like Grave, it was easily close to seven feet tall, but that was where any similarity ended.

The thing wasn't a person at all.

It was a nightmare made real.

The abomination loped toward him. Ropey cables of shifting sinew connected joints that bent and shifted in all the wrong ways. As Fine backed away his mind scrambled, grasped for something familiar in the creature's anatomy, some touchstone to ground and absorb what he was presented with, but the task was impossible.

The withered and parched remains in the pits only hinted at what was headed for him now.

Were those mottled oily things up on the creature's trunk scales, feathers or fins? Were the quartet of milky pools above lidless eyes, the gashes on either side, gills, mouths, ears?

Fine felt himself begin to come apart, unspool. Whatever resource he usually called upon to power reason was being siphoned away, used as a raw and dirty fuel to drive the fear thundering through him. The creature was almost upon him, and he couldn't even run. The part of his mind that had once known how to was lost.

When its hands, claws (too many fingers, too many joints!) finally seized his arms and tugged him close, like a spider plucks a web-snared fly into its grasp before spinning it into a cocoon for later dining, the only thing between his terror-dilated eyes and the creature's vile visage was the thick glass faceplate of the EX-SADS' helmet.

Those lidless cloudy pools seemed to stare into Fine's soul, and then a maw opened below them. It had been invisible before, lost among the scales or feathers or fins. As it widened a ring of wet fronds tipped with what looked like bone were exposed.

The maw gaped open for a moment, then oscillated, issued a piercing roar, a siren of dread, quite literally a cry from another world.

Hot piss flooded Fine's suit.

The creature lifted him, and rotated, ambulating toward the spiral of pits nearby.

Its limbs bent and twisted as it began to fold itself down. It took Fine along with it, swathed in its embrace, until they were curled up like the husks surrounding them, the creature big spoon to Fine's horror-stricken little spoon.

How long they lay there was beyond him.

He knew only that the last thing he saw, as the hordes of madness besieged the crumbling fort in which his sanity now cowered, was grey goo spill over the lip of the pit.

# Chapter Fifty-Five

Gabe's hands met the huge rock he had just seen crash down on top of Holly and Jin.

More rock was still falling, lumps small and large bouncing off him as he searched with his hands more than his eyes. He was well aware another piece the size of this one could come down at any moment. The light from the fallen floodlights was growing weaker by the second as the seabed threw up more and denser silt.

He located Jin first.

Groping through the murk, his friend's face, teeth gritted, suddenly appeared before him. Gabe immediately spotted the cause of the expression: Jin's leg was trapped under the rock. He set his shoulder to the rock and heaved against the seabed. Jin used his free leg to push, too, and was finally able to drag his crushed leg free.

Amid tumbling stone, Gabe continued his search for Holly.

Then Jin suddenly grabbed his webbing and jabbed an urgent finger to the left. Gabe followed him and found his wife, or part of her.

Holly's arm protruded from under a slab of rock. Together he and Jin tried to lift it. The slab hardly budged. They swam around to the far side. This side of the slab was higher but buried in other lumps of rock. He began to lift and roll them away.

The slab was covering a pocket of the seabed.

They hurried to move more rubble, the rocks still falling around them.

The gap was perhaps just wide enough now. Gabe crawled down and fumbled blindly. Then his hand fell into Holly's, and he felt her fingers snap closed.

He pulled, his broken ribs roaring in painful protest, and felt her move.

He redoubled his efforts and felt her slide towards him. He climbed further out and Jin was able to get a hold on her arm too.

Together they hauled her from under the slab of rock.

The ground underwent another upheaval.

More rock rained down, bouncing and tumbling as the shelf shifted and crumbled, torn apart by the efforts of something long buried seeking to break free.

Then Holly was with them. The fallen floodlights offered enough of a glimpse to confirm they had her. Gabe had no idea how she was, he just knew she was alive and kicking, and that was good enough for him.

It was almost impossible now to see anything more than inches away.

The three of them set about getting themselves clear of the still cascading rocks and the shuddering wreck.

Like a beacon in the dark, Jin saw it first, a feeble but sure light ahead.

As they closed in, it took shape.

It was the diving bell.

## Chapter Fifty-Six

Carson Grave was a survivor, and part of being a survivor was knowing when to cut the dead-weight loose to prevent the ever-trailing reaper from closing his distance.

He had been spat out of the chamber and made it away from the worst of the falling debris. The ruins were shaking, and while he had no idea why, it wasn't difficult to see the result. At some point in the distant past, the huge shelf of rock that had broken away and crumbled to bury them was being disturbed, sliding off into the abyss that reached thousands of feet below.

He had toggled his EX-SADS to assist his escape, and the mode had drunk deeply from the rig's power. His readout now informed him that the suit's battery would soon automatically default back to normal, to ensure it reserved enough power for its wearer to reach the surface.

Grave charted a path for the diving bell, peering through the silt-choked water at the display on his wrist, using the tracker to locate it. The readout insisted he was close, and sure enough, a halo of light soon appeared ahead.

The diving bell grew clearer, and finally, his hands gripped the cage welded to its exterior. He tried his coms; beyond the ruins they should have re-established contact with the ship.

"Feeney?"

The expected voice came back, but it sounded rattled, "Boss?"

"Raise the diving bell. Fast as you can."

"Who's with you? I'm getting readings from a few of the others. Holt and Kenner and Stiller are showing vitals but not responding. The rest… I got nothing. Nothing on Fine or Oblonsky either—"

"Feeney, I'm assuming you didn't hear me the first time. Get this damn thing up to the surface, now."

There was a brief pause, and then, "You got it."

Almost at once, the diving bell began to move, commencing its slow and steady ascent.

Feeney was back, "Just so you know, Boss, I don't know what the hell is going on down there, but if you're hoping things are better up here you'd better think again. We had trouble, half the fucking deck is ablaze and the crew are herding folk into the lifeboats."

"Sit tight. I'll take care of everything once I'm back on board."

## Chapter Fifty-Seven

It, the thing that had once been Atana, knew it was being torn apart, but unlike the man howling and thrashing in its unshakeable embrace, it felt nothing. Strangely, all it could think of was the fresco Atana had seen in a cave on Crete thousands of years ago, and again on the bodycam footage from Mervin Pickering's lab.

The story of a champion, a saviour who had sacrificed herself and turned on her own to save the denizens of a tiny island she had grown to love.

And it with its memories restored, it could attest to the truth of the story.

It recalled the vessel hurtling to the seabed, where it was intended to rest for all eternity.

It recalled taking human form to the vessels' walls and escape.

It recalled the collision as it escaped and the vessel crashed into the seabed; not the depths of the trench where it was supposed to lie, but a shelf of rock on the cusp.

It recalled the avalanche of rock that had buried it and the other escapees.

It remembered all the things it had forgotten, or had perhaps fought not to remember, the truths hidden from the woman who had been set free when the earth had heaved ages later and spat her and the imprisoned dead out into the ocean.

Washed up, she had wandered blindly into the forest, a wasted wraith, a stranger, owed nothing, with nothing to offer, not even the explanation of who she was. The people who found her had taken her in and cared for her. She had been shown compassion and kindness. She had been loved.

These distant descendants of the people the champion had fought to save had guided her to that singularly intoxicating, chaotic and wondrous state of being we simply call humanity.

But these memories were not the champion of the story's memories, because it was not the champion. The being that had taken human form, that had survived and become Atana, had been one of the champion's pursuers. The being that recalled all this had been one of those set on destroying the insignificant lives on this insignificant planet; had been the very threat the champion had sacrificed its own life to defeat.

But all this had been hidden to it – to her – for millennia. With no memory of who and what she was, given a second chance, she had learned what the champion had learned before her: what it was to truly be alive.

It was a debt she could never hope to repay, but she had done her best. She would finish what the champion had started, and save mankind.

## Chapter Fifty-Eight

The milky beacon of the diving bell began to climb; someone had reached it, and called for it to return home to the ship above.

Gabe and Jin adjusted their course to follow its trajectory, using it to guide them through the pitch-black depths. Holly and Jin, both injured, were struggling to keep up. Gabe slowed his pace, and the three of them kicked for the surface.

The diving bell soon outpaced them, but its sister cable which had powered the floodlights near the ruins remained, and they stayed within reach of it until slowly the impenetrable dark transitioned to a deep blue. In time the cable became visible, as did the movement of other creatures of the ocean surrounding them. They continued to follow the thread that promised to lead them back to the ship's dive room.

When eventually they climbed, battered and bruised, from the moonpool into the dive room, they were met with the sound of cycling alarms.

The diving bell had been hoisted clear and rested on its track nearby. Whoever had ridden it up was gone.

Like Holly and Jin nearby, Gabe heaved up seawater and drew a ragged breath. His side protested, broken ribs no doubt knitting together, healing, but not healed enough yet to save lending each breath a sharp stab of pain. Jin looked equally beaten up; his leg had been crushed, was still a mess, and Holly looked in even worse shape.

But they had reached the surface.

Now they needed to get as far away as possible.

Whatever Atana was planning, Gabe was pretty sure it was best observed from a distance.

—

Carson Grave had not lingered long in the dive room. He had abandoned the diving bell the second it cleared the moonpool, jumped into the dive room and headed for the door, and from there for the upper deck.

He instigated the disengagement process from the EX-SAD rig. The battery readout was a hard red; soon the exoskeleton would cease to have power, and he would simply be stomping around in cumbersome fancy dress. The command was confirmed by the operating system, and dozens of internal seam locks began to twist free.

A wearer was supposed to be stationary while the rig completed the process, but Grave had no intention of hanging around. He shrugged and shook off its parts as he went.

The helmet was discarded first, lifted from his head and tossed to the ground, soon joined by a left sleeve thrown carelessly down. The other arm and chest and back plates followed. Finally, he stepped from the lower half and, feeling considerably nimbler in just the thermal bodysuit underneath, rapidly wound his way up through the ship.

Shrieking alarms attested to trouble, as did the deserted and occasionally bullet-scarred path ahead. When he reached the deck, he found a blazing inferno across its middle section. Something combustible in the litter of hastily-stacked cargo exploded as he watched.

The crew had taken charge and were guiding everyone to the lifeboats. Some had already been lowered into the water and were busy getting clear of the DSV.

If they hadn't already, the authorities would soon take note. This was not the way for someone like him and his unit to remain under the radar. He needed to put a healthy distance between himself and this crazy mess, ASAP.

He turned and tilted his eyes up, past the bridge, to the helipad at the uppermost head of the ship, and sprinted toward the steps.

—

Gabe, Holly and Jin stumbled up through the vessel. Following them like breadcrumbs, they encountered piece after piece of one of the fancy ADS rigs the mercs had been wearing, strewn along the corridors. Gabe's eyes fastened on the helmet as he passed it, still bearing the name of its most recent wearer: GRAVE.

The man who had invaded their home in Brooklyn, stolen their grail, attacked Atana and stolen hers before, and Torsten's, captured him, maimed him, destroyed his mind... This was the man who had almost succeeded in killing Gabe back at The Shell, who had severely beaten Holly.

Not as a crusade, not for a greater good, or even for evil, but simply for money.

Only he had acquired something else along the way. He had taken a far more valuable bonus. In between stealing one of the grails for Benedict Fine and handing it over, he must have used one. Gabe had put him down at The Shell, but he had got right back up.

An immortal, conscienceless, killer for hire…

They negotiated a few more corners, and finally, Gabe saw them: the doors leading out onto the main deck. They threw them open to a deck ablaze with angry orange flames and rolling black smoke.

On the side furthest from them, a lifeboat was being lowered into the ocean. Others were already bobbing on the waves around the vessel.

It was then Gabe saw the hulking figure climbing up from the bridge to the ladder leading to the helideck.

Grave.

It wasn't difficult to work out why. Gabe turned to Jin. He and Holly weren't pilots, but Jin was proficient.

"Jin, how does flying us far away from this mess sound?"

Jin and Holly looked where he was looking, saw Grave clambering up the ladder.

Jin nodded and they set off, sprinting across the deck in the direction of the bridge.

Gabe had just begun climbing the ladder to the bridge when the gunfire started.

He was committed. There was no time to do anything but clamber up and hope to find cover before something hit him.

Not all the mercs had got off the ship, then.

Below him, Holly and Jin ducked behind a rail and returned fire. Gabe heard Holly shout up to him.

He didn't catch what she said; there was a small window to catch and stop Grave and secure the helicopter, and it was shrinking with each second.

## Chapter Fifty-Nine

Grave crested the ladder and emerged onto the helipad.

Moments later, he was slipping into the helicopter's cockpit. His preparations were minimal: the aircraft was kept ready to fly at a moment's notice. He fired it up. The blades began to spin, quickly picking up speed. Working for Benedict Fine had been lucrative, and the squad he had assembled had served him well, but the whole shebang was coming apart at the seams.

The time had come to consider what fresh opportunities lay ahead for a man with his special qualities.

He heard gunfire from the deck below.

—

Gabe climbed the final few rungs of the ladder leading to the helipad and stepped off onto the helideck to find the chopper's lights on and its rotors spinning.

He swung his Sig to draw aim on the cockpit and advanced toward it.

He cleaved to the fuselage and edged forward, ripping open the door to the cockpit.

It was empty.

He frowned, where wa—

The blow struck him square in the back of the neck, smashing his face into the frame of the cockpit door. An instant later and a big hand seized his wrist and smashed his gun hand into the door.

He lost the Sig, heard it clatter to the ground.

Then he was yanked back and thrown down, slammed onto his back to look up and find a huge neoprene covered foot racing towards him. He rolled sideways, barely escaped it stomping his face.

He failed to manage the same trick for the hefty right kick that followed, the blow connecting perfectly with his broken ribs; his whole torso exploded in pain. A hand seized his scalp, lifted and smashed his face into the ground. Something above his right eye caved in.

Then he was being hauled to his feet, one-handed. The other hand was curled into a fist which delivered a powerful right cross that shattered his jaw.

He swung back, his right eye blind, his left not much better, through a bright explosion of pain and a fug of faltering consciousness, and scored a wild hook. Unfortunately, the mercenary leader seemed to soak it up with little appreciable concern.

Quite the reverse, in fact. As the vision in Gabe's left eye momentarily cleared what swam into focus was Grave's grimly impassive face, soon blotted out by a powerful headbutt square into Gabe's own face.

Gabe lost himself again.

And then he felt himself being raised, his feet lifted clear of the ground and carried somewhere.

A margin of clarity bled back, slowly, and with it a rush of air like a whirlwind blowing the darkness away.

He looked down. Two hands gripped his webbing. Below them lay Grave's stony face. He tilted his gaze up, towards the blur of rotor blades above his head, getting closer by the second as Grave thrust him higher.

Holly and Jin exchanged bursts of fire with the cluster of mercs across the deck, short salvos, each side testing the other's capacity before committing to a concerted push.

Until something happened which caused both sides to quit firing.

The dive support vessel seemed to be rising.

The entire horizon around the vessel had lowered and was still lowering, as though the ship was levitating out of the water. It was another few seconds before the true situation became evident: it was the water beneath them that was being pushed up. As the radius expanded it became impossible to miss the massive bulge that had swollen around the ship.

The lifeboats surrounding the DSV at a judicious distance began to lean and slide down the outer edge, drifting away on the cascading water.

Then the DSV itself began to list, tilting sideways as the budge intensified.

A shrieking, deafening boom threw the whole massive ship violently onto its starboard side.

Across the deck the mercs tumbled from cover, one or two bouncing and falling over the guard rail and into the sea. The others were scattered, left scrambling for something to cling to. Holly and Jin might have fired on them, if they hadn't been busy desperately clinging onto something solid themselves.

A wall of water exploded as a colossal shape blotted out the port side horizon.

Holly caught a momentary glimpse of the mass: huge, building-sized, so much larger even than the vessel it had shunted aside as it ripped clear of the water and shot into the sky.

—

Gabe beat at the face and arms of the hulking mercenary in a frenzied attempt to avert his imminent decapitation.

The blades were a roar now, inches from his scalp.

In less than a second or two they would smash into his skull, and that would be the last he would know about it, about anything. Even the grail's gift wouldn't be able to repair that kind of damage.

Suddenly a massive boom rang out, a mixture of screeching and rending metal, and the entire helideck tipped violently sideways.

The giant holding him was thrown sideways, forced to surrender his grip. They both hit the tilted deck and began to slide.

They weren't alone.

The helicopter beside them began to slide too, its skids scraping a path across the platform. While Gabe and Grave could scramble for purchase and were able to slow their descent, the chopper quickly reached the edge of the platform and flipped off, but not quite over.

Its leading skid jammed into the gap between the thick steel bar and the grilling encircling the helideck. Its progress abruptly terminated, its upper portion was left hanging over the edge, almost on its side, rotor blades still whirling, but now sideways on, a deadly blur right in the path of the sliding Gabe and Grave, ready to slice and dice as they reached them.

Gabe found himself sliding at a slower rate than the mercenary. His neoprene diving skin was providing more friction than the thermal body liner Grave wore.

Until the giant reached out and snagged Gabe's ankle.

Suddenly the giant was sliding slower and he was sliding faster.

Gabe almost missed it as it skidded by: his lost Sig, smashed from his hand when Grave had slammed his wrist into the fuselage. He threw out a hand to scoop it up.

His fingers folded around it.

They continued to slide, Grave's powerful grip around his ankle. The rotor blades were dangerously close now.

Gabe emptied the magazine into Grave's arm.

The grip vanished, and suddenly the giant picked up speed. Gabe offered gravity a helping hand via a swift boot to further separate them.

Grave shot forward into 400-500 RPM of spinning titanium airfoils. They made short work of him, grail's gift or not.

Gabe had no time to cheer: the same fate still awaited him. He tried rolling to escape the reach of the blades, but it wasn't going to be enough. He was still sliding closer every moment, and not veering away sharply enough.

He was only a few feet away when the helideck began to rock back on its axis, and suddenly he was sliding a great deal slower. He missed the whirring blades by inches, hit the steel ring and scrambled to claw a hold in the grating, winding up with his legs dangling from the lip of the steel ring.

But not for long.

The ship was already fighting to regain its equilibrium.

When it righted itself a moment later and the helipad returned to its usual horizontal orientation, Gabe was flipped back up and rolled away from the edge. He wasn't alone. The helicopter sprang back at the same time, and slammed down on both skids at the edge of the deck.

For a moment or two, Gabe simply lay there, looking up at the still spinning rotor blades to his left, content to let the grail's gift do its work fixing him up.

It was Holly's cry that snapped him back to the here and now, and reminded him things were far from over. He looked across to see her climbing up onto the helideck, Jin close behind.

They ran over and helped him up, carrying him into the back of the helicopter. Jin slipped into the cockpit and soon they were rising, up above the ship.

Gabe looked out of the window, down, at the lights of the lifeboats surrounding the huge vessel whose deck was still burning.

The ship was sinking. A huge scar had been ripped along one side where something massive, something which had spent five thousand years buried at the bottom of the ocean, had been torn free, pointed at the heavens, and sent far, far away.

Gabe closed his eyes.

It was as over as it was ever going to be.

# Epilogue

*The Hida mountain range, Honshu Island, Japan.*

"You're still sure about this?" Gabe asked. They were ferrying the last of the provisions from the camp.

Jin stopped and smiled, the same warm but tired smile Gabe realised had replaced the one he had worn when they had first met.

"Yes, Gabriel. I'm sure."

The plan had been Tokyo, or at least, that was what he and Holly had believed until Jin had made his intentions clear. Now the plan would be Tokyo, but only for him and Holly, once they'd helped Jin find a different place on the island for himself.

They had hiked into the mountains, along the Azusa River to Kamikochi, and from there into the mountains, carrying enough equipment and supplies to reach the less-travelled and more precarious climbs. After almost a month of searching, Jin found what he was looking for, and they had made camp.

The last ten months had been odd, a strange mixture of trying to digest what had happened, and how the world had interpreted what had happened.

The disaster that had befallen the Oculus was widely reported, but received particular attention due to who had been on board and the strange events which coincided with its sinking. Rumours and theories flew like crazed bats around the world.

What wasn't a matter of debate was its resting place, some sixteen thousand feet down in the Hellenic trench to the southwest of Crete. This naturally presented a significant challenge to reach, for salvage, but also impeded any potential investigation. Numbering the lives lost by those who had gone down with the vessel was no simple task, either. All the ship's logged crew members had made it to the lifeboats. Accounting for Fine Tec's technical staff was slightly trickier. Hard documentation of names and roles was scant. Even less certain was the whereabouts of some sort of security contingent who the survivors insisted had been aboard the vessel, but who were similarly absent from the ship's manifest. All had mysteriously vanished in the immediate aftermath of the sinking.

Of course, the biggest question, and without doubt the one the media were interested in, was what had happened to the famous tech billionaire Benedict Fine.

Both crew and technical staff attested to his presence on the ship in the hours before the sinking, yet no one reported seeing him on any of the lifeboats. Had he escaped by helicopter? A number of survivors claimed to have witnessed the aircraft leaving the site, but it was dark, chaotic and they might have been mistaken. The pilot had been directed away from the fire on the deck to one of the lifeboats, but it was always possible someone else might have been capable of flying it. The aircraft could have flown away, with Fine aboard, but it could also be lying thousands of feet below the sea with, or buried under, the rest of the wreckage.

If Fine had escaped, though, where was he now, and why hadn't he come forward?

Conspiracy theorists were having a field day.

If it was a kidnapping, no one had issued demands for his release. If the sinking was a terrorist attack or an assassination, no one had claimed responsibility.

The whole incident was riddled with more questions than answers.

Without doubt, there had been a fire on board, involving equipment which was reported to have been hurriedly stored on the main deck, although this didn't explain how the vessel's hull had been compromised, causing catastrophic and fatal flooding. It also did little to account for the multiple reports of gunfire, too. Fine Tec's lawyers were far from helpful, keen to protect the firm from criminal action and adverse publicity, and not just in respect of the incident itself.

If the investigation into the purpose of the vessel's work was mired in confusion, the expanding probe into the wider Fine Technologies organisation it had sparked only led to further irregularities and peculiarities. It was a giant ball of tangled twine that no one had even begun to unravel.

Benedict Fine had been an eccentric individual, had never hidden the fact, had even made it part of his personal brand, but it seemed he was also a man willing to break the law, deliberately falsifying and obfuscating to protect the technology he had developed and the privacy he wished to maintain. There had even been leaks hinting at the cover-up of an armed attack on his facility in Iceland.

So bizarre was the whole circus of events that it became a challenge to discern fact from fiction. Cretan residents reported an object streaking into the sky from the ocean. Air traffic control even supported the claims, but common sense and simple science indicated faulty data, as nothing could have moved as fast as the anomaly they recorded.

Gabe, Holly and Jin watched the chaotic and messy coverage unfold, and the public slowly lose interest. A billionaire had drowned, and the company he had built were conducting the appropriate public relations and legal damage control. The world would go on, never knowing how close it had come to erasure, and never needing to know, either.

The grails were gone, as were the vessel that had brought them and the seed of extinction that lay within it. Mankind's history would remain the one men and women had recorded, and the future history would lie in their own hands.

This would be his and Holly's last trip to the cave. The next, Jin would take alone.

They slipped through the narrow fissure, Jin first, then he and Holly. Shuffling along the narrow channel, and finally into the modest pocket of space beyond. There was just room for them to stand upright, either side of the casket, if they bent their heads a little.

Gabe removed the copper flask of whisky and the one filled with honey from his backpack and set them against the walls of the cave. The casket had been assembled in the cave. Spartan, lightweight but tough, made of plastic that would survive more than a thousand years before it began to degrade.

Gabe imagined his friend inside it, sleeping for centuries, perhaps many…

Setting down the provisions from his own backpack, Jin looked up and caught Gabe studying him.

"Why now?" Gabe asked. "Why not at least join us in Tokyo, we can—"

Holly's hand found his arm, a quiet plea to shut up. He stopped talking. They both knew Jin had made up his mind.

Their friend smiled at them.

"I'm tired, Gabriel. What better remedy than sleep?"

—

Back at their camp, they ate and drank. Holly didn't hide her feelings.

"What will we do without you?" Holly asked.

"I would hope you can live something close to ordinary human lives. Go where you like, when you like, make homes that are not required to be fortresses too, settle and know the comforts of domesticity, or travel if you prefer, so far and so wide that when you circle around even the places you last visited are fresh and exciting again. Most of all, live lives where life is at the centre, freed from a promise, unburdened, untethered to a mystery. The grail is gone. We discovered enough about its origins not to lament its absence."

"And one day you'll wake and come find us?"

"Nothing could stop me."

There was more said, but these were the words with most weight. Those that followed were, for the most part, no more than a feeble effort to stave off his departure a little longer. Testament to his character, he did not hurry them, allowing them to call time on their last evening together.

Letting go is hard.

Eventually, in the waning light, they accompanied him back to the cave.

Holly hugged him.

Gabe too.

They concealed the entrance and commenced their hike back to camp.

Neither wanted to wait until morning, so they chose to walk through the night, under a star-scattered sky, under the moon, the unfathomable reaches of the cosmos, a realm in which time was measured on a different scale from that imposed upon the creatures who inhabited the small blue rock beneath, who counted their existence in years rather than aeons.

Save for a few, whose allotment lay somewhere in between.

The End

Also
by John Bowen

Vessel

Where the Dead Walk
Crows Cottage

Death Stalks Kettle Street

## Acknowledgements

Thank you to my wife Caroline and my kids, Henry and Freya,
to my mum, Carol Thornton, my stepdad Tony Thornton, and my dad, John Bowen snr, and to Richard Daley who sufferers my daily ramblings.

Thank you to all those who helped out and offered valuable feedback and corrections. My mum, mentioned above, and the amazing author, Kath Middleton. Your keen eyes amaze me and saintly patience boggles my mind.

Finally, thank you to kick-ass thriller author, and my brilliant editor, Joel Hames.
Trust me, any mistakes you may find will not be his.

Cheers guys.

Printed in Great Britain
by Amazon